Praise for

Jacqueline E. Luckett and *Searching for Tina Turner*

"Fans of Terry McMillan's insightful dissections of love and life will appreciate novelist Luckett." —*Library Journal*

"The pace quickens until it becomes un-put-down-able... I can't wait for Luckett's next." —*Midwest Book Review*

"Jacqueline Luckett writes about relationships in a way we can all relate to." —Examiner.com

"In her debut novel Luckett delivers a strong, likable heroine who comes through her crisis by recognizing her true worth and empowering herself. Luckett's triumphant tale will rally readers of all backgrounds." —*Booklist*

"Ms. Luckett spins a sparkling tale of a woman's rise from emotional pain and obscurity to independence and power. Tina Turner as a mystery character is pure ecstasy!"
—Deborah Santana, author of *Space Between the Stars: My Journey to an Open Heart*

"An incredibly gifted writer... Bravo, Ms. Luckett!"
—Renee Swindle, author of *Please, Please, Please*

"Luckett sculpts lovable, complex, and beautiful characters."
—NewWorldReview.com

Also by Jacqueline E. Luckett

Searching for Tina Turner

Passing Love

A NOVEL

JACQUELINE E. LUCKETT

GRAND CENTRAL
PUBLISHING

NEW YORK BOSTON

Grand Central Publishing
Hachette Book Group
237 Park Avenue
New York, NY 10017

www.HachetteBookGroup.com

Printed in the United States of America

First Edition: January 2012
10 9 8 7 6 5 4 3 2 1

Library of Congress Cataloging-in-Publication Data
Luckett, Jacqueline E.
Passing love / Jacqueline E. Luckett.—1st ed.
p. cm.
Summary: "A novel about a woman in search of the truth about her roots in the magical city of Paris"—Provided by publisher.
ISBN 978-0-446-54299-9
I. Title.
PS3612.U259P37 2012
813'.6—dc22

2011008635

For all who understand that the past is just that...

In Paris, I began to see the sky for what seemed to be the first time. It was borne in on me—and it did not make me feel melancholy—that this sky had been there before I was born and would be there when I was dead. And it was up to me, therefore, to make of my brief opportunity the most that could be made.

—James Baldwin, "The Discovery of What It Means to Be an American"

Passing Love

1

The phrase *depuis quand?* (how long?) is used to question actions or events started in the past and still going on in the present.

la frousse (lah fruhs)	fright
chercher (share shay)	to look for
indécis(e) (ahn day see)	undecided, indecisive
remettre au lendemain (ruh meh truh oh lawn duh man)	to put off until tomorrow

---

She'd waited all her life to go to Paris.

As for the reasons why the dream of speaking French in France, of standing beneath the Eiffel Tower at the stroke of midnight, of lingering in sidewalk cafés took so long to come about—she chose to evade, not explain them. Her greatest fear, the one she carried like a locket close to her heart, was that in taking too close a look at the days that composed her fifty-six years, the dam that confined her existence might break and release a river of regret for all the places she'd never visited, the books she'd never read, the things she'd never done.

With the given name of Nicole-Marie Roxane, she believed the choice was not her own. Bowlegs, a widow's peak, and French, her inescapable and defining particulars. People asked if she was from Louisiana, teachers inquired how she (a Negro girl, they said) could have not one but three French names. Her neighbor to the left of their stucco bungalow (who never let anyone forget her Louisiana roots), Mrs. Albert—*ahl bear*, no hard T, *chérie*, spoke Creole French whenever she wanted Nicole to walk her miniature poodle or inform gentlemen callers that she was otherwise occupied. *Merci*. Her father, clicking through false pearly-whites, used his military French to teach his daughter basic phrases when he wasn't absorbed in one of his beloved books. "Comment-allez vous, Mademoiselle Handy?" A greeting so formal for a little girl. "Comprenez-vous, Nicole?" Nicole, never Nicki, not from her father. *Oui, oui*.

All of that, and the blue book.

Years ago Nicole discovered it, slightly bigger than her nine-year-old hand, in the trunk at the foot of her parents' double bed. Secrets in a cedar box. A sampling of their lives before she came along—a wispy bed jacket, a woman's suit covered with an enraged dragon spitting embroidered threads of red, orange, and yellow flames, a soldier's cap and jacket bound in sheets of brown paper and pungent mothballs, a manila envelope filled with her father's Army discharge papers, their birth certificates and marriage license, dozens of crisp hundred-dollar bills, a military patch with the three stripes of a staff sergeant stitched in parallel rows beneath the pointed top, a worn French paperback—*Cyrano de Bergerac*—and the blue book.

Saturdays when her handyman father had an emergency repair and her mother ran errands best done alone, Nicole was left to entertain herself the way only children were in the sixties—without ever feeling lonely, neglected, or scared. The minute her father's run-down truck bumped the curb at the end of the driveway, Nicole bolted down the hallway to her parents' bedroom and claimed it as her own. Eventually, her snooping refined itself into a routine that never varied: check the dusty space beneath the bed, her mother's panty drawer and jewelry case, the cedar chest, and, close to Christmas, the deepest corner of the one closet in the compact bedroom. Without fail, she inspected the antique hope chest to see if the contents had changed. She slipped the peach bed jacket over her shirt, its fluffy sleeves swallowing her thin arms, and daydreamed about the meaning of such a sheer and dainty garment. She marched with the soldier's cap tilted on her head. Left. Left. Left. Right. Left. Her fingers traced the embroidered dragon on the gabardine suit in search of the reason her mother no longer owned a single outfit as elaborate as this one.

Nicole never touched the money, but she took the blue book—a French dictionary. Under the cover of night and fuzzy blankets, she practiced the phonetic pronunciations, whispering French phrases instead of girlish secrets into her feather pillow. Every noun and verb transported her to a place miles from Berkeley and its dreary summer fog: *bonjour* (bone zhoor), *comment allez-vous* (come mawn tah lay voo), *bien merci* (be in mare see). Every phrase meant passage to another reality. *Paris* (pah ree).

Weeks after the discovery of that blue book, confidence settled in. Three weeks before her tenth birthday. When, at last, Nicole decided to surprise her father, she waited by the back door. It was easy for Nicole to love him. Tall and trim, he was strong enough to lift her with one hand and interested in her—had she memorized the short Langston poem he gave to her; eaten lunch alone or with friends? Nicole lived for the light of his smile, his approval, his explanations of poetry and politics. He was the parent who played hide-and-go-seek indoors, told her she was beautiful, read to her, and described the Eiffel Tower, tallest of all structures in Paris. To her nine-going-on-ten-year-old self, he was handsome and fascinating, an expert on the world, on Paris.

When he came through the door, Nicole jumped into his open arms. "Tiens, Papa . . . la famille . . . est ensemble . . . maintenant." Spoken to another aloud, her sentence had a choppy, yet musical tone. *Tee ehn, pah pah, la fah meel eht ahn sambluh maa ten nawh.*

Astonishment beat out her father's toothy grin. He never questioned how she learned this new phrase—"the family is together now"—without him. He replied as if the most natural occurrence in the world were his daughter chattering in the language that he, too, practiced. "Vous avez raison, Mademoiselle Handy. Je comprends."

Her mother snapped at child and husband celebrating the newfound vocabulary. "That nonsense needs to stop," she yelled, not looking away for one minute from the chicken frying in a cast iron skillet. "Best to make sure you've got your arithmetic finished, missy. French won't do you any good in this life."

And then the blue book was gone.

Nicole searched high and low. She refused to ask her mother the dictionary's whereabouts, understanding that the mention of it was an admission of theft. Had she brothers or sisters, she would've pummeled them with her fists or pinched them until they confessed. In the following hours or weeks that seemed an eternity in her young mind, her father stopped speaking French. He avoided her hazel eyes and shushed his child when she demanded why. *Pourquoi?* When, at last, he answered, his harshness surprised Nicole. "When you're a big girl, you can go to Paris and speak all the French you want." But she missed this connection to her father. *Le français.* No phrases whispered behind her mother's back. No practice. No spinning the black globe in the living room to seek out the patch named France, as if no other countries had existed.

Paris. Not how she'd intended, but Paris nevertheless. Sixty-one hours before boarding the nonstop flight from San Francisco to Charles de Gaulle. Twenty-nine whole days in France, plus one to get there and one to come back. Vacation hoarded over the years. Nicole poured a tall shot of one of Mexico's finest añejo tequilas into a crystal glass. Years ago she'd bought the hundred-dollar bottle for a special occasion. If this trip didn't count as special, she figured she didn't know what did.

A smattering of travel paraphernalia topped the coffee table: luggage tags, an airline itinerary, a shuttle service schedule, emergency numbers and security codes for the rental apartment, her brand-new passport, five hundred euros in denominations of five to fifty. And a notebook, Tamara's gift—a combination journal, address book, and log of miscellaneous events and information. A means to capture Paris. Nicole ran her fingers over her friend's angular cursive.

Even as they planned their trip, Nicole realized Tamara must have had a clue that her health wasn't the best. The last time she saw her, Tamara had looked years older than her forty-three: bloated middle, face drained and spent. Beneath Tamara's loose gown, her collarbone jutted and a bone poked where a rounded shoulder should have been. A white canister hung from a slim pole on the opposite side of the hospital bed. It beeped—a persistent and unwanted reminder—and administered intermittent doses of morphine, a nurse in a plastic box.

"I'm not afraid, Nicki."

Nicole pressed a glass of water to her friend's lips. Over the course of a few months, weight had dropped from Tamara's heavy frame. After her biopsy, the doctor pronounced the diagnosis with certainty—pancreatic cancer. The discovery was too late, and the insidious disease had reached her liver.

"Did I tell you my daddy preached? I delivered a sermon every now and again. I was pretty good. Tonight, I'm going to preach to you. I figure me in this bed, acting pitiful, is the perfect setup to get you to change." That was when Tamara pulled out the notebook and wrote on the inside cover, *Be wild. Dance in the streets. Take French lessons. Walk the wrong way home. Don't play it safe.* "This is your mantra, Nicki. Promise me you'll go to Paris, no matter what." Determination edged Tamara's tone like a mother's counsel to a confused child.

Nicole sat on the edge of Tamara's bed, straightened her back, and repeated the pledge. "I promise to go to Paris, no matter what."

The shock, the cancer's rapid consumption of her friend's body, and the isolated grieving accelerated this decision. The afternoon of Tamara's funeral, the dam burst sure as the rain started when the pallbearers lowered the casket into the ground. Tamara's death did what years of procrastination hadn't. Nicole got the lesson—live; play, don't watch.

She settled on the floor beside the fireplace's deep hearth and stuffed newspaper under the manufactured logs. Four matches held to the edges and smoke burst into dancing flames; a frolicking light show of yellow, orange, and red tipped with blue. The real estate agent had hesitated to show her the run-down 1940s bungalow, but she fell in love with the house, the garden filled with hydrangeas, the turquoise blue lanterns tacked under the eaves, cooing rock doves, and the morning sun shining through the windows. The fireplace cinched the sale; visions of frosty nights stretched out in front of it, the toasty scent of burning wood, crackling flames, and her man's arms around her. Married, divorced, or single, she could count the evenings she had snuggled there in the twenty-one years she'd owned the place; not one man had turned that image in her head into a long-term reality. Hand to heart, she held the place that ached with the need to rest against the shoulder of a full-time someone who cared.

The tinny ding-dang-dong of the doorbell's chime broke the quiet and caught Nicole off guard. Only one person had the gall to stop by this late at night without calling ahead.

Nicole first met Clint Russell when she was twenty-three and he was twenty-eight, compact and husky, irresistible and charismatic beyond his years. He'd sized up the volunteers at the conference registration desk, then swaggered to her station. "You know you have simmering eyes," he'd whispered and requested directions to a meeting clearly posted on a sign behind Nicole. "You mean shimmering," she'd corrected, thinking he referred to her makeup. "I meant exactly what I said: simmering. Bubbling underneath that crisp blouse." Not her first love, but her first lover, they spent ten months together.

Three and a half decades since he left Oakland for the East Coast and his failed promise to return and pick up where they left off. Even though her beloved friend was no longer present, Tamara's voice was in Nicole's head, nagging, as she often had. "Forget Clint. If you kicked him out of your life, you wouldn't even know he was gone. What does he do for you?" Never had she answered her friend and now Nicole sat motionless, while the doorbell chimed nonstop, frustrated that she could both love and not stand (or resist) this man. Forgetting him, her ex-husband, all the men who'd failed her—awkward loose ends of her past—was what she needed to do. Maybe she'd figure out how in Paris. Maybe not. Nicole poured a second shot of tequila into her glass, sipped, and considered a third.

Maybe she wouldn't open the door.

Five years ago, she'd heard the chatter when he came to the law offices—not his name, simply the description of the attractive lawyer collaborating on a case with one of the partners. Clint recognized Nicole when he passed the word-processing bullpen. Time had been generous. Clear skin. His shaved head defied a receding hairline. His suit shouted power and money. "You have simmering eyes, Ms. Handy." He played with the line that caught her attention back in 1975. "And I do mean your eye shadow."

They went from lunch to dinner to an expensive hotel to bed. Bored and fighting the lingering loneliness from her divorce, Nicole surrendered to his spell and let Clint fill that hole without his ever mentioning and her never inquiring about a wife.

After five minutes passed, she opened the door.

"What took you so long? I came to check on you." Clint passed his suit jacket to Nicole and headed straight for her bedroom, ignoring the fire, the papers on the coffee table, newspapers and assorted junk mail spread over the dining room table that he usually complained about until she organized or tossed the whole mess out. She followed and watched him stretch out on her queen-sized bed and pick at the striped duvet. Nicole stood at the side of her bed, crossed her arms, and breathed in his faint smell—cologne mixed with hours spent polishing the fine print of contracts, and pressuring any associate and administrative staff within reach of his booming voice.

He fingered the elastic waistband of her flannel pajamas. "Such practical nighties."

What, Nicole thought, would he say if she asked if his wife wore flannel pajamas or slinky negligees or tied her hair up in satin scarves at night? "You came to apologize?"

"No, baby. *You* owe me an apology. I've been waiting for it."

"My timing was wrong. I'm sorry, but you should be sorry, too."

In the five years since they'd taken up with each other again, Nicole had convinced herself that Clint kept a separate phone for her calls, one left in his car or office, free from discovery or suspicion. Raindrops had sprinkled the mourners during Tamara's funeral and flattened Nicole's spirit. Later, she'd checked her bedside clock on the hour, every hour, from eight o'clock on. By midnight, she'd tossed and turned herself into a blanket cocoon. By one, she was wide awake, and by two, her whole body ached for comfort. Clint's cell phone rang until his husky voice came on the line.

"If this is an emergency, it better be good." He fumbled with the phone, creating an echo, but not before Nicole heard a lilting voice, and in that moment that woman in bed with him was no longer simply the wife, but Eleanor.

"Tamara's funeral was today." Nicole stuck to her rules. Not even in boozy hazes or feeling pitiful had she succumbed. She sensed he'd moved from the bed to a safer place to talk.

"I'm sorry your friend died, Nicki, but I can't talk. You'll ruin everything."

Tonight, without noting the six weeks since her crazy

middle-of-the-night breach, Clint whistled a mindless tune. Nicole had resisted phoning him. Anger, she supposed, was why he hadn't called her. Six weeks ago, she might have welcomed this impromptu visit.

"My friend died...the least you could've done was call me back."

"Eleanor grilled me the rest of the night. When I got to the office in the morning, all hell broke loose. I know Tamara meant a lot to you. I'm sorry. I really am." Turned out that his firm, he, had lost a multimillion-dollar client and he was left with no opportunity to debrief before another contract was in the works. "It's been crazy. You know I would have if I could have."

"But you didn't, and I guess that says it all."

Nicole stared, watching Clint take in the room. Piles of clothes covered the floor, the bed, the sofa bordering it—each item awaiting a packing decision. He pursed his lips. "What are you doing? What's this mess?"

"I'm going to Paris. I leave in two days."

"Paris? I figured since Tamara passed, you'd change your mind."

"I made a promise." She had the passport, the tickets, the place to stay. No refunds. No turning back. *I promise to go to Paris, no matter what.*

"I love you, baby, but you're not a woman to be in Paris on your own. You'll never make it."

"When I planned to go with Tamara, you implied she wasn't sophisticated enough for a trip to Paris."

"She wasn't."

"Have some respect."

"I call it like I see it—that's what I'm paid to do. And my opinions haven't worked out so bad for you." Clint pulled her on top of him. Nicole squirmed out of his hands and shifted to the other side of the bed. "Stop complaining and admit you like having me around."

"Sometimes I wish I didn't." She wanted to say, "Watch and

see," but doubt inched up her throat—the same uncertainty that had kept her from Paris for so long. He was her rock. His opinions were as important to her as water to the lavender shrubs lining her garden. She'd taken every tip he'd given and doubled her investment accounts, replaced her aging car, refinanced her mortgage, and made herself trustee of her aging parents' will. He listened when she fussed about her job, sent flowers, wined and dined her at dimly lit restaurants. Even though he'd never met her, he had a knack for helping defuse her mother's subtle tantrums and nagging over her daughter's single status, her hair, or her weight.

"If you wait, I'll take you to Paris." Clint wiped his face with his palm and sat up straight. "I shouldn't have lost that deal. Incompetent associates. Contracts. Wheeling and dealing. I think I billed ninety hours last week, and it's getting worse. I can't bear another of Eleanor's black-tie, five-hundred-dollar-a-plate, dry chicken dinners." He ignored Nicole's stiffened pose and slid his hand onto her thigh. "You keep me grounded, Nicki. I don't know if I can keep it together. Don't go to Paris. Stay here. I can get away for a long weekend. Santa Barbara? You love nice hotels."

One second. For one second she allowed a semblance of joy to spread along the width of her mouth. She marveled at him, as important as the big-shot partners she worked for, wanting to take care of her. Nicole envisioned a rare, entire weekend—forty-eight hours—the ocean, the salt air, strolling aimlessly, holding hands without the worry of discovery, and luxuriating in an expensive hotel room.

"Do you think I'm stupid?" She slapped Clint's hand and shoved him back against the pillow. You want me to change my plans because . . . your wife didn't appreciate my call? It got you in trouble? You're addicted to your work?"

Her pajama bottoms loosened with one quick yank as if she'd planned her next move. She pounced on top of him and adjusted her frame. Neither fat nor thin, Nicole held him under her. He whistled a single, long note, and released to her control. She bit his lip. He turned away. She was sick of him, his bribes and his part-time love. Sick of his big white house on a hill. His Saturday night tuxedo dinners and Sunday brunches at restaurants with one-hundred-eighty-degree views of the Bay. Sick of his four kids in private school and his damn latest-model Jaguar. His law partnership. His dimples, his idea of what made her happy. She unbuttoned his shirt, unzipped his pants, and marked him, left red imprints on his belly, forcing him to do his best to avoid the evidence of his infidelity. Without hesitation, Nicole pressed him into her, and rode him, tightening and squeezing her thighs to make him feel her pain. She rode him, her buttocks slapping against his thighs, her hands forcing his shoulders into the pillow. She rode him without kisses or foreplay. He never spoke, never shouted for her to stop. He moaned. He came. She didn't. Nicole backed off of Clint and ran to the bathroom.

In the shower, she rubbed her skin until it colored under the hot water, soaped and scrubbed her graying pubic hair until every drop of Clint's quick release slid between her legs and down the drain. Without bothering to towel dry, Nicole threw on her robe, took a cigarette from the pocket, and went back into the bedroom. She watched Clint zip up his pants, tuck in his shirt, and smooth the creases. His face was flushed and blank and covered with satisfaction.

"What got into you?" He smirked and waved away the smoke Nicole blew into his face.

"You got what you came for."

Arms open, he moved to hug her. When Nicole stepped aside he tugged at her again, holding her in his arms. "I'm sixty-three, Nicki. Losing this deal, after the work I put into it, was a heartbreaker. Baby, we have no guarantees in this life. Think about it. I am."

"And that means what?"

"Stay and find out. Paris is a tough city—you can't speak French, you don't like to travel, and certainly not by yourself. You can't be alone."

"You don't know that."

"I know you. You have routine, baby. Not spontaneity. Stay." He held her hand. "I need to see if this, us, will work more than three nights a month. I love my kids. I won't hurt them. I respect my wife, but I don't love her. I haven't for a long while."

"Why now?"

"Because the clock is ticking fast. Stay. With me. We can go to Paris on our honeymoon."

2

Mississippi, Spring 1944

Martha told RubyMae, at least twice yearly, that the day she was born, the afternoon sun had carried a red hue over its round self as if Jesus's blood had dripped onto the brightest star to welcome her newborn babe. To RubyMae, that peculiarity of red sun meant she was born to be exceptional. It augured a fate to live and die beyond Sheridan where her parents were born and bound to die, where her grands and great-grands and the greats of the greats—ancestors, the slaves she had come from—lay in the red dirt still waiting for Jesus's hand to lead them to freedom.

She was one of those women born under the sign of dissatisfaction. Nothing mother, father, or friend did brought her happiness. When she reached thirteen, she complained of a burning deep within—she came to call it longing. Her mother called it restlessness. Now and then, RubyMae swore it kept her fingers from pushing buttons through hand-stitched holes on starched white blouses, somber skirts, and dresses full on high to her neck that her mother, Martha, made her wear. The impulse pushed, nigh on to a living creature. On hot nights she squeezed it, rocked herself quiet with its ache. It pushed her to not come when she was summoned and run wild in the street where the neighbors whispered behind their hands.

The longing kept her in front of the mirror where she stared at her face, tugged at her skin, ran fingers through her hair and pondered how it must be to stand at the head of a line, to be addressed by voices filled with respect, not lust. To be white; lady not gal. Later, after first blood stained her panties, she pondered the feeling of a man's lips on her own. Her thinking stretched to a world without a staid big sister, a demanding church with lengthy sermons, and commandments that kept her from breathing. Had Martha known, these feelings were the kind best done away with the stick behind the kitchen door or the back of her hand. Instead, RubyMae was marked a lazy child, a dreamer.

But there was meaning to a blood-covered sun. Though she had never seen that huge ball of light covered in such a way, RubyMae knew it was different and so, too, was she. So instead she made friends with the moon that showed itself whole every month. The moon was her kin, and RubyMae gave herself to the waxing and waning of its love. She watched it turn from yellow to silver as it moved from the trees to winter puddles or summer blossoms past Sheridan, past Jackson and Clarksdale and past Tennessee to places her schoolteachers marked on a yellowed wall map. With the waning moon her head spun, her heart pumped fast, the soles of her feet itched.

On this night, the moon was at its roundest, primed for the eccentricities that came to pass when its surface was so close to earth. The air bristled against the fine hairs on RubyMae's arms with the breeze of possibilities. The longing goaded her out Lurlene's window, through Martha's garden, the scent of ready-to-pick radishes spicy in the air, past the caged rabbit and down the darkened street toward a waiting car. At the black sedan, RubyMae tucked and tugged at the dress Lurlene lent her. The curve of her breasts burst from the low neckline.

"Hurry!" Lurlene's whisper blended with the wind rushing

through the tall pines. She opened the back door of the sedan, slid to the far side of the leather seat, and motioned for Ruby to get in. The two mustached men grinned not at the women's eager faces, but to what was spilling out of the front of RubyMae's dress visible in the car's dim interior light. The girl had worked her manipulations on Lurlene for weeks to get the older woman to take her along. Lurlene got a companion and a little protection from these two men she just met; RubyMae got the chance to wear makeup and a dress that fit her like it never had Lurlene, and have a bit of real fun. "Chester's behind the wheel and LJ's riding shotgun. This is RubyMae Garrett."

"Ruby, just Ruby." She extended her hand to LJ's, letting it hang midair, thinking a limp hand a sign of womanliness. From the moment Martha had taken her in as a border, Lurlene and Ruby were drawn to each other. On occasion they slept in Lurlene's narrow bed, talking through the night about the opposite sex and what ladies could do to catch a man; getting along in the way Ruby and her big sister never did. Ruby latched on to Lurlene, understanding even almost six months before she turned sixteen that a woman who described herself as a beautician, but never touched a hot comb or lifted a curling iron to any woman's head, save for her own, might well have a lesson to teach her.

That was how Ruby came to be sneaking out Lurlene's bedroom window at eleven o'clock on a night filled with moon glow. She was testing. It took the four of them little conversation, several ditches, a very bumpy road, and two slow swigs each from a pint bottle of bourbon to get deep in the woods. Here and there the eyes of a skunk or a possum glowed in the headlights. No other cars, no signs of humans or good times until they turned down a lane marked with a washboard nailed to a tree stump. The joint at the end of the road seemed like a living space, not the rowdy place Ruby had expected. It was compact, neatly built, and surrounded by beams from car headlights. Music spilled out the windows, sneaked under the joint, and swirled fast as tumbleweeds.

"It's just a shack." Ruby giggled. Men and women dawdled on the steps or by the door, anxious to be near the music blaring within. Some stood waiting in the dirt for the room to clear out so they could refill the space. Most were dressed up; men in suits with wide lapels, women in close-fitting hats or bareheaded with hair marcelled in deep waves. Light skin, brown skin, dark skin, and every shade of colored in between glistened with the sweat from the warm night.

A wailing saxophone followed a singer's plea, a cinder from a raging fire ignited that place in Ruby. The music grew loud over the wails, mostly women's, of appreciation. The piano and bass stopped and started, stopped and started, and alternated the second ditty following the saxophone's lead. Ruby pushed past Lurlene and their men friends to the head of the line.

"What kinda horn is that anyway?" Her question was addressed to no one in particular.

"That's a saxophone, baby," Chester answered with a big grin. "Stick with ole Chester and he'll teach you."

When Ruby entered the crowded room, a musician occupied the farthest corner. Standing with his saxophone in his hands, fingering the keypad in the way that he would for all his breaks that night—absentmindedly. Moving through the room, she felt his attention, unsure until Lurlene schooled her that his was the instrument that had taken her breath away. She sighed and Chester, who had attached himself to her right side, mistook that breath for timidity. He grabbed her arm, swung her so that her dress flared, exposing her short legs. Chester held her. His arms begged her to feel the rhythm of the music and the desire rising in his pants. Ruby felt the want, saw it in the men that glanced at her, and she jerked away. She felt it from the saxophone man. Her body responded before she could think or will it to do differently. She stepped slowly, aware of that clinging dress, its fabric soft against her thighs. Years later she would remember telling herself that night was not for dancing, but for watching and sensations she had yet to understand. Instead, she conserved her energy, this power she discovered her body had, and popped her fingers, ignoring the sheen of sweat collected at the pit of her throat.

The saxophone man sauntered from his corner to the band, which seemed to separate for him; even the piano player seemed to scoot the upright piano and his stool away from the center. Moses, she would call him when they met, because the crowd parted so wide for the man. But merely once that night, because, he made a point to let her know later with the most serious of faces, he had no interest in Moses or the Bible. "Arnett," he would say, "is my name. Arnett, no middle name, Dupree."

Arnett put the saxophone to his lips and blew, the notes soothing and sad. They sweet-talked Ruby, and she let the call of the saxophone work up her arms and down her spine. She squared her hips in a way she knew was nasty because Lurlene had shown her when they had practiced what Lurlene termed "seducting." That was how Arnett worked her. He removed the felt hat from his head and covered the saxophone's bell, turning the music from blaring to muffled. He blew one long note that reached for her soul, and she let it fly.

They met in the middle of the room. Had Ruby been a woman by age and experience, she would have waited for him to come to her. She moseyed to where he had situated himself amidst a cluster of women, their finger waves shiny under the bare lightbulb. To a woman, the five of them jockeyed for Arnett's attention, twisting this way and that, showing off painted lips and supple curves and touches of whatever else was available to a good-looking, saxophone-playing Louisiana man.

Ruby stood among the women—chickens posing for the rooster—and grinned. Her lips, ample and tempting, were her best feature. She parted them enough to reveal slightly crooked teeth. "Ripe." Arnett grabbed her hand with the assumption of having known her forever. "Ripe enough to bite. Why haven't we met before?"

She should have known. She should have known by that line and mocked him and rushed to Chester's arms because, despite his puffery, that young man meant no harm. Unable to decide which one influenced her most—the liquor, the moon, or the burning that demanded his comfort—she held on to Arnett's hand.

"Right here, Moses!" Her eagerness drew the smirks of the women beside her. "I mean Sheridan. I been in Sheridan—that's where I'm from."

She was tickled by his laughter, but confused by the women's titters. Yet they fell away, moths parting a light gone cold. With that simple and slick line they, too, might have fallen for just the taste of Arnett. They understood that with Ruby's naïve reply, Arnett had chosen.

He strode to his corner, Ruby following as if she'd had no other choice. She squeezed past dancers and drinkers and entwined lovers to that corner. When she joined him, Arnett pushed her hair from her ear, so that his fingers brushed her lobe. The saxophone hung from a strap around his neck. The J shape of the instrument pushed into her torso. It was cool and sharp, surprising, not hot from the warmth of his music. He put his face close to hers.

"And who, baby love, are you?"

"My name is Ruby."

"Ruby, Ruby." Arnett picked up a glass jar from the stool beside them. He swigged back a long taste of the amber liquid and spoke again. "Ruby, my jewel."

Ruby tilted her face to meet his. He was sharp and cool in that hot and musty room. Thick hair slicked back in natural waves from his wide forehead. Lashes long and brows—the kind women envy—evenly arched over deep-set eyes. A hint of hair above his lips; a faded line, as if he hadn't made up his mind whether or not he wanted a mustache.

Arnett lit a joint and touched his thumb to Ruby's chin, parting her lips. He exhaled into her mouth so that she tasted the bitter reefer. She coughed the smoke into her throat and let that smoke set her free. She ignored the fumes threading through her hair, the liquor on her breath—these telltale signs of where she had been, the likelihood of discovery. Ruby ignored the harshness of her mother's backlash if her daughter was not asleep in her bed, driven as Martha was by swift anger when Ruby did wrong. Never did she think of Lurlene, LJ, and Chester, though to his credit she'd watched him shift his attention to a big-boned woman.

"You're a pretty one." Arnett fiddled with the cut-glass brooch pinned to the shoulder of Ruby's dress. "Pretty as this fancy glass flower. Sparkly. How old are you, anyhow?"

Ruby arched her back. "How old do you think?" She waited for Arnett to stop laughing.

"You Bricktop and Josephine rolled into one." He kissed her. Had she been able to think, she knew he must play his saxophone with such need as she felt in his kiss—her first real kiss. Their tongues fit into one another; found pieces of a puzzle gone missing.

It was Arnett who turned from Ruby. "Come back and see me when you're legal."

He strode, the back of his jacket hugging his body, moving not from her but to the band. He slipped the reed from the mouthpiece, tested its pliability with a swift bend, then slipped it back into the neck and began to blow.

Ruby waited in his corner. He never came back. If she had been woman in body and mind, she would have known better, would have known to get the hell out and never come back. As it was, Ruby was saved by Lurlene. "Girl, you let that guichee Creole put a spell on you?" She led Ruby from the corner and into the night. "And don't tell me you don't know that's a grown man you messing with."

3

French is a living language. Memorizing vocabulary lists and conjugating verbs in their various tenses is necessary, but the language is best learned in conversations.

la maladie (lah mah lah dee)	illness
travailler (trah vy yea)	to work
aller (ah lay)	to go
joli(e) (zho lee)	pretty

Impatient in the spacious seat of the transatlantic flight, Nicole tinkered with every button and switch on her armrests until she found a comfortable seat position, pleased she'd upgraded to business class. After two movies and five chapters of a forgettable book, she gave herself permission to daydream. Whenever Clint popped up in her head, her stomach knotted in protest. Taking a cleansing breath, she dismissed this musing and what she characterized as his proposition; he'd called it a marriage proposal.

It was bad enough that her mother hadn't taken to the idea of Nicole's going to Paris when she'd shared her plans three weeks earlier. The elderly woman had sidled into her kitchen on frail legs and jerked her cane at Nicole as if she were a displaced animal in her mother's glass menagerie needing to be reminded of her place. Clint didn't simply think she lacked follow-through; he didn't believe in her. Queasiness proved her own uncertainty. The airplane began its descent. Nicole peered out the window at the unfamiliar territory below, released the negativity, and let her thoughts drift to the blue book.

Over the years, the memory of the dictionary refused to fade and rendered the navy cover, the language and pronunciations, the tissue-thin pages larger than they had been. If she felt comfortable with the man sitting beside her, she might have poked him and described the book that generated her love of French. She giggled, reverting to her nine-year-old self first discovering the blue book.

Yesterday she'd spoken a few phrases to her father. Not since the dictionary disappeared had they toyed with French. No recognition of the language they'd shared. If he were healthier, he would have celebrated her trip with a Langston Hughes poem written in the city where the poet had spent time or recited a verse of his own composition. Instead, her father settled into his plastic-covered recliner and recommended she take along an umbrella. "I'm going to speak French in France, Dad." Nicole tried to jiggle his brain and make him remember when they'd shared the language and he'd promised Paris was in her future. "I'll be fluent when I get back," Nicole teased. In a single moment of clarity, her father had focused on his daughter. "Oh, baby, your mother will be happy."

She missed that blue book. She missed her father.

The flight attendant's announcement alternated between French and English. It wasn't the ten-hour flight, the drone of the engines steady and low, the tremor in her foot that cramped her calf, or the bona fide French that marked themselves as the sensations and images to remember years from now. It was her body's reaction to the pilot's downward turn toward the City of Light—a hint of motion sickness and what Nicole understood was anxiety. How far would reality fall short of the dream?

In Paris, the sky will always be blue, she prayed, God will love me there. Life will be sweeter, filled with adventure not found on the streets of Oakland or San Francisco or Berkeley. The Eiffel Tower breaking the skyline. The Seine flowing fast beneath its many bridges. Stepping out of a cab, her feet touching the sidewalk, it will be home.

The taxi driver cut through the traffic on the invisible border surrounding Paris. "Le Périphérique," he said. In the sunlight of this June afternoon, the city showed off the way an ardent suitor does at the beginning of a perfect love affair. *Regardez-moi*: statues—men on horses, animals with wings; fountains, countless bridges poised over the Seine. Roundabouts. Métro signs with curlicue lettering. Gray, yellow, verdigris. Pockets of green gardens and red geraniums. Steeples. Each scene a snippet from posters, guidebook pages, advertisements for a perfect getaway. Her dream had come true, not quite how she'd imagined, but true nevertheless.

"Est-ce que tout va bien, Madame?" The driver looked at Nicole in the rearview mirror and touched his hand to the place on his face where tears striped hers. He grabbed tissues from the passenger seat and passed them to Nicole.

"It's beautiful," she mumbled. At home, the flatlands of Oakland and Berkeley abutted the base of hills speckled with eucalyptus trees and homes. Virtually every glance westward exposed a body of water or a bridge or the peaks and valleys of San Francisco's skyline. Home was a different beautiful. "Jolie, très jolie!"

Paris, no matter what. This new love wooed and enchanted. Nicole opened to it, taking in every gargoyle and wrought iron balcony, every rooftop and streetlamp beyond the windows of her cab, willing and eager because, forever and for always, she would only have one first look at Paris.

The concierge, Monsieur Large, introduced himself when Nicole entered the lobby. Monsieur was not large. He was gaunt and his head came up to her nose, or at least that was Nicole's estimate, given the man's proximity. Monsieur lugged her suitcases into the compact elevator and demonstrated, complete with hand signals—he spoke as little English as Nicole did French—how to hold down number one for what Americans call the second floor, and RC for *rez-de-chaussée*, the entry-level floor of every French building.

Opening the heavy wood door, Nicole knew she'd hit the jackpot. God bless Tamara. God bless Tamara's friend's naughty Swiss ex-husband who rented this apartment to fund his alimony payments. A collection of antique chairs and tables. Built-in bookcases lined with leather-bound books. Crystal chandeliers in the middle of a high ceiling. Traditional herringbone plank floor. A wall of mirrors.

After Monsieur Large dragged her heavy suitcases into the living room, Nicole pushed open one of three floor-to-ceiling windows and inhaled: a hint of river, exhaust fumes, and early afternoon. Without stretching past the windowsill, she saw bridges to her left and right. On their second date, she learned her ex had visited Paris. Her wedding present to him was a scrapbook of his disorganized Paris photographs. Not understanding their logic or connection, she'd put together an album, only to have him peel photos of Paris's most popular attractions from between the cellophane sheets. "When I take you, you'll see they're all wrong." Placement right or wrong, the Seine before her now was the exact replica of what he'd rearranged: water rushed through open arches supporting each level structure and lapped against concrete embankments. Booksellers attended their stalls, pedestrians, joggers, and bicyclists navigated traffic. Iron, glass, masonry, and elaborate rooftops. Beyond the windows, cars jammed the street, the Quai des Grands-Augustins—her street now—and a view of the Île St.-Louis beyond the Seine.

A first promise, even her ex's first promise, was the sweetest and the toughest to forget. Let the past stay where it belonged. What did he care if she was in Paris or Outer Mongolia? They hadn't spoken in years. Seven years of unpredictable flashbacks of the loss of a cunning man who'd broken his vows and his promise to bring her to this city. In Paris she was supposed to work on letting go of the past. Stop. Live.

Nicole hauled her suitcases up the spiral staircase to the second-floor bedroom and paced the length of the room. Her cell phone pinged twice inside her leather handbag. How did the cliché go, she thought: you never miss your water till your well runs dry. Her hands trembled as if she'd had too many cups of the strong black tea she loved. She reached for her notebook and reread Tamara's challenge: *Be wild. Dance in the streets. Take French lessons. Walk the wrong way home. Don't play it safe.* Staying inside was not an option—twenty-nine days left to unpack, to shake off the fatigue, to rest. This was Paris.

The streets were wonder-filled observed from the cab; with the cobblestones uneven beneath her rubber-soled shoes, reality hit as solidly as the jet lag. Outside, releasing to the sensation of both, Nicole closed her eyes, fought the oncoming drowsiness, and listened to the familiar: short bursts of horns, the screech of tires, gunning engines, the whisper of the summer breeze. This was the din of home. The difference was in the snippets of French, and when she opened her eyes again, the difference was in the view.

Her phone pinged again. Nicole removed it from her purse and glared at the screen. Clint's proposal had been a cliché—the married man, at last tired of his wife, proposed to his mistress. That last night they were together, he'd taken the cigarette from Nicole's hand and stubbed it out in a nearby ashtray. "Well, what do you have to say? I asked you to marry me."

"You didn't say the words."

"Does that make a difference?"

"If I chuck my trip and stay in Oakland to help you through this latest crisis, or when it's over..." Clint, Nicole reminded herself, had dangled the hint of marriage before, qualifying it with his children's needs and his wife's social position. "... what's to say you won't change your mind?" The angry sex had worn her out. She wanted him to stay, wanted him to leave. To leave and make the decision easy and put him into the past, a place to glorify and regret their relationship. If he left, never to return, the option of "no" was easy. Nicole giggled.

"It's not a joke, Nicki. I'm serious."

"I'm not sure I want to be married," she blurted, surprising herself and Clint.

"You've got to be kidding."

"Me and you. Yes. But permanently?" Infidelity had broken up her marriage. If Clint could be unfaithful to his wife and leave her as he said he wanted to do now, what was to say, Nicole considered, down their own married road, that boredom or stress wouldn't prevail? "Let's leave us the way we are for now." He'd saved her from the sadness of divorce; she'd escaped loneliness. A little bit of someone, married or not, was better than a whole lot of no one at all.

That was her decision: a definite maybe. Nicole deleted the voice message without listening to it and read the text. CRAZY HERE. WANT 2 COME BACK EARLY? THOT ABOUT WHAT I ASKD? Clint's offer, she reasoned, was an effort to keep her in Oakland, not necessarily a decision to take her as his wife.

Beyond Nicole, the Seine flowed at least fifteen feet below street level. She'd never seen the Mississippi. Her parents spoke of the mighty river so wide, the current so fast, the cargo-laden barges alongside tugboats. The view of the Seine was as reassuring and calming as the San Francisco Bay.

"Puts the postcards to shame." Nicole giggled at her thought, spoken aloud as if a friend were standing beside her.

"Wasting my Paris time on Clint," she whispered and wiped the sheen of sweat from her neck. On an island in the middle of the river, the spires of Notre Dame poked at the sky. The panorama stopped her in her steps. The June sun was hot, the air tense with humidity. Nicole clapped her hands. "I did it!" She was hot and cold, happy and happier all at once. Paris was simply Paris. If hers was a photographer's eye or a painter's hand, she reflected, she'd capture Paris and make postcards. Postcards for her parents, the hunched woman who delivered her newspaper, even Clint.

I'm okay, she'd write. *I am here. In Paris. All on my own.*

4

Mississippi, Late Spring 1944

All Ruby wanted when she went to that place in the woods was to experience a juke joint, taste what her PapPap called hooch, have a little fun and learn about life—either which way, hers was forever shifted. Some girls she knew set their hearts on recipes and picket fences, wedding veils and white gowns, babies and a good man. Ruby dreamed of things a fine musician could provide: silk dresses, fancy shoes, and trips to cities dotted with buildings touching the sky, anywhere outside the confines of Sheridan, Mississippi, population 2,576. For days after she met Arnett, she suffered from distraction while her teachers spoke of proper sentences, while she succumbed to the habit of biting her fingernails nearly to the quick. While brushing her hair, changing the bed linens, and eating her meals, all the while thinking of Arnett's lips blowing into the saxophone and into her, the taste of smoke mixed with spearmint gum, the tickle of his mustache. These thoughts, these sensations made her knees tremble even now.

What a grown woman might have classified as mere flirtation, Ruby interpreted otherwise: not as love, not yearning. Destiny. A future linked to Arnett's. Twice she declared this to Lurlene before convincing her to take him a handwritten note. Lurlene explained to Ruby that she was merely experiencing her first longing for a man and not to take the feeling as seriously as the dilemma of what she wanted to do.

"I'm going."

Lurlene watched Ruby now, the girl, not the almost woman she had been in that juke joint fourteen days earlier. She reeked of her mother Martha's control: hair thick with pomade, braided and bound with no hope of stray hairs going free; black skirt old-woman shapeless, clearing buttocks, past knee to calf, socks, and clunky shoes.

"Your mama find out, she bound to whip *you* and kick *me* outta here, and then where would poor Lurlene go?"

"Then you shouldn't have taken him the note. But you did." Ruby wrapped her arms around her friend's ample frame. Lurlene had gone again to that shack in the woods with Ruby's lavender-scented note secure in her brassiere. In her childish hand, Ruby pleaded for Arnett to meet her in town this very afternoon. With no assurance or certainty of his coming, she merely trusted that he had fallen, too.

"Girl, I'm nigh on to twenty-two and not half bold as you. Not even a woman. Least not like that."

Ruby was gone for Arnett, and it was too late to come back. It was in her face, the fluttering lashes, the blush on her cheek, the distraction. It was in the place between her legs that she dared not name, the place Martha pointed to when she wanted her daughters to make sure they were clean.

"Listen, RubyMae, you best forget that man and stick to boys. Arnett is a musician, honey, and a saxophone player to boot. I used to love me a sax man, and let me tell you . . . a saxophone played right is as close as a person can get to God and a woman can get to good loving. And the combination?" Lurlene picked up the hem of her dress and fanned herself the way she would if summer heat had crept up her legs and into spaces godly women were not supposed to think about. "Lord, the combination will spoil you forever."

Martha didn't watch daughter and boarder move from the spacious porch down the steps to the street. Nor did she note her daughter's quickened pace, her lightened step. Lurlene and Ruby dawdled, letting the neighbors see the two of them and confirm they had been together. Gone was the brooding stride Ruby had maintained when ordered to run errands or go into the center of town. At Ruby's direction, the two friends parted at the short road leading to the courthouse square.

The plan that came together in Ruby's head had to do with providence. Not the sort the preacher went on about Sunday mornings involving the Almighty and Heaven. The kind that made two or three events come to pass at the same moment without preparation—it happened when she met Arnett, and she wanted to make it happen again. Ruby was set to run into Arnett in front of Mr. Lewis's ice cream parlor between one and two—a believable happenstance, considering the sun's heat.

Men, and women with children in tow, strolled on either side of the street, listless in the afternoon mugginess. Few lingered near the ice cream parlor except two barefoot colored boys examining the coins in their hands and calculating the cost of two cones. "Mr. Lewis, don't 'low no credit!" The shorter of the two boys punched his companion's arm before taking off, leaving behind a wake of dust.

On the far side of the street, a colored man lingered in the shade of the dry goods store, hat cocked to his left, left leg over right. Smoke drifted from his cigarette to nowhere in particular. He seemed lulled by deliberation. Ruby sucked in air to slow her pace to make sure this was the man she expected. No one in the whole of Sheridan stood straight as Arnett. It seemed to Ruby that none of the boys at school stood at all. To a tee they acted foolish, yanking at her hair and running off.

The urge to run to Arnett rushed over her as it had the night she followed him to his corner. She paced before the little store, thinking to trifle with Arnett same as she did when one square-headed young man knocked on the Garrett door. The young man had stammered and shifted the posies he'd brought from one hand to the other, waiting for permission to keep her company. She had not waited for Arnett in the juke joint, and with Lurlene's advice ringing in her ears, Arnett, Ruby figured, needed to understand that she was worth the wait.

Selling ice cream and dry goods to whites and coloreds was how Mr. Eugene Lewis supported his family and kept himself in fancy suspenders. Following Jim Crow's rules, he kept "WHITE" and "COLORED" signs affixed to the two doors of his establishment. The signs were plain and clear for all to see, for every colored man, woman, and child to heed. A believer in partial if not whole truths, Ruby stepped into the ice cream parlor through the door marked "colored" and ordered a vanilla ice cream cone. It was the white man's habit, and her game, whenever they were alone in the tiny store, to talk to Ruby in a tone reserved for white folks. "RubyMae, don't you ever want to taste another flavor?"

"It's the tasting that precipitates experimenting, Mr. Lewis. I know what I want."

She batted her eyes, knowing such an action between a colored girl and a white man was open to interpretation. Clothed as she was, Ruby felt his glare from the top of her head down to the clunky shoes on her feet.

"Well, don't go letting that ice cream spoil your appetite."

"No sir, I won't." She set two nickels on the counter.

Because Mr. Lewis didn't bother with Jim Crow when his white customers were not present, Ruby stepped to the door marked "WHITE." Without looking back at the elderly man, she sashayed right through it, imagining life in a place where signs didn't confine her use to a specific door or toilet or water fountain; where a colored girl did not have to tolerate lecherous glances for a minute's worth of equality.

Mr. Lewis set his attention on Ruby's backside and she watched for Arnett. Neither of them noticed the white boys, close to Ruby's age, posturing against the wood siding. Ruby surveyed the two boys at almost the same minute she noticed Arnett move to one of two posts supporting a flimsy canopy. He pushed back the sleeve of his jacket, and to Ruby, it struck her that he was going to leave. She picked up her pace.

"Hey!" she shouted. In her hurry to get to him, she plowed straight into the boys. In that one flat second, she examined them, then stared dead in their blue eyes and motioned for them to go on. They bowed deep, caps to ribcages; a towheaded boy and a second one, puffy in the face, two competing Casanovas ready to play the same game.

Ruby recollected neither of the two. Sheridan was not large compared to Jackson and, maybe, Biloxi, but she recognized newcomer from citizen. In Sheridan, coloreds knew their whites and vice versa. Everyone knew she was colored because everyone, colored and white, had seen her all over town with Martha and Paul. Everyone knew she got her color from her daddy and her temper from her mother.

"Y'all want another cone, miss?" The towheaded boy was the braver of the two. His face was covered with freckles that matched the color of his dirty hair. He showed her his grubby dollar bill, proof that he was able to afford floats or a ticket to the movies, if that was what she was partial to. "I favor strawberry, myself."

She continued ahead, disregarding the boys and their inquiries. The other boy stepped closer to Ruby. "How you keeping so fresh in this weather, miss? I can hold up one of them pigtails so's you can get air on yer neck." He smirked and reached for Ruby's hair.

Mr. Lewis stepped into his doorway. "Y'all leave that colored gal alone now, and go on back to where you came from."

Ruby lowered her head and separated herself from the boys,

aiming toward the reason she had come to the ice cream parlor in the first place. She caught sight of Arnett. His view of her was as clear and straight as hers was of him. Nothing on his face showed that he grasped Ruby's predicament. She stepped to the curb. The pudgy-faced boy examined her as he might a June bug tied to a string.

"Well, I'll be gotdammed! I heard tell of these whitish negras, but I ain't never seed one." The towheaded boy whooped and stuck his face right in hers, forcing Ruby against the large window of Mr. Lewis's store. "Hey, brother, this gal been trickin' us. Acting white." He rechecked the "WHITE" sign and moved to touch Ruby's hair.

"Don't you know no better?" The second boy poked his finger at her chest. Ruby sidestepped to the right, keen to escape. They blocked her. She moved in the opposite direction, and they blocked her path a second time.

"Either let me pass or be on your way." Her command was loud enough for anyone close by, and surely Arnett, to hear.

"Ain't no monkey gonna make a monkey outta me." The towheaded boy cleared his throat and hocked spit onto her ice cream. The thick glob stuck to the ice cream, then proceeded down the cone. His flexed arms dared her, or any colored folk nearby, to make a move.

The boys positioned themselves on either side of Ruby. Ruby pursed her lips, prepared to spit at the unruly young men, not caring that the consequences of her action might cause trouble for her and her family. She inched backward, knowing where white folks were concerned reckoning was not a colored girl's privilege. Surveying the street again, from the boys to Arnett fixed to his spot, Ruby saw the brim of his fedora set farther down his face and his interest in the details of the soil beneath his polished shoes.

"Get on outta here." Mr. Lewis flapped his hands the same as he would at a flock of bothersome chickens. "Shoo, now! Ain't no need for trouble. This is a quiet town. We get along with our coloreds." He moseyed back into his store and stepped behind the counter. It seemed to Ruby that he placed his hand beneath it.

"Don't know where you're coming from," he bellowed, "but best tend to your business, and get on back."

The boys paused, seeming to consider Mr. Lewis's alert; they were old enough to know better, but young enough to respect their elders.

"Ain't worth it, brother." The towheaded one frowned at Ruby. "Not for one little nigger gal."

They scooted past, knocking Ruby off the sidewalk, their heavy boots noisy even in the tamped dirt. The abrupt motion sent the ice cream down her skirt and into the street. She went to the gutter and wiped at the milky mess. When the boys were completely out of view, and it was clear they had no intention of returning, Arnett came to her.

"You see what they did?" Ruby threw what was left of her cone into the dusty street. She kicked Arnett and he stumbled from the force of her small foot. Then she stomped on the cone, the vanilla cream dotting the vamp of her shoe, and mashed the ice cream until it blended into an unrecognizable muck.

"You saw! And you didn't do a damn thing."

"I swear I didn't know it was you them boys were messing with. Until it was too late." Arnett bent to wipe his shoe with a handkerchief from his left pocket until its shine matched the other again. Her face, the lips that had hypnotized Arnett, were subdued in their natural state. He lifted one of her long braids and held it in his hand. "I wasn't going to let them hurt you, you know."

Looking like the girl she was, Ruby sucked in air through her teeth, nothing moving except her nostrils. She snatched her braid from Arnett's hand. "I had them fooled, till that ice cream man spoke up."

"It was that man that saved you." He followed her, taking her elbow—a helpful colored gentleman with no other purpose—until her trembling stopped.

Ruby yanked her arm from Arnett's grip. "You didn't even try to stop them."

"Ruby, my jewel, you are a dear one...but it seemed, from where I stood, those boys were messing with a white girl and I wasn't about to be no martyr for a *white* girl. Before I knew what was happening, I'd be hanging from a tree." Arnett's hand shook when he fingered her long braid again. "I'm taking this as a sign. I shouldn't have come."

"Shame on you, Arnett, no middle name, Dupree. Are you telling me I can't count on you?"

"I'm telling you I got plans and I'm not letting anyone change them." He adjusted his belt buckle, straightened his back, and widened the space between his feet. His stance gave the impression of a man well over the twenty-five years he'd claimed a fortnight ago.

Without the certainty in her daylight emotions that she had exposed in the dim light of the juke joint, Ruby shuffled closer to Arnett. She wanted his arms, firm as they had been when they met, holding her again. Not that caution had been on her mind that night, but right now, comfort was what she wanted.

"Any other time, any other circumstance, I'll be there for you."

"Promise?" For all of her not knowing and just feeling, even in her anger, Ruby could not resist Arnett's gaze. "Because you have to promise, if you want me."

"I can't seem to help myself," he whispered, quickly kissing the top of her head. He checked for folks interested in a man paying too much attention to a girl: the man beyond them who swept without cleaning, a white woman who scrutinized him from beneath her wide hat with attention bound to get him in trouble.

"This wasn't a good idea, Ruby my jewel." He took his lighter from his pocket and held it so the swirling letters of his initials, AD, were forever imprinted in Ruby's mind as they were on the gold. In one continuous motion, he lit a cigarette, tipped his hat, and left before Ruby had the chance to beg him to stay or find out when he planned to come to Sheridan again.

5

By using routine greetings, the beginner can practice the language and initiate polite communication.

ça va? (sah vah)	how is it going?
comment vas-tu? (coh mah vah tue)	how are you? (familiar)
bonjour (bone zhoor)	hello
au revoir (oh reh vwar)	goodbye

The phone rang and rang. Traffic advanced in three directions. A triangle-shaped fountain bisected the boulevard, its front a statue of a winged man, sword in hand, standing on top of a slain dragon. Water spilled from below and into a pool guarded by snarling winged creatures, half lion, half serpent—the fountain of St.-Michel.

Squire rejected answering machines. His definition had become a family joke; they were, in his opinion, "an opposition to the telephone's communicative intention." Opposition was a word Squire collected. Periodically, opposition crept between Malvina and Nicole, and he had been the referee: in this corner matriarch and maker of rules—Malvinaaaa Handeeee; and in this corner, dutiful daughter—Nicole-Marie Handeee. Ding. The night Nicole told her parents she was going to Paris, Squire paced from the den to the kitchen in a compressed circle that widened with every short lap. "Malvina, I can't find my keys. I need to go to work."

"You can't go!" Malvina fussed, leaving Nicole unsure whom her mother meant to overrule. Malvina pressed against a tattered wingback chair and dropped her voice. "I can't handle your father on my own. I can't do it."

"We'll find a nurse to help until I come back. I'll make the arrangements before I leave."

"I won't tolerate strangers touching my personal things."

"Then what do you want me to do, Mother?"

Nicole had helped Squire to his chair and flipped through TV channels until a show caught his interest. Back when he was the family's dinner-table intellectual, Squire scorned TV, except for his westerns. He quoted Plato, Descartes, and Aristotle from the books stacked beside his recliner. He memorized speeches—King and Kennedy. At Friday night get-togethers, he posed by the fireplace and recited Langston's poems. Squire stretched out in his favorite chair, eighty-five years of age and content to watch cartoon characters bicker to canned laughter.

"You can't go gallivanting all over the world. I need you here. I was hoping you'd move back home, for a while." Malvina pushed on her cane again and hobbled to the kitchen. Her face directed at the counter, she adjusted the toaster then the coffeepot, flicking the on-off switch. "You owe us, Nicki. It's your duty."

It wasn't the physical act of caring for her parents. Five years of Wednesdays. Fifty-two multiplied by five, and then some. Help rooted in love, not duty. Nicole already whispered names of friends and neighbors in her father's ear, read to him, helped him untangle past and present. To pay the bills and visit the doctors month after month with little hope, to be greeted by name at the drugstore, to sleep in her childhood bedroom—responsibilities that were not burdensome, separately. Taking them on daily, every night, week, month, year, was a job.

"Hello? Hello?" Long distance not withstanding, Squire's voice was weak. If he slept at all, Nicole was no longer sure. He was now an early riser.

"It's me, Dad. Nicole." She crossed her fingers and turned right at a busy intersection, most of which was taken up by the Boulevard St.-Michel and a plaza crazy with movement. "You okay?"

He didn't reply right away. "Today is good, Nicole. A good day. You coming over?"

"No, I won't be out your way. I'm in France. Remember? I miss you."

"Today is good, baby. You coming over?"

She paced the width of the fountain and responded to her father's looping question as if she'd hadn't heard it before. A circle of conversation, an updated version of the joke, "who's on first?"

"Pass the phone, Squire." Malvina's voice was loud in the background. "Stay in bed. We get up at seven, remember? Nicki, how's Paris?"

How, she considered, to describe what she saw to a woman whose travel experience had been a one-way trip from Mississippi to California. "It's great, Mother. Really great. The best."

"Make sure you don't go moping, thinking about who promised to take you there and what he did to keep that from happening." Malvina breathed noisily, waiting, Nicole suspected, for her to agree or disagree. "The bank statement came. I guess I'll balance the checkbook, unless you want me to wait for you. When did you say you were coming back?"

"I got here a few hours ago, Mother." To her left, a youngish man with a serene face raised his hand in a polite wave. Nicole smiled—lips, no teeth—and stared at the tourists collecting in organized groups on the nearby bridge. Women in running shoes and white anklets, men in Bermuda shorts and black knee-highs, maps in hands, cameras on straps dangling from reddened necks. "Let me enjoy being here, before I start thinking about when I have to leave. Anyhow, I'm letting you know I arrived. All is well."

"Don't get friendly with strangers. I read about women getting kidnapped and turned into sex slaves."

As a reader of newspapers, not books, stories with a negative spin attracted Malvina. Her warnings framed Nicole's ambition. Often they'd kept her from venturing far from home, traveling or eating the food if she did, socializing on the Internet, and putting gas in her car after sunset.

"Not to worry. I doubt anyone's interested in women with gray roots and too big to fit into Paris-sized clothes."

At a take-out restaurant close to the Pont St.-Michel, the bridge linking the Left Bank to the Boulevard du Palais on the Île de la Cité, Nicole selected a ham and cheese sandwich. "Bonjour, Monsieur. Jambon et fromage, s'il vous plaît." Her first French spoken, not counting the cab ride and the few phrases mumbled to her father before she left, since freshman year when a professor declared that her accent was terrible and her pursuit of the melodious language a waste.

"You are well come, Madame."

Grateful for his friendliness, Nicole tipped the vendor and sat at a nearby table. In the middle of her bite, a heavy hand tapped her shoulder. Malvina's warning of mayhem transferred from California to France. Turning to face the source, she secured her hold on her purse and vowed not to be the victim of a crime. Minutes ago this very man had waved to her and now he stood beside her table. Wrinkle-free skin, clean-shaven, fortyish, Nicole guessed. His shirt was buttoned up to the collar where a tie should've been; inches of cuffs exposed below his jacket sleeves, white socks beneath the hem of his pants.

"You are American, oui? Yes?" He rushed his request, Nicole supposed, to maintain her attention.

Amidst the French conversations within her hearing range, this man's heavily accented English was a surprise. She frowned; at the man, then at his hand on her shoulder and figured if her glare didn't confirm her country of origin, then she didn't know how to cut her eyes as well as she'd practiced.

He removed his hand. "Forgive me, I do not want to be rude. It is easy to identify American women. French women do not... they do not walk so fast and stiffly. *You* are American." His dimples had a magic all their own and Nicole wasn't able to tell if he was conscious of how they worked their indentations in his cheeks, a subtle invitation. "Allow me to present myself. I am Ousmane Diallo. I want to talk to you." His silhouette darkened her table and guidebook, a dead giveaway, beside her waiting baguette.

The sandwich crept back up her throat with a sour repetition. *I want to talk to you* was a sorry line she'd fallen for thirty-some-odd years ago, thinking she was special when a good-looking guy came on to her at a frat mixer. She left with him; to defy Malvina, to test the waters. She didn't remember "Good-Looking's" name or his fancy talk or how he came so quickly in the backseat of his car. Fast enough to get them back into the mixer and pretend he was getting her a drink instead of moving on.

"Many Americans do this talking."

Nicole shook her head. "I'm afraid that's not possible."

The cheerfulness dropped from Ousmane Diallo's face, making him seem boyishly sad. Not broken, rebuffed. "You are certain?" Erect and silent, Ousmane's posture pleaded for Nicole's agreement. His arms hung from his shoulders as if they, too, were perplexed and unsure what should happen next. He bowed and headed for the bridge.

When they had agreed, a year ago, to make the trip to Paris together, Tamara and Nicole met for drinks to toast their excursion. A man at the bar sent cocktails and a request to join them. Tamara winked at the man. "It's easier to say yes when there's two of us." She spoke for Nicole's benefit because, alone, Tamara had little use for "no." The man turned out to have the best sense of humor, and they had joked and talked until the bar closed. A little assistance right now was what she needed.

Oh, how she missed her friend.

Don't play it safe. If she let go, and truly committed to Tamara's advice, she could be a modern-day version of Diahann Carroll (younger and accompanied) in *Paris Blues* and have an adventure by simply agreeing to this proposition. She could meet Ousmane's friends, speak French, go to a dinner and enjoy a meal that combined the best of Africa and France.

Long past the tautness and the gray-free hair of youth, Nicole believed younger men did not see her. Age or narrowed perceptions, her radar for detecting if this man was serious or suspect was weak. *Talking* to the African Man wasn't a bad idea. A person to *talk* to. To engage in conversation for the purpose of learning the language. Talk. He wanted to talk to her not *talk* to her. "Ousmane!" Nicole called out, loud enough for him to hear and low enough to avoid embarrassment.

Ousmane turned on his toes, his smile filled with perfectly even, perfectly white teeth. He rushed to the chair opposite Nicole. "Merci, Madame."

"I will talk to you." No need to clarify American slang. "How do we do this? Do we speak French or English?"

"We speak a little of both. We do not have to make all our decisions now."

Oh, yes they did. "Why are you in Paris?" Clunky, she realized, but a conversation starter.

"Ah, Americans have the questions. In Senegal, I was a teacher of science. My parents wanted an engineer. But I am a lover of literature, not thermal units, copolymers, and dielectric strength—these terms I know in English, you see. I make my studies at the Sorbonne in French writers of the twentieth century. Now, I complete myself with André Breton, Cocteau, and Proust." Ousmane tilted his head and winked. "After, I work at the grand Bibliothèque Nationale."

He went on to tell Nicole about his love for learning and for Paris, and his parents' resistance to both. When he finished, he relaxed in his chair. "I have an idea for you. This is your first time in Paris, *oui*?"

Nicole confessed it was.

"Then, I propose to you an adventure. I will show you a special place not in your guidebook."

"I don't know you, and I don't know Paris."

Ousmane opened his wallet to a plastic card case and showed Nicole his Sorbonne registration and an identification card. "Voilà, my *carte d'identité*, which must be carried at all times. *Regardez*. You will be safe, this I promise. We take the Métro. It is very, how do you say? Public?"

Nicole inspected Ousmane's card twice before handing it back. There was only one way to break out of the ordinary. An extraordinary city demanded extraordinary action.

The St.-Michel Métro station was a cavernous maze of tunnels lined with white tile, bustling and complicated. Flights of stairs veered off to the left and right. Several stations, Ousmane described with the air of an experienced guide, were large and long enough to have moving walkways. At the iron gate close to the enclosed glass ticket counter, Ousmane showed Nicole how to read a giant wall map and identify the station to which she'd return. At his urging, she bought a packet of ten tickets. "They are easier to use for when you are in a hurry." He showed her how to insert the ticket's magnetic edge to open the turnstile. They waited on a crowded platform for the Number 4 train, bound in the direction of Porte de Clignancourt.

"We are going to Barbès-Rochechouart. It is not many stops from here." He pointed to the linear map above the exit door listing Line 4 Métro stops in order.

They sat side by side on the molded seats. *Ka-chunka-chunk*, *ka-chunka-chunk*. The train's hypnotic rhythm, and an occasional grin from Ousmane, eased Nicole's nerves. She focused on the station names spelled out in black against white tiles, a reminder she was not at home. Four or five stops beyond the St.-Michel station, the dress and the complexions of the riders changed. At home, where check marks classified race on school, credit card, and housing loans applications, she would've said more people of color entered and exited the train. In France, she'd read, being French was the most important descriptor. The train drew closer to their destination; language morphed and expanded from French to the unfamiliar. Twists and turns of the tongue that Nicole was unable to identify. Exiting the station, the city had changed.

Ousmane stretched out his arms. "This is Little Africa!"

Neither Nicole's cream-with-coffee skin nor Ousmane's pecan brown were the exception as they had been in the Place St.-Michel. Dark and light—not white, but shades of every skin color in between. Bob Marley T-shirts. Men and women dressed in fabric with magenta, yellow, red, and turquoise combined into pleasing patterns and swirls. Comforting odors, some fresh and a few sour, pervaded the air: the perspiration of hardworking citizens rushing home, cobs of corn roasting on an open grill, popcorn, churros, fresh-cooked beignets, curry. A man hawked gold bracelets encircling his palm. Another man, of Arab descent, and his young sons sold shopping bags made of African cloth, yellow, red, green, and black. A one-eyed boy stared. Nicole believed her brown skin fit well in this *arrondissement*. His stare proved she was out of place. No tourists here.

A metal bridge hovered above them, interlaced strips of steel studded with round-head rivets, underneath it, a teeming street, a city all its own. They waited for the traffic light to change beside a newsstand with papers whose headlines were written in French and a language with scimitar-curved letters. Palm against her elbow, Ousmane escorted Nicole to the Boulevard de Magenta.

"I call this the street of weddings. In one block many stores are for marriage clothes."

Ten-foot display windows up one side and down the other, crowded with wedding finery: purple, pink, turquoise, and lavender bridesmaid dresses; salmon, beige, gray tuxedos with velvet lapels. African salesmen dressed in bright-colored tuxes supported their weight against the storefronts, and peddled their goods. "Entrez, entrez, Monsieur et Madame. Nous avons des wedding dresses magnifiques!"

"Non, non," Ousmane replied and ambled with Nicole past a fifties-style beauty shop and the smell of hot flatirons against hair, chemical relaxer, and hair spray. He waved at shopkeepers or stopped to shake hands. Ousmane was attentive with an old-fashioned style. He guided her through the neighborhood, stepped aside and allowed her to precede him when the sidewalks narrowed. Brown-skinned mothers lugged their children and picked through tables of clothes bound together with rubber bands. Women in plain cotton hijabs tried on footwear from tables set up in doorways. A neon sign advertised a tattoo parlor.

"Now, to the other side of the station. We are too late for le marché Dejean, the market where they sell the foods of my country."

Nicole scrutinized his profile as he led her past shops filled with neat piles of linens, checkered plastic tablecloths, tagines. His dimples gave him the appearance of a mischievous teen. Nicole giggled, unable to remember when her day had been filled with so many twists and turns.

Up to last evening's flight, the sum total of Nicole's experiences were an infinite recurrence of ditto marks. No pets. No kids. Fixture in a law firm along with mahogany desks and leather swivel chairs, ditto since 1977. Breakfast: boiled eggs, toast. Lunch: tuna/dark rye; extra mustard, no tomatoes. M–F ditto. Popcorn and peanut butter; salami on rye. Cookies, ice cream, pie. Weekly dinner with parents. Married at forty-nine. Divorced at fifty-one. A few vacations. Girls' nights out. Tea not coffee. Hard liquor not wine. Choosing men without thinking. Ditto. Ditto. The Monday-to-Friday commute to San Francisco and return to Oakland. Seeing the same faces weary from lawyering, administrating, copying, computing, decision-making, shopping, clock-watching.

Blue triangle banners hung from lightposts and named the area. "This is Goutte d'Or, golden drop. It is the name of the vineyard that existed here and the wine it produced." Ousmane seemed determined to give every fact about his neighborhood. They strolled past mobile phone stores brimming with customers crammed into compact spaces as if the phones were free. A woman moved down the street with her hands and feet, her head angled backwards, her middle twisted. Men of all ages clustered in groups. "They are North Africans."

Alone, Nicole might have been nervous, and she didn't want to think why. She raised her camera and focused the lens on a passing family. The woman was dressed in African garb, her baby secured to her body with a large piece of fabric. The man was outfitted in a long white flowing top with matching pants.

"You see my friend inside the store? He is working. And here the women? How they are dressed in their babus? How they have purchases and food for their families in their hands? What would you say if they pointed their cameras on you?"

"Sorry." Not one of Nicole's guidebooks related any description of Little Africa. Modern architecture mixed with old, new compared to the center of Paris. She tucked the camera back in her bag.

Ousmane accepted her apology and motioned to Nicole to make a one-hundred-eighty-degree turn. "That is Sacré-Cœur." Rooflines converged, like an artist's trompe l'oeil, into the spiked domes of the famous basilica. The top, its exterior white and gleaming, peaked above the buildings at the end of the street, five blocks away.

"We are behind the church, the highest in Paris. Little Africa is what can be seen if a person climbed to the top and looked eastward." They stopped at a café centered at the tip of the triangle where the street split in two. "I have shown you my Paris, and I have talked. Now, you must talk. In French."

"My French is nowhere near as good as your English," Nicole confessed. "I know a few basic sentences, a bit of vocabulary, and very little grammar. I signed up for a class at the Alliance Française."

"This is good, Nicole! I will help with your French and you with my English." He brushed his hand against hers. "You will give me your telephone number. Non?"

Nicole removed her notebook from her handbag and pushed it toward Ousmane. "It's easier if I call you." He wrote four sets of double digits separated by dashes.

"In truth, Nicole, you must call me at the Bibliothèque Nationale. It is where I work. My wife, she does not understand this talking business."

"Your wife?" Nicole chuckled under her breath. "Married."

"There are the occasions when I... *comment dit-on*? You Americans say: to stir up things, eh?" Ousmane allowed his dimples to flirt when, apparently, he wasn't supposed to.

"Thanks, but no thanks." Nicole watched Ousmane frown again. Paris promised to get rid of the ditto marks. This was a start. Daunting as it was, Nicole loved that she'd accepted Ousmane's invitation. She chuckled, indifferent to what part of his story—the engineering, the love of French literature, whatever—was also a lie. When, she considered, was she going to learn to tell the lies from the truth? Either way, she hadn't come this far to spend her vacation in the company of a married man.

6

Mississippi, November 1944

By the time Arnett came back to the two-room juke joint, Ruby had turned sixteen. In that six months her body had not so much blossomed as rounded. Intentionally or otherwise, his absence had caused her to brood. When Lurlene let it slip that Arnett was back on the circuit, back in the shack where they met, Ruby demanded and got her way. This night Lurlene helped her climb out her bedroom window into the pitch-black night and a sedan that smelled of wet dogs. They rode in near silence—the skunks, the possum, and the battered sign showing the road into the backcountry.

What the months had done to her body, they did to her confidence as well. Ruby allowed no hopeful boy, or soldier waiting for her letters, to have her for his own. With no idea of his plans or the prospect of his return, she claimed herself as Arnett's. It was with this on her mind that she sashayed toward the packed shack, head held high.

A chubby woman blocked the door, in her hands a tin can of pocket change. She was the gatekeeper to the dancers cramped in the narrow space. Ruby followed Lurlene and her newest suitor, a big spender who lisped. Men squeezed close to women they knew or wanted to know. Women rocked back and forth, their bodies open invitations to whoever came along. A few men alone, drinks in hand, held up the wall behind them and watched Ruby and Lurlene, the men smacking their lips like the two women were finely blended sipping bourbon.

Ruby brushed invisible lint from her dress and waited, as Lurlene had instructed. At the table with the tin bucket that passed for a punch bowl, Ruby ladled the liquid into a short glass. She put the glass to her mouth, letting its edge part her lips, and looked for Arnett huddled in his corner.

A thin smile loosened the right side of his face. He ambled toward the couch pushed against the wall. The piano and bass began a light intro along with the two musicians: a medium-sized gray-haired man, bent as his battered saxophone, and Arnett. The man spoke his name, "Red," and folks clapped before he stepped opposite Arnett. The two men began to play, tossing music between them. Red, then Arnett. Arnett, then Red. At the start, their exchange was not loud or fast. One man riffed off the other, adding in notes, speeding up, slowing down. Red played measures from a quick piece. Arnett ran his fingers through his wavy hair, letting the crowd know he had not heard the music before. He cocked his head and listened. When Red was done, Arnett grinned, put his lips to his waiting mouthpiece, and blew Red's notes and his own; worked his fingers up and down the saxophone's shiny body sure of his own rhythm, caught between blues and jazz and a style of music with no name. He threw new notes together for Red, mellow and careless ones. The notes were free to stray. Arnett and Red went on until folks stopped dancing, hypnotized by the dueling instruments. Twenty minutes into this set, Arnett tossed the man a wicked grin and answered Red's last challenge by repeating the same melody. When Red picked up the beat, Arnett didn't stop. He blew, making each note longer and hotter. He blew, scarcely taking a new breath, until beads of sweat collected on his forehead and crept down his face. He blew until women and men chanted, "Yeh, daddy. Blow." He blew, succumbing to his frenzy, his knees shaking, his body rocking his saxophone, tilting until his back arched and his knees pushed him upright. He blew until Red threw up his hands and put down his sax. He blew until his last long note, taking for itself a mind of its own, drifted into the room and out into the night. Then he opened his gray eyes that tinged on blue and found her, making Ruby unsure he knew where he was.

He did not go to his corner where she waited. He went to the center of the room where men handed him watered-down brandy and slapped his back and women thrust their bodies to his body, their lips to his lips, waiting for him to blow his fever into them. A big-boned woman, small-chested but sexy, Ruby decided—if one cared for her type—was one of these women.

"Don't go doing anything you'll regret," Lurlene chided.

The sight of Arnett got Ruby's head to throbbing, girl silly and grown woman ignored, jealousy brewing together.

"Stand your ground. Let him come to you," Lurlene whispered in Ruby's ear.

Arnett talked to the small-chested woman, who pawed him in expectation of possession, until a new set began. All the while him staring at Ruby, searching her face for a reaction until she nodded.

He played again. He blew the one note for himself, then turned his attention to Ruby and played the rest of his song for her. When he was done, Arnett headed straight for her, took her drink and downed it. He fingered the blue brooch on her dress.

"It's my good-luck charm—it brought you to me. You like it?"

"A girl like you deserves the real deal."

His voice was honeyed and deep as his last note. She wanted him to talk, to know him. To know if he liked her and how he'd learned to replicate notes without referring to papers. She wanted him to help her with the ditties on the radio she sang along with or made up in her head. But the sweat and the yearning so open on his face, told her to hold on. And she did.

Someone put Billie Holiday on the record player. Thick cigarette smoke curled around the music's slow beat. Without his seeking, or her giving, permission he put his free hand on her elbow and steered her past the dancers, the lovers, and the near-drunk. The chubby woman stopped them at the door.

"Where you goin', sugar man? I thought we were taking a ride in your car." She cut Ruby a mean glare and slipped her hand into Arnett's pocket. "You know what you getting into, li'l girl?"

Ruby went to speak, understanding the woman was challenging her right to be with Arnett. She clung to Arnett, watching the woman rub his thigh. Arnett neither budged nor backed away, but held on to Ruby's arm.

"A girl can't do what a woman can." The woman ogled Arnett's crotch thick with her touch, then cackled in Ruby's face. "This ain't no boy, baby girl, this a man, and if you don't know what to do with him, as you can see, I can teach you a thing or two."

How they got to his car, she never remembered. The distance of the music, close enough to hear the beat but not to understand the crooner's lyrics. The hood of the car shiny in filtered light from an unknown source. Arnett held her against the cold steel of the car, his hands all over her. "After this night, you ain't nobody's woman but mine."

"Ruby!" Lurlene's call broke the spell, not a shout but a firm command, a schoolteacher to her student. "Come on back, Ruby." Her voice blended with the night, the low thrum of the music far behind them.

With one breath in, Ruby thought to call to Lurlene, to follow her back to home and her warm bed. With one breath out, her body opened to the ache. She wrapped him in her arms; that flow, that hot longing, released. The saxophone against her replaced with his lips and hands. He kissed her again, and she kissed him back, her silence Lurlene's answer. They held on to one another, quiet until Lurlene's calls stopped. The night no longer black, heavy with the smell of pine, the lonely chirp of a cricket, water dribbling from a nearby pump. And heat mean as the hottest day on this cool night.

He opened the car door and helped her onto the broad seat. Then he peeled off her dress and slip, her bra and cotton panties, until she was naked on that backseat, in the middle of those woods. He read her from head to toe; sniffed her. Her without words, but the merest of sighs. When Arnett shook off his shirt, awkward in the confines of the car, Ruby gasped. Not as she might have, this being her first time. In the dim light, his half-nakedness was less shocking than the gash stretching from his ribs to his pelvis. The scar long as if a doctor had sewn in a zipper to bind his left and right together.

Ruby ran her fingers the length of his scar as if she had learned the lesson of his fingers on the saxophone, as if touching a bare man were for her an unexceptional occurrence. "What happened?"

She broke his magic; stopped his wandering hands, not understanding that waiting was familiar to him. Waiting for his turn to play or pausing in a song, holding his lick for the moment to jump back in and pick up the rhythm. Arnett held his stroke.

He described how, on the road, he made up stories for his buddies—enemy strafing, a switchblade fight on the streets of New Orleans, a jealous woman's kitchen knife. He confessed to his disinclination to tell the truth, choosing rather to tell stories that made him a hero. He admitted that Ruby's tentative touch made him want her to know him as a teller of truths, a keeper of promises.

"'Forty-two. Camp Claiborne, Louisiana. Filthy swamp of a place. Army gave white soldiers the high ground near the highway and the buses to take them to town. They quartered us on swampland. No PX. No nothing, Just water moccasins and rattlesnakes. Even the damn German prisoners had it better." He licked her fingers like he had his stiff reed.

"Couldn't go nowhere or do nothing but sit in that marsh and pretend backwoods hoogies didn't want to mess with us awfully bad. They didn't care for colored boys carrying guns. It's our war, our country, too. Patty boys had ice and water. They kept us confined to our area, kept us working, hauling, washing, serving their food." He spoke, his breathing controlled. He'd messed with firecrackers—his habit of caring for what he shouldn't instead of what he should do. "It was the Fourth of July, and on Independence Day, I love sparklers and firecrackers. Ever since I can remember every Fourth of July me and my brothers had firecrackers. I was missing my brothers, missing my celebrations, so I lit a firecracker and a fool guard shot me. I set myself on fire. Lucky I didn't lose my fingers." He clenched and opened the fingers on his left, then his right hand.

She set Arnett's hand, his left hand, on that longing spot, not caring about his story, his scar, just him and this feeling meant for him alone to satisfy. "Shh," she whispered.

Arnett pressed his mouth to Ruby's lips, his breath became hers. He held her in his arms so that she was neither girl nor woman but flesh-and-blood saxophone—her body the tube, her hips the U-shaped bow, her nipples the keypad for his composition. He dragged his wet forefinger on her nipple, flicked the warmth of his tongue against her until he became stiff and hard. Picking up his rhythm, her thighs, their muscles flexing, moved with him, squeezing until he groaned. Rocking with his beat, Ruby released to Arnett, to this excitement surging through her body, to the possibilities of what was to come.

7

Practice conjugating verbs in each of the three basic tenses. Past, present, and future can be combined in both speaking and writing.

rencontrer (ron con tray)	to meet
le hasard (luh ah sar)	chance
avoir de la chance (avwahr duh lah shahnce)	to be lucky
choisir (shwah zeer)	to choose

"Bonjour, Madame. Comment allez-vous?" Monsieur Daudon balanced a cigarette between two fingers and his thumb when he brought it to his mouth. His charm had lured her inside a week ago, as it did this afternoon. A fixture as weathered as the sign above his head, he stared at passing traffic, at workers with lime green plastic brooms sweeping clogged gutters, at Nicole. She considered, again, the irony of the burly man smoking in the entry to a store of fragile, flammable goods. He dragged two caned chairs from inside the door, in what had become his habit since Nicole had included him in her daily routine, and dusted the seats.

Self-guided tours and meals at neighborhood bistros gave

Nicole a sense of the city and its citizens. Solitary evenings left her still unsure if she had made the right decision to take this vacation on her own. Tamara must have known, and that was why she demanded a promise, knowing Nicole's best quality was that she tried her best never to break one. Parisians were not unfriendly but reserved, by American standards, and protective of their privacy. In the lines of the *supermarché*, boutiques, and museums where, at home, conversations with strangers were spontaneous, Parisians were formal and kept to themselves.

For three straight days, Nicole had passed by Les Petits Secrets, greeting the owner with the basic "bonjour" and "comment-allez vous." On the fourth pass, she'd practiced the lesson of connecting learned from the African Man. Curious, she'd entered the store and expanded her conversation with a well-rehearsed phrase describing the weather, "Il fait très chaud aujourd'hui," though the weather had been mild, not hot, as Monsieur Daudon had corrected. When Nicole made it clear that she was in search of a gift for her father ("Je cherche un cadeau pour mon père"), he asked, "What is your father fond of?" That was how she learned that Monsieur Daudon spoke English.

It was a game—finding mementos for Malvina and Squire and peering through antiques shop windows at porcelain pipes, heaps of vintage newspapers, and delicate pieces of European history. After scouring two stores in as many *arrondissements*, she found a beginner French textbook for English speakers, a child's cookbook with a recipe for a chocolate cake, *la tête nègre*, in the shape of a head topped with hair of cotton ball frosting, and a poster of the trumpeter Sidney Bechet. Monsieur Daudon proved to be the friendliest and most helpful of all of the shopkeepers. Cigars from the *tabac* and jokes that lost their punch lines in awkward translations had helped.

Colored crystal, teacups, saucers, and other collectibles filled shelves and glass-faced bureaus. Before Paris, Nicole avoided stores overrun with knickknacks and other people's memories.

Too close to the curios cluttering Malvina's breakfronts. Les Petits Secrets had become a substitute for Tamara, but mostly she found joy in being greeted by name. A *brocanteur*, Monsieur Daudon styled himself. Hints of a once-attractive man lined his sagging face. A bushy crew cut covered his flat head, and he rubbed his thick mustache whenever he expressed an opinion. No need to worry if Monsieur was married, his habit was to tug constantly at his wedding ring. Monsieur Daudon and Nicole had come to an understanding.

Nicole settled into the sturdy chair and lit a cigarette, prepared to pass the afternoon. Nowhere to be. No one waiting. She forgot about her father's mind shutting down, her mother's dependence on cane and daughter, Clint's proposition. Splat. No pomp. No circumstance. No I love you. Now on a daily basis he sent messages, which she ignored, lists of where to go and what to eat reminding her, she supposed, of his value.

Through his exhalations Monsieur gossiped in English. The fish he bought at the *poissonnerie* turned out to be smelly—a sign that the fishmonger was not doing well. The *boulanger*'s baguettes were salty. His best news was that a shipment was due any minute. Monsieur had purchased a mere three dozen battered and crumpled boxes without checking the contents. The hour was neither guaranteed nor its delivery predictable.

"Madame, you can pick *un cadeau* from zees boxes." He aimed the tip of his cigarette at his bulky body so that the smoke drifted into his face. "Your parents, they will enjoy, non?"

Nicole pulled a *Paris Match* from her bag without bothering to tell Monsieur that predicting what her father might enjoy was impossible. Personal details never entered into their conversations. In the days since they'd begun their visits, Monsieur hadn't invited her to meet his family in the rooms he lived in above the store. He hadn't questioned why she'd come to Paris alone, and she'd never volunteered a reason, keeping personal details to herself, as he had his, not wanting to translate the words for dream, escape, and obligation. Thirty minutes of French. Thirty minutes of English. That was their bargain. Clint swore she'd never get close to anyone French. Between Ousmane and Monsieur Daudon, he'd been wrong, and Nicole considered that his proposal was wrong as well.

"Let us see what zuh *gendarmes* blondes are doing this week." Monsieur Daudon mixed his languages. Franglais. He scooted close enough to browse the magazine's glossy pages, but not close enough to breach personal space.

"'En fait, les mariages de la plupart des mannequins se termineront certainement par un divorce, dit un psychologue qui a écrit un livre...'" Nicole read. Monsieur corrected instead of cringing at her mispronunciations. She was long past shame for her hatchet job of this beautiful language. Instead, she waited for Monsieur to reread the sentence and repeat his corrections until Nicole mastered them. *Mariages*—mah-ree-aahj. *Mannequins*—man-nay-can. Each syllable for marriage and model spoken phonetically, similar to the phrasing in her long-gone blue book.

Monsieur continued his loose interpretation until a tan van rumbled to a stop. "Zis fancy guy says marriages of famous... models go... pffft."

Nicole flipped to an article on caves in Southeast Asia. Monsieur decoded the captions, not with exact translations, but with concepts. He slapped his healthy thigh, as he did whenever she chose to use her dictionary. Nicole searched for *chauves-souris*—bats (literally bald mice)—proving the fat paperback worth toting around. Frequently, he came upon a forgotten definition—this one, *été assourdi*—and checked his thick Larousse for the meaning: was deafened. He allowed Nicole to correct his pronunciation and followed her example, accentuating the beginning and ending "d."

After the driver parked, Monsieur Daudon waved him inside. He flicked his cigarette on to the street, then pushed the right, then the left door open to his shop, his signal that the session with Nicole was at an end. Neighbors came from both sides of the street, hunters on the prowl, a mix of men and women who seemed to have reserved this midafternoon. They, too, were waiting for Monsieur's cache.

The deliveryman wheeled odd-sized boxes through the door, while Monsieur Daudon described his purchases. "Zay belong to people dead or too old to care. Zay need money. Zees are from an apartment. A room so filled, I could not fit between zem all." Monsieur Daudon was working on "th," which was as tricky for him as the throaty "reh" of *très*, *faire*, and *cher* were for Nicole.

The driver finished unloading his truck. All three aisles were overcrowded, including one already crammed at the far end of the store. Hushed conversations, breaths of anticipation low as the buzz of bees in a field of lavender. Monsieur Daudon beckoned with his arms, encouraging all to step close, and delivered a speech with the ease of one who'd given it often. He spoke rapidly, leaving Nicole to take clues from the neighbors. A woman, with a gray streak and stern face, bolted toward a stack and picked through an open container until she found a brass figurine of a monkey holding an umbrella and lowered it into her wheeled shopping cart. Then she began scavenging through other boxes in the area she claimed for herself.

Two shoppers, a young woman and a middle-aged man, judging by his paunch, courteously tussled over their discoveries: brass spoons and tiny forks, a jar filled with pearl buttons, a lace tablecloth, a tin of wooden clothespins.

"Dépêchez-vous! Madame." Monsieur waved his hands. "Vite, vite!"

Men and women marked off their territories and Nicole deciphered the command to hurry. Faithful customers settled in, while Monsieur opened two bottles of wine. Glasses passed from hand to hand. "Salut," a woman toasted. One aisle over, a man, dressed in a vest over his white shirt, a beret, and round spectacles, opened a magazine and began reading. Paper crunched. Boxes scraped against the planked wood floor. No box was opened, no item removed without careful examination and commentary.

Nicole dashed to the less crowded back section of the store and four boxes stacked two high. She separated a hand-tucked top and grinned, knowing Tamara was smiling down on her; sending a little "I told you so" message along with her blessing. Postcards bound with lace, four tarnished silver teaspoons, three wooden candlesticks with melted wax, long turned brown, stuck to their bases. The second box reeked with rank-smelling perfume from something stuffed inside a suede pump. It was a bottle attached to a rubber bulb for spritzing, the perfume dark as oil through the cut glass.

Records, 78 RPM, protected by brown paper sleeves, covered the top of the third box. In the late fifties, her parents had stacks of these in the bottom of their hi-fi cabinet. Seventy-eights and Friday nights: neighbors, fried shrimp and rice, Schlitz beer. Until her parents shooed her off to bed, it was Nicole's job to wipe dust from the records before Malvina stacked the turntable, set the stylus into the groove, then danced with Squire.

Square sets: Louis Armstrong, Benny Goodman, Artie Shaw. Vinyl albums: Miles Davis, Duke Ellington, Ornette Coleman, Mingus, Coleman Hawkins, and Bud Powell. Sarah Vaughan. Charlie Parker—lots and lots of Charlie Parker. Coltrane. Names and jazz over and above what she knew. Nicole had no idea of the value of her find, but someone long ago had loved music. Loved jazz. Nicole raised her hand.

"Voilà! You have found. *Trouver.* For your list Madame." In the motes of dust drifting through the afternoon light, Monsieur Daudon's silhouette turned ghostly. When he reached Nicole, he refilled her glass and permitted her to stow the records under a pine table.

The sun hid behind the property facing Monsieur Daudon's. He flipped on the brass chandelier and light spilled over the room. Fairyland. Paris. Nicole wanted to shout it out: *je suis à Paris.*

She hurried now through what was left. Embroidered dishtowels and mismatched cups. A whiff of mildew. Newspapers. One, crisp between her fingers, dated August 25, 1944: the Liberation of Paris. A front-page shot of a cheering crowd lining a street, handkerchiefs and scarves raised high. Men, women, and children watching a parade of tanks marked United States Army. Soldiers, their helmet straps unbuckled beneath their chins, standing upright in the tanks' hatches.

Deal seekers gloated over yards of fabric and arcs of silk flowers shaped to fit a small head, in the same style Malvina wore when Nicole was a girl; a man's suit, a copper tea kettle. Behind Nicole, the man in the beret opened his last box, splotched with a liquid long dry. The mildew scent of a library's stacks spread over the room. Picking through the layer of books, he held up a copy of Richard Wright's *Black Boy*, the words *Jeunesse noire* printed beneath its English title. "Oh-la-la!" He picked through the rest, then hoisted the box onto his shoulder and presented it to Nicole. She scanned the titles: books by black authors.

"Regardez, Madame. You want? Non?"

His offering was filled with books. Books from another era, Nicole judged, from the copyright dates. *The Stone Face* by William Gardner Smith. Baldwin's *Go Tell It on the Mountain* and *The Fire Next Time*, *La Reine des Pommes* by Chester Himes.

"English." He shook his head. "I read no English."

"Merci beaucoup." Nicole was pleased the man wasn't giving them to her because she was the sole black person in the store. This was a history lesson: African American newspapers dating back to World War II—*New York Amsterdam News*, the *Chicago Defender*, *Atlanta Daily World*—headlines of black soldiers mistreated in the armed forces, desegregation in Arkansas, four little girls killed in Alabama, freedom fighters vanished in Mississippi; clippings from the passage of the Civil Rights Act of 1964 and Martin Luther King's and Malcolm X's assassinations.

An eight-by-ten black-and-white photograph slipped from between the books and fluttered to the floor. It was not frayed, but worn as if fingered often. In the photo, a troop of black soldiers stood at attention before a flag stilled in the midst of a breeze. The numbers of the company and Quartermaster Corps were hidden in the furls along with half of the insignia of the United States Army.

"Oh my God!" Nicole shouted.

She picked through books, shaking each one by its spine, searching for others. The picture in her hand was her only reward. A young man erect and serious before the cadre—their right hands frozen in salute—faced a white officer in a captain's hat, round, not pointed, different from the hat of the soldier before him. Three white soldiers, their posture defensive, flanked the captain. The officer, of seeming importance by virtue of his stiff-legged stance and aura of authority, was pinning a medal on the jacket of the singled-out soldier. The soldier's face was familiar, handsome, and proud. His mustache, well manicured and thin. A dimple dented his right cheek and his right cheek alone. Nicole grabbed her reading glasses and re-examined the image of the single soldier. He towered over the captain, with shiny boots on big feet and a sharp crease in his pants that screamed perfectionist. Even in the aged photo the man's hands were strong and capable: long fingers, trimmed, even fingernails. She squinted and stared again, knowing but not catching on.

The lyrics of a '70s song Nicole loved for its repetitious refrain and depiction popped into her head; a description of an old woman's hands. She loved the lyrics because she loved her father's hands. Saturday morning hands jutting from the bedcovers after she tugged at his nose and put her face close to his. Despite her giggles and pleas, he held on: "I've got you in the vise." Her hand enclosed in his gently clenched fist, the security of knowing he meant her no harm.

Grandma's hands: that riff, that whine pounded in her head. Her father's hands. Brown like almonds, soft like gloves, clean like Sunday morning. Not partial to his hands when they spanked for talking back. His steady palms atop her eight-year-old hands on the steering wheel of an Oldsmobile 88—him guiding the enameled wheel, her thinking she was driving.

Nicole flipped the photo, checking for a clue, a how or a why. On the back of the photograph, six words were written in ink that had not faded. *Darling, I am Forever yours, Squire.* Even handwriting. Tapered. Controlled. The tail of the Q extended beyond the letters following it. How often had she watched his hands write his name on report cards, permission slips, and checks? His hands now withered with age and roped with thick veins. Nicole loved her father's hands. Sought men whose hands had the same strength, beauty, promise of security and unconditional love. Meticulous shaver, waxer of cars, trimmer of hedges, mower of lawns, carpenter, handyman.

What the hell were his hands doing here?

8

Mississippi, Winter 1944

Arnett showed up on the porch exactly five Sundays after he first made love to Ruby in the backseat of his 1939 Ford, two bouquets of scraggly snapdragons in hand, grateful for a home-cooked meal and prepared to play Ruby's game to the hilt. Martha peeked through the lace curtains on the door's oval window, then adjusted her dress, the bun twisted at the nape of her neck, and straightened a portrait of her cousin until Arnett knocked a third time. When she opened the door, Arnett stood at attention like he'd learned in the Army and permitted Martha to inspect him from the brim of his felt hat, past the broad lapels and double-vested buttons of his wide-legged suit, to his spit-shined shoes. He didn't move, allowing her to inspect him and consider the bouquets in his hand. When he thrust the flowers at her, in the hurried fashion of a bearer of a bad-news telegram or a notice of a delinquent insurance payment, Martha accepted them without a thank-you and directed him to the parlor.

Behind Martha, Lurlene waited in the entryway, Ruby close on her heels. He handed his second bouquet to Lurlene, who curtsied and shook his hand. Ruby and Arnett had agreed to his plan to see each other openly, not in the car in the cold meadow beyond the city limits, not in the town square, not with every juke joint woman waiting for her to fail, for her turn to be over as if she were a successor in line instead of his true love. Every one of the women refused to believe when he held her hand, not one of theirs, how intrigued he was with every inch of his Ruby. How right before them he ran his fingers over her face, her hair, her body, memorizing each part. How he breathed in her ear when they were together and afterward, spent from lovemaking. They did not know that he read to her from the newspapers; articles on the war, the end of meat rationing, FDR's plans for a fourth term. Or that they talked about living in a place where color did not matter. He conceived the plan, telling her had they not been so far gone, so secretive, so filled with unmarried passions, he would have marched up to the Garretts' door and introduced himself. This visit to her home proved he had not forgotten his upbringing and that his love for her was real, not a backseat affair. If her parents met him, had a chance to know him, their open love was possible, even at Ruby's age. What would Martha's opinion matter if she assumed her daughter was settling for Lurlene's leftovers?

"Mrs. Garrett, allow me to introduce Mr. Arnett Dupree, of New Orleans. And, Mr. Dupree, this is her daughter, RubyMae." Lurlene presented him formally, pretending the two had never met. Arnett shook Ruby's hand, holding it long past the common courtesy Lurlene's introduction necessitated, faltering in his pretense.

The two girls fussed over Arnett, Martha observing Ruby then Lurlene then once more Ruby's anxious countenance. When Ruby closed in on the man, Martha ordered her to the kitchen.

"Li'l Mary's in the kitchen, Mama." Ruby referred to the helper Martha hired when a combination of boarders, guests, and friends gathered at her dinner table.

"Watch your mouth, RubyMae Garrett." Martha suggested Lurlene go to the parlor where Ruby's PapPap sat listening to the radio. "Let Lurlene be with her company."

In the kitchen, Martha lowered her voice. Sharp as she could be when it came to Martha's moods, Li'l Mary had the sense to keep whipping the mashed potatoes.

"RubyMae, keep away from that man. One, he's courting Lurlene, and two, you got a decent man waiting for you to grow up. That Arnett Dupree is a fop and a failure if I've ever seen one. Don't you be a woman who's a fool for pretty men. If Lurlene were my child, I wouldn't have let him in."

Deciding it was risky to gape at her mother's beady glare, Ruby focused on the whipping stick in the corner; the limber branch was Martha's favorite for chastisement. Ruby rubbed at her thigh, the sting of her last whipping months ago for the tangled lies she'd told even before meeting Arnett still fresh in her mind. In that moment, she shivered against the urge to snap the knotty stick in two and toss it into the dining room's sputtering fire, knowing her mother's inclination to keep her on a righteous path.

"He's Lurlene's beau." Ruby turned to hide the color rising in her face. "No way for me to know."

Martha emptied a pot of string beans into a china bowl. "Don't go getting ideas. I watched you. That's Lurlene's friend and—"

"—It's not Christian to judge, Mama."

Martha stopped, the pot in her hands stock-still, between sink and faucet. Her back straightened, a warning that prayer or a shower of sermonizing was coming on. "I'm not beyond using my stick, company or not, RubyMae, if you speak to me in that tone again." She lowered the pot to the sink, stepped close to Ruby, and popped her daughter's arm with the palm of her hand. "I know his kind. Thinking that good hair, light eyes, and lashes fit for a woman, and his city suit will get him whatever he wants. Hear this: no good will come of that man."

Martha turned from Ruby and proceeded to the dining room. Picking up the crystal dinner bell her deceased mother had inherited from the white woman she worked for, Martha rang the call to supper. The diners assembled around the table dressed with a lace cloth. A total of ten in all including Mr. Sanders, the almost blind second boarder, Mr. Montgomery, the widowed neighbor Martha had chosen for Lurlene, and two soldiers, one of whom was Li'l Mary's only brother.

According to her fixed pattern for guests at her Sunday table, Martha started at the far end of the table by the parlor door, and PapPap dutifully obliged by seating himself in the chair with carved arms at the head of the table. Martha sat opposite him at the other end, close to the kitchen. Had her eldest daughter been there instead of college a hundred miles from home, her place would have been on Martha's left where she now directed Lurlene. Ruby sat at her PapPap's right. Boarders on Martha's right, guests on the left filled in the chairs according to Martha's whim—a last-minute decision she made based on personalities and inclinations. She seated Arnett alongside Lurlene and the widower directly opposite her boarder, so that Lurlene was better able to appraise that man's decency. When Li'l Mary set the last of the food at the the far end table and seated herself beside her brother, Martha nodded for PapPap to do his part, and at her command everyone joined hands.

"Lord, bless this food, the fruits of our labor, your bounty. We share this humble meal and find gratitude in your blessings. Amen." PapPap recited his one prayer, varying its length for Easter, Christmas, Thanksgiving, or his appetite.

Martha spoke next. "In his benevolent generosity, the Lord has blessed us with abundance. We are indebted to Him. We will honor Him by holding fast to His word and speaking the truth in all that we say and do. Bless our family, living and gone on. Bless the colored men prepared to protect this country. Please, everyone, share your blessing." Martha turned to Lurlene.

Lurlene acknowledged the family. RubyMae was grateful for Arnett, but she kept that thanks to herself. Li'l Mary prayed for her brother's safety. And the blind Mr. Sanders praised the Lord. After each guest, Martha nodded her approval, until she got to Arnett and cut him off with a request for the sweet potatoes.

"Thank the Lord, and bless the cook," Arnett said.

"Mr. Dupree, you're a strapping young man." PapPap helped himself to double portions of creamed onions and string beans before sending them down the table. "Why ain't you in uniform?"

"I was in the Army down in Louisiana, but I got wounded. Honorable discharge." Arnett shivered despite the fire burning behind PapPap. "I play the saxophone, sir. My Creole grandmother on my father's side gave me a toy saxophone when I was nine." He stopped to pile biscuits, sweet potatoes, and homegrown collards on his plate. "I carried that toy everywhere. To school, all through the shotgun house we lived in. My father was a trumpet-man. All he did when he came back from the last war was talk about playing all over the streets of Paris with Jimmy Europe's band in 'Mo'mart.' He'd sit me on his knee and describe Josephine Baker dancing buck-naked on the stage, and how the Frenchies loved her. I enlisted 'cause of my old man's stories."

Mr. Montgomery, partially deaf, uninterested, or a bit of both, changed the subject. "Seems the papers gone on about war coming to an end in Europe and the Pacific. America done lost lots of boys on D-Day. Colored and white stormed Normandy. Double war, I say." He went on, describing the latest letter from his son. "At Fort Huachuca, Arizona, colored troops had a fight on their hands before they even saw action. White officers, folks in town. None of 'em care for so many colored men in their vicinity."

"Let Arnett finish. He's going to Paris!" Ruby said, eager for Martha to know her Arnett. PapPap, she had learned, was an easy man to bend to her thinking. Ruby caught herself and dropped her head. "At least that's what Lurlene says."

Lurlene dished a heaping serving of mashed potatoes on Arnett's plate. She giggled when he touched her hand with the enthusiasm of a man intrigued, and Ruby saw that her friend was not entirely disinterested. Ruby avoided gazing at Lurlene and Arnett and tried not to see that their age seemed to make them fit together well.

"Ain't no Jim Crow in Paris. A colored man eats anywhere, drinks anywhere. Goes wherever he wants, whenever. That's what my daddy did." In Paris folks ignored the color of a man's skin. Freedom. Freedom to fit right in. Freedom to drink coffee, hell, languish over it at cafés without regard to skin color or hair texture. "I'll get there. I will."

"And your folks, Mr. Dupree. Do they agree with your ideas?" Martha patted Lurlene's hand, but she stared at the young widower she'd invited to meet her boarder. "Lurlene has no mother. I guess you could say I'm watching out for her."

"Don't matter, ma'am. I'm a man. It's what my daddy talked about when he came home from the war. My head got so stuffed with his stories, seems sometimes like they're my own." Arnett grinned. "I'm a musician, that's all I ever wanted to be. Come the end of the war, I'm heading straight for Paris and I'm gonna make it big."

"I'm sure a lot of men want to 'make it big,' Mr. Dupree. But I'd say not many do it playing music. It takes sacrifice. Mr. Garrett here provides for our family. That's what we've taught RubyMae. And her sister, off getting her education, lives by that rule as well."

"Well, Mrs. Garrett, I don't aim to take care of anyone until I damn well can." His hands shook under Martha's icy gaze, and everyone but Martha turned away when his fork dropped onto the shiny pine floor. "It's been a long stretch since I sat at a proper table, ma'am. I hope you'll forgive my language and my manners."

"Poor manners, Mr. Dupree"—Martha glared at him, then Ruby—"and crude language are the easiest of sins to forgive."

9

Questions are formed in a number of ways. Start with simple phrases beginning with the phrase "what is?" (*qu'est-ce?*).

répondre (ray pon druh)	to answer
poser une question (posay een kes tee on)	to ask a question
interroger (ahn tair oh zhay)	to question (in class)
qu'est-ce que c'est? (kehss kuh say)	what is this?

The question was the question: not how did the snapshot get to Paris, but who was it for? Not all men were saints—her philandering ex-husband and married boyfriend were proof—and that could include Squire Handy. Though her father's past wasn't any of her business, curiosity spurred Nicole.

As calls notifying them of friends' deaths increased, Malvina and Squire Handy regarded the phone as a bearer of bad news. Nicole didn't care for the phone either, not because of bad news, but because five-minute check-ins turned into hour-long conversations. Emails and texts allowed for revisions and eliminated misunderstandings. Right now, she wished she could text her mother.

Malvina answered on the seventh ring.

"You won't believe what I found." Nicole described the soldiers, the insignia, the hands. Her father's hands. "How do you think it got here?"

Malvina responded with a line from the song about Paris in the springtime, ignoring Nicole's story. Her voice was melodious and clear, a talent shared with no one except husband and daughter.

"Mother, did you hear me?" Nicole recounted the photo's details, not the inscription, happy for a reminder of how dashing her father once was. "Do you think Dad will remember?"

"Calm down, Nicki. You know what they say: we all look the same. It's probably Bob. You know he and your father favored one another. Even when you were little, you got the two confused."

"I'm not confused. It's Dad." Nicole stared at the photo. True, her uncle Bob and her father, two years apart in age, were often mistaken for twins. But this was her father. And those were her father's hands.

"How's he supposed to remember a picture from sixty years ago when he can't see it? Mornings it takes a minute before he remembers me."

On their initial visit to the neurologist's office, Squire sat between Nicole and Malvina. When he focused on a poster (this one of the brain, the red and blue neurons marked to show the flow of blood in and around the cerebral cortex), Malvina handed the doctor a piece of paper and waited for him to read it, reminding Nicole of a boy hiding his beloved's note from the teacher.

The doctor gave Squire a list of words. He was to remember all five. "Penny. Telephone. Red. Box. Monday," the doctor read, his tempo deliberate. The rest of his questions were polite inquiries between two new friends becoming acquainted with another. His next question, the name of the president of the United States, put joy in Squire's face. "Come January, Barack Hussein Obama. A black president, and I voted for him. Never thought I'd see the day."

"What's the day and year, Mr. Handy?"

Squire screwed up his face and peered straight at the neurologist. "Let's see. The Giants won the pennant in 2002. Beat Atlanta in the playoffs, then they beat the Cardinals."

Nicole pushed her hands against her chair's thin armrests until they creaked—Monday, 2008—and silently commanded her father: *read my mind, Daddy.*

The doctor admitted he was an avid baseball fan, too. "And how old are you?"

Squire beamed and recited a ditty the poetry lover in him enjoyed. "Eighty-five and still alive." In the ten minutes that the doctor went on with his questions, half of which Squire got wrong, Nicole's spirit sank. When, at last, the doctor requested Squire repeat the five words, Nicole trembled as if the doctor were testing her.

"Please, Mother, hand Dad the phone."

Fumbling replaced silence. How to find answers when past and present befuddled his mind? After the doctor had confirmed Squire's diagnosis, Malvina immediately called Nicole. "It's Alzheimer's, but don't tell your father." Squire's disease was a sneaky thief. It affected his temperament, and his ability to call to mind long-term events was often better than short, depending on the hour.

"Nicole?"

"Dad, were you in Paris during the war? Do you remember having your picture taken?" Slow down, she reminded herself. One question, then the next. "I found one hidden in a book a man gave to me."

"A man gave you a book?"

"Yes. Well, no. I found a picture of you in a book. And you wrote on the back of it. You signed your name. Remember?" From the other side of the street, a blue-eyed cat scurried toward Nicole. The cat meowed and settled near her feet.

"I hear a cat," Squire announced. "Never lock eyes with a

blue-eyed cat, Nicole. If they're blue, you better run." This from the man who should've been a teacher or a college professor, instead of a carpenter and under-the-table fix-it man. It was the oddest advice she recalled him ever giving. His chuckle reminded her of the visit to the neurologist's office, and Nicole had no idea what could come out of his mouth next.

She wanted him to act as exacting as he had when he collected multisyllable, obscure words—philter, brummagem, virago—their definitions and pronunciations, in a black accountant's ledger. The evenings when he read aloud, trying to share his love of unusual vocabulary or poetry. Her father hadn't read to Nicole since she was fourteen. One Sunday night, he'd handed her his tin of Virginia tobacco, and she'd packed a wad into the bowl of his reddish pipe. He puffed, while Nicole held the ebony lighter she gave him for his forty-second birthday close to the pipe until the smoke plumed. He flipped through the book he'd chosen until he came to the page he searched for.

"'Ruby Brown,' by Langston Hughes." He hadn't read this poem before. He cleared his throat, his habit before he read aloud.

"She was young and beautiful
And golden like the sunshine
That warmed her body.
And because she was colored
Mayville had no place to offer her,
Nor fuel for the clean flame of joy
That tried to burn within her soul.

One day, sitting on old Mrs. Latham's back porch
Polishing the silver,
She asked herself two questions
And they ran something like this:
What can a colored girl do

On the money from a white woman's kitchen?
And ain't there any joy in this town?"

Squire's voice carried to nearly every corner of their two-bedroom bungalow. Malvina rushed into the living room at the end of the second verse. She wiped her sudsy hands on her apron, patted her foot against the floor, and waited for her husband to stop.

"Squire Handy," she chided. "That's no poem for a child."

"Aw, Malvina, it's only a poem." Squire never lifted his eyes from the page. "Nicole doesn't care. Do you, baby?" Nicole shook her head, eager for more. Through the noise of Malvina's foot and the sharp squawking of his name, Squire continued, toying with the meter until a pouting Malvina went back to her kitchen.

"Never lock eyes with a blue-eyed cat," Squire repeated now in the same tone he'd delivered the shocking poem that had ended with the scandalous implication of how the woman eventually earned her living. His warning traveled from the mountains and rivers, the skyscrapers, the ghettos, the interstate highways of forty-eight contiguous states to the ebb and flow, the whitecaps and swirls of the Atlantic, and into Nicole's cell phone. His bewildering counsel was new for Nicole. But the cat stared at her, its expression taunting. Its bushy tail swung back and forth as if to say that even it knew her questions were a waste.

"He's not himself, Nicki." Malvina spoke so sharply that Nicole realized she'd been on the extension for the entire exchange. "Go on, Squire, say goodbye. You need your rest." Her mother seemed trapped between love and loving duty for her husband of fifty-nine years.

"I'm no dog you can boss," Squire yelled in the background. "You think you're fooling me? I know what you really want." This was not her father. This man was unpredictable and cranky.

Unlovable without warning. Her father was the man who'd stayed in the hospital, sat beside her mother day and night until she recovered from her stroke. Her father was the man who'd confessed at her wedding that he tried writing a poem, but was out of practice, then held her as if she were leaving on a long trip from which she'd never return and whispered in her ear, "I know you think your mother and I are old-fashioned, but we love you and every day we've tried to prove it. We did our best, and I have no regrets."

"It's alright, Squire. Nicki, hang up now. It costs a lot of money to call from France. We'll take a nap." Malvina Handy abided by the standards of her southern roots; hers was the generation of women that deferred personal desires to their man's. In sickness and in health; her man's needs before her own.

"Do you want to hear what he wrote?"

"I told you, Nicki. You don't listen. Your father gets agitated, and I never know if he'll get back to himself. He's better when you're here. How long before you come back?"

A calendar with the dates of her trip circled in red hung from a banana magnet on her parents' refrigerator. She imagined her mother staring at that calendar this very minute, counting the now twenty-four days before Nicole returned even as she questioned her daughter. The image of the two of them was clear in her mind: her mother leading her father down the hallway to their bedroom. Not a big woman, but not a petite one either, her mother assumed fragile mannerisms. Since her stroke eighteen months ago, she depended on a cane, refusing to wean herself off the rubber-tipped aluminum stick as the doctor had encouraged. In her mind, Nicole visualized her father squinting, creases framing his mouth. She'd witnessed him in this state when she gave her mother breaks. Sleep wouldn't help him, but for her mother it signaled blessed relief. This was not the moment to hint that coming home might not mean coming back to them.

Nicole felt caught in a cliché between aging parents and her own midlife crisis. A pawn in a game predisposed to rob her father of his pride, his doting chauvinism, his manhood.

"But what about the picture? Do you have any ideas?" The cat meowed and trotted in circles at Nicole's feet even as it seemed to whimper its sympathy.

"Don't be silly, Nicki. What can I say about something I can't see? And anyway, I told you not to go."

The phone cut off without warning, the noise tinny and final. Malvina's abrupt disconnect meant *why don't you pay attention to what I tell you*, and in this place Nicole had no wish to succumb to that pressure. Years of experience taught her that they both needed a short period of noncommunication to cool down. What she needed was to get lost.

Blocks from Monsieur's store, a modest crowd had converged around several women dressed in flouncing patchwork skirts and peasant blouses. The women's skin tones were dark to near-white, copycat images of Nicole's family. Inside the circle, the women taunted one another until the tallest, her curly hair tumbling to her shoulders, turned to the audience and delivered a short speech and handed out flyers printed on bright orange paper. The title of the advertised play was so ambiguous in Nicole's mind that she could only translate it as something about women without a country. The actresses held themselves with a playful authority so Nicole took one, believing that in Paris, the unexpected held potential.

Hypnotized by the pied piper thrill of it all, Nicole trailed the dancers. Where they turned, she turned; her on one side of the street, them on the other. Eventually, they disappeared behind a wooden gate. She settled in the front of the whitewashed theater, prepared to wait until the performance started. A habit from youth, when Squire dropped her off early at the movies so she could have her pick of seats a few rows from the screen and the thousands of dots that composed the images.

The doors to the compact playhouse opened and Nicole hurried to sit near to the stage and the exact middle of a row of red upholstered chairs. She waited, eager for the close-up connection between actor and audience. "Sit farther back, and don't focus on the dots," Squire had reminded whenever he dropped her off. "You need to see the whole picture." Movie screen as life lesson.

A tall man slipped into the seat beside Nicole as the house lights dimmed and the women filed onto the stage. She hoped luck had hit again and she'd have another chance to talk. The actresses high-stepped to a conga's rolling beat until the theater was no longer a room crowded with secondhand chairs, until the scent of frangipani seemed to waft through the vents, the lapping waves of a turquoise sea, the scent of jerk chicken became what the audience believed surrounded them.

"Nigger!" one woman shouted. Even with a French accent, the tag was harsh. No snickering, no heads turned in Nicole's direction. In Paris or at home, she was comfortable in her skin. The photo she'd discovered was a reminder of the names America had created for blacks. Black soldiers were called nigger even as they fought and died for their country. Had they felt free on this soil? Had *Forever* meant freedom to her father in France?

In unison, the women shouted again, a multihued Greek chorus. "Nous allons vous dire l'histoire de ce qui arrive lorsque les actions des hommes deviennent pire que leurs paroles." In French class, the instructor spoke in a measured pace. These women spoke at a brisk, conversational tempo and Nicole sensed a challenge.

The man on her right, his hand cupped over his mouth, spoke into the side of her face. "This is the story of what happens when men's actions become worse than their words."

Onstage the women twisted their bodies into the hull and bow of an imaginary boat, their angles and curves realistic. They rocked with the rough motion of an angry, imaginary sea while each woman revealed her story—lost and dead children, false promises of freedom, a master's shameless hands. Abandoned hope was obvious in their arms, their faces, their grunts and choppy dialogue. Despair transcended language.

When the actresses finally exited the stage, the audience was enthusiastic, but subtle with their applause. Nicole whooped her very American appreciation better fit for a concert. Her translator joined her, and without speaking they sensed they must either stop their raucous cheering or at least fall into harmony with it.

"Laurent Bésson, Madame." He extended his hand and waited for Nicole to introduce herself.

Chaos. His energy reeked of deliberate, designer chaos, and he seemed far too disordered for his age, which, she decided, was late fifties. Salt-and-pepper hair twisted in colliding directions, in charge of him instead of the other way around. The collar of his crisp white shirt askew, his leather jacket aged and marbled. She identified it; loved seeing it in his roots, the crinkle of his graying hair so tossed about his head, roots. The brown in his skin; his lips, and the breadth of his nose. Africa.

"Enchanté, Monsieur, de faire votre connaissance." A clipped, Nicole thought, but grammatically correct response.

"You're very brave. These offbeat places aren't usually in the guidebooks. Especially without an interpreter."

Oh-la-la! English without a trace of accent. Nicole was ready to talk for the purposes of conversation. A chance for dialogue, translations, an insight into living in Paris. "Not brave, curious. Great play!" Her giggle was the equivalent of a nervous preteen's. Tongue-tied by the meeting, *rendue muette par la rencontre*, the very phrase she'd mastered in class that morning. "Um, it was all in French."

"It's Paris." Mr. Chaos raised his right hand in a quick salute and blended with the crowd exiting from the center aisle before Nicole found out how he'd known she didn't quite get that one, powerful line.

10

Mississippi, February 1945

Ruby rapped on the glass until Lurlene pushed back the lace curtain and let her vision adjust to the dark outside. When she opened the window, Ruby tossed in her purse and shoes, latched on to the icy sill, and lifted herself into Lurlene's bedroom.

Ruby had taken to sneaking out and running in the black dark down the road to where Arnett waited, neither of them giving sensible consideration to the consequences. Often they parked in the woods where the owls hooted into the winter night. One particularly cold evening, they rode to the town one over from Sheridan where Arnett and his boys were playing. Foolish as it was for a colored man to be on a Mississippi back road that late at night, it was reckless to be on the road at any time of night with an underage, colored girl light enough to pass for white.

"Lordy, RubyMae, you both crazy. You gonna get caught, and I don't want to be a part of it no more." Lurlene eased the window shut and secured the latch.

"He loves me." Ruby licked her thumb and erased the lines drawn down the back of her bare legs, imitating stockings.

"Girl, you just a one-night stand stretched out over a couple of months. That man is fine, baby doll. Louisiana fine. And he's not the type to stick to one woman, especially one that might put him in jail. He bound to have women in every place he play. You probably the youngest and, for sure, the most foolish."

"I'm what he fancies." Ruby unpinned her hair and shook it free of the twist she wore to make her seem older. Her lips were covered with lipstick, deep red in the light of the lamp. "Jealous?"

"If I had a mean nature, for sure. Early on, men reckoned I was a female they didn't have to work to get. I'm a one-dollar, one-drink woman, a good time at the end of a short drive, and I don't mind. There's plenty to distract myself with."

Ruby situated herself at the dresser and held out her pearl-handled brush to Lurlene. Lurlene brushed Ruby's long hair until she reached one hundred strokes. Then she picked up the comb and parted her friend's hair down the center and plaited four braids.

"And, baby girl, in your shoes? I'd be scared. You're my play sister, not my competition. That's what I should've done from the beginning with the men, that Arnett with them bedroom eyes blinking danger. I didn't think—that's my problem."

The door opened without a creak or a knock. Martha in her white nightgown, the unlit hall behind her, resembled an oversized haint that on any other night would have tickled Lurlene and Ruby. A switch wobbled in her hand, the very one from behind the kitchen door.

"I hope you realize, Lurlene, that since I'm considering using this switch on you, you should be contemplating where you'll be sleeping tomorrow night."

"Mrs. Garrett, ma'am, you got no right. I'm grown." In the year Lurlene had boarded with Martha Garrett never had she witnessed such sternness on her face. She backed into the far corner and out of Martha's whipping range.

"Complicity is as great a sin as commission." Martha turned to Ruby, her voice subdued and steady. She picked up Ruby's shoes and fingered the damp, mud-speckled soles. "Did you think I was born a fool, RubyMae? Did you think good folk wouldn't talk? Did you think I wouldn't smell the liquor and the smoke?" Dropping the shoes onto the floor, she raised her right hand. "That man with his sugar-coated lies for a fool girl. You think I didn't see? You've been with him."

The switch fell first on Ruby's back, snagging the dress Arnett had given her. The switch fell next on Ruby's legs, and welts, imprints as big as the branch itself, popped red on her calves. Martha reached for the bulky scissors, the ones she used to cut heavy cloth, in her pocket.

"'Do not let me be put to shame, for I have called to you, Lord. Put the wicked to shame, reduce them to silence in Hell.' Don't you know a good man don't want a tainted woman? You have sinned with that man, RubyMae. I saw your desire and his, at supper, and I should have corrected it then. I should have thrown him out. I should have kept you under lock and key."

Martha grasped Ruby's shoulder. Hers was a strong grip accustomed to harvesting vegetables from her garden, and hoeing rows and scrubbing her house from top to bottom without help. It was then that the girl began to call for her PapPap and tried to wriggle from her mother's grip, but when Ruby squirmed, Martha pushed harder against her shoulder.

"Don't bother your father. It's a mother's duty to teach a daughter." Martha sniffed Ruby's hair: cigarette smoke and the mannish scent of Arnett's sweat. She snatched a section of her child's fine hair and yanked, pushing her free hand down against Ruby's shoulder.

"All that type of man cares for is good hair and good times."

"He loves me, and I love him," Ruby shouted, twisting from side to side. She tried her best to catch sight of Lurlene, to get her help. But Lurlene stood frozen in the corner sure as if snow bound her there, arms folded against her chest, holding herself from harm.

"If he loved you, there'd be no backwoods carrying-on." Martha grabbed a loosening plait, opened the scissors, and mashed the blades against Ruby's hair. The strands spun fast; threads of a thick rope chopped from itself. She hacked with the blade so that the ends of Ruby's hair mirrored ragged strands caught in a machine. "If this be your crowning glory, it is also your shame."

"I haven't done anything. PapPap!" she shrieked and pushed against Martha.

Martha grabbed the second braid, putting her knee on her daughter's lap, and hacked again. Then she snatched layer after layer of hair with no order or commitment to style, so that when she was done Ruby's not quite red hair was a patchwork of uneven pieces. The shout from Ruby's lips came from deep in her lungs, loud and long, forcing her hands against her head, groping for hair that was gone. "See what you've done, Mama!" She lifted the clipped braids and held them to her head as if to put them back where they belonged.

"I can forgive a lie, RubyMae. I cannot a whore. If this is the only way I can teach you, then so be it that you never forget."

Ruby pushed against Martha's legs and knocked the big-boned woman to the floor. From where Ruby stood, her foot poised high over Martha, she was prepared to stomp the air out of her mother, until she saw her reflection in the mirror. Red lipstick smeared her face. Hair chopped. Plucked worse than a scared chicken. Ruby slung Lurlene's robe over the mirror, seeing herself ugly as never before. Martha stumbled to her feet and slapped Ruby twice, the band of her wedding ring leaving a gash on her chin.

After Martha left her room, Lurlene threw her belongings into three suitcases and left. "I'll tell him," was all she said, and that in a velvety voice close to Ruby's ear. In the four days before Arnett knocked on her door, Ruby refused to leave her room, knowing her mother could do nothing worse than she already had. When Arnett showed up, he banged on the door until Martha threatened him and PapPap held her out of the way. "Step through my door and you'll pay."

"You don't have a switch, ma'am, big enough to do damage to me," Arnett announced. "Ruby!" Up the stairs he ran, pounding on the bathroom door, on the near-deaf boarder's door, and on the door where Martha and PapPap slept in separate beds. He pounded on the door of every room until he found Ruby. Her face was swollen from crying and the sadness that had overtaken her, and she looked younger than her sixteen years and five months.

Ruby clung to Arnett. He walked her to the other side of her room and made her stand in the corner so that she could gather her strength while he jerked at dresser drawers, threw open the armoire doors, and dumped her belongings on the quilt spread across her bed. Arnett worked at a madman's pace. He grabbed the quilt's four corners and tied them together in the fashion of a hobo bundle. Ruby reached under the mattress of the second bed to the spot where her big sister kept her money for the wedding she so desperately desired—the silver coins counted and recounted, the bills folded and refolded, the sum recalculated whenever she came home from school. Ruby took the money and searched for what she could find in her room to let her sister know she meant no harm; that she loved her. She reached into the back of her dresser for the cut-glass brooch her sister had skipped meals to buy and wrapped it in the lace handkerchief that had held the money. Then she returned brooch and hanky to her sister's hiding place.

Hand in hand, Arnett and Ruby rushed down the stairs to the entry and out the door, neither of them hesitating at the threshold.

"Go on!" Martha's voice was loud and firm. "He ain't nothing, and you'll never be nothing either."

Ruby listened for the screen door to slam behind them, for the latch to click, the house to shudder when Martha shut the door. No such noise, loud or sharp, occurred. Only the breeze that dusted their faces. Arnett and Ruby ran down the porch towards his black sedan, the motor sputtering its threat to quit. He tossed the bulky quilt into the trunk. Ruby took her last glimpse at the house where she was born, where she had hunted pastel eggs on Easter mornings, where her mother and her PapPap's lives were destined to end. She stared at the oval window, sensing her mother's vigilance behind the delicate lace she herself had tatted, PapPap silent behind her. She had no idea of where she was going or how long she might be gone, but seeing this place again was not what she wanted to do.

11

Cognates are French words comparable to English ones in spelling and definition and are easily recognizable.

la famille (lah fah mee)	family
la classe (lah clahss)	the class
un souvenir (uhn sue ven eer)	a keepsake
aider (eh day)	to help

Three and a half days later, neither the conversation with her mother nor the photo disclosed any new information. Nicole set the photograph, a perfect fit for its Eiffel Tower frame, on top of the marble mantel. Her father—sharp and unafraid of the future. Was he thinking of his promise when he saluted the officer? And the men behind him. What part had they played in the war America didn't want its black countrymen to fight?

No, it was best to take a break, let go, and not forget, but become friends with the mystery. Paris didn't labor over its past, the city lived with it—revolution, occupation, literature, fashion, jazz—settled in the mortar between the cobblestones, on the tongues of tour guides and double-decker bus drivers. Best to follow its example.

Nicole left with a specific goal in mind. Today she decided to walk home the wrong way, a good plan for this grayish afternoon; her goal a silly one—no left turns. Her wanderings led to a covered passageway—an ancient mini-mall—and shops where she was neither sore thumb nor ugly American. Not that stationery vendors and boutique clerks spoke French to her, but once she greeted them with a friendly *bonjour*, no one bothered her or stared.

By late afternoon, Nicole returned to the Quai des Grands-Augustins with the help of an English-speaking merchant who sold her a souvenir set of postcards and two totes covered with *oui, oui—c'est Paris*. "You are right, Madame. Right, right. Your right turns will take you to the River Seine and your quai facing it." The intentions Nicole wrote and the books inspiring them—*The Law of Attraction*, *The Secret*—repeated themselves in Paris's streets: bliss lay in the journey and the destination.

"Bonjour, Madame." Monsieur Large, the concierge, delivered his greeting, as he did morning or night or whenever she left or returned. She had no idea how he knew her comings and goings. It didn't matter; his protectiveness reassured.

"Il y a un petit paquet à votre porte, Madame." The concierge waved a wizened hand and gestured to the floor by his door, making it clear where a *paquet* waited for Nicole before the door of the two-by-four elevator closed.

The package was painstakingly marked on both sides as if customs agents were unable to read anything but their beloved French, as if destined for delivery by a barely literate child.

NICOLE HANDY
c/o Monsieur Large
157 Quai des Grands-Augustins
PARIS FRANCE 75006

Her name and address was written in the large letters of a style of handwriting taught years ago and practiced and practiced until the O's, the A's, the open loops of the P and G were perfect circles.

The uninterrupted letters connected without evidence of fountain pen lifting from paper; a smooth, tilting cursive written by a woman indifferent to rules imposed by the airway bill's narrow rectangles and squares.

Malvina had been precise in wrapping. Two boxes nestled inside the larger one; the first, labeled with the Johnston & Murphy logo, had once held a spit-polished pair of the dress shoes Squire wore to church, lodge meetings, baptisms, and funerals. The shoebox bore most of the weight of the entire package, sending a sharp twinge through Nicole's right thumb, the joint where arthritis had chosen to settle. The length of the shoebox caught her off guard. She had never been interested in the size of her father's feet, but the line of shoeboxes stacked on the top shelf of his closet had fascinated her. Snooping through that closet, she had resisted the temptation to rearrange or scratch tiny marks on the surface of his perfectly kept shoes, to see if he noticed.

A sandwich-sized plastic baggie, filled with two pieces of white cardboard cut to fit inside, slipped to the floor when Nicole opened the smaller box. Inside the cardboard sandwich, its edges jagged from the pinking shears she used for crafts, Malvina had written a note so that Nicole could read it and look at the picture opposite it at the same time: *I am not bitter. Just old and tired.*

The aroma of Malvina's cookies drifted from the open box. The smell and sensual photo brought Nicole back to the Sunday nights of her childhood. Malvina knitting through all the acts of Ed Sullivan, Squire immersed in a book waiting for his favorite western to come on. Nicole browsing through the family album.

She'd studied the album the way she never had her schoolwork; thick black pages filled with photos of play aunts, uncles, cousins, and friends secured by white triangles at each corner. Malvina cooing over chubby toddler Nicole in a wooden playpen; Squire tucking her into bed; toddler Nicole again, long fingers entwined in pigtails, standing beside cousins with whom she no longer had common interests. The black-and-white photos exaggerated the hues of her family's skin: Uncle Rufus over a barbecue pit, fat and grinning at meat nearly the color of his skin; Auntie Mary, skinny and pale, caught in a moment of jitterbug bliss; Malvina picking flowers, her ruddy complexion glistening, hand on hip, bobby sox and oxford shoes; Squire in an Army helmet, elbows on the hood of a military truck, his head cocked away from the photographer, flirtatious.

The image of this nameless woman always caught Nicole's eye.

A feather boa draped over the woman's bosom, leaving her shoulders bare and exposed—nude, but not quite. It was impossible to tell if she was black or white. Her sultry attitude was colorless and impatient, as if she had been caught unaware. "Why don't you ever get fancy, Mother? Who is she?" Lipstick was Malvina's makeup, reserved, for the most part, for special occasions and Sunday mass. When she was twelve, Nicole asked again on the night the Temptations sang "My Girl" on national TV. Neither parent gave a straight answer. This simple question seemed a ball in a perpetual ping-pong match tossed between parents until Malvina's lips puckered no, and Squire refocused on his book.

It was then Nicole accepted that hers was a family of secrets: s-e-x, Mississippi, the woman in the photo. Even now, it was mysterious and dreamy; shot at an angle, the woman's head rested on a satin pillow, hair parted so that curls fell on both sides of her face to her long, square chin. The lashes of her almond eyes stretched under brows perfectly arched; a mole prominent on the woman's face, a beauty mark. The black mole, a polka dot against the woman's pale skin, was dead in the center of her right cheek. In the photo's lower corner the woman had written: *For you my dearest, with all my love.*

Less than forty-eight hours ago, she had asked a question. Her answer was a shoebox, a photo, and a note smacking of despair. A twinge hit, bitter on Nicole's tongue. The taste of all not being right; a wrenching gut clutch. A reminder that she was just a black girl in Paris, when she wanted to be a woman in charge.

Silver-colored duct tape bound the lid to its bottom. The frayed tape peeled off easily, leaving an imprint that reminded Nicole of a finger turned pale beneath a ring worn for many years. She passed her hands over it, palms up, then again palms down in the style of a faith healer divining sickness below the body's surface.

Fifty-six years of living and arguing with Malvina Handy. Nicole wanted candor, none of this beat-around-the-bush nonsense. She stormed into the kitchen, turned around, and marched back into the living room. The package hadn't gotten bigger or sprouted wings or turned to dust. It was the same yellowed shoebox.

A faint hint of lavender rose from the box when she removed the lid.

12

Summer 1948

When Arnett gunned his noisy engine outside her house back in '45, Ruby thought the rumble was a trick of her imagination. Arnett hadn't let her down and his loyalty fortified her. The weight, the meaning of the shut door, hung between them like the smoke from Arnett's cigarette. "I'm keeping to my plan, Ruby," he told her. "Except now, the plan is me and you. I didn't come after you for it to be anything less." Driving from that house, neither one of them turned a head or deliberated over what was left behind. Forward was the direction that interested Ruby; she never glanced back to see if, perhaps, her PapPap had run out of the house, waving his large hands for his baby girl to come back, to change her mind, to be the loving daughter again.

A believer in fairytales and backwoods stories, Ruby reckoned she was in store for happily ever after. The shortsightedness of her impressionable sixteen years and the freedom from her mother spurred that belief. Ruby had become all too familiar with the geography of Mississippi and Louisiana by the time she and Arnett arrived in New Orleans. Biloxi to Bogalusa and cities, on and off the map, where Saturday nights helped colored men and women forget their Monday-through-Friday blues. They traveled Highway 61,

Arnett entertaining the crowds, putting his soul into every song while Ruby, jar in hand, guarded the door and collected folks' hard-earned money, both expecting free meals and lodging in return. Woodville, Natchez and Port Gibson, Memphis. East, west, north, south, Ruby found them the same. One-night stands. Two-week stints. Women offering themselves to Arnett. Men doing the same to Ruby. Tumbledown colored motels where crickets competed for rooms, shabby hotels, nights in Arnett's sedan and no hot meals.

Every month or so, Arnett reached into the jacket lining of the worst of his three wool suits and carefully removed their savings. This inclination to secure his money on his person kept Ruby like a shield at his left side and got folks to mistaking protectiveness for dependency. It was she who demanded they sit on the bed of whatever motel or boarding house they occupied at the moment, and separate the bills by denomination. Together they counted, watching the stacks go up and down depending on the number of gigs Arnett got or meals they skipped.

"Baby, you got to chip in," he'd plea whenever his wad of money shrank.

So naïve was Ruby that she expected Arnett, like her father, to be the one who brought in the money and supported the two of them. "Mama never worked, and I just don't see why I should." Her PapPap's railroad job and Martha's tiny store and her rabbits, fat enough for folks to feed on for a week, eliminated the necessity of dependence on white folks. No need for Martha to work on the other side of the tracks or watch white folks' children or iron or scrub their clothes.

"But you ain't your mama and if we want to get to Paris, we got to sacrifice."

She obliged by looking for jobs in beauty parlors, sometimes with an eye out for Lurlene, thinking she could press hair. She asked in ice cream parlors, thinking of Mr. Lewis's store and assuming that her love of the icy treat made her an expert of sorts.

Rejections, polite and otherwise, came at every turn because of her age, her color, her lack of experience, or all three. Mostly, she worked on Arnett; smoothing his hair with her pearl-handled brush and tickling his lips with hers when he calculated their money deficiencies, her argument always the same: they saved half of every nickel and dime they earned—when were they going to have some fun?

Persuadable as he was when it came to Ruby's honeyed arguments, Arnett put his foot down when the cash she had taken from her sister came close to running out. "Baby, until we get straight, ain't no other way. I promise in Paris we'll be rolling in dough and living the good life."

Once Ruby adjusted her attitude, finding jobs came quickly. A single knock on the back door of a dignified mansion or tips from other women on the road. White folks rejoiced at the cheap labor. Until they reached New Orleans, Ruby scrubbed clothes on corrugated metal washboards and cared for children she couldn't abide, never sticking to any job over two or three weeks, the extent of her tolerance or Arnett's need to follow the music.

"It won't be for long," Arnett promised, nights he rubbed petroleum jelly mixed with glycerin into her reddened hands. And that was how he stretched his promise from one year to almost three.

Rampart. Esplanade. Canal. Just after they arrived, Arnett guided Ruby to the French Quarter, showing her where he had been and what he had done in this city he had visited often, when in truth his visits had been limited to two. She learned that from his mama shelling shrimp on the porch of her roadside shanty. Ruby had mentioned to the pale woman that they were on their way to Paris, visiting to speak their goodbyes. "His daddy was a wishful thinker." His mother had snickered. "You young. French Quarter, my ass. Better love it, sugar, because that's as close to Paris as you gone get."

This second week, they sat in a darkened hall waiting for

Arnett's turn to go onstage. Ruby's whole body dripped with sweat. Fierce and different from home, the New Orleans heat was a cloying humidity that frizzed her hair and smelled of the Mississippi River. She'd taken to powdering with cornstarch to keep her thighs dry. The folds of every garment she wore clung together, leaving her rumpled and sticky. Arnett fingered his saxophone's keypad, committing the notes to his fingers.

This was the third night Arnett was playing a real club. Every session had been packed with folks white and colored, colored sitting in the back and lining the walls. A place with tables where a man behind a bar served scotch or bourbon or gin poured from bottles with labels. A place where big-name musicians jammed and the crowds were committed to the music, not dancing or smoking or finding someone to spend the night with.

Ruby worked on the crooked knot of Arnett's tie, declaring that she was sick of scuffling for work in towns backward as the one she had left. "We got to get going. This club ain't doing us any favors."

"You're mad 'cause you cleaning tables, not singing."

"It's that and more."

Before Ruby met Arnett, music was entertainment, consolation, and an aching for the gift of a fine voice. She had no expectation of performing until she met Arnett and he explained music, the notes on his saxophone, how to move people's bodies and their hearts with a song.

She pointed her finger in his face, a habit Ruby had taken to lately when Arnett wasn't making money. "It's time to get noticed—you or me. How else are we getting close to the Atlantic Ocean and the ships to take us to Paris?"

Arnett shoved her finger out of his face. "Never do that again, RubyMae. I ain't that kind of man. Didn't you get enough of that at your mama's house?" Did she want to go back? Hadn't he saved her? She kissed him, and dabbed at his sweat until he forgave her for pointing, and she forgave him for taking so long.

"There's got to be a way, Arnett."

"I'm doing the best I can, baby. Don't nag. Let me get steady work under my belt—get folks to know my name and respect me when I call for favors." He reached for the glass of brandy set next to his left foot. "I can't take the nagging—Ma'dear used to nag, so much... I hate it. I'll keep my promises, but it takes time."

"The time is now, honey. Roll some French words in your mouth and spit them through that sax." Ruby caressed his cheeks. "Go on and play. Get hired, then we can do what we want."

Beads of sweat dampened Arnett's body. The shirt Ruby had ironed stuck to his skin and the strands of his black chest hair underneath. Ruby reasoned, hot as it was, her man was wet from the jitters that expended him in the moments he doubted—getting the two of them to Paris, her love, his abilities. How this sudden doubt had come upon him, Ruby didn't know, but she guessed that the longer they went unnoticed, or well paid, the less likely they were to get to Paris—otherwise they'd be there by now.

Arnett stepped to a crowded wooden platform with a piano on his right side, and the drums and bass on his left. He was composed, despite the setup not being exactly how he'd asked. Arnett scoured the audience for Ruby. She watched him from the back of the room. A shiny, heavyset man in a suit talked nonstop and inched closer to Ruby with his every sentence. She focused not on the dapper man, but on Arnett. "Go ahead on, baby," she called out and went back to serving drinks to the coloreds in the crowd.

The band jumped into a tune; swing jazz that Arnett had practiced with them earlier. He kept up with the piano and worked in a short solo between the bass and the drums. To Ruby, working to keep the customers happy, he seemed slow to catch on. He held back, not outshining the other musicians, but keeping up with them. The crowd, and every woman, was with him—heads bobbing, fingers snapping. Sweat poured down his face, sopped by his now-soaked shirt collar. He was searching for it, the beat, waiting to take over and show the men on the platform he had what it took to play in the Big Easy. His playing was tuneful, but Ruby never heard that break, that chance to shine. To her it was a sign; of what, she wasn't ready to consider.

The dapper man from the bar approached Arnett when the set ended. Curiosity, disguised in the business of collecting dirty glasses, propelled Ruby near the stage, so that she was better able to hear the two men.

"Freddie Jones." The man shook Arnett's hand. "You play pretty good. Ever been to New York?"

"I got my mind on a bigger place," Arnett boasted.

"Ain't a whole lot bigger than New York, my man." Freddie Jones released an easy burp from deep in his throat, comfortable, as if it were a part of his standard vocabulary.

Ruby set her tray on a cocktail table and stepped past the man to Arnett's side. Arnett put his free arm on Ruby's shoulder, clarifying for this and any other man looking at her the fact that she was his.

"You need a musician's card. Not many coloreds get their hands on them, but if I can take care of that, would you be interested?"

"Yes!" Ruby shouted.

13

Fall 1950

Zigzagging their way to New York and living off the generosity of others, when they finally arrived in that city, Freddie Jones was nowhere to be found. Ruby went to the center of Manhattan in search of jobs in department stores and employers mistaking a fair-skinned Negro woman for white, until she gave up and found work in a Harlem drugstore. Before Arnett found a transatlantic liner cheap enough to take the two of them to France, he swept barbershop floors, scrubbed hotel bathrooms, and hauled garbage. He stockpiled and spent. So greatly did he want to please Ruby's expanded appetites with the rhinestone baubles and nightclub evenings she coveted that he did not resist spoiling her whenever his paychecks allowed.

They waited until after the Germans surrendered, the last Marine fell on Guam, the bombs dropped on Hiroshima, the thousands of near-dead Jews stumbled out of concentration camps, the treaties were signed, and the victories declared. They waited until after the colored troops returned to the States, to Jim Crow and its believers. Soldiers, colored and white, came home from the war, some in coffins, some without arms or legs, some with scars inside their heads that made them crazy when they talked of war and bombs and carrying off the dead. They waited until brochures and newspapers and travel agents declared that Paris was safe again, her arms open to America's citizens and dollars.

"Where's the Eiffel Tower?" RubyMae Garrett stood on the gangplank of the ocean liner that had carried her, Arnett, and a thousand passengers from New York to France, thinking the busy loading dock before her was Paris. On the road, Ruby had never read a book on France. Arnett had yammered with anyone he met who'd been to or had friends in Paris. Ruby scanned fashion magazines left behind in the places Arnett cleaned. Details of how to get to France and what to do when they got to Paris, she left to Arnett.

"This is Le Havre." Arnett pulled out his notebook. Neither his cash nor the black book ever left his person, except for when he bathed or made love to Ruby, and then it wasn't far from his reach. Arnett's address book had swollen enough to require the aid of a hefty rubber band to hold it together. It covered geography and French phrases, names of clubs, including Chez Inez and Haynes Restaurant, and cats he hoped to see in Paris. For the most part, he held on to his father's stories and kept a list from World War I: Casino de Paris and Le Duc, Bricktop and Chez Josephine, Eugene Bullard.

"From here we take the train to the Gare St.-Lazare in Paris."

On the dock, and at the huge train station, everyone, everywhere, and in every direction Ruby looked was white. Not one person shunned them or forced them to step to the back of the line or sit in the last train car. For every Frenchman who tipped his hat and greeted them, "Bonjour," Ruby poked Arnett's side.

"Told you," was all Arnett said. Ruby released the breath she wasn't aware she'd held since stepping off the ship and understood that never, in any place they had visited, slept in, or driven through in the U.S. had she ever felt free. She pondered what this meant to a colored girl in Paris. Every sign, poster, and voice was incomprehensible and, suddenly, Ruby realized how far they had come.

After they settled into a cheap Latin Quarter hotel with a twin-sized bed and a toilet, but no tub, at the opposite end of the hall,

Arnett made love to Ruby. They rocked and they reeled on that narrow mattress; the thrill of it all pushed him deep into her, urgent and gentle all at once—Paris love. The satisfaction that had eluded Arnett on the road. Not his love, he constantly reminded Ruby, but the unease that rode him and caused him to doubt his ability to get to this place or satisfy her. "Ruby, my love." He held her now, sniffed her hair, teased her with his tongue; they coupled a second time and a third. "I kept my promise."

They roved the city and held hands like newlyweds on their honeymoon. Arnett wanted to see Montmartre, even after hearing that most of the clubs of his daddy's day no longer existed. Notre Dame. The Louvre, from a distance without the need to see the art inside. The Eiffel Tower. From the cobblestoned streets to the clocks in the middle of cement walls, the neat rows of rectangular windows, to the general politeness of whomever they came across—no stepping aside to let French men or women pass by; no lowered heads or wary glances. They greeted the waiters who encouraged them to try escargots, drenched in butter and parsley, with bonjours and bonsoirs. No one paid attention to their race. Any restaurant within their budget was theirs to enjoy without fear of not being served because of the color of their skin. They forgot Jim Crow and looked straight at French white folks when they needed directions or help understanding a menu. Not one idea, person, or place did Ruby find objectionable in this city, except, maybe, the occasional Turkish toilet where she had to squat, not sit, to do her personal business.

It didn't take much for Ruby and Arnett to learn what folks had told them about the city had changed since the war. Ruby trembled with it—the rush to return to normal. *Hurry up, hurry*, the city cried to her: Paris is Paree again. As they wandered all over Paris, they were unaware which streets had been crumpled and aged by war, and which smudged façades had simply suffered from centuries of tarnish or were soon to be sacrificed to the new wave of renovation. Seeing the scaffolds cloak buildings where the famous and the royals had lived, and the gray tarps hiding facelifts and restorations, it was clear to Ruby that Paris was a city of change. Change gave the two—city and woman—a common goal.

Arnett and Ruby had no idea how long it had taken to repair all the Germans had done to the City of Light: the signs renaming *rues* to *strassen*, Nazi flags, stiff-legged soldiers marching the length of the Champs-Élysées, tanks and rules, curfews and rationing, ancient statues destroyed for the value of the metal, women with heads shaved for carousing with the enemy. Jazz musicians from New York to Kansas City to southern backwoods had heard that the war forced jazz underground. Germans had not tolerated it: branded it African music, banned the Negroes left in Paris from performing in nightclubs. It was a contagious art.

Paris had survived, jazz survived—it was all the talk on the ship—the way good things do, with the help of Europeans who played that music on the radio, disguising song names. With the help of the young, the philosophers and intellectuals who rushed to the Left Bank, eager for new thinking and new music. French musicians claimed a piece of it, coddled it, loved it, Frenchified it. Jazz had survived the Occupation; the beat had been too strong.

Arnett made one or two friends, piano players with particularly tender personalities who played the music until he learned every nuance, measure, and beat. He discovered that Freddie Jones had moved to Paris. He didn't call right away, telling Ruby that he was concerned about using the French telephone. It took three weeks before he worked up the courage. When he reached the man, Arnett spent five minutes reminding him of who he was and how they met. It wasn't until he described Ruby as the waitress in the New Orleans club that Freddie decided they should meet.

The Club St.-Germain-des-Prés was located in the middle of a dingy block in the sixth *arrondissement* that Freddie Jones described as the heart of jazz in Paris. The music intensified with each step down the stairs. The club was narrow, the ceiling lumpy and arched, dug from layers of ancient Paris. Table abutted table, shoulder grazed shoulder, and dancers grooved in whatever spaces were left. The bar was close to the stage so that when the joint was live and at its best, clinking bottles and glasses became a part of the groove.

"A few clubs up near Mo'mart. Bricktop's doing okay. There's rumors she's going home. Bechet is still here. But"—Freddie nodded to the crowd—"this is where the big shots come. Lots of cats, American and French. This cave is where the action is. The best place to start looking for gigs."

"Cave, Freh dee. En Français, c'est caahve." Freddie's woman, Yvette, exaggerated her pronunciation. "Pas caaave." Freddie had taken a fancy to Yvette shortly after he had arrived in Paris. They lived together in a residential hotel. She was learning English, "And I am to teach him French. But he is not the good learner."

"Will you teach me?" Ruby scooted her chair close to Yvette.

"Mais oui, chérie," Yvette hugged Ruby. "I teach you and you teach me. Oui?"

"Freddie. Not frehhh dee," Ruby corrected. The potential of Yvette's cooperation reminded Ruby of Lurlene. Lurlene had sent Arnett, but she had cowered in a corner, without interfering, when Martha punished Ruby, then vanished, never to be seen or heard from again. Trusting Yvette meant believing in friendship not just between two women, but two women, one Negro, one white.

Yvette hugged Ruby again, and Ruby hugged Yvette back, knowing it had been a long while since anyone, man or woman, but Arnett had been so affectionate. Ruby's age, her poorly stitched dress, Arnett's constant flinching when Freddie introduced him to a couple of musicians and suggested he audition in one of these clubs, caused Yvette to whisper into Freddie's ear and him to bob his head. She held on to Ruby's hand. "You will like our Paris, chérie. You will be très happy here."

When the club closed in the early morning, Freddie chuckled loudly and looked from Arnett to Ruby, then he opened his wallet and paid for their drinks. He passed francs to the cabdriver, pushing Arnett's money aside. "Naw man, it's on me."

It was Yvette, seeing the dilapidated exterior of the hotel Ruby and Arnett were living in, who suggested they move, and Ruby who confessed to the weariness of five years living in cars, hotels, and motel rooms.

"It might be nice to have a place of our own."

"Big Freh-dee et moi, we will help."

14

Correspondence presents a unique form of language exercise. It offers the beginner an opportunity to practice proper spelling, commonly used phrases, salutations, and closing lines.

avoir peur de (ah vwar purr duh)	to fear something
étonner (aay tawn ay)	to astonish
bouleverser (bool vehr say)	to upset
que faire? (kuh fair)	what to do?

The box was filled with letters stiff beneath Nicole's fingers and divided by wide rubber bands into three groups—a dozen or so in each section. No bows or ribbons or sachets. No fragile tissue hinted at their content. The addresses on the top batch were from Malvina to Squire, Malvina's flourishing handwriting less controlled back then. Nicole decided they were organized by dates imprinted over airmail and three-cent postage stamps; no random collection of memories. Malvina's top letter was dated before Squire was deployed overseas; before blacks had been allowed to engage in combat.

September 1943

Dear Squire,

Surprise! Bet you didn't think I'd write, but I promised. Remember?

It's quiet in town. I can't tell if it's because colored and white boys have volunteered for the service and are off to basic training, or because summer is winding down. The leaves of trees seem anxious to fall, and birds are abandoning their nests.

I saw Lena Horne (oh, she's so beautiful) in Stormy Weather. I cried when she sang. I can sing but, oh, to be Lena, even for a minute. I saw the movie twice because the ticket taker never came upstairs to check on the colored section. After the weekends, I go back to my chores and preparing to leave for school. I'm learning to cook. I make a mean apple pie and knit, too. Mama's a master, but I'm not very good. My stitches are rough, and my rows are crooked. I'll try my hand at a scarf or a tie and surprise you when I'm better.

I hope you don't think I'm silly telling you all my doings, but I hoped to take your mind off of the war. We learn what's happening to our men by word of mouth—and often it's not good—but Roosevelt and Patton are considering colored soldiers in combat. Here's hoping that if you go to Europe, folks will be polite and respectful. You must be missing home. Hope you and your friends enjoy these cookies—I've been perfecting a special recipe. I'd be happy to send what you need, be sure to let me know. Please write, Squire. I think you know how I feel.

Always,
Malvina

When, except for New Year's Eve and Valentine's Day, did she recall a card from one parent to the other, or her parents hugging or standing close for the sake of touching? No matter how she tried, she was unable to visualize an openly amorous Malvina and Squire Handy. Theirs was a pristine love: distracted pecks on the cheek before work, errands, or bed. Up until Nicole was nine, cold or afraid of the dark or lightning or sleeping alone, she regularly crept into their bed, into the distance between their bodies, and fell asleep, awakening in the morning undisturbed in the same spot.

That nosy nine-year-old Nicole, poking through her parents' room and her mother's nightstand, was a sucker for secrets. The rumbling feeling now was far from thrilling. Save for her father's mention of the blue-eyed cat, no history of bad juju existed in her family. No superstitions, no throwing salt over a shoulder or saving discarded hair in a glass jar. Caution pricked her insides. A breeze slipped under the windowsill and ruffled the photograph into a mini tailspin. It drifted from the coffee table to the floor, where Nicole left it. Had both her parents been dead, she might have felt better. But that curious kid lived on inside Nicole; she selected another letter.

August 1944

Dear Malvina,

How are you and how are your studies going? I'm anxious for this war to be over so that I can get started on mine. Though the details are not mine to give, I can tell you that ■ Express is a chance for Negro soldiers to prove that we've got what it takes to fight. We have all stepped up to the challenge. The trucks are loaded with supplies. We rarely stop to eat, and when we do French farmers sell us eggs and chickens and scrawny field rabbits that we cook at night on the hood of our trucks because the engines are so hot. One fella has mastered this so well we nicknamed him Cook. Ha. Ha.

If we're lucky, we can get a few hours break in Paris. I saw the Eiffel Tower off in the distance. Did you know it has 1,665 steps? I don't know if I'd ever be able to make it to the top. I have to admit all that height makes me nauseated. No chance to see it up close because the Germans occupy Paris. Between our uniforms and skin we're obvious. Wasn't smart to be so public and in plain view. So, we roamed a neighborhood, stopped at a café and then started our duties all over again. Thank you for the treats. I hope you don't mind if I share your cookies with my buddies.

Your friend,
Staff Sgt Squire Handy

Besides the bits and pieces Squire shared during flashes of the civil rights struggle on the nightly news and the Black Panthers fighting the Oakland police, he hadn't discussed his tour of duty with the Army. Thinking back on it now, Nicole realized that, except for the French phrases he learned during the war and the snapshots of him in his uniform pasted in the family album, his letter revealed details he never had.

Years ago, Malvina had admitted to Nicole that she had never loved anyone but Squire. "I'm not a syrupy woman," Malvina had commented, picking lint off of her housedress and rolling the little pills in a ball between her fingers. "You know the sort. I do what has to be done." Her admission came when Nicole announced she was getting divorced. It had stayed with her these years since—barring the evening when she was nineteen and Malvina caught Clint necking with her daughter on the front porch—because the two of them never spoke of love or any topic remotely intimate.

Nicole dreaded that gene. Detachment. Her ex's lame justification for womanizing. So hooked was she on Clint that first time, that first sex, the remembrance of him practically made her come even after he left for Washington, D.C. Years later, detachment came in handy after he wooed her from routine, saved her from boredom, brought desire back to her body. When he admitted to a wife and kids, Nicole trusted aloofness was what he wanted.

Watching him come and go at any hour. Watching him shower away her smell, his guilt. Nicole hadn't justified being with a married man, even one she'd loved thirty-three years ago—when there were no wife and children. Before she closed her door behind Clint, there was passion. Many nights, after he went back to his wife, she huddled in the warm spot he left on the mattress and wondered if his wife greeted him with distance. Her ex, Clint—she wanted to keep the past dead. Nicole sighed at what passed for affection between her parents. Even from an adult perspective, she never imagined her mother engaged in a passionate kiss.

A shorter, second stack. Envelopes of all shapes and sizes, thick and thin. The top letter from Squire to Malvina. With age, his handwriting had come close to illegible. In his seventies, Squire had showed Nicole how he practiced his penmanship, reemphasizing that clear, dignified handwriting was the calling card of an educated man. He proudly flipped through an accountant's ledger where, for years, he copied words and definitions, poetry and lengthy paragraphs from his Great Books into that journal and at least four others. Nicole removed a letter from his stack. Behind it, and the many following that one, was a second letter addressed to someone else.

September 1943

Dear RubyMae,

The Atlantic is an angry ocean. From the day we got on the ship, I felt the churning waters beneath all this steel. The platoon doctor said I was suffering from seasickness and said I should toughen up. And I wasn't the only one. He was angry. "You colored boys need to adjust to living on a ship." When he claimed none of the white boys fussed, I told that man my stomach didn't distinguish between colored and white, and that he needed to give me a remedy before I died on that ocean. Needless to say, he did not take my complaints seriously. There has not been one day that I have not thrown up or have otherwise felt poorly. I hardly sleep. We're stacked flat as pancakes on narrow bunks. They swing and lurch when the water is rough, and it is mostly rough. But, I have done my share of the work.

No different from home, we're separated from the whites. You'd think this is the place to get along. We don't know how we'll need each other when we get near the fighting and all of us trying to save the world from Hitler. The fact of the matter is most colored troops won't see action, but that shouldn't matter. We're all doing our part. Little tiffs come up now and then. They feed us after the white soldiers have eaten, but it makes not a bit of difference to me. All I eat is mashed potatoes, rice, and soup as clear as I can find. Some fellas just eat candy bars.

The other day, some of us stepped into the mess hall (that's what I call it, there are hundreds of names for every part of this ship) before the white soldiers had finished. My bunkmate, Tyler, figured it didn't make a bit of difference if we ate a little early. If we got to die together, surely you think we could eat together. They put him in the brig. The MPs said my buddy was trying to start an insurrection—now what riotous trouble can we get into on a boat? No place to go, no place to get away. I'm not even sure any of these colored boys know how to swim. These officers must think we're stupid. But I think they're scared. White Northerners never saw these many coloreds in one place before. And the officers from the South, well, I think they're as scared, but for different reasons. I'm hoping that being on boats together and fighting a common enemy will make us equal when we get back. America should be proud of all of its soldiers.

I miss the feel of the earth between my fingers. I miss watching crops grow. I miss you. I keep thinking of your hands, how you can't hold all that hair of yours at the back of your head, how the loose strands brush up against your face, how you smell when you step close. I wish I could bottle that scent and sniff it every night and make the other boys green with envy. Oh RubyMae, I pray that you will wait for me. That's how I keep myself sane. That's how I let go of the thought of throwing myself overboard rather than go on suffering this terrible twirling in my gut. Oh, how I hate the ocean. Please write. I know I'm coming back. Nothing is going to happen to me. I want you to be my wife.

With all my love,
S

The letter slipped from Nicole's hands. Why had her mother sent these letters? She searched for a second note hopefully less dramatic than the first. Nothing. She checked the third batch for an answer. All the letters were addressed to Squire Handy in this grouping. A dried sprig fell into her lap. The brown stem hinted at an aged residual of that herb, the faint fragrance of lavender. The handwriting was rectangular and deliberate as if the writer had contemplated each letter of the alphabet before finishing it. So worn was the rubber band holding these letters that it had lost its elasticity and fell apart when Nicole tugged at it. The letter, addressed to Private Squire Handy, Portageville, Missouri, was postmarked Sheridan, Mississippi.

October 28, 1943

Dear Squire,

You write so many letters! I promised so here's mine. I told you even when we were in the midst of talking and you always interruptd. I'm best at speaking not writing. Don't say I didn't tell you. right now Sheridan is tolerble. Colored men of all ages have gone off to the Army camps. We hear talk of riots and fights between colored and white soldiers, the military police and even the folks in the towns near their camps. PapPap says that colored soldiers from the north are just now finding out about the real south. I guess Mister Jim Crow don't live up north. As far as marrying goes, I don't want you getting your hopes up. My skin itches just knowing the whole world you get to see. I want to see it too. I want to do better then spend my life where folks are happy doing the same thing over and over again till they die. It's what I know and it sits well with me. You are my good friend. Who knows me best? Your two ears and good heart are my friends and I don't know what I would do if you didn't listen to my gripes. Tend to yourself. I will pray for your safety.

Your friend
RubyMae Garrett

Nicole's hands trembled, and the letters sighed when she riffled them like a flip book of stick figures—the musty smell of mildewed paper. No animation here. A few sheets were onion-skin thin and folded into themselves with borders striped red, white and blue for airmail delivery. R. Garrett. R. Garrett. R. Garrett. Ten times, at least, written clearly in the upper left corner.

January 1944

Dear Mother and Father Garrett,

I cannot tell you where I am specifically, and if I did, the Army censors are on the alert, but I can say I am in France. Recently, my platoon had a scare. We got caught in the strafe of an enemy ■■■■■. No one was harmed, but as you can well imagine after such a close call, I'd rather be at home. But for now, I want to pin my hopes on the future. Surely, holding on to it will bring me back safe and whole.

I am writing for your permission to make RubyMae my wife. I know our RubyMae is young and spirited. I can help her become a fine wife and motherhood will help her to mature into her responsibilities and settle down.

I am saving most of my pay. For all the years you have known me, I have been a hard worker and an honest man. I can provide for RubyMae. I plan to return to Sheridan. My father is ill and he wants me to run the mill for him. When he is well again, I am going to enroll in college. I'm thinking that Alcorn will be a good fit, as I want to become a teacher.

My troop has not seen the action the 92nd (Negro) has in Italy and our fellas in the Pacific. Our troops take care of the basics, duties we won't get medals for. A lot of folks believe that the colored man is aggressive, but not smart enough or capable of fighting this war. They say we need the training promised when we enlisted. What that all boils down to is that few of us get to the front lines. But when we do we surely put up one hell of a good fight. Most stay behind. We do laundry, fix trucks and jeeps. We clean up behind the fighting troops picking up their waste. We register the dead, a sad duty indeed. The locals are nice. They offer good will and gratitude.

Keep me in your prayers. I pray for your blessing. I'll be proud to be a part of your family.

Yours truly,
Squire Handy

Nicole combined the three sets of letters and sorted them into chronological order. She shoved cookie after cookie into her mouth. When the dozen was gone, she started in on wine and set her wristwatch on the table. Too early to call, the minute hand seemed to take forever to make its way around the hours.

July 1944

My Dearest,

Did your folks tell you about my letter? I hate that our letters don't match up. I am so lonely for you. A few fellas share, but your letters (as few as I've gotten, smile) are mine alone. But how can you put a smile in a letter? I see you in my mind, tossing your head back and letting your arms fly when you run. That's what I miss most.

Today, I received two pieces of good news. I've been promoted to staff sergeant. It's a non-commissioned officer spot, meaning I've gotten a little raise, the responsibility for 60 men, a truck pool and no authority. Here's a picture of me getting my new stripes. Uncle Sam has put me, and all of us Negro soldiers, in an awkward position. Negroes are not in charge of troops. All the officers are white. Here we are, willing to die for our country and we can't even lead our own men. They don't trust that we can do the job, any job. With the little training they've given I hope to prove that I can. After all, the last time I checked, we all bleed red (and God knows I have seen the blood). Every Negro man here is fighting two wars. I'd venture to say, not one of us in this Army understands why we face such prejudice and segregation. I thought I left all of that at home.

2nd piece of news. I hear talk of a special unit that transports ■■ from ■■■ to ■■■. The Redball Express. I'm going to volunteer for that unit. I'll be a driving fool. Not on the front, but in on the action. I tried to write a poem, but each one I write ends up being about you. Here's one.

> *When day's bright sun drops to its nest*
> *And silence bestows my ears with peace*
> *I surrender, weary soldier at night's behest,*
> *To dreams that will not cease.*
> *Dark speck of beauty 'neath your eye*
> *Tumbling lashes angels envy*
> *In sleep I release a moan, a sigh*
> *And yearn for your lips mine to be.*

I keep my book of Langston's poems wrapped in a tarp under my shirt. I'm sure that great man would snicker at my sad attempts to rhyme. I read from his book often, careful not to ruin the pages, and pretend I'm reading to you. The fellas tease me, for sure, but by and by they settle down, and I know when I read, they are thinking of their loved ones as well. Please write.

Darling, I am Forever yours,
Squire.

November 1944

Dear Squire,

I had a vision in my sleep last week that I bought a train ticket with silver dollars. I swear I heard them jangling. When I woke up I was soaking wet and happy even though the air through the window blew icy cold. When I went to close the window that pearl handled mirror you gave me fell to the floor and broke into a thousand pieces. That was a sign. I don't want any bad luck, so I owe it to tell you that I have met someone. His name is Arnett Dupree. He's not from Sheridan. He's like me. I'm sorry, but I won't change my mind. Don't worry about me. We'll always be friends.

RubyMae

Nicole felt sorry for her father. Him feeling love. Ruby loving somebody else. She was hooked, wanting, but not wanting, to read.

February 1945
Alcorn College

Dear RubyMae,

Thank God you're safe. Don't be fickle, sister, please think about what you've done. It's not too late. Mama tows the line, but you're a fidgety girl, and with two children, she had to put her foot down. Don't hold it against her.

What about Squire? I figured, sooner or later, you'd tire of his attention—toying with him when he came around—but he wants to marry you. I've been corresponding with him since he went off to boot camp. If he mentions you—what should I say? He thinks of me as a friend, classmate, and your big sister. Every soldier needs friends at home to let him know how much his sacrifice is appreciated. I've sent cookies and if my stitches get better, I'll knit a scarf or two for him and when he wears it, he'll think of me. Friendship can be a seed that grows into love.

You may not want anything to do with Mama and PapPap right now, but please stay in touch with me, sister. Let me know where you are and what you need. We've not been close, but we are sisters. And no matter what you've done, or where you are, family is family.

Love, Your Big Sister,
Malvina

Nicole knocked the box from the table and pushed the windows open until the din of late night filled the living room. Without checking her watch, she dialed her parents' number. Malvina answered before the first ring ended.

"You have a sister?"

Malvina responded as if they'd paused an ongoing conversation. "Did you finish them?"

"The letters? No. Feels like I'm eavesdropping at your bedroom door." Fatigue and adrenaline raged a battle inside Nicole's head; she wanted fatigue to win. Her eyelids drifted shut without her wanting them to. "Did I really need to know about this triangle?"

"I hoped you'd be interested."

"Interested? You send a bunch of letters that you've saved for years thousands of miles. I find out my father was in love with someone else, and that someone was your sister. Yes, I'm interested." Nicole waited for Malvina to explain, pleased the connection cooperated with a slight delay.

"I never got along with RubyMae, there was such a difference in our ages."

"Dammit, Mother." No different from most children, Nicole wanted to believe her parents told the truth, no matter what: the Tooth Fairy left cash; Santa Claus brought Christmas toys; no one remembered the woman in the photograph. "You lied. You said you were an only child."

"She had everything; you see her. She was beautiful. Light-skinned. Good hair, eyelashes. That beauty mark. Thin lips. Indian nose." Malvina never lingered in front of a mirror. Even when she carried more weight, clothes hung loosely from her wide shoulders. She pinched her nose, and Nicole's, hoping to reshape them to pointed, not flat against their faces. "She turned her back on her family. She threw her good life away. Acted common."

And she had my father, Nicole wanted to say, conscious that that response was inappropriate from a daughter to her mother. "A lot of sisters don't get along. I'm so sorry she hurt you, Mother." Nicole paused, waiting for her mother, despite this rambling, to tell her story.

"He was my classmate, my age. You don't understand, Nicki. It's not how she looked it's what she did. She hurt your father. She hurt me. She cheated us." Behind Malvina's silence a TV voice shouted to a screaming audience to guess the dollar value of a big prize.

"And the letters?"

"I read them. Hers. His. All of them. I don't think your father ever had a clue, and I'm surprised you never found them. You were such a nosy child."

"So Dad loved your sister. Then he loved you."

"I was always in love with him." Malvina heaved a lengthy sigh. "If your father could see you. If he could speak for himself."

"Well, he can't. You could've told me you had a sister. Dad was in love with her and obviously, she rejected him, and moved on. Almost sixty years, Mother. Dad loves you. I love you."

"No way for you to know, Nicki, since you don't have any, but babies have a spot on the crown of their heads." Malvina lowered her voice as if the background noise weren't enough to keep what she was saying from Squire. "I don't know why it sticks with me, that's your father's habit. Fontanel—that tender spot where the skull's bone hasn't come together. Every time somebody had a baby, my grandmother used to go on about that spot, almost a wound. It was so fragile and took so long to close."

"You forget I have friends with kids."

"We all start out with a soft spot. RubyMae is my spot, and even if she was gone, I could've sworn she never went away. Watching. I owe her, and you know I'm not a woman who tolerates debt of any variety. After what she did to me, to us, I owe her."

"You won. You married Dad. Why do you owe her at all?"

"I expected your father to tell you... RubyMae, my sister, she's your *real* mother. The one who gave birth to you."

15

Paris, 1951

"Baby, you stuck, again?"

Arnett nodded, the most he'd do before any audition. Six years with Arnett, six years of auditions, and Ruby chattered, all the same, when she was supposed to wait and let him replay the notes and progressions in his head and figure out if his E-flat was in tune.

"Cogitating." His explanation for holding music in his head, his mental preparation for the audition.

Ruby waited for his spell to be done. Only the ability to read music, understand the measures, the clefs and symbols, could change this near trance Arnett fell into before and after practices, rehearsals, and auditions. Back in the States they had, he had, plenty of friends interested in big band jazz and not the underlying harmonies of this bebop mesmerizing everybody but him. He learned the difference between quarter notes, whole, and half ones, but not what they meant lined up together with tails and bold lines connecting two, three, or four of them.

All in all, where his lack slowed Arnett down, Paris made Ruby antsy and keen to be a part of the city. Beside her silent Arnett, she read the signs of the businesses on either side of the street. "*La boucherie, la crêperie, le salon de thé*." Her passion for the language was convenient. Ruby never fretted that Arnett's accent was better, figuring his ear was trained to pick up the nuances between *un* for one and *un* for a or an.

"Soon I'll speak French so good—perfect. And no one will be able to tell I'm not French. *Le tabac*—the tobacco shop; *la laverie*—the laundry; *la boucherie*—butcher shop."

Arnett didn't bother with translating when Ruby did it for them. He spoke French to musicians who spoke little English. He came to Paris to play music and music needed no translation.

"Say *libraire*, Arnett. Leeee brrrrair."

Arnett rarely repeated what she said save for "cigarette," spoken the same in English and French, and *châteaubriand*, because on nights when they ate hot-water soup with onions, he spoke of big, fat, juicy steaks.

"I bet you think that means library. Nope. Bookstore."

The more bebop became popular, the more it required rhythmic phrasing, improvisations, and substitutions and variations, the more Arnett rehearsed. When they reached where the Boulevard St.-Michel ended at a bridge, Arnett descended into a stairwell and rehearsed the last of a melancholy song, leaving Ruby to pace before the fountain of the angel, raised sword in hand. In Sheridan, one statue stood on the side of the courthouse—a prim, frowning man holding a Bible. In Paris, statues were elaborate. This one was a warrior. A holy warrior with wings.

Waiting for Arnett had become what she did in Paris. That and taking in the details. No museums with paintings older than the whole U.S. of A. It was the cement gargoyles and metal curled like spools of ribbon that fascinated Ruby. The shops devoted to tobacco or flowers or bread and the women smoking over cups of the strong coffee she loved practically white with milk and sugar.

From nowhere, Martha overtook her musing. Her mother liked her coffee the same way. Reflection hadn't come upon Ruby since she'd come to Paris, or even on the back roads before then.

She shuddered, not remembering when she let go all thoughts of mother and father, home, lightning bugs, and chinaberries perfuming a summer night. Perhaps it was during the months she wore scarves and close-fitting hats waiting for her hair to grow back into a style that made sense. Or when she stayed at Alcorn waiting for Arnett to make arrangements and Malvina begged her little sister to return to her senses before both mother and God forgot her. Not in the years since her hair had grown into the wavy bob she now wore had she dwelled on home. Too much to see and do.

Arnett emerged, packed his alto saxophone into its case, and guided Ruby closer to the fountain. He reached into his pocket for two coins, then handed one to Ruby. "Make a wish."

"I wish to stay in Paris." They had bumbled through French red tape and each gotten a *carte de séjour* and identification papers. Ruby felt born again. She changed her name from RubyMae to Ruby; on her passport, on all the forms. Ruby Garrett. "Forever." She brushed water from her thirdhand suede pumps bought in the flea markets near Clignancourt and linked her arm into Arnett's.

"I wish for enough money to buy my Ruby a diamond ring." He rubbed the coin before tossing it in the water, then kissed Ruby's ring finger. "It's going to happen, Ruby. Our wishes are gonna to come true. I feel it."

Head high, beret tilted at an angle that shadowed her face, Ruby steered Arnett to his umpteenth audition this month, inside the Club St.-Germain-des-Prés, where a left-handed Charlie Parker blew everybody's mind in '49. Three men waited for Arnett: a Big Apple tenor saxophonist who played with his fedora set low on his forehead, a pianist who went by the name of Poppa because he seemed to be the oldest Negro in Paris who stepped off the boat to play music, and the manager behind the bar. Arnett unlatched his case and lifted his saxophone with his left hand from the red satin cradle. He assembled it, every time the same, wetting reed before putting on the neck strap, then attaching the mouthpiece to the neck and the neck to the body and so on. Then he played the seven notes of the scale, trilling a couple, and waited.

When the music started, Arnett jammed loud and clear, leaving no doubt for the men that he was hungry for this gig. He harmonized, coordinated flats and sharps with the crazy beats the tenor sax laid down, instead of working against the rhythm; he played till his chops tightened. The second sax player gave him a run for his money. With a piano and a guitar Arnett was fine. Alone he was the man. Give him a solo on "Since I Fell for You" or "That Old Devil Called Love" or any song women swooned to, nobody beat him. He kept up with familiar, overplayed ditties and songs, "Autumn Leaves" and "Baby It's Cold Outside," but when it came to improvising, what he tried to do at the moment, and this bebop, hot and new to the scene, that was changing the beat of jazz, his fingers let up. Ruby picked up a note to cover his mistake and scatted, mimicking Ella and Sarah, but without either woman's knack.

The manager walked to Poppa at the piano. Ruby watched the two men, unable to catch their conversation, and reminded herself to ask Arnett why the husky piano player bothered to audition since his reputation kept him playing any night in any club of his choosing. The bartender squeezed between the piano and Poppa, shaking Arnett's hand in passing, and stretched beyond him to the tenor sax player, the both of them nodding when the man whispered into the bartender's ear. Arnett's shoulders tensed along with his jaw.

"Come back, tonight. All tree of you. Bien?" The bartender's message not quite without accent, proof he had repeated this one line over and over to the many saxophonists, trumpeters, pianists, drummers, and singers who passed through his door and down into the cave. "Arnett, we will split between you and the tenor sax. You and I, we will talk. This is okay?"

"I got it," Arnett grunted and dismantled his saxophone in reverse sequence and shoved a cotton sock down the bell to soak up the spit and keep the bow dry. He laid all the pieces in the black case and fastened the left latch then the right. His every action began with his left, including him and Ruby in that left corner of the juke joint.

"Money is better, Monsieur. Comprenez?" Ruby frowned, knowing to a musician talking meant payment in booze, reefer, or a meal at the café above, occasionally horse—enough to get high, not addicted—instead of the francs they needed. She hadn't gotten the gist of finding the best prices on eggs and stale bread when that was all her money could buy. She was better at purchasing chicken parts or a little meat on the days Arnett was paid in cash.

"I got it, baby." Arnett tipped his hat to the manager and moved to the narrow steps. Outside, they soaked in the afternoon sun and adjusted to the light and the familiar streets of St.-Germain.

"Why do you let him do that?"

Arnett shrugged. "I'm Joe Below, low man on the totem pole, Ruby, and that's how they pay at the bottom. Which way will it be, sugar?"

Whenever he presented this question, Ruby licked two fingers and raised them in the air. "Only so many ways to get back from here, but the wind is blowing in this direction."

They continued from the club to rue de Seine and the triangular Hôtel La Louisiane. The scent of down-home cooking leaked from the lobby and into the street—beans and rice, mustard greens, and hot grease that had fried one too many chickens. Home to Bud Powell, and his wife Cupcake, and the other famous musicians whose names glowed on club billboards. Arnett peered into the tall window and searched the lobby for a friendly face or an invitation, not to eat but to bask in the company, a jam session, an after-hours set.

From the sixth *arrondissement*, Arnett and Ruby wove through Paris, unwilling to hail a cab or take the Métro, to save their *francs* and *centimes*. Early on, Ruby and Arnett lived as well as a country girl and a backwoods musician could without steady income. Now they were far from that. They wandered different parts of Paris whenever they went out. Over the Pont Neuf, toward the Opéra Garnier, to the Boulevard Haussmann, up the rue des Martyrs. Twilight, "*L'heure bleue*," Ruby whispered, was not settled in the sky when the two returned to rue de Vintimille.

"Damn!" Arnett plopped onto his straight-backed practice chair. He fluffed the pillow Ruby had hand-stitched for him to cushion the caned seat and tucked it under his butt. "Seems between auditioning and fooling with you, I've used up most of my rehearsing time."

"I think you got it, baby. Why don't you rest?"

"I can't rest, Ruby. Can't you see? Cats are out to get me and the only way I'm gonna stop them is to play the hell better." He stuck a reed between his lips, then slid the supple piece onto the mouthpiece and tightened the ligature. Arnett puffed twice and practiced flats and sharps, the quarter notes and eighths. His shoulders followed the up-and-down movement of his sax. His feet measured the rhythm. He swung from side to side. He stopped playing and opened the record player.

"Damn," he grunted. "If I take my mind off it, you know." He fumbled with a tall stack of jazz records. Arnett played records to work on fingering. And the cat with the best fingering, and left-handed to boot, was Charlie Parker. "Come on, Ruby, help me."

Ruby and Arnett traded places; she to the stack and the player, Arnett to his chair. When he stopped playing, she lifted the stylus from the groove and replaced it where Arnett had begun. Often, Ruby stayed with him, her attention undivided. Now she yawned and tried to work the kinks out of her neck. An hour into this ritual, Arnett signaled Ruby to turn the player off and went back to his track. He hunched his shoulders again; fingering the keys of the practice tune. He once told Ruby that in his head he played like Parker. Who, she considered, did he think he played like now.

When Arnett's body and mind were engaged with the music, his playing was soulful. He played the song's refrain every which style he figured out, in many tempos and keys: slow, to learn all of the notes; fast and wild; low, in case it was requested. Music filled the room and flowed from the window, into the streets and over the rise and fall of slate tiles, turrets, and rooftops.

"Arnett? Arnett? You need me?" Ruby spoke underneath the music. It was clear from the angle of Arnett's brow he was in that place with room only for his music. She snatched her notebook and her blue French dictionary, and ran out the door.

16

The verbs *devoir* (must, ought to) and *falloir* (to have to) are used when communicating obligation, duty, necessity, or need. Their meanings are similar; their usage varies.

se fâcher (suh fah shay)	to get angry, to lose one's temper
être en retard (eh truh ahn ruh tar)	to be late
mentir (mahwn teer)	to lie
la vérité (lah vear ree tay)	the truth

We didn't...I didn't mean to hurt you. I was keeping her from you, not the other way around." Malvina made no effort to muffle her sobs. The aged hurt came clear across the transcontinental connection and planted itself in Nicole's core. She allowed Malvina to cry because her mother, this mother, rarely showed her emotions; because when Nicole had suffered her great crisis of divorce, her mother let Nicole cry and refused to let her name herself a failure.

RubyMae Garrett stared at Nicole from her portrait, captured in a time warp, eternally young and sexy—aunt and mother. Years ago, Nicole had pretended to be her, the beautiful lady, twisting the sharpened tip of Malvina's eyebrow pencil into her cheek, marking the same spot on her face as RubyMae's. Wanting badly to have a mole, to be as pretty as the lady. The secret of the family album revealed. The missing link to hair texture straighter than Squire's or Malvina's; almond-shaped eyes, embarrassing ears, skin even and unblemished, close to theirs in hue but not near it in tone.

"RubyMae... that RubyMae. She was a mess." Malvina's voice slipped into her Mississippi roots. Fifty-seven years, and her sobs carried pain. Pain, Nicole believed, from knowing the man she loved loved somebody else. "I hated her. I don't even care if she's dead or alive."

"And is she?"

"Is she what?"

"The whole truth, Mother."

"I love you, Nicki." In the background, wood knocked against wood, the noise constant and rhythmic.

"You aren't going to tell me, are you?"

"Hush now, Squire." Malvina described Squire's preoccupation with the earthquake-proofed cabinets he didn't remember how to unlatch. "I've got to go, Nicki, or your father will work himself into a frenzy."

"Go? You can't *go*. What happened to Ruby? What happened to her and Dad? Don't you dare hang up, Mother. You owe me." Malvina had used the same phrase when she'd asked Nicole to live with them, take care of them. *You owe me*. When she said it, Nicole was convinced her mother was reinforcing her child's responsibility. "I want to talk to my father."

"Son of a bitch. Dirty, rotten sonofabitch," Malvina cursed, surprising Nicole. "He's the strong one, not me. He should be telling you. I wanted him to."

"Where is this woman, your sister, my... mother, RubyMae?"

"I... we... last we heard, she lived in Paris."

December 1950

Dearest Ruby,

I convinced Malvina to give me your address in hopes that you won't mind. I know it seems cruel getting your sister to tell me where you are, but we've talked. She accepts my feelings and remains my good friend. You tell me. Maybe I'm a fool. Well, in any case, she wants you to know your folks are fine. Your father is graying. Your mother's little store is thriving. My father passed recently. He suffered from cancer of the throat. Understanding how deeply it had gone into his system, he gave up and accepted a slow death. He wanted me, not my brothers, to partner with him at his mill as I did during his illness in the four years I've been back home. Not a week after Daddy passed, a white man from a mill outside Jackson served me with papers. Mister Rufus Lee claimed Daddy had signed his rights to our mill over to him as payment for a debt that man refused to describe. Folks, colored and white, were buying our lumber instead of his. Lee never let me read the crumpled paper he waved over his head. Even the saw went quiet when the sheriff and his deputy came up behind me. These men threatened me with their presence and their false documents. We went to court, but without any proof of payment, I lost the mill. Sadly, Daddy was a better father than businessman. I received less than half its worth, or should I say old man Lee stole the mill from me for practically pennies.

My feelings are conflicted. I loved and respected my father. I confess that war changed me, and I tried to tell him. Even though my brothers were in the war, they didn't think the same as I did. I became aware of the world and the prospects for Negroes! My father's is not the path I want for myself. These circumstances bring me to the reason for my letter, which I hope finds you well and happy. The government is allowing soldiers, including colored soldiers, to take advantage of the latest GI bill. The money is for new homes or education. I've chosen education. You know

I love poetry. Not that I'm any good at writing it, you've seen the evidence of that (smile), but I'd like to teach it, and so I'm planning to attend the Sorbonne. I've been practicing my French I learned during the war and I can put together clumsy sentences. They have special language courses and I will have a tutor, so my semester will be spent on the language and civilization. My biggest challenge will be learning French and staying on top of the twenty-five hours of classroom work required by the bill. But, they say living in a country helps you to learn the language quickly.

I am compelled to say that I'm not coming to Paris for you, RubyMae. I'd be lying if I said it wasn't because of you. I can't get you out of my head. I need to see you. I need to hear your voice. I know you have a man. I do think that if he respected you, he would make you his wife. You may not want to hear that, but I'm a man who speaks his mind.

For the most part Sheridan is quiet. We've got a swelling equal rights movement afoot. For all of us who fought, or lost their lives, only to come home to Jim Crow, nothing could be better for the South and the country. Are we ready to be equal citizens? Is white America ready for us? is the question. The answers are unclear. Every southern ex-soldier I know is trying to readjust to Jim Crow. Already, newspapers report an ex-Navy man beaten by a mob of white men when he refused to step aside for them on the sidewalk. Whites tell us that we were spoiled in the war and to quote the butcher on Maple Street, "You boys think 'cause the Frenchies let you disrespect them, y'all can do the same here."

How must it feel to roam the streets and not understand one word or fear lynching for speaking your mind or facing a white man or woman without turning away? Is that the promise of France? Is that why you are there? The taste of freedom Negro soldiers got in France and Italy and even in the Pacific has spoiled us for the rest of our lives. I pray to God that is not so. I don't plan to make my living outside the USA, but I do know that I deserve to be treated like a man.

I expect to be in Paris by August. When I'm settled, I'm hoping you'll see me. I look forward to climbing the steps of the Eiffel Tower, standing under the Arch of Triumph, and seeing the great Notre Dame with you. Forever and always yours,

Squire

Nicole lit a third cigarette and puffed until she was cloaked in smoke. She paced, fluffed sofa pillows, rearranged guidebooks on the bookshelf, set dishes in the kitchen, poured a glass of rosé, slathered cheese on a baguette, contemplated the screeching birds, possibly bats, flapping in the night sky.

1951

Squire,

I don't care that you're coming here. Just don't expect a thing from me. A new me lives in Paris. Ruby. I bet if you saw me on the street you wouldn't know me. You might even pass me by. This Ruby doesn't bother with country ways. This Ruby works at a shop near Montmartre. She's speaking French and delivering fancy hats to the rich ladies from England and America who come to Paris to spend their husbands' money. She takes the little extra they tip her in ivory envelops for bringing their hats to the fancy hotels they stay in and buys skirts and sweaters and sits in cafés smoking (yes smoking) cigarettes and drinking coffee. The Americans think I am French—just quiet or shy. And the English women don't care. So don't come thinking I've got to be saved. I am right where I want to be. And if you accept that, then we can be friends. If not, just keep yourself over at that Sorbonne and leave me alone.

Ruby

Nicole stared at her reflection in the dining room's mirrors; fine wrinkles etched the corners of her mouth, breasts threatened a downward slide. A breadth to her middle, despite daily outings. Legs and ample bottom her best assets. Height from Squire. Hair dyed dark absent its natural tinges of red. She'd unconsciously taken on Malvina's habits: a finger in the corner of her mouth when she worried, constant squinting despite excellent vision. Somewhere in Paris there was a glimmer of herself in another woman's face. Nicole picked the bottle of pink antacid from her purse. She swallowed and waited for its thickness to work.

At this moment, she needed to talk.

The tumble to Clint's attention, the second time, had been effortless because the man made her feel out of the ordinary, because he didn't find a fifty-six-year-old woman unattractive, because they already knew each other. Apart from her father, no other man besides Clint had cared or paid attention in years. No matter how she fought it, she relied on Clint. For his financial advice, his levelheaded knack of homing in on issues when she couldn't make up her mind to leave her firm or train as a paralegal or sell her house. He parsed facts into manageable parts, easily determining where to begin or let go.

"Can you talk?"

"I'm alone. Zoning out in front of the TV." Clint's code for napping. Sometimes at his office, he told Nicole he'd zoned out before meetings or after long lunches. Sometimes, after sex, he'd zoned out before returning home.

"I shouldn't talk to you," Clint said. "You've been rude—not answering my calls or texts. Have you changed your mind?"

"I want to tell you what's happened." She described the letters and her mother's revelation. "Long story short, Malvina's not my mother. My 'real mother'—she said it, not me—who's also my aunt, I think that's right, is a woman named RubyMae Garrett. And to top it off, she lives in Paris." *My* Paris, Nicole thought, the one right outside *my* window.

"So that's why you *had* to go to Paris?"

"If you don't know why I came to Paris, then you don't know me."

"I know you, Nicki."

"Then help me understand this damned situation. Help me figure out what to do. My mother's not my mother, and my father's a liar. Both of them are liars."

"Don't be so tough on them. At least wait until you know the whole story. Do you want to come home?"

"I don't think so."

"Your mother hid the truth for the better good. She probably feels free now that she's in charge, instead of your father." He yawned. "She has no idea of the size of Paris. Let's hypothesize: she believed it was possible to run into a woman on the streets of Paris who resembles you and blurts out that you're her daughter. You think you're shocked now..."

"This RubyMae, Ruby, is my mother. My mother, Malvina, is not my blood, at least not mother-daughter blood, considering the two are sisters, but I am who I am because of Malvina Handy. I don't love Malvina less. Or RubyMae at all."

"Aren't you the least bit intrigued?"

"Yes, I'm curious, of course. It's like breaking into their cedar trunk all over again." Curious—to see if Ruby's butt was on the high side and if she pivoted on her toes when she turned. To hear her speak and match her delicate bones. Decades too late, the answer to Malvina's cautions and accusations: too fast, too slick, too self-confident, too adventurous. To please her mother, Nicole had stripped those adjectives. Red for stop. Green for go. Caution painted yellow. Yellow like her life. Swinging backward, standing still. Poetry without motion; beginning and predictable end.

"Finish the letters."

"I don't know if I can. Not all at once." Nicole wondered what she'd inherited from Ruby that had caused her to choose a married man. "I don't care for this Ruby."

"You don't know her."

"I already know I don't want to be the sort of woman she was." Nicole sighed. "The woman in the letters..."

"You're drawing conclusions without a complete set of facts."

"You're right. I guess, when I think...aren't I doing the same as she did? Messing with somebody else's man?" Nicole let herself believe Clint's boredom with his wife's fancy balls, her need to be president of this and chairwoman of that. She believed him when he branded her uninterested and uncaring.

"It's not the same."

"I don't want to be responsible for another person's grief." Even with his lame excuses, Nicole thought, the woman Clint deceived hadn't left him, and that meant his marriage wasn't as bad as he protested. "Not if I can help it."

"Now don't go jumping to conclusions. Our relationship is completely different." Clint sucked in a deep breath and released it. "I proposed—"

"No! You're married."

"Then why the hell did you bother to call?"

"I guess...there was nobody else. But really, when I think about it, I called to say goodbye."

17

Paris, 1951

Arm in arm, Yvette and Ruby turned the corner. A woman with a bandanna knotted twice under her chin waved from her table of violets, a vendor selling baguettes from a cart tipped his hat at the two women. Yvette blonde and pale, Ruby close to redheaded, curly-haired and a shade darker in comparison to her friend.

By the end of their fifth month in Paris, Ruby and Arnett had settled into a furnished apartment. One room, *une pièce*, the *propriètaire* described it, long and wide with a window overlooking the street below. Yvette had introduced her to the shopkeepers who spoke a little English until Ruby learned what she needed. Yvette's kindheartedness kept Ruby going the weeks she tried running errands and shopping on her own by pointing to what she needed: toilet paper, coffee, milk, sugar, and fruit. Today Yvette gabbed in French and Ruby repeated her phrases: What does it cost? Is this your best price? When will my clothes be ready? Can I pay a little now and a little later?

"Your French, chérie, becomes better. Soon you will not have a need for your poor *amie*, Yvette."

"Mais non, Yvette. Toujours. We'll be friends forever. Allons."

Ruby found two chairs at a café. "That Arnett's gonna practice till we go back to the club. He'll nap, he probably won't eat, and I know he'll take at least two sips from that bottle of brandy in the back of the closet he thinks I don't know he's got."

"Ruby, you are lucky to have a handsome man. And Arnett, he loves you. You are not happy?" Yvette sighed. "Oh, chérie, I wish my Freddie loved me with such passion."

"Mais oui! He loves me very much. But we're broke. If Arnett doesn't get this job—I don't even have enough for coffee." Six years ago, Ruby felt in her bones that Arnett would rescue her. She believed no man could love a woman with such fire and not want to take care of her. "But I didn't come this far to be poor. I want things, Yvette. A room with a toilet and a tub to start with. Clothes and fur coats sharp as the ones on St.-Honoré, a chance to sing, and for Arnett to be famous."

"Chérie, life is not easy. We must do what we do and try not to think so much. After that, then you must ask yourself if you have found Paris all that you wanted, eh?"

"No place else I'd rather be. I love Arnett. I love Paris. We made wishes this afternoon, at St.-Michel's fountain. A wish brings change." Ruby opened her arms as if to embrace the drizzle. No fields of dandelions, no green lawns soaked with spring rain, no magnolia trees or June bugs to catch and bind with string, no lightning bugs on ring fingers. Not the smell of red dirt or its dust on her shoes. "It hasn't been easy, but no matter what happens, I'm going to be a woman who lives with no regrets."

"Ruby!" Arnett's voice rang out from the other side of the street. His saxophone dangled from his strap. The instrument thumped against him as he paced from one side of the street to the other. "Ruby, where are you?" He'd played for so long that, for Ruby, his music blended with the neighborhood din—the bling of a bicycle bell, the clacking of wooden wheels against the cobblestones, the patter of rain.

Ruby tilted her chair back ever so slightly until she merged with the customers inside the restaurant.

"He will see me, Ruby, and then he will know that you are here."

"Un moment, je t'en prie." Ruby scooted back, her chair moving quietly over the planked wood floor. "Sometimes a girl just needs a minute."

"Ruby!" Arnett rushed to the café, hair tousled from fingers working through his waves. "I didn't know where you were."

"You were in one of your spells, baby. I'm here. See? With Yvette."

"I had a vision, at the fountain." He stood before their table and ogled the two big men seated behind the women. Arnett glared until the men looked elsewhere. "I didn't know where you were and I wanted to tell you."

"I'm right here, and you found me." Ruby soothed Arnett in the voice she used when he wallowed in uncertainty. "I'm fine. See?" She waved at Yvette. Ruby guided Arnett back to the rue de Vintimille and up the five spiraling flights of stairs, him holding her hand and angled into her side.

"You gonna be fine, baby. Just play the way you do for me. I'll be there."

"I been thinking. You don't need a diamond, do you, Ruby? We'll get married. Go back to the States. You love me, Ruby, right? Even if I couldn't play, you'd love me."

"What are you talking about, Arnett? We aren't going anywhere and, of course, I love you." She sniffed his breath. Brandy.

The door to their room was as wide open as the window beside the narrow bed. Ruby guided Arnett to the bed and removed his saxophone.

"Arnett, you're just worried. That's all. We're fine. Tonight's gonna be fine." She laid the sax in its case, slipped out of her dress, and hung it over the back of his practice chair. "You need to rest."

"We have to get married, Ruby. Gold bands, that's all we need. One for you and one for me. Then home. Maybe New York or New

Orleans. We can make it in New Orleans. Food on the table every night. Hot water. I'm tired, Ruby. Plain old tired."

"We're fine, baby, just fine." On the bed beside Arnett, Ruby held him until his clammy body went limp. She rocked and hummed a little "God Bless the Child" until he drifted off, leaving her to ponder why Paris had lifted her up and done exactly the opposite for her man.

18

Idiomatic expressions are unique to every language. Words combine to create a new thought or an idea quite different from the separate meanings.

mauvaise perdante (mow vayz pehr dahnt)	sore loser
chercher dans tous les coins (share shay dahn too lay kwahn)	to look high and low for
avoir l'air de (ah vwar lair duh)	to seem
flâner (flah nay)	to stroll without purpose

January 1952

Dear Malvina,

Paris now has a distinct chill. Winter is upon us. Here are a few postcards for you. Paris is different. I almost can't put it into words. Not many Negroes congregate together—you know how the church at home is the place where we welcome new folks. In Paris, Negroes want to celebrate this new freedom without having to worry about being Negro—we can all just be. Plain and simple. Many of the Negro men I've met love it here because they walk down the streets with a white woman (a few have 2!) on their arm without threats. If there are any, they come from Americans. I heard a story of a white man from the States who asked a French woman why she was out with a "nigger," and the French woman slapped the American for insulting her and her friend and told the American that he should be ashamed. We both know that would never happen in the States, let alone Mississippi. And if it did a lynching would surely follow.

I confess that the mightiness of this place is intimidating. You wouldn't believe the buildings. Not so tall, except for the Eiffel Tower, as gigantic and long and wide (see postcard of the Louvre) as if folks just kept adding on rooms and sections until they couldn't. So many statues and bridges. The bigger streets are boulevards, and they are wide as any two blocks put together in Sheridan. And busy, this city is busy (and noisy) with pigeons, and people and bicycles.

Often, when I touch these grand structures, I feel their history talking to me, telling me what uprising or revolution, what famous man or woman, king or queen walked the same streets I do. The best is the smell of bread—which I have come to eat every night—baking in the boulangerie, that's the bakery where they make baguettes, long skinny rolls of crusty bread (but cornbread's better!). I enjoy the little pies (tartes) and croissants, but I'm trying my best to avoid treats as I'm watching my budget and my budget is helping my waistline. I keep myself to a daily food allowance of 200 francs (61 cents)! You'd be amazed at what good food I can find. Other students are in the same shape. I'm not alone.

In Paris white men do not disrespect me. At last I understand what it means to be truly free. It's a blessing but, to tell you the truth, my friend, I miss home. No matter how I try, I can't seem to get a hold on this language. I use basic French: oui, non and merci. I remember to say bonjour and bonsoir to shopkeepers. But when anybody speaks to me, even my teachers, I cannot get what I've learned to come out. Not knowing the language makes me feel lonely. So, I'm glad to get your letters. I got lost the other day without the map I carry with me everywhere. I had to get directions from a man on the street. Gauche is left, droit is right, à droit (that little mark changes the meaning) is straight ahead. I got the directions so confused that finally I gave the man my handkerchief and he drew a map for me, complete with the names of the rues (streets) so that I could get back to the school.

I have three classes (poetry and beginner French conversation and grammar especially for all the Americans and foreigners who have enrolled here) and most of my day is spent on my work. Not knowing the language makes it tough. But then, I'm not afraid to work. I hope you and your family had a good holiday. Your letters and care packages mean a lot. If, by chance, you send another, I sure would appreciate a Doctor Pepper. And Mennen Brushless Shaving Cream, I don't particularly care for the kind they have over here.

Your Friend,
Squire Handy

The question, she decided, was one of impact: how was she supposed to feel? Today, she passed plane trees without admiring their speckled trunks or the church's vestibule overflowing with visitors interested in architecture not prayers. *Am I where she had been?* Nicole peeked between the cracks of a rusty open door. Had Ruby done the same, curious to see what was within? Right in the middle of the plaza of St.-Sulpice, it hit Nicole that these lies gave a new context for her parents' actions.

When Nicole was a teenager, Malvina encircled her with a moat of can'ts and don'ts: home by ten, no male company, no dating until eighteen, depending. Advice streamed from Squire's lips. How his coworker's husband cheated on her so bad that forty years later she still complained about his "fornicating" ways. Or the neighbor's husband, a "no 'count drunk and philanderer—educated, but no 'count." Rarely a good comment for the young men Nicole brought home or who came to the door to pick her up. They were too short, too tall, too dark-complected, too light-skinned, too moneyed or too poor. Too ambitious, too passive. Too slick, too shy. Nicole sat through Squire's lectures every Saturday morning. Most men lied, pretended to want a woman's love, and most often, carelessly tossed it aside. Squire never taught his daughter what was important in a good man. "Look at your mother." All along, Nicole assumed he meant, look how good he was to Malvina, how he cared for her.

The French lesson for the day was under way when Nicole slipped into a chair at the rear of the classroom. One student sported nose, brow, and lip piercings. Another wore a spiked Mohawk dyed in shades of shocking pink. All Nicole had in common with them was the inability to speak fluent French. The instructor rattled on, referring to the newspaper article in his hand—an announcement of an impending transit strike.

Each night she practiced pronunciations and memorized vocabulary lists. At every class, the instructor praised her progress. She brought in lists of new vocabulary and presented them to the instructor for extra credit. Ruby and her damn letters. Nicole rose and declared to the instructor, in English and French, that this was her last class and left.

Put your thinking cap on, woman. Out the gate of the grand language school, down the steps and off to the closest *tabac*. Time to connect these puzzle pieces. The clues were in the letters: a return address, the American Express office, two names, and perhaps even the boxes in Monsieur Daudon's shop. If she never tried to find RubyMae, the not-knowing would be a grudge she'd hold against her parents when they needed support, not resentment. Her questions needed answers. Did her father see Ruby in her? Did her mother question what of Ruby was in her sister's child?

Cell phone cards, pouches of tobacco, Swiss Army knives, gum and mints lined the *tabac* shelves. Nicole paid for thirty minutes on the computer. In the search box, she typed: rue de Vintimille, the street name on her letters. The name of a three-star hotel with the same name popped up near the Moulin Rouge and Pigalle. Then iterations of RubyMae's name—RubyMae Garrett, Ruby Garrett, Ruby Handy, then Ruby Dupree. No luck. Nicole combined RubyMae Garrett with Paris, tried it with Mississippi, spelled Garrett with an extra E, one T. Garretts popped up with one T, two R's, one R two T's. She put their names together: Squire Handy RubyMae Garrett. Squire and RubyMae Handy. Permutations bordered on complex, uninteresting mathematics. No matter how many combinations she tried, she couldn't get a feeling for any one of the RubyMae Garretts—author, historian, scientist, librarian, 1959 homemaker of the year, heroine of a romance novel. No one by that name lived in Paris.

Arnett Dupree. A common name. No luck. Nicole had no inclination to pursue his history. She discovered Squire's enlistment records charted on a table divided into two columns. His serial number the primary statistic in that scanty file. Madison County, Mississippi, 1922, were Squire's place and year of birth; his birth into the Army, Shelby, Mississippi, 1942.

Browsing along the information highway, it occurred to Nicole that the assumptions concerning her mother had been wrong. *He should be the one telling you.* Her father, keeper of secrets. Not the father she adored. The generous man who lent money and didn't care if he got it back; the set of tools he brought on every visit to Nicole's to tinker with the leaky faucet, the running toilet, the blown fuse. Consoling when Malvina had a stroke, that brush with death; measured recitations of Langston's poems, his secret journal Nicole discovered filled with his poetry—that was who he was.

From behind the counter, the tobacconist cleared his throat. His signal to finish because the man pacing in the doorway was in urgent need of the computer.

When Squire wanted to prove one of his theories, he'd gone to the library for the answers, his arms so loaded with books that he had no room to pick up Nicole. Of the two men whose acquaintance she'd made in Paris, the African Man, Ousmane, married or not, might be able to help, and he worked at the library.

By the age of fifteen, libraries and her father's infatuation with books had lost their charm for Nicole. Library as babysitter, as place to meet nice boys, as reliable locale to tell the parents she was when she really wasn't. (Oh, that Nicole? Such a smart girl, spending so much time at the library.) Not one library was as impressive as the one before her. The Bibliothèque Nationale was a palace; a house of books the length and breadth of a generous city block. A sign, written in four languages, directed her past a boutique window decorated with flying pig statuettes and to the rue de Richelieu. Double gates, flags, and its name carved into the stone above marked the entrance where she surrendered her purse to an African security guard and passed through the metal detector.

The foyer was a corridor of remodeled beauty: a glass-enclosed bookstore, marble counters, a reading room—cordoned off by carts filled with three-foot lengths of steel poles. Nicole peeked through an open door at blue walls and table lamps, wooden desks comparable to church pulpits, and imagined Hugo, Dumas, de Tocqueville laboring inside the circular room. Farther down the hall, a curved staircase wound up to the second floor. Its steps carpeted in red and accessorized with brass rods reminded Nicole of the grand staircases in the Sunday open houses Malvina and Squire visited in ritzy Oakland neighborhoods where homeowners' association covenants kept blacks from living, not looking.

Beyond the stairs a security guard sat inside a kiosk, his arms long enough to touch the sides without effort.

"Bonjour, Nicole!" Ousmane wore the same thin suit and brass badge as the security guard at the gate. "I did not believe that we would see each other again." Ousmane chuckled; a warmth that reminded Nicole of Squire.

"Bonjour, Ousmane. I need your help. I hope you don't mind."

Ousmane straightened his uniform. "I am most happy to aid a beautiful American."

"I'm trying to find a woman." Nicole stepped back from the counter, her distance polite, her message clear: not interested. "My mother was in Paris after World War II."

"Your mother is French?"

Before she could reply, a thin woman barged into Nicole's personal space at the counter and tittered a fragile, uncomplicated request. The woman observed Ousmane's nametag, her cadence that of weary parent to young child. "Manny." Nicole disliked this familiarity typical of Americans who changed Richard to Dick or Suzanne to Suzy, shortening a name down to a basic element without the name holder's permission. That was why, except for family and true friends, she insisted on being called Nicole.

"The Champs-Élysées?" The tourist said *champs* with an accent that suggested she meant a group of fighters. Nicole laughed and the fragile titterer stared at her. "American?"

The vacationer's equivalent to name, rank, and serial number. If her French had been fluent, Nicole wouldn't have denied her citizenship, but teased. Not because she didn't love America or feel comfortable in her own skin. Black woman in Paris, she had the freedom to blend, the absence of questions.

"Attendez. Wait, s'il vous plaît," Ousmane pleaded to Nicole with the perseverance of their encounter near St.-Michel. Nicole stepped to the side of the kiosk. Ousmane reached for a yellow highlighter and a map from beneath the counter—not the job she assumed he'd have with the education he'd described. Nicole decided to read another letter.

August 1951

Dear Sister,

I'm apologising up front. I know I haven't written except for money. I shouldn't even be sinding this letter, but I haven't got anyone else. My friend Yvette would help if she had money, but her and Freddie's in the same shape as me and Arnett. we work where we can without the papers we need. But we're not different from a lot of other coloreds here. Most of us are poor—but loving Paris. So many saxophone players have come here, Negro and white. So many musicians and not enough work since big shots from the States are starting to come over. jazz is so hot, there isn't room enough for everybody. But, I know Arnett is going to come out on top. It just takes time and, as you say, I'm used to having my way, right away. I'm grateful for whatever you can send, but $100 (about 35,000 francs after I exchange it) will keep us in food and pay this month's rent.

Thanks for whatever you can do.

Ruby

The letters fit together, like ingredients in a recipe. Didn't matter if it was from Squire, Malvina, or Ruby. One letter answered the other.

October 1951

Dear RubyMae,

This is all I can spare. I guess would-be singers make even less than teachers. And because I am sending my money to you, it's what PapPap used to say, if you want a favor then you've got to listen to the lecture that goes with it. No one will ever be as truthful with you as your sister. Remember that. It's my duty to tell you you cannot have everything you want. Being in Paris, doing who knows what with that two-bit musician you ran off with, doesn't give you the right to think that I'll always be here for you. Or, for that matter it doesn't give you the right to keep Squire Handy on a string. Before he went into the Army, you had Squire wrapped around your little finger even though you didn't want him and you knew I did.

Many would call you simply greedy. I won't do that. But I will say to you sister, I can't find any reason why you should have two men. You have to make up your mind. Now. Squire is in Paris to get an education, and no one knows his love of poetry better than I do. But if you think I believe for one minute that he's not in Paris because of you, you forget I'm the smart sister. Let him go, RubyMae. Starting now. That's what I want for my savings I'm sending to you. I cannot let my own flesh and blood fail. Let him go and send him back to me. I don't care if he thinks he still loves you. I don't care how long it takes. I can cure him of that. I can give him what he wants: a home, babies, a family. Love. Not wanderlust that will nag him forever. He belongs here. His roots are here, what's left of his land is here. I am here.

RubyMae, call it quits and come home. Or, if Arnett is as good a man as you say, he will take care of you and help you to build a better life. Let me do the same for myself.

Your Sister, Malvina

"You are sure you have come to visit me for this reason, Nicole." After the visitors left, the dimples in Ousmane's cheeks flirted with Nicole again. It was impossible for her to discern whether his behavior was natural or calculated charm. "You have reconsidered talking?"

Nicole showed Ousmane the envelopes for the two letters in her hand and the clues written in her notebook. He retrieved a red book from his backpack beneath the counter, *Paris par*

Arrondissement, and found rue de Vintimille, the address printed on the boxes waiting for her at Monsieur Daudon's shop, and the American Express office on rue Scribe. "Both rues are in the ninth *arrondissement*."

"How do I get the information? Forms? Fees? How far back do the records go? Can you go with me? Do you think I could take care of the paperwork by myself?"

"S'il vous plaît." Ousmane stared at Nicole, puzzled. "You must talk slower. I can show you these places, when my work ends. To find your information will require much effort and I am not sure if I can. I am happy to be of help but..." He shrugged again.

"I know." Nicole scowled, understanding that signs came in all shapes and forms. "You can't, because your wife and kids are expecting you. No thanks." Nicole left the stall accepting the message the Universe confirmed.

19

Paris, 1951

Ruby wanted him to take her picture, unconcerned that she didn't know him well. Seeing him was a sign. Three men in the last week—one American, one Italian, one French—had handed her a business card behind Arnett's back with the promise of making her a star. Did she not have the portfolios that models and actresses carried with them? She heeded their interest, wanted the glamour they promised, at last realizing it was going to be a long stretch before Arnett's saxophone bought a ticket to fame and fortune; her face might bring it sooner. The little photographer was the man to make that happen. She had no plan to tell Arnett, knowing three facts where her man was concerned: he was determined to play his music, fussy when it came to spending money save for essentials—which, for him, included cigarettes and liquor, and not the crunchy meringue cookies and fancy trinkets she adored—and he didn't want her to see men without him.

Ruby dragged a cigarette from her purse and waited for the photographer to offer her a light, aware of the square-headed drummer who reminded her of Squire. She scanned the room, flabbergasted by the idea that someone from home, Squire of all people, could find Club Tabou. The crowd was jumping and ready to raise a nightlong ruckus. Men and women danced so close that one half-turn meant changing partners. Arnett played, crammed in the space passing for a stage, his focus on Ruby when he should have put his mind on this opportunity for a permanent gig.

Except for the new holes hunger forced him to cut into his belts, Ruby couldn't measure what disappointment had done to him. Arnett seemed slight to her now, scrunched inward, slumped shoulders. In fact, she viewed him these days in Paris, and every one they spent getting here, as shrinking each time he stepped on a stage. Might have to do with the kinds of gigs he came upon, his inability to read a lick of music catching up with him. When there was no work in the clubs, he played for rich white folks from the U.S. and all over Europe who partied every night of the week. Some days he picked up a little money from enthusiastic tourists when he played near the Eiffel Tower until the gendarmes made him leave. Or might have been the musicians, and a few jealous women, finding fault behind his back because his woman accompanied him everywhere—auditions, practice, gigs, after-parties—until they put a stop to his bringing her to jam sessions, protesting it wasn't right for a lone woman to be amongst a room of men with the drinking and the carrying on. Might have been the French musicians who were taking gigs they believed by right were theirs.

The photographer obliged her with the flame of the matches he kept on his person, he assured her, for good luck. Every Negro man in Paris knew or wanted to know who Ruby was. He tipped his head. They were regulars, Ruby and Arnett, as he was at Tabou, Caveau de la Huchette, Chez Inez, and other clubs in St.-Germain.

"I'm on the verge of being somebody," she said. Cigarette smoke drifted, like wispy fog off the Seine, from the pinkish hall of her mouth and into his face. "I see you with your camera. You any good?"

"I'm gonna photograph all of them." He squinted into his camera's viewfinder, rotated the lens, then snapped. The silver contraption in his hands was elaborate and complicated, unlike anything Ruby had seen back home. "You watch. My pictures will be famous."

"I want mine taken for when I'm famous, too."

"And what does your man have to say?"

"I should be the one worrying, don't you think?" Ruby winked, a lazy motion that sucked his attention better than a hoodoo spell.

"I don't think nothing, dahlin'. I'm not the one at his side. I'm not the one they call his shadow."

"My man is happy when I'm happy." Ruby smiled again, reflecting how often Arnett held on to her in Paris. Little by little when men ignored Arnett, and out-and-out stared, he kept her close when, she supposed, seeing the number of women who ogled him, it should have been the other way around.

"I'm most inclined to work with these cats." The photographer watched that smoke drift through the portal of her red lips. He swallowed hard at her lazy wink that seemed to hold promise. "If that man of yours will let me, I'd be glad to."

"You just worry about me, Mister Man, and I'll take care of Arnett."

The photographer lived on rue Christine, a narrow street near the Club Tabou. He claimed a famous New York Puerto Rican gangster owned the building and let him stay in the studio at the top in exchange for watching the *propriétaire*, who might not be forwarding the rents. A week later, Ruby mounted the last flight of stairs, her shoes pattering against the polished wood. Most of the clothing, books, dishes, cameras, makeshift darkroom, and general mess the photographer lived with was hidden from sight. When he opened the door, he craned his neck and checked for Arnett lagging behind her.

"I told you, it's a surprise." She looked at the room, keeping any opinions she had of the untidiness and the wall of tall windows to herself. In her hand Ruby held a black satchel. She dropped it on the threshold and waited for her pulse to catch up to her breathing. From the doorway she headed straight to the bank of windows anchoring the cleanest corner of the room and peered into the street below.

"Ain't you got no mirror for a girl to check her face? And where am I changing?"

The man chuckled and aimed his camera at a screen covered with a rough, Army-issue blanket. Then he nodded at the sole mirror in the room perched above a sink with paisley print fabric stretched to cover three sides. Ruby scanned the room, rechecking the window and the street below.

"And what, my Mister Man," she said, strutting behind the screen, "will you be doing while I'm behind this skimpy cover?"

Turning his back, the man fussed with his camera's knobs and lens, deeply absorbed in f-stops. He listened to Ruby's jabbering.

"Me and Yvette been trying on outfits. We decided, I decided, on this."

When she emerged from behind the screen the photographer whistled low. Ruby strutted again to the bank of windows, observing the street from the side of its frame, hidden from anyone below.

"What does that man of yours let you do on your own?"

She tossed back her head and spun in a circle, letting the slinky silk catch the open window's breeze and cling to every inch of her body. The time when a spark of attraction might have been a possibility was gone; the split second of hope this photographer, and a bunch of other men, colored or white, held on to when she looked at them. With Arnett at her side day in and day out, no man had a chance. She rummaged through her satchel and finally withdrew a feather boa, a magazine, and a wide piece of satin.

"I know exactly what to do. We'll fix your bed, put this on top, and you can get to work." Ruby primped in the mirror, added lipstick to her already red lips, then went about the task of turning the bed into her romantic stage. She opened the worn French fashion magazine to a dog-eared page and handed it to the photographer. A woman lay on a chaise lounge, irresistible and certain, bundled in a cloud of fabric so no one could tell if she was naked or clothed.

Ruby draped the satin remnant over the dingy bed linens. With each tuck of the sheet and thump of the pillow, she moved with unspoken trust and without a care that her stiffened nipples poked at the thin fabric of her gown. She arranged the feather boa as low as she assumed, judging by the photographer's open mouth, appealed to men and lay on the bed.

Ruby made her adjustments; the photographer made his own. He pushed back the flimsy curtains, opened the second window, and let the afternoon breeze into the room. He positioned eight lamps, a few tall, several short, all without shades, on all sides of the bed, diffusing the sunlight on her face.

"Ready?"

"Oh, I'm not quite ready. Relax." He went to the dresser, set a record on the turntable, and adjusted the volume on a woman's warbled, moody ballad. "That's 'La Vie en Rose,' Edith Piaf, to get you in the mood."

"Just take the picture, baby. You got a clock in here?"

They bantered back and forth. He teased for a smile. Ruby gave him two and stretched like a cat seeking a warm spot, her skin glowing in the combined light. She had darkened the natural mole on her cheek, making it coal black, deliberate and accentuated. It captured the photographer's attention, a subject all its own, and he focused on it, letting her hair, her face, her shoulders blur in a pose he swore was art.

From beyond the flimsy door, assured footsteps echoed on the stone stairs. Ruby froze and held her hand in the air for the photographer to do the same. Fingernails scratched on the door. Ruby held her breath; the photographer clicked the camera and cocked his ear. Three forceful raps shook the door again before the knob rattled.

"Monsieur, c'est moi!" a woman cried out. "Est-ce que vous avez du sucre? Je n'en ai pas."

"Non. Pas aujourd'hui." The photographer whispered to Ruby that the woman wasn't interested in the least in sugar; she wanted to know who the lady was. "Je suis occupé, Madame."

He turned to Ruby motionless, her hand above her head. "What's the matter, dahlin'? Don't your man know where you are?"

"You forgetting English? I told you it's a surprise." She relaxed back on to the bed. The boa slipped, exposing cleavage and firm skin. Ruby watched the photographer, harmless in his military clothes, snap when the light, the angle of her head, the drape of her hair was perfect. "If I'm gonna be somebody, it's what I got to do."

"Watch the door." He opened the door to the empty stairwell. "Pretend you're waiting for Arnett, not scared or tired of him. And he's coming through that door, ready to give you the best loving he knows how."

She followed his instruction and in her mind saw Arnett's face when he was happy, when he worked his saxophone, when he pushed into her. The warmth of his mouth, his firm tongue moving downwards from her navel, hot sweat on a cold night, his hands playing her in the darkness. Ruby closed her eyes. She focused on her man, her mind considering a mixture of want and trepidation that he might find her and not understand why she lay half-naked upon another man's bed. She lowered her lashes. The photographer snapped once and once more, and he caught her eyes opening. Caught them so it seemed as if Arnett's footsteps, the songs he whistled, him coming through the door right this very second were all she ever wanted in the world.

20

An elision, a coming together or connection, is a smooth and fluid transition between words that creates fluent, pleasant pronunciation.

l'ami(e) (lah mee)	friend
une rencontre fortuite (een rahn con truh four too eet)	a chance encounter
ce soir (suh swar)	this evening
pourquoi pas? (poor qwah pah)	why not?

Instead of rushing with the crowd, Nicole stepped to the side. Before her, the Opéra Garnier was an island in the midst of the bustling traffic and intersecting streets. Golden angels perched on the roof. Streetlamps, their oversized white bulbs remnants of the 1800s, guarded the entrance.

The lobby was a secret behind its stone façade; rich reds and gold leaf proof that a luxurious history had constructed these walls. Massive chandeliers, statues of sculpted muses, electric candles. The draped stage was equally elaborate. Trumpets played a brief refrain of the U.S. national anthem, and the opera began. *Aida*, *Carmen*, *The Barber of Seville*, and this, *Madama Butterfly*, the last of the classic operas on Nicole's to-see list. Now the story of abandoned love and a child separated from mother hit close to her new truth. Unlike the fragile Butterfly and Mother-Aunt Ruby, Nicole had never faced that problem.

The velvet curtains parted, their center swinging up and into a beautiful scalloped frame on either side of the stage as the U.S. naval officer, Pinkerton, and his Japanese marriage broker inspected a place to live. Was this staged drama, Nicole guessed, a version of her story? Did this opera have to remind her of her parents' lie? Had her father taken her from Ruby? Questions for the ever-expanding list in her head—where was Ruby, and how did her baby end up with Malvina and Squire? Nicole loved *Madama Butterfly*'s romance, detested the officer who wooed then abandoned his naïve and loyal Cio-Cio San. Or maybe the Butterfly was not naïve; she was simply in love. Complete surrender, the ultimate sacrifice. Was that Ruby?

Questions demanding answers. Three acts and three hours later, the final drapes floated shut after four curtain calls, and by then it was clear to Nicole that the hole Malvina had opened required filling, if this mother and daughter were ever going to function as whole again.

The well-dressed crowd bustled through the outer doors. Nicole dawdled on the edges of conversations, trying to decode their expressions.

"Didn't your mother ever tell you not to eavesdrop?" The voice came from behind. Nicole jumped. Chaos Man. Flanked by youth; attractive, sexy, and thin youth. A lanky man on his right, a tall woman, about twenty-five, holding tightly on to his left arm. The man winked and bowed slightly. "Where will I see you again, Madame? The Louvre? Notre Dame? Laurent Bésson, in case you don't remember, from the play."

Oh, she remembered. Paris may well be the City of Light, the City of Love, but for Nicole it was also the City of Coincidence, the fulfilled prophecy of an inspirational message folded in her wallet: *Do not be alarmed at surprises as you take your journey's path; accept and be delighted.*

"If I we were better acquainted, Monsieur, I'd say you were following me. I've had my ticket for weeks." Nicole shivered on the inside, feeling sultry and shy and demure—not who she believed she was. She adjusted her dress, glad her outfit complemented her legs. *C'est dommage.* Too bad the woman on his arm was so young. Judging from the ogling ladies in the lobby, Laurent was a man women watched without the slightest hint of reserve. He was American in his flirtatious arrogance, French in his etiquette, and assumptive in his body language bordering on conceit. Salt-and-pepper hair, earring in his left ear, a fashionable five o'clock shadow—meant, it seemed, to mask pitted skin. The chaos that seemed accidental at the theater was evident, different clothes: linen shirt and pants, lightweight cashmere overcoat, designer shoes.

"Touché, Madame. I'll take jazz over opera any day." Without missing a beat or a hint of braggadocio, Laurent went on. "But I'm working." A magazine had accepted his pitch for a perspective on the Opéra Garnier and the Opéra Bastille, where the opera company moved in the late eighties, and the state of opera in the City of Light. "Allow me to introduce my daughter, Michelle Bésson, and my son, Alexandre Bésson. They're the opera fans, their mother's influence." He nodded in deference to their knowledge and swore that without them he'd be lost. "I'd planned to listen to a few CDs, not sit through hours of an actual performance."

"C'mon, Dad. I saw your tears. You cried at the end." Alexandre squeezed Nicole's arm. "Dad mentioned that you were alone at the play and now you're here. By yourself?"

Nicole nodded. If the grin on her face was as wide as she sensed, she guessed she must look a bit idiotic, but after six days in Paris alone, she missed chitchat. Loneliness, curiosity, and Paris.

"We're waiting for the *salle* to clear. Michelle and I have a friend in the opera, and Dad's going to interview her. Join us?"

God bless this young man, a carbon copy of what his father must have been like thirty years ago. Nicole pulled her pashmina—red, the color that highlighted her skin tones—over her shoulders and followed without a second thought. Laurent led them backstage.

"Do you mind a question?" Nicole lengthened her stride to match his, taking one and a half steps for his every one.

He straightened, instantly guarded. At the backstage door, he flashed a journalist's pass to an attendant who stepped to the side. Laurent waited for Nicole to follow his almond soap scent.

She continued without his answer. "You were so sure I was American when we met. That is, you spoke English, even after I introduced myself. Is my French . . . *that* bad?"

Frown lines melted and his posture reverted to casual. Laurent chuckled and placed his hand on Nicole's back, guiding her to the stage. "Your French is very formal. And you cheered so . . . enthusiastically. Americans tend to be very emotional in public. And then there was the dictionary in your lap."

"Very funny." Chitchat was good.

Several cast members waited onstage. The floor was striped with different-colored tapes indicating, Michelle shared, cast positions during the performance. A large X marked the spot where Madama released the Navy man from his promise, and hers. Alexandre hugged the woman who played Suzuki, Madama Butterfly's servant, who in turn rushed to Michelle and Laurent and kissed each of them on both cheeks.

"Colette Deschamps, je te presente une amie de Papa. Nicole . . ." Alexandre paused, waiting for Nicole to complete the traditional French introduction.

"We're being impolite. Nicole is learning French . . . or I assumed . . ." Laurent grinned and headed for the far corner of the stage, taking the singer with him. He pulled a hand-sized recorder, notepad, and pen from his pockets and began to interview her.

"Colette never talks to the press, but she'll blather to our father all night—if he lets her. See? She's hooked." In perfect English, Michelle volunteered a few personal details: she was from New York by way of Montréal and Paris. "I'm an actress. Father mentioned that he sat beside you at my play. I hope you enjoyed the performance. Were you able to understand us?"

Nicole stared at Michelle and realized she was the last woman to "jump" into the water. "I got the gist, not the little details. I'm a beginner."

"Before you ask, no, the n-word isn't new to the play, but the choral challenge was; reactions ranged from outrage to appreciation." The reviews were amazing, Michelle finished. The troupe was headed to the annual July festival in Avignon.

"Use your French, and don't be shy. That's how you learn." Michelle's voice carried a smoker's huskiness, and sure enough, she took a cigarette from her pocket and glared at her brother.

"You can hold that cigarette out all you want, chérie. I refuse to facilitate your bad habit." Alexandre reached for Michelle's cigarette. She pouted and slapped her brother's hand.

"Alexandre and Dad are born-again nonsmokers." Michelle tossed her head. Her hair was curlier, her skin browner compared to her father's. She and Alexandre could've passed for twins. Laurent was lanky, and the body type seemed to run in the family. "But they're trustworthy." She flipped a metal lighter and leaned close to the flame.

When Nicole admitted she was an off-and-on smoker, Michelle hooked her right to Nicole's left arm. A young version of Tamara, already marking her years with international adventures. Michelle punctuated her conversation with her hands. She waved one toward her father.

"He gets lost in his stories. Fifteen minutes or five hours—once he gets going it's hard to know when he'll stop." Michelle nodded to the exit doors, and they proceeded in that direction. "We're headed for Chez Papa in St.-Germain. Come with us."

The four reunited in a candlelit corner below a precarious loft. Music graffiti—song titles, verses, clefs, autographs, and names difficult to decode in the dim light—etched Chez Papa's brick and plaster walls. At the bar beneath wooden beams, the bartender poured champagne, wine, and Johnnie Walker Red. An enormous abstract canvas of a naked woman rumored, Laurent whispered to Nicole, to be a celebrated American folksinger, hung from the ceiling near a wooden guardrail. Framed jazz LP covers lined the loft's banisters. They were of the same vintage Nicole had found at Monsieur Daudon's: Coltrane, Ellington, Monk, Memphis Slim, and Max Roach, among others. Nicole's music preferences were loosely defined by a touch of opera, sixties Motown, Marvin Gaye, a little psychedelic funk, and a mishmash of different music, except country-western.

Straight-up jazz, easy listening, Nicole lacked the proper music vocabulary to ask what type of jazz they were going to hear. The musicians played what turned out to be jazz smooth enough for her to enjoy, and she relaxed in the ups and downs of the trills and the bass whispers. At the end of the set, Laurent described his work. He'd freelanced all over the world for the *Washington Post*, the *New York Times*, and a couple of French news magazines.

"I decided fifty-nine was too old to keep dodging bullets and traipsing through barrios and favelas for the sake of a story."

"Since when are you shy, Dad?" Michelle rapped her father's arm with the flat of her palm. "Usually we can't shut him up. He can talk for hours about work."

"For whatever reason, Dad's being modest. Trust me, it's an act." Alexandre patted his father on the shoulder. "What he won't tell you is that he wrote a front-page article for the *Washington Post* when he was twenty-four. Let me see . . . Should we list the prizes?"

"What Alexandre says is true—you should also know our father's untrainable." Michelle nudged Laurent.

He switched to his children's memories: their international travels, but distinctly American selections in language, schools, and home base, the creative streaks they inherited from both of their parents.

"Mon dieu! When he starts yakking about us, instead of talking with you, it's our cue to leave. You're on your own, Papa." Alexandre and Michelle left, offering their goodbyes in the French style, with kisses to both of Nicole's and Laurent's cheeks.

Laurent waved. "They're usually not this friendly to strangers."

"They're fun. Obviously, they adore you. But I'm curious. You changed earlier." Nicole watched Laurent's body language shift to an awkward pose, his second this evening. "Back at the opera, I watched your face change when I asked a question. What happened?"

A woman stepped beside the piano. She toyed with the lyrics of "Night and Day," making the thirties' song new. Laurent's face transformed; open and cool. He tugged at his thick hair. "When they hear English, lots of American women have the same question—what are you? A man, I usually say. Most don't get the sarcasm, but they come back to it. It's annoying."

"It's not a question I hear much at home. Why here?"

"Curiosity. Ignorance. In the States every black person is just that—black, African American, Negro. This is an international city where skin tones reflect every culture in the world. Paris is different. Americans are obsessed with race. You'd think Obama's election would've changed that. It's not that I don't want to talk race or deny it. Too many other issues to deal with."

"Men never ask about race?"

"It's the same as shaving off a mustache. Men never comment. I met a woman who told me my face invited female conversation. She called my comportment an invitation, like a schoolteacher." Women, he described, often engaged him in tête-à-têtes.

His face was open and approachable—features spread wide on its surface. When he angled forward, the gesture encouraged whoever sat with him to do the same. His demeanor invited, Nicole observed, intimacy, and it was probably one of the reasons for the success his children described.

"The 'invitation' isn't conscious, necessarily. I give my standard list of hot spots. I listen. You never know where a good story will come from." Yes, he lingered for as long as they amused him—a minute or a pleasant hour depending on their questions or their answers to his.

Counting the opera, the backstage visit, and the hours in the club, Nicole calculated they'd spent over half the evening together. She checked her watch. Laurent slipped his hand over her wrist.

"For the record, my answer is consistent. French mother met black American father in Paris after the war. Educated in the States, lived in South Africa, Barcelona, and a few other places I'd rather forget. Back in Paris since the nineties."

"I wish I understood how people cram so much into one life."

"I say it's a damn shame to waste it—but globetrotting has been my downfall. Ruined my marriage. Alienated my kids. Our relationship hasn't always been good, and even now, it's fragile. There've been a few years when they didn't speak to me. It's the price of those awards I don't brag about any longer." He huffed, the breath noisy and strong enough to snuff the votive candle's flame. "Forgive me. I can't remember the last person I told that to, at least not one I just met. But now you owe me your story. Any particular reason you're in Paris?"

"I wish my story was exciting. If I were writing a book or researching a story or thinking about moving here—that'd be something." Nicole spoke to herself and Laurent. "You don't know how far from the truth that is. Actually, I'm here because I've wanted to be here for as long as I can remember. My plan was to shake up my life."

"And what's the matter with that? Or why have a reason at all?"

Laurent motioned to the waiter. Nicole put twenty euros on the table, which he promptly pushed back.

"Or what if I discovered that I'm not who I thought I was."

"It's Paris. We thrive on discovery."

"My mother sent me a bunch of letters dating back to before I was born. Hers. My father's. Letters from a woman I'd never heard of before three days ago." Nicole's conversation flowed with the ease that comes when strangers share personal stories, the lack of history and worries over consequences. "So," she sighed, "if you found out your mother is *not* your mother but your aunt, that your mother was, is, living in Paris, could you find that woman if you just happened to find yourself in the city where she was last known to be?"

"That's the best question I've ever heard." Laurent brushed his shoulder against Nicole's. Their clothes crackled with static electricity. "I'd hound my mother and my father for the truth."

"My mother's in California. My father's on a trip to never-never land. I went to the Bibliothèque Nationale. Except for exploring another beautiful part of Paris, not one new piece of information."

Chez Papa's lights switched from dim to bright. Laurent bid his goodbyes to the owner's wife at the piano and the band drinking at the bar. Outside the night was sticky. In the early morning mist, the lights of the jazz club's neon sign tinted their skin an icy shade of blue. Rue St.-Benoit was filled with late-night strollers; except for the darkened sky, it could have been in the middle of the afternoon. Nicole accepted Laurent's offer to walk her home, liking how it felt—moseying through the streets with a man, a nice man, in the humidity of an early Paris morning.

21

Paris, January 1952

Ruby wasn't mad when she got Squire's letter. She was preoccupied with winter and the expectation of snow. Not for one of her four hundred fifty-some odd days in Paris did she miss Mississippi. Not the nasty dust and the ever-present pollen, not the snakes that sheltered themselves in the blackberry bushes in the backyard, nor the need to pretend that every white man and woman was the best or the smartest. Stepping aside, waiting at the end of lines, finishing every sentence with ma'am or sir, not out of politeness or respect but fear.

And now Squire was in Paris, ready to agitate memories she no longer wanted. Here she toyed with newness: changing her name, learning French, working to speak it as if she had lived here all of her twenty-three years. He would be scared, this dear friend; his nature was to hold steady for the predictable. He was anxious, that Squire, and that was why she refused to be with him. Squire guaranteed traps: wife, mother, colored woman.

Four months after he'd arrived in Paris, he knocked on her door. Between the transatlantic voyage and another bout of motion sickness, Le Havre and finding the train to Gare du Nord, getting used to the routine at the university, the language, the *francs*, *sous*, and *centimes*—it took that long. Not that she counted, as she did the length of her stay in Paris. She simply sensed it. Four months before the shuffle of his feet on the five flights of worn wooden stairs and his knock on number 21. Did he take the Métro? Did he sit in cafés, stand under the Eiffel Tower in the rain, stroll past the windmills of the Moulin Rouge and see the dancing girls, their costumes scanty, their legs kicked high into the air?

Squire was so simple.

Nevertheless, here it was, his one-two knock in the middle of the day. Not the *propriétaire* seeking the weekly rent, not one of Arnett's buddies wanting to practice a few tunes, smoke a little reefer, and pilfer the macaroons hidden in the pocket of her winter coat.

If her figuring was right—and she wasn't any good at arithmetic—her last visit with her friend was before he shipped off to war, before she met Arnett in '44. So different from Arnett, Squire considered her fragile, and that was how she presented herself to him. The coming of her monthly blood had changed her by the time she met Arnett. She was afraid to see Squire's face, afraid it had aged with war, its stories tucked in the creases like the GIs who stayed on in Paris, or rejection after rejection in Arnett's face.

Squire was smiling when she opened the door.

His complexion was unmarked; he'd grown a thick mustache. He stood before her, crossed and uncrossed his arms, jittery from the situation or the discomfort of his black fedora and suit. His hand-knitted tie registered not a bit of this sophisticated city. Ruby reckoned her sister had made it for him, knowing her taste for needlework. Malvina had tried to teach Ruby the art of knit and purl, but the clashing of needles, the winding of yarn, the patience it required were unsuitable for a woman with Ruby's busy nature. She considered inquiring after Malvina and her sister's opinion of the man she wanted going off to Paris where the woman he really loved lived. Instead, she let her blue dress and the lace edging its low neckline, the cleavage exposed under the shawl she wore to protect her from the weather's chill speak for her.

"Well, well, well. Staff Sergeant Handy. Took you long enough."

Squire's coal black eyes traveled from Ruby's face past her flat midriff to her legs. Ruby saw it, the hunger, as if he were starving. As if he wanted to take her in his arms and hold her, his lips on hers until she no longer breathed.

"Well, what do you know? Little RubyMae isn't little anymore."

"It's Ruby, Squire Thomas Handy, and I'm a woman." Ruby let him take all of her in, used to men's roving looks, their eagerness to touch, to smell her lavender perfume. In that minute, they were back on her parents' threshold—her glad to see him, but wishing he was somebody else she was yet to meet; his hound-dog face, a scrawny bouquet behind his back, ready to do whatever he must to gain her attention.

"Have I changed?"

"Cleaner than the last time I saw you." She rested against the doorjamb, neither inviting nor rejecting his presence. "Unh, unh, unh. Squire Handy, all dressed up. And in Paris. What you been up to, Bud?"

He grinned at the nickname she gave him when they were young and he was momentarily shorter. "As you can see—" Squire stretched into his wiry frame and saluted, a soldier without uniform. He hovered eight inches above Ruby's five-foot-four frame. "Been getting my feet wet." Paris was wearing him out, he told her. He held out his hands for her to inspect the effect of months of nail biting, getting from his hotel room on the rue Champollion to the building with Sorbonne Université de Paris etched into its façade, trying to find baking soda to ease his digestion, adjusting to the meager portions of food he'd allotted himself, avoiding spending all of his seventy-five-dollar-a-month GI Bill stipend. He changed the subject. "Even with those high heels on, I can see the top of your head, including a few strands of gray."

Ruby ran her fingers through her hair, feeling for the rough texture of the gray filaments Squire described and pouting when she caught on to his joke. They lingered in the doorway; him straining his neck past her shoulder for signs of Arnett, her savoring the means she had to tease him by prolonging his entry. But Arnett's footsteps, his shrill boogie-woogie whistle saved them from whatever they separately wanted to happen—Ruby that Squire would leave; Squire that Ruby would leave with him.

"Looka here, looka here." Arnett stopped on the landing. "Who you letting in, Ruby? Ain't no music-playing cat 'cause I'd know him." He strutted, positioning himself between his woman and this man, surveying Squire. Arnett fingered Squire's homemade tie and snickered. "I'd say from his tie and that suit, Ruby, this is your Mississippi man."

She heard, in the timbre of Arnett's voice, a new reaction—anxiety, sarcasm, deliberation. He glowered at Squire, and Ruby stepped back from her friend. Arnett had already threatened Poppa for staring at his woman. She rested her hand on the back of Arnett's head and it slid, on its own, down his neck to his back and stayed put. Arnett looked at Ruby and kissed her. His kiss said, *I own this woman*, better than anything he could have spoken.

Ruby melted into him and let go of a moan. When she withdrew from his embrace, she wiped lipstick from Arnett's mouth with her thumb. "Arnett Dupree, meet Squire Handy. He goes to the Sorbonne." She repeated Sorbonne with a fault-finding lilt.

"Well, I say we need to celebrate his arrival. Give us news from home. You country boys still hiding from the white man behind women's skirts?"

Arnett pushed the door wide open and scrutinized the room, the bed, the position of the chairs beside the metal table, the upholstery on the back of the wingback chair he'd found in the neighborhood. He touched this and tapped that, inspecting for rearrangements, in the manner he did even after Yvette's visits, and a hint that Ruby's friend had recently arrived or was ready to leave.

Waiting for Arnett to settle in, Squire focused square on his competition. That Arnett was not the man for her was the flicker Squire waited for in Ruby's eyes, and Sorbonne or not, it was what he had come to Paris for.

In honor of Squire, they went to Café Tournon. Ruby mixed English with French and shared Arnett's cigarettes before finally lighting one of her own.

"Man, you mean you been in Paris for this long and you ain't been to a club?"

"Nope. My studies keep me pretty busy, and I guess I was more interested in testing what I'd learned during the war. Every time I passed a man or woman, I tipped my hat and looked straight at them, and no one looked away or called me a name. Not one woman was afraid."

"I can go into any salon and get my hair pressed. Eat and drink, we go wherever we want. They don't care," Ruby said.

Squire looked straight at Ruby. "It's everything folks described. During the war, Negroes and white soldiers mingled a bit with the French in the countryside, beyond Reims and Normandy. We, meaning us Negro soldiers, were respected."

"What kinda cat are you?" Arnett gulped his drink and started to order another when Ruby shook her head no. "Clubs are hot, man. Best way to meet folks. Lotta cats from the States pouring in, making competition—not to mention the Frenchies wanting to take the music from us—but you, schoolboy, don't have any competition."

Squire stared at the seven Negro men seated in the café, seven more than he'd observed together since he'd arrived in Paris. The few at the Sorbonne didn't bond like stateside Negroes were inclined to do; given the high ratio of whites to everyone else, some of the Negro students melted into Paris.

"You ought to come here. Catch a French sweetheart. You see that cat in the corner?" Arnett pointed at the man hunched in the corner, a large fountain pen in hand, writing furiously on sheets of white paper. "That's the cat wrote that famous book and won a prize. And if you go to Les Deux Magots, you'll see famous white ones, too." Less doh maggots. Arnett made no effort to pronounce the café's name correctly.

"You've got it wrong, Arnett. Lay duh maa go. Les Deux Magots. You say it, Squire." Ruby thumbed through the pages of her blue dictionary. "*Auteurs célèbres*. Famous writers."

Squire's French was stilted, but after two drinks—two over his usual—his tongue loosened, but held on to Mississippi. "Lah doo mah jo." When Ruby scowled at his poor accent, he confessed that no matter how much he tried, mastery escaped him. It got to be he never put his dictionary back into his pocket, holding on to it in the style some men did an unlit cigarette or a rabbit's foot. He was an American in France, with a hundred-word vocabulary, who showed vendors the names in his book for what he wanted in food, beverages, or clothes.

"You're all right by me, Square Squire—that's what Ruby calls you, you know." The closer the clock ticked to midnight, the faster Arnett rocked in his chair; he downed brandy until he began to slur. When the hands on the clock above the bar's mirror stretched to half past eleven, Ruby, Arnett, and Squire headed for the steep steps of the Café Rouge.

"Boris Vian, my man on the trumpet. Ronald Herbert on drums. Poppa on piano," Arnett shouted over the music. A tall white man poured his soul into his trumpet. Men and women danced alone and together in the middle of the room.

Squire nodded without any indication that he recognized the names.

"Bebop!" Arnett strained above the music. "What do you think?"

"Not a music man. I prefer poetry," Squire muttered.

"Man, I can't make money and I play music. How the hell you gonna make money with poems?" Arnett scratched his head and left to join two men waving him to their table. Ruby inched past the dancers and gripped the outstretched hand of the photographer still sporting his Army uniform, leaving Squire on the sidelines.

Squire watched Ruby spin on the floor: fast, faster, then fast again, her skirt swinging, her fingers popping to the beat. He tried to catch on to the erratic rhythm and waited for a slow song to dance with Ruby, to hold her in his arms, to feel the changes in her body. When another man grabbed Ruby's arm, Squire turned to climb back up the abrupt stone steps. He stopped when the trumpet player signaled to Ruby. "Viens, viens, Ruby. Il faut que tu chantes."

Chanter: to sing. A verb Squire had conjugated. He had never heard Ruby sing. Malvina's voice—loose as molasses in hot sun—he had heard in the choir. Ruby joined the musicians on the platform and whispered the title of her song in the piano player's ear. She hooded her brow with both hands from the glare of the bare light bulb overhead until she saw Arnett.

Ruby started a French tune akin to a lulling ballad Edith Piaf might have sung if she chose now to perform in any of these crowded cellars. She started off gently, her chance to build tension, then released to a spirited refrain that she carried for one short verse. Her voice wasn't strong, but it captured attention. For a minute, dancers stopped dancing, talkers stopped talking, drinkers stopped drinking. When the music quieted back to where it began, she stepped off the platform and into Arnett's arms. Squire watched the two of them in the middle of that club acting like no one was in the room except them.

"You'd be better off without me," Arnett whispered in Ruby's ear and shushed her, held her so that, despite her efforts, she couldn't free herself from his grip, or tell him how silly he was acting. "That Squire seems to be a do-right man."

Squire watched them, Arnett holding Ruby, her not struggling to be free of his arms. The music blasted and ricocheted off the walls. Squire yearned for a signal that he was important to her, too. Without one, he waited until the loneliness, the weight of the vocabulary and grammar left on the desk in his room forced him out the club.

Map in hand, he plotted out the quickest return to his hotel. He wove a crooked path to the fountain of St.-Michel where the road became familiar. If his footsteps could have been traced, or his long trail of homesickness, they would have burned a patch up and down the boulevard, so often he trod that route. Four months and Paris had neither wooed nor cast a spell over him. No one told him that memorizing, reviewing, cramming without sleep or food to keep up was going to swallow him and any minutes he had free. No one told him that the bond Negroes relied on back home would be abandoned in this place and leave him lonely and frustrated and sad.

No one told him Ruby would be so much in love.

22

Paris, February 1952

It was the early part of their day, two o'clock in the afternoon, between waking and going off to the clubs. Despite the bleakness of the sky and the threat of rain, Arnett perched on the sill of the window, a bottle of brandy at his feet. He resembled a painting framed by the window with slate roofs, turrets, and the mixed light of Paris behind them. Arnett's practices varied based on the weather, the week, what Ruby needed and where she wanted to go. If he was stuck cogitating, he practiced his embouchure, the way his mouthpiece sat in his mouth, and the beginning notes of songs. Or he improvised tunes already in his head. Depending on his mood, he played whole songs starting as if accompanied by a trio of piano, drums, and bass or a singer to break into a song. Today, he held the saxophone without playing it or fingering the keys.

"Are you trying to kill the both of us with that window open?" Ruby drew her coat across her chest, protecting her from the cold, and backed herself to the opposite corner of the room. "Arnett, do you hear me?"

"I hear you, baby." Arnett balanced himself on the windowsill dressed in his overcoat and gabardine striped pants, the weakened sun dancing on his sax and each particle of dust on the pane. "I was thinking I've had enough of Paris."

Ruby glared at the half-empty bottle on the floor. "You been drinking, Arnett. Don't go getting gloomy on me. I can't take another day, let alone a month of this."

"I feel it. My fingers tell me so."

"Don't do this. I belong here. We belong here." Ruby rushed to the window and held her hand to Arnett's forehead. "It's the cold, Arnett, and the dark sky. Shut the window and get in the bed. You're making yourself sick."

"Yeah, baby, I'm sick. Sick of not understanding why being good on the back roads doesn't make me good in Paris."

"We're fine, Arnett. We can try the south of France. Take a break from the city."

"You're freezing. Hot water for breakfast. No work. It's not what I promised, Ruby." He stared at Ruby's frameless picture propped on the dresser. His birthday gift. He'd bordered on tears when she told him the photographer was going to show it to important people and make her famous.

"I'm fine, you're gonna be fine. We can make it. If you tried again, Poppa might help."

Arnett removed his red spit rag from his pocket and stuffed it down the saxophone's bell. "Know what Poppa said last night, baby? 'Mothafuckah,' he was serious, 'you one sorry-assed cat. Can't keep up no matter how you try. Might as well hand that pretty woman over to me and take your sorry self back to Loo'siana, 'cause brother, you ain't never makin' it here.'"

"He's jealous, Arnett. Why you let him talk to you like that?"

"Go away from me, Ruby. You deserve better." Arnett watched Ruby, her teeth chattering from the draft. "Remember how your ache burned? Well I got one, it's cramping me, cramping my fingers, and I don't know what to do. Leave me, Ruby."

"I'm not going anywhere. Please, Arnett. The cold is making you crazy."

Arnett stared at Ruby hard as the night he watched her in that decrepit juke joint. "My Ruby, my jewel." She offered that smile that brought her to him. He saluted with his left hand, his right arm unmoving, a branch refusing to bow in the wind.

"I have what I want." Ruby moved to Arnett. Before she stepped, before her slipper dropped to the floor, before she yelled, *What the hell are you doing?* Arnett was in the window one second and then he was gone. He didn't scream or shout or call out Ruby's name. The speed of his falling body combined with the wind. Then a loud thump identical to a tree fallen in the middle of the night because its end had come.

"What the hell are you doing, Arnett Dupree? You come back here, you hear me? Come back here!" Ruby stuck her head out of the window to see her man sprawled in the street. "Don't you do this. Come back here!"

Throwing open the door, she ran down the stairs, her feet thudding against the hollow core. Five flights. "Easier going down than up," Arnett teased when they handed over the first week's rent. Ruby sped, her hand on the polished banister, skipping steps where she could.

She ran down the narrow stairs, the silk of her slip swishing under her coat. Halfway down she felt the cold. Another ten steps and she didn't care. In the hall a woman's scream rose louder and louder, and it wasn't until Ruby ran the length of the lobby and pushed the door open on to the street that she recognized the high-pitched tones of her own voice.

She screamed even louder when she saw Arnett's body up close. Between the fall and the car that had collided with him at the moment his body neared the street, his body sprawled, unmoving. His hands clutched his saxophone, showing the world his concern for it, not himself.

"Come back here, Arnett," Ruby shouted, dropping to her knees. She shook him, ignoring the blood streaming from his nose and ears and reddening his white undershirt, his overcoat bought the winter in Paris after they arrived. Ignoring the mess spreading onto the cracks of the stone-paved street, and the crowd, gawking, whispering about her man.

"Merde!" the driver cried out.

Yanking at Arnett she managed to cradle him in her lap. The humming came next, unconscious and soft; then she rocked him. "God bless the child," she sang. "God bless the child who's got his own." She repeated the line over and over because that was what he needed, because she didn't know what else to do. His body was warm, his clothes sticky and wet with the rain that began to fall, and she felt his heartbeat slowing. Thump. Thump. Thump.

23

As vocabulary and circumstances expand, questions can be formed with the same pronouns and adverbs—who, what, where, when, how, and why—used in English.

pourquoi? (pour qwah)	why?
quand? (kahn)	when?
comment? (coh mahn)	how?
qui? (key)	who?

Lamplight danced on the damp, uneven cobblestones as moonlight might, if that yellowish orb was shining. Nicole stumbled, focused on Laurent's mellow voice instead of her feet. He hooked his arm into hers and she held on to him for support, not the amorous possibilities of that proximity. They walked slowly, new friends, open and curious.

"I came to Paris because it's what I've wanted since I can remember. I'm embarrassed it took so long." Nicole lowered her head. "For years, I filled folders with travel tips on Spain, Brazil, Africa, the beaches of the Côte d'Azur, Provence. And Paris. Obscure museums. A restaurant in the Louvre that serves a fantastic lentil salad. Sunday afternoon picnics on the canal. Tarte tatin recipes."

Laurent waited for Nicole to continue, proof the inquisitive tourists he disapproved of were right. Her descriptions came quickly because she didn't want to stop until the thought was clear in her head. Writers who'd gotten off their respective butts to have experiences and penned the articles she saved. Women who meditated with Buddhist monks or sailed the Mediterranean, or fell in and out of love with penniless boy-toys, moved to cities where they were friendless and they didn't care.

"My friend Tamara did whatever she wanted. I envied her adventures, anyone's adventures. She was my safety net. She pushed me. And then cancer happened and she was gone, and I couldn't go back on my commitment. I lived with my parents until I was twenty-five. Never owned a new car. Worked the same job for thirty years. I don't have stories. I have ditto marks. I've wasted my life."

Clint had never heard that admission. Not when she was twenty-three and so impressed by his seeming sophistication; not years later when he slept in her bed. Hesitation and dread were not what he wanted.

"Now it's my turn to apologize. It's not my style to ramble."

"It's late. It's the champagne. It's Paris."

"I miss my friend—no 'what are you?' from Tamara because she'd want to get to the action. I was on my own when it came to the opera, otherwise she was in for whatever. I'm blathering, aren't I?"

"Don't let me stop you." They turned onto the Quai des Grands-Augustins, now empty of foot traffic and cars.

"I'm glad she pushed me, but I wish she were here. I love this city. It's magical. I want to sing and dance and people-watch and explore every part of it. Is that silly?"

"If you love it, you love it. I feel the same, most days."

"I want to make sense, but I can't. My dad could if he were here. He loves words and writes terrible, corny poetry. Paris is in my bones, I felt it in the music tonight—highs and lows weaving through my body making me part of a bigger history. I'm home. I feel at peace. But now I have a reason, a real reason, to be here."

"I don't know you, Nicole, but I do know this: you don't need an excuse, and you don't have to rationalize. You're here, that's what matters."

They reached Nicole's carved door. On the opposite side of the street, the Seine flowed silent and clear of the glass-topped *bateaux-mouches* that cruised up and down the river daily.

"Dad loved Langston Hughes. Now he has Alzheimer's. They need me to take care of them." Nicole described the impact of Squire's disease and Malvina's stroke, then explained how she found the photograph and the records, and the letters her mother sent without warning.

"Your mother—"

"—lives in Berkeley."

"Your birth mother," he corrected, "is the most tantalizing question of all." He spoke with certainty, as if he believed Malvina Handy had postponed filling in the blanks to allow Nicole to search for the answers. Knowing Malvina Handy as she did, Nicole was certain her mother put off filling in the blanks because this situation was untidy and she didn't tolerate messes. "It might make a great story."

"That's the second time you've mentioned that. Are you planning to steal my story, Monsieur?"

Laurent blushed. "I confess I've been accused of putting work ahead of... I don't know your story. But, I'm willing to help you if you'll let me."

"All I have is the letters. Lots and lots of letters."

Laurent and Nicole sat side by side on the maroon leather couch, a tray of cheese and the meringues Nicole had discovered in a *pâtisserie* on the rue Jacob on the coffee table. Laurent picked through the letters, pausing to compare postmarks, as if it were three in the afternoon, not the early morning, and listened to Nicole summarize the letters.

"After a while, a pattern will evolve. I'll make a timeline from the letters you've finished. You read."

April 1952

Dear RubyMae,

I hear from Squire that your friend killed himself and you witnessed that tragedy. I do feel so sorry for you. For you to have traveled the world and stayed with him for so many years, without being married, speaks to the love that the two of you must have had.

Providence has sent you a message. There are greater needs to be taken care of at home than being frivolous in Paris. You need to make peace with Momma. PapPap is not well. Neither one is getting any younger. Dr. Brown has not discovered what is wrong with PapPap, he may have the sugar. He has lost weight, enough that he no longer fits his clothes. And he's so ashen. But the truth of the matter is that since you left, he has not been the same. He goes for stretches without speaking between "good morning" and "good night." The doctor says that if his health stays this poor, he won't see Christmas.

Come home, RubyMae. I know what I read and Paris seems fast. It cannot be easy for a colored woman alone. Your family is here. The Bible speaks of a child's obligations to family and parents. I'm doing my part. What about you? PapPap will get better if he sees your face, if he knows that you are all right and safe. I hope to never know the pain of never seeing my own child again—I believe that that is what is wearing at him.

Your sister,
Malvina

"I was thinking: if this was a piece I was working on, how would I find RubyMae?" Laurent's voice was scratchy.

"The return addresses on the envelopes?"

"She may not live in the same place now. No, better to work on the angle of blacks in Paris in the fifties. If we were at my place I could go through my files."

"Well, let's go," Nicole responded without checking her watch. This spontaneous change of plans from the woman who took, roughly, a lifetime to get to Paris.

The taxi dropped them off at the Réaumur-Sébastopol station, which, along with the rest of the Métro, closed by 1:30. From the Métro to his apartment, Laurent made it clear that he'd bought in this neighborhood on the verge of, but far off from, gentrification. He led her through a gauntlet of men and women primed for a police lineup—if they did that in Paris. The hotels on either side of the narrow street flashed hourly rates in bright neon. Women lined the sidewalks in a fashion show of temptation: a red patent leather suit with matching tilted tam, tops cut low enough to display pinkish aureoles, skirts cut high enough to show off the bottoms of well-rounded buttocks—ladies of the night. Their pimps, nowhere near as fancy, posed against gleaming motorcycles big as compact cars. The women welcomed Laurent in throaty French and, judging by how close they came to him, she guessed the advanced vocabulary was especially for his ears. He returned their greeting, whispering to Nicole that after five years of his disinterest, they'd agreed to his friendship.

They entered his building through doors of sable-colored wood carved with intricate swirls and thorny vines; they were worn and in need of paint. The whole place needed several coats of paint. Inside, the hallway was dark and the elevator out of order. Halfway up the stairs to the fourth floor, Laurent chided Nicole. "With all that huffing and puffing, I can tell you're a smoker, whether you'll admit it or not." The *I-quit-and-you-should-too* smugness his daughter, Michelle, had described. Without the breath for a snappy comeback, Nicole stuck out her tongue.

His place was not at all chaotic. Two buttery leather sofas faced each other, pillows lined evenly across the back. Books shelved against plastered walls. Crown moldings, plank wood floors. Bright art on cream-colored walls.

While he made coffee, Laurent outlined the structure of Paris's city government, giving depth to Ousmane's description: each of the *arrondissements* was an administrative department with its own city hall and birth, marriage, and death records. "That's where I got my birth certificate."

He paced from the dining table, its legs carved with swirls, to the French armoire embedded with bits of glass against the opposite wall. A physical thinker, he yanked the tasseled key hanging in the lock, opened the doors, inspected the insides, then closed the doors. Walking again on that same path, he reviewed Nicole's options. He rubbed his head with the flat of his right palm as he paced. At the baby grand angled between ceiling-to-floor windows, he played a couple of chords and marked the notes on the lined paper covering the music holder. At that minute, Nicole deciphered the mystery of the disheveled Laurent.

"The key is to figure out who your mother is at this moment—if she's alive, that is."

"Not my mother. The woman who gave birth to me."

"If that's how you feel, why are you trying to find her?"

Nicole rose and paced the unfamiliar room with the same preoccupation Laurent had. Ever the obedient daughter, she was following Malvina's unspoken order: now that you know who she is, find Ruby.

"I'm loved. A little spoiled. I can't say that I connected with my mother the way some of my friends did with theirs. We've had our disagreements. Now, I think she was afraid I'd turn out like Ruby."

From freshman to senior year in college, Malvina decided Nicole should live at home. Listening to Squire's occasional lectures on sex or the implications of sex gone wrong, Nicole assumed they were cover-ups for the real lesson: keep your legs closed until you're married. The night Nicole introduced her parents to Clint, she tiptoed in hours past her midnight curfew, wine strong on her breath. She found Malvina waiting in her room, sour-faced, teeth clenched, foam rollers outlined under her nightcap.

"I won't let my child turn wild." Malvina tugged at Nicole's dress, the belt she had worn before she left home now stuffed into her handbag, lipstick smudged outside the lines of her thin lips. "There's more to love, Nicki, than the feelings you get when a man puts his hands up your dress. Sex isn't love. Love is waiting until what you want comes your way."

Nicole grabbed letters from her purse and tossed them onto the marble surface of the antique dining table. "Curiosity. That's what it is. And duty—my mother's big on duty. Making me put my needs second. She does. Otherwise, I would've thrown the letters out."

"Have you finished them?"

"I put off Paris. I put off the letters. It's what I do."

"The worst part is over. All that's left is filler."

Laurent sat at his desk and thumbed through a Rolodex. "I know of a couple of black Paris tours, the owners might have an idea or two." He picked up an envelope. "In the fifties, a lot of expats used the American Express office as mailing address. I don't know when they stopped that service, but since 9/11, no mail accepted. We'll contact the ninth's *mairie*, uh, town hall to you, and try directory assistance, check out ship manifests from the forties and fifties—they couldn't keep records of race, but they could nationalities. We can check microfiche copies of newspapers from back then—they might list Arnett as a musician."

"I don't get it."

"It's pure research, that's all, merely finding a source. You have to read between the lines. The most important lesson I've learned is to stick to a lead. No matter how slim the thread is or how long it takes. What if Ruby uses one of these addresses? That's why we need the stationery. Start writing."

June 20, 2009

Dear Miss Garrett,

My hope is that this letter has reached you and, when you double-check my name on the envelope, you continue reading. Yes, the last name is Handy. Malvina and Squire Handy are my parents—at least that was my truth up until last week. In the midst of my explorations, I found a war photo of my father with an inscription, I believe, meant for you. After I mentioned it to Mother, she sent me letters: yours, hers, my dad's. I've learned that my parents are not who I thought they were. I am not who I thought I was. You already know the truth.

Mother had a slight stroke eighteen months ago. Now she has a noticeable but slight limp. Dad has Alzheimer's. The disease makes it difficult for him to remember his present, let alone his past. He can't connect the dots between you and him or how I came to be raised by him and my mother, and Mother refuses to say. If you recall, it takes a lot to keep her from whatever she sets her mind to. Mother suggested I find you. For me or for her, I'm not sure.

I don't want anything from you, except to fill in the history between the four of us and the chance to recover from the shock of finding out this secret so late. I think, after so many years of staring at your image in our family album, I want to see how close you come to that woman now. I'm not sure what your feelings are. I'm not sure this letter will reach you. I am sure I want to meet you. What happens afterwards, we'll leave to that moment.

I can receive mail where I'm staying. My plan is to leave Paris on July 12th. I hope you'll consider meeting me before then.

Sincerely,
Nicole-Marie Roxane Handy
(1) 33 83 04 86
157 Quai des Grands-Augustins,
Paris

Three identical letters. Her best attempt to invite contact, not reveal frustration. Nicole wanted to rush to the American Express office on rue Scribe, to stand by the door, stare at every woman passing through, dare Ruby to check her out, see her reaction to her face, and shout, "See me!" She sealed the letters inside stiff white envelopes that Laurent addressed to Ruby at each location written on her letters.

Nicole rubbed her hands together, surprised at their moisture; not anxiety, attraction. Enough to make her want to pull Laurent down to her and muss his crazy hair and peel off his shirt. He must have felt it, too, because he stepped close and kissed her.

24

Paris, February 1952

Minutes after Arnett drew his last breath, Hardy Powers, Freddie Jones, and Socks Mandrake, all small-time musicians living on the floors above and below Arnett and Ruby, formed a circle to protect Ruby. Big brothers in the cold. Socks, a skinny man who wore white socks no matter how dressed up he was, said later he thought he saw a large bird diving from the roof. Ruby felt but did not see him. Felt his skinny arms tug at hers, heard his Harlem accent urging her to move away from Arnett. She held on, ignoring him. Freddie Jones came after him, as disquieted over his friend's death as he was the commotion disturbing his sleep. When he stepped past Ruby and saw Arnett's limp form, he started singing a down-home church song, "Swing low, sweet chariot." His voice was as rich as his ebony skin. Chatter ringed Ruby; Arnett's body, Socks and Freddie. *Mort*, Ruby heard. Dead.

With a few signals between them, Socks and Freddie accepted the heavy blanket a neighbor pressed into their hands. Freddie searched Arnett's dampened pockets and came up with a roll of francs and dollars, which he thrust into Ruby's hand. He motioned for Ruby to stuff the money in her bra as he'd watched Yvette do. Ruby obeyed.

"You have to let him go now, girl. Ain't nothing you can do for him." Hardy carefully pulled the saxophone from Arnett's loose grip. Taking the handkerchief from his pocket, he clutched the sax in his hands and lifted it to the rain, falling heavily now, to rinse away the blood. He wiped the instrument, the raindrops battling with him all the while. "You take this, Ruby, and don't you let nobody talk you out of it. I know you're not thinking right now, but it'll help later."

Ruby saw Freddie, Hardy, and Socks, men not quite old enough to be her PapPap, but older by ten or fifteen years over her twenty-three. They were grown men with grown men's experience. Grown like her PapPap who she had pushed out of her mind for years but longed for right now. "What am I gonna do?" No one spoke. The question had so many answers, she expanded it. "What am I gonna do with his body?"

The rain beat, washing the streets and drenching them all to the bone. It was Freddie who asked for the second blanket. Together he and Socks wrapped Arnett, taking him from Ruby's lap, leaving her clothes covered with bits of debris that they brushed off. The body thudded against the cobblestones.

"Don't hurt him!" Ruby screamed.

"He's beyond hurt now, you know, don't you, Ruby?" Socks stared into Ruby's glazed eyes.

Holding Arnett's body, they managed to wrap him from head to foot. Blood and rain blended together on the heavy wool. "We got to get him outta here before the gendarmes come."

Together the three men maneuvered up the winding staircase. Ruby headed for the room now hers alone and motioned for them to lay Arnett on the bed. "Naw, Ruby, not in there." Living and dead were soaking wet, but Arnett's body was messy and wet; they carried him to the bath down the hall and set him in the tub.

Ruby's eyes reddened from tears that did not stop. Noises came out of her mouth, muffled by sobs. She tried to form words. In her head, it was right. When Arnett went over that ledge, Ruby was sad and mad and sorry. Mad that he left her, left her in a place where they were supposed to be happy, and sorry that they hardly ever were. Sorry for herself, sorry for him. Just steps from the perfection Arnett promised. All of these days and years in Paris. At last she spit out the city's name. "Pair ess—Par. Is." Two separate pieces. One for her. One for Arnett. His Is now her Was.

Someone draped her robe on her shoulders and a towel on her head. Tying the sash of her robe over her old coat, she held vigil over Arnett, the saxophone in her hands, until Yvette and another woman came with a washbasin and lavender soap.

Ruby watched, tugging at her hair, dropping the strands to the floor. The women wiped the blood and released stool from Arnett's body with an affection that surely would have gotten all three of them killed back in Mississippi. Ruby dipped a towel in the scented water. This was not the face of her man. This man's face was tinged with black and blue bruises, already threatening to further darken. This man's eyes were not staring at her, wanting to give her the world; they were not interested in her. This man's hands were cold and going stiff, unable to hold her or wipe her tears or guide her through the Paris streets.

The passing hours were of no concern to Ruby. Now she wore a sweater and skirt, with no awareness of how they got on her body. Her lips were chapped, her nostrils red, her hair in her face. Her friends were with her. At home, women from church handled the details; covered the mirrors, arranged for food, spread the news in the community, and figured out where folk should be buried. Neither mother nor father knew that their son had died—no letter written, no telegram sent. That would come later. Yvette and Freddie, Socks, and Hardy were family.

Arnett's body lay stretched out on the bed. Ruby watched the French women, the white women, pull at Arnett's arms to finish the task of preparing him. Rising, she stepped to the chest of drawers and picked up her pearl-handled brush. She brushed Arnett's hair with the vigor she did her own—one hundred strokes to make it grow and shine.

"No need to brush, chérie." Yvette pressed her hand to Ruby's until her friend stopped. The second woman kissed the cross on her rosary and began her prayers, working bead after black bead between her fingers.

When the women were done, Ruby stuffed Arnett's dented saxophone into his case, dismantling it as she had seen him do. She hid the case behind the wingback chair and rose to her feet, stepped to the closet for Arnett's good suit. Yvette positioned herself at the top of the bed near Arnett's head. The other woman stepped to the right and Ruby to the left of Arnett's body.

"The left is his good side." Ruby fingered strands of his fine curls from his face. He needed a haircut. With the tiny sewing scissors from her pocket, Yvette clipped a curl from Arnett's hair and placed it in Ruby's hand. Together the women turned Arnett's body left and right and put pants, shirt, jacket, and tie onto his cooled corpse, reminding Ruby of the day her mother had prepared her grandfather's body after he dropped dead in the middle of Easter Sunday dinner.

Ruby searched every corner of the room for a piece of her, a token, for Arnett to keep with him. A memento for all eternity to carry to whatever place he'd gone to. Not the photo of her, not his records or the player or the bottle of brandy he loved. She put her pearl-handled brush inside his jacket pocket, where it hid unseen and offset the bulk his body had lost in the crush of the fall.

News of Arnett's death spread quick as if they lived in a country town instead of this city of millions. They came from all over;

black and white, men and women. There was even a little food: baked chicken and a poor substitute for a sweet potato pie that Ruby never touched.

Yvette and Freddie stood by her side in place of her mama and PapPap who might have if she'd married Arnett and made her peace with them. It was Yvette who kept the well-wishers from her, who kept trying to make her eat to keep up her strength. When folk walked up the stairs to number 21 to pay their respects, they found themselves at the end of a line that snaked past Arnett to Ruby seated at the window. It was Freddie who thanked everyone for coming, who shook hands when Ruby held her own close to her side. She accepted the hugs, the comforting sentiments, and counted to herself the number of well-wishers in the tiny room, but she did not shake one hand.

Amazing, a few men whispered to each other, how beautiful she was even in her grieving. She shed not a tear. Not when well-wishers suggested she send Arnett's body back to his kin. Not when Poppa approached and praised Arnett's potential. Not when the undertakers came and shrouded him in black before they carried his stiffened body down the stairs and into a black hearse. Not when they buried him in the poor man's cemetery far on the edge of Paris where there was room enough to bury the dead without crowding the living.

How Squire found out about Arnett, Ruby never asked. After that night weeks earlier when she and Arnett had taken him to the club, she never saw him around St.-Germain again. Not carousing in the streets late at night before or after the clubs closed, nor sitting in cafés, nor roaming the streets of Montmartre. He showed up at her door, without warning, eight days after Arnett was buried, flowers in one hand, fedora in the other. To anyone else he was a man who knew Paris. To Ruby he was home.

25

In idiomatic expressions, the basic verb *avoir*, to have, completes physical or emotional feelings.

en avoir pour (ahn av vwhar poor)	to need, for it to take
avoir de la chance (av vwhar du la chahnse)	to be lucky
avoir envie de (av vwhar on vee duh)	to long for
avoir faim (av vwhar fahm)	to be hungry

Sunlight peeked through the shutters. Morning. Late morning. Vague memories crowded Nicole's awakening: Laurent covering her with blankets, crying on his shoulder, cuddling, without expectations. They had slept together: her on the couch, him folded onto the chaise. She wasn't drunk; but the hour, her anger at the letters made the act of moving, of raising her arms, her head, any part of her body difficult. Sex would have been easier, she thought, watching Laurent at his desk waiting for her, impatient as a neglected puppy. One-night stands rarely came with strings or emotions. For the moment, she wanted to listen to the silence and pretend her life hadn't made such a crazy shift.

When he saw Nicole was awake, Laurent started in as if their conversation had never stopped. "We'll talk to Loot. He's a veteran. A lot of GIs stayed in Paris after World War II. A few had illegal papers so they were able to work. A few returned later—my own father included. Between five hundred and nine hundred expat blacks lived in Paris after the war. They might not have known each other, but chances are music lovers ran in the same circles. When I want to get in touch with him, I visit his hangouts—the sixth or around Shakespeare and Company or by the Seine where he takes photographs. He must have a thousand shots of Notre Dame."

"You really think he'll help?"

"It's up to you, but I believe it's worth a try."

Laurent glanced down the path near the Pont St.-Michel stairs to the cement bank edging the even-flowing river. Floating restaurants, pink geraniums hanging above their decks, bobbed in the wake of the passing boats. A bride and groom posed before a camera, senior citizens sketched Notre Dame. Having a companion felt right; Nicole sensed this wasn't the time to be alone, and whether or not it was because Laurent was familiar with the city or because he cut at her isolation and anxiety, she didn't know or care.

"Loot could be anywhere. Ready?"

"You ask if I'm ready, and I'm thinking—am I ready to see Ruby?" Nicole snapped. "Sorry. I don't mean to take it out on you." Years, she remembered, of arguments, of loving and not loving Malvina, peacemaking tears, and Malvina's off-and-on backup through each of her mistakes. Lies and tough love.

"Remember, it's your choice. We'll stop whenever you want, but let's see what we find and then you'll be better equipped to decide if you want to go on."

From the Seine they went to the little bookstore whose reputation overcompensated for its floor space. The interior of Shakespeare and Company was a book lover's fantasy, every wall covered from beamed ceiling to checkered floor with books by English-speaking authors.

"This store is as popular as it was when it opened in 1956. There's even a little bit of black history here." Laurent ran his fingers over a few volumes. Nicole watched him examine the titles and take one from a shelf. Books lined one wall of his living room. An organization Squire, for all his love of books, never imposed on his.

"The owners held a reception for Richard Wright the same year they opened. Baldwin signed copies here of *Go Tell It on the Mountain*. Your father's favorite, Langston, read in the sixties. Abbey Lincoln sang and read poetry. I guess that's why Loot loves it here. It reminds him of the past." He greeted the cashier by name and introduced Nicole.

"Loot." The English cashier paused to think. "It's been a while since he's been here. Be sure to mention he should stop by if you see the old fellow. We miss him."

"I'm not sure I was prepared to see him anyway." Nicole took Laurent's hand and held two of his fingers to her carotid artery pumping fast under the skin of her neck.

"Well, lady, best to get ready, because with Loot, it could happen"—Laurent snapped his fingers—"in a heartbeat."

Left Bank. Right Bank. Paris was a maze separated by the Seine. All *les rues* didn't lead to the river, but the streets, *les quais*, alongside it made it easy to traverse *arrondissements*. They arrived at Boulevard St.-Michel. Every step Nicole made in Paris brought her back to this monument, her neighborhood, and tempted her senses. Juice dripping from hanging cones of roasted lamb sizzled into metal pans. The spicy opposition of hummus and lamb-filled falafels. Vanilla crêpes. Blooming yeast and crusty bread. The damp smell of the gutter.

Two blocks before the apartment Nicole was beginning to call home, they turned onto rue Gît-le-Coeur and stopped in front of the Relais-Hôtel du Vieux Paris.

"I've been known to get carried away. So tell me if you're bored." He squeezed her hand and went on without waiting for an answer. "In the forties and fifties hotels were the cheapest accommodations. Artist, writers, and musicians, anyone who didn't have much money, lived in them. This used to be the Hôtel Rachou. Chester Himes, the writer, lived in here with a two-burner gas stove in his room. It's where he wrote part of his prizewinning *La Reine des Pommes*." Laurent led her up the street and past the *passage* she'd stumbled upon during her adventure of right turns. "If you're interested in black Paris, this is the place to be."

"What about your friend?"

"If Loot's here, I guarantee that as long as he's drinking free coffee, he'll stay put. And if we don't catch up with him today, then we'll try another day."

They zigzagged until they reached rue de Seine. Nicole peered into storefronts and down side streets, listening to Laurent's descriptions and hoping to see a black man old enough to have been in Paris since the war. Laurent stopped at a plain, rather contemporary structure. Block letters spelled out "La Louisiane" on a red doormat.

"At one time, Hôtel La Louisiane was considered the center of the jazz universe, so many musicians stayed here over the years, Miles, Coltrane, Bud Powell, Lester Young, Chet Baker, Mal Waldron, Archie Shepp, Charlie Parker, Dexter Gordon, Ben Sidran, Wayne Shorter—to name a few."

"Show-off."

"What? I dig jazz." Laurent grinned, a lopsided expression Nicole was growing fond of. "I'm a journalist—a journalist with a jones for jazz. What can I tell you?" His father loved classical music and thought jazz a waste of his son's talent. "One in a list of reasons why I'm not partial to the man."

The hotel was unimposing, without an engraved plaque, Laurent mentioned, to describe its former inhabitants and accomplishments. Brass plaques all over Paris touted the famous, the literate, the conquering: Picasso painted *Guernica*, Balzac penned novels, Richard Wright lived and wrote, Monsieur so-and-so fought or died.

"Gossips say Bud Powell's wife sometimes locked him in his room to keep him from drinking. Musicians cooked in the lobby, and apparently the smell of red beans and fatback was so strong that it was often mistaken for a restaurant."

Professor of history or tour guide or a man, Nicole decided, who didn't have many chances to share this information. Laurent motioned in another direction and described the jazz clubs that had enticed music lovers from all over the world: Tabou, Club St.-Germain-des-Prés, Café Rouge, the Vieux Columbier. Jazz made St.-Germain special. The medieval cellars, *caves*, and the wacky kids, *les troglodytes*, who couldn't get enough of the music. The existentialists: Sartre and de Beauvoir. The equality: black or white, French, American, bourgeois, and commoner. "Club Tabou's long since been converted to a hotel, but in the fifties it was where Boris Vian—the white Negro, a few christened him because he wrote *J'irai Cracher Sur Vos Tombes*, 'I Shall Spit on Your Graves,' pretending to be a black man—author, trumpeter, and jazz fan, played his heart out. Literally."

After checking several places, they entered a rectangular-shaped café on rue St.-André-des-Arts where coffee was priced less for patrons standing at the bar. An elderly black man leaned against the counter. He was dressed in a soldier's uniform, the olive now faded to a pale green mixed with yellow as if he'd exposed sleeves, cuffs, and collar to the sun. A reminder of the sixty-plus years passed since the real need for his getup. His torso seemed to fit the uniform, but the sleeves and legs were too long, a sign that his body must have shrunk over the years.

"Loot, my man!" Laurent slapped Loot's back affectionately and introduced Nicole. "Can we buy you another coffee or have you had enough?"

Loot's age was as mysterious as Laurent had intimated. Hints of wisdom seemed pocketed in the grooves on either side of his mouth and nose; his brown cheeks were sunken, having lost their natural plumpness, and a narrow ring of blue circled his irises. Nicole figured, from Laurent's wink, that this was Loot's way—coffee, gab, information.

Loot held up two fingers and bowed in Nicole's direction. He lifted her right hand and kissed the back of it. "Lieutenant Harold S. Jenkins. Enchanté."

Within seconds, the barista set two demitasse cups of coffee on the zinc counter. Down went the first, fast as a shot of tequila. "Ahhhhh. This one reminds me I'm alive." He sipped from the second cup. "And this one's to give thanks that I am. Have you been to Paris before, Ma'amselle?"

Nicole shook her head.

"St.-Germain wasn't this ritzy when Baldwin and Wright were here. Did Mr. Newspaperman tell you that when Jimmy got here his room was so cold he wrote in cafés all day long, just to keep warm? Or did he bother to mention that Duke Ellington, Beaufort Delaney, and Henry Tanner, the artists before them, and others set their feet on the very cobblestones you just came in on? *Mon dieu!*"

Nicole fumbled through her purse and slapped Ruby's picture on the counter. Everyone wanted to give her a history lesson. "Do you recognize her? Did you know her? Is she in Paris?" Loot brushed his free hand against the photo with a tender mix of longing and admiration.

Laurent pressed into Nicole's side and whispered, "Let him tell you on his own." He turned back to Loot, giving the impression that he'd simply whispered an affectionate message into his lover's ear. "Nicole is in Paris on vacation. She's trying to find her birth mother. RubyMae Garrett."

"I'm not your daddy, am I?" Loot chuckled and sipped from his cup again. The fine grooves on his face spoke to experience beyond Nicole and Laurent's, separately or combined. "I'm kidding. For as many ladies as I been with, I have not one child—so

I figured"—he adjusted his pants and winked at Laurent—"musta been shooting blanks. *C'est la vie, n'est-ce pas?*" He sipped more coffee. "Weren't many colored women around then. Most came with their men. Inez Cavanaugh came to sing and dance, but her husband came with her. Paris was harsh for some colored folks. Some had a time learning the language, couldn't say but *franc*, *oui*, *bonjour*, and *merci*. Then the French, their arms wasn't all that open. Oh, they were good. And color-blind for the most part, better to us than they were to the Africans or Algerians, but it was tough to break into the culture. They weren't letting foreigners into their inner circles. Was easier for us men, I suppose. A little chocolate got us a long way." He grinned at his double meaning. "And some picked up nasty habits from white GIs."

Loot dug deep into the pockets of his loose wool pants and pulled out a pair of glasses bound at the hinges on both sides with wide tape painted the green, black, and yellow of Africa on one side, red, white and blue on the other. "I been in Paris since after the war. I've seen them come. I've seen them crash and burn, succeed and fail." He pushed the glasses onto his face, rubbed his chin, and flattened a nonexistent hair on his shiny head.

Nicole followed his inspection from the part in the middle of Ruby's hair to the long lashes, the mole, the space between her lips, the bush of feathers. At the age of twelve, she'd locked herself in the bathroom, draping sheets of toilet paper around her neck imitating the woman's boa, and wondered how she could be pretty. Wondered how, with Malvina for a mother, kinder than she was pretty, it was possible to overcome what she'd inherited from her parents—wild, unmanageable hair, hands and ears too big for a girl.

With this wizened man beside her, Nicole tried to visualize Loot as the swarthy military man he must have been and the fights Laurent mentioned he bragged about. Fights with French husbands over their wives conned, seduced, or both with U.S. Army–issue cigarettes and chocolate. The twinkle in his eyes, a tad short of haughtiness, said he wanted to be that man again, to do what his body couldn't, over and over again with the woman in the picture.

"I took that picture." He stretched his arms out wide and stepped back from the marble counter. "No way I could forget her. Ruby."

At that moment, Paris became forever different for Nicole. "What happened to her?"

Loot danced to the center of the room and sang in French. Cane in hand, he shuffled between the tables speaking French where he heard German, British, or other foreign accents until they dropped euros into his outstretched hands. It seemed he was going to loop the tables and return to the bar. Instead, Loot left. Laurent and Nicole waited, believing he'd carried his routine to the curb. Nicole rushed after him, almost tripping on the top of the metal loading door in the middle of the café floor. For all of his years, Loot moved quickly down the street and out of sight.

"Catch him!" she shouted. "Make him come back."

"Don't bother. It's his way. I told you he was kooky."

Loot's story was unfinished. Nicole plopped into a chair. Laurent sat beside her, silent.

"I really appreciate what you've done, Laurent. But I'm tired. Inside and out. I want to go home." She wasn't sure, after she spoke, if she meant the Quai des Grands-Augustins or Oakland.

26

Paris, February 1952

"Why didn't you call? Why didn't you find me? Don't you know, girl, I would've been here."

Between Squire's return and Arnett's mistimed death, Ruby had refused to sleep in their bed, could not bring herself to touch the sill or the window where Arnett had fallen to his death. She grieved, fought the advice of everyone, including Yvette and Freddie, to take a boat home. "A single colored woman is better off here with a man's protection," Freddie Jones had spoken in a voice that meant he was speaking for every Negro in Paris.

Huddled in the wingback chair, Arnett's saxophone cradled in her arms, she touched the mouthpiece to her lips, seeking a last taste of Arnett. She fingered the keys where his fingers once played and pondered and plotted her future. By the fifteenth day after Arnett fell from the window, Squire had come to her door and Ruby had a plan.

"I didn't know how to find you."

He'd left the club so quickly that only night she'd seen him, he'd forgotten to tell her where he lived and how to reach him, how to visit if or when she decided to leave Arnett.

Squire turned his head from Ruby, so flat was the light in her eyes. Slowly, he took in the room: the bed's military corners, the covers folded back and tucked into the mattress so a dropped coin could bounce off the white surface. The window curtains held shut with a clothespin. A blanket lay crumpled on the wingback chair, cups, their bottoms covered with coffee dregs, were in the sink and on the table beside a caned chair. Ruby's face was sallow and empty of the glow Squire had studied that first afternoon he made it up the stairs to her apartment.

"Come out this place. What's with you? Hungry?"

"You still stumbling, Bud?" Ruby teased like she hadn't in a while. Her words escaped freely as they had the day she ran out of the room, unaware that she spoke them.

"Only around you."

Squire dropped his bouquet into the basin and placed his hat, coat, and jacket not on the bed, but on the closet door. Then he picked Ruby up and sat in the big chair. He wrapped the blanket over them, tucking the ends behind his shoulders. Ruby rested her head into the crook of his neck and wept until she drifted off to sleep.

They awoke hours later to a sky turned the last of dusk's dark orange and a chill in the air hinting at snow. All over the street and for blocks beyond, lights turned windows into glowing rectangles. Without warning, Ruby jumped from Squire's lap and hummed the song Arnett had written for her, an intersection of the big band jazz he loved and the blues. She picked up the cups. She stuffed clothes into the closet, pushing Arnett's pants, shirts, jacket, and ruined overcoat to the back. After all this was done, after order was restored to the room, Ruby opened the curtains and dusted the ledge.

"Yes," she said at last, as if sleep hadn't crept over them or hours hadn't passed since his question had been put forth. She ran her fingers over the bed. On rainy days when Arnett had no job, they had put a record on the player and stayed in bed to keep warm, talking and loving and sleeping, neither one of them moving far from their spots until the record needle had to be reset or nature demanded. "Let's go."

Squire, his face brightened from the nap and Ruby's mood change, got up from the chair and set the blanket at the foot of the bed. He stepped once, then twice toward her, waiting for a signal that she meant out of here and back home to Sheridan and out of this city that he detested—the language that went by him so fast, the food heavy with butter, not enough salt, no hint of a smoked ham hock. Back home, back to him. Squire straightened his back and thrust out his chest. First lover or last, that Ruby could be his was all that was important.

When Ruby stepped behind the closet door to change her clothes, Squire went to the dresser. Coming into the apartment, he'd taken notice of the photograph; Ruby in a movie star pose, her shoulders bare, her lips open and waiting. The dedication promised Arnett forever. He slipped the photo into his inside pocket and moved to the other side of the room.

Ruby shut the closet door and stood dressed in the outfit Yvette had given her and altered for the differences in their dress size and height. The black dress hung loose; her body thin from lack of sleep, from hours of sleep, from not enough food. She and Paris had that in common: dogged after the madness of war—solemn and trim. When she opened the door a few weeks ago, she had been a mix of the remnants of the innocent and daring RubyMae that Squire loved and the bodacious and knowing woman Arnett had won.

Now her bearing carried the flair of an experienced woman confident in where she was going and what to do once there. Squire watched her take each stair tread. Watched the seam of her stockings drop down to her thin ankles and tiny feet. Watched the hem of her somber dress swing back and forth in a one-two rhythm all its own. Her hat's loose netting covered her face, and

Squire fought the urge, knotting his fists inside his pockets, to take that hat off of her head, run his fingers through her hair, and kiss her until she moaned as she had when he watched her kiss Arnett.

They went down the rue de Clichy past the tall columns of Ste.-Trinité church, past places new to Squire. Ruby went before him in her high-heeled pumps, never stumbling on the brick or the curbs or stepping in the spit on the streets. They continued until they came to Haynes Restaurant.

Squire peeked through the window at the folks eating, drinking, and generally having a good time, and making him think it was a Saturday, not a Thursday, night. "You sure?"

Ruby inspected his face, then gazed through the restaurant window for herself. She didn't care. Not tonight, and maybe not tomorrow. To be out, to speak French, to be in the company of folks who made music to chase the bad times; a taste of what was now and forever beyond reach for her and Arnett. She pouted. "You worried about your pocketbook, Bud? Worst case, I can sing for my supper." Her finger moved to his lips before he answered. That Squire didn't have enough money was clear enough in his frame, his clothes looser since his last visit.

The dining room was filled to capacity with Negro and white singers, dancers, writers, and artists. Folks of all kinds, some Ruby knew and some she didn't. There were a few musicians without and with French women, and two Negro women with French men, all of them testimony to the freedom Paris allowed—to love without scrutiny, to wash away loneliness regardless of skin color.

Ruby looped her arm through Squire's and circled the room, introducing him as her friend, and Arnett's, from back home. Men pressed francs into her hand and Squire pouted until Ruby squeezed his arm. Finally reaching the table where Freddie Jones and Yvette sat, she said to Squire, "They were Arnett's buddies. Ne t'inquiète pas."

"Don't worry," Yvette translated for both Freddie and Squire. "Ruby is becoming good with French, non?"

"I couldn't say," Squire replied, "I'm having a time with the language myself."

"Then you must talk to me. You must practice. That is what me and Ruby did before..." Yvette patted Ruby's hand. "Isn't that right, Fred-*dee*?"

"That's right, baby." Freddie winked. "Man, it took me a while to pick up the lingo, and I still don't got it down. But I make it without offending too many." He yanked at Squire's jacket. Freddie was a big man with hands large enough to wrap his trumpet's lead pipe and valve slide, if he needed to. His was a big man's voice that he struggled to keep low in deference to Parisian dignity. Occasionally, he slipped; he had when Arnett killed himself. He'd shouted at his friend from his window. "Arnett! Now why'd you want to go and do that, man?" He almost shouted now. "Eat, man, it's on me. You must be missing ya mama's cooking. And if that's the case, you come to the right place." The big man's face was sincere, and Freddie waited for Squire to speak as if going to the Sorbonne meant he had answers. "Me and Arnett talked a lot. But I'll be damned if I understand why he jumped outta that window..."

27

Pronouns substitute for nouns and refer to persons, places, or objects. The interrogative pronouns *qui* (who, whom), *où* (where), and *que* (what) are used when questioning persons or situations.

moi (mwah)	me
il, elle (eel, ehl)	he, she, or it
la sienne, le sien (lah see en, luh see ehn)	hers or his
aller (ah lay)	to go

It was as if he were waiting for Laurent to leave. Five blocks later his hand stopped Nicole dead in the middle of the street. "I've been watching for you, Ma'amselle." Loot peeked from behind Nicole's shoulder. His grin was facetious, the joy of his ambush obvious. "I wasn't sure if you're the one interested, or your friend Laurent is doing a story. He's wily, that one. He has a way of getting information from folks."

They went in the opposite direction, and Loot strolled casually, pausing at a *tabac* and an open bar, speaking to customers and owners alike. No one rejected his greeting. A few saluted, others raced toward him.

"Are you saying he'll take advantage of me?"

"I'm saying I'd rather tell *you* what I know. Your mama, your story." He halted in front of a neat stack of espresso makers displayed in a window. His sigh either a hint or admiration of the artful display. "I really do remember her."

Inside, Nicole ordered espresso—one for her and three for him—and Loot scoured the room before selecting a cushioned bench. He sat facing the large window, claiming his superstition was a throwback to the war when many a soldier was killed, sitting with his back to an open space, by a vigilant sniper. Just as he drank greedily not forty minutes ago, Loot slurped down coffee number one, then tested the second cup. "When the opportunity comes, I get my extra coffees *très chaud*, so they won't cool down before I'm ready."

Nicole nodded, a schoolgirl learning her lessons—don't be late, don't speak until spoken to, don't let Loot's coffees get cold. Her obedience was calculated to avoid his running off again, leaving her, and his coffees, behind.

"I hail from Beaumont, Texas. Haven't set my foot on American soil since 1946. I was at Normandy on D-Day—part of the 320th Antiaircraft Artillery Balloon Barrage Battalion. Don't most folks know blacks were on that beach, but we were. We were important in the war. Don't let anyone make you think different. From the beginning white folks, even Roosevelt, didn't want us to fight. Highfalutin generals afraid to put guns in our hands. Assumed we cared more about shooting them than the Germans. Fools. They came around."

The patches on his sleeves were large enough to see the uneven stitching. The fabric was less coarse and not the same as the original uniform either in texture or color. Different from the jacket Squire stored in the cedar trunk—thick wool that scratched when she rubbed it against her nine-year-old face. When Loot began sipping his second demitasse, Nicole realized he wasn't going to jump up and dance out of the restaurant. "Tell me what you know."

Loot paused like an actor onstage prepared to deliver a punchline. "After the war, no one here harassed us. We were ordinary men going about our business. If a black man was in uniform, *mon Dieu*, we were celebrities. Folks' faces lit up. Women kissed us; men shook our hands, glad we helped kick out the Germans. A few defended us when white soldiers wanted to get in our faces and start that old racial crap. Folks back home were convinced we were here for the women. Like that's ever all a nigger ever wanted: a white woman. Not true. For the first time in our lives—especially for the men from the South—we were whole men. The women came naturally."

Nicole set the photograph in front of Loot.

"She went by Ruby. Not RubyMae." Loot stared. The second hand on the clock on the wall behind him skipped around the dial until he finally looked away. "The day I gave her that print, I told her to go back home. No listening for that one. Ruby Garrett and Arnett Dupree—pree rhyming with tree. He played a good sax. Not that I was any judge, but those musicians were jealous—couldn't one man have talent and a fine woman, too."

Loot checked his third cup of coffee. Caffeine jitters were nowhere to be seen; his hands were steady and he was relaxed and thoughtful. "Ruby dressed French, little sweaters, berets and straight skirts, scarves around her neck. Walked like them, too. A proper and sexy motion. She soaked up French fast.

"She was the most beautiful woman I'd ever seen. Wasn't a man, black or white, who didn't set his aim on Ruby Garrett. You hoped if Arnett wasn't with her, you'd have a chance. Ruby was only interested in Paris and Arnett and singing. She wanted to sing."

"And what did she end up doing?"

"She was whoever and whatever she wanted to be in Paris. French, American, white, Italian, Spanish. I got around the city back then. Many's a time I'd see her chatting, flirting with white men, pretending to be what she wasn't. You're going to have to figure out that one for yourself." Loot wiped the corners of his mouth with a paper napkin and stared at the photo in his hand. "You're her daughter all right. Skin browner. Same nice eyes. Hair color. Can't tell from the black-and-white, but I remember. I lost track of her."

"And what do you suggest I do? Keep this in my hand and compare faces to hers? Stand in the middle of the street and call out her name? Or should I make posters and slather the walls in the Métro?"

"No need to get snippy, Ma'amselle. In that, you remind me of her."

He stretched to his full height, which Nicole estimated must have been reduced by at least two inches given his hunched back and shoulders. Loot beckoned to Nicole with his forefinger. When she stepped to his side, he bowed, took her into his arms, and danced a graceful two-step. Not that he was impoverished or needy. Not that he'd given a hint or signal that he needed it, but after he threw back the last of his coffee, she stuffed euros into his hand.

"Eh bien, Ma'amselle Nicole, I wish you the best. But if you were my daughter, I'd tell you this: be careful what you look for, because you might not care for what you find." Without examining the bills, he inserted them into his pocket. Then he kissed both her cheeks and glided out the door.

Loot blended into the Parisian afternoon. Save for Laurent's method of scouring the nooks and crannies of this neighborhood, Nicole didn't know how to contact him. Except for taking the picture, she didn't know how Loot fit into the whole scrambled puzzle or, assuming she found Ruby—dead or alive—whether he wanted to know. Ruby was part of Paris's past, history not revelations. Between the glow his face radiated when he spoke Ruby's name and his self-conscious grin, he reminded Nicole of a boy with a crush. That allure, Nicole knew, had skipped her. What had she done to make men fall for her? The answer to that question alone was worth finding the woman.

The warm afternoon bordered on stifling. Nicole decided sleep was the solution after her late night with Laurent, Ruby, her parents. She chalked it up to a meteorology term learned from the local TV weatherman: convergence—an upwelling where unpredictability trumped the expected—and headed back to the apartment distracted by the sudden loose ends complicating her trip. She needed to finish the letters and talk to her mother. Malvina, she knew, was Mother; Ruby was Ruby.

No matter what happened between her parents and Ruby, Nicole trusted that she was loved. From kindergarten, hair parted in two braids bound with white ribbon and starched middy shirt tucked into perfectly pleated skirt, up to before she left for Paris and her mother had taken a wad of cash from her pocket and shoved it into her hands. *Shhhh. Don't tell your father.* Another damned secret.

Her cell phone buzzed when she closed the door behind her. The bright screen flashed Clint's name and office number. Nicole turned off her phone and settled on the couch. Finished. Over. Done.

"Too bad." Nicole pointed to the letters on the coffee table, "I can't do the same with you." The letters were as addictive as Clint had been. Random or in order, the whole situation was crazy.

May 1952

Malvina

Yes, my beloved Arnett is gone. It hurts to write that.

Sister, I will not leave Paris. I've seen the world, or all I want to see. Paris is my home now. I cannot think of living elsewhere. News from the US travels to us. A man by the name of William Gardner Smith writes for the Pittsburgh Courier. Negro tourists thinking I'm hungry for US news pass his columns to me. He writes about Paris for the negroes back home and understands that many of us are content here. That we have taken up French ways and some of us have learned to like the policemen who salute us when they pass. I know there's buzz about equality for negroes, but I can't be a part of it. If you were here you'd understand what I mean. We don't even have to think about being equal—we are. I go everywhere I want, speak my mind. White men open doors for me and buy me coffee and ask me to go to dinner with them.

It seems that this is all I ever do, but I need to get situated. Can you help? Can you send a little money to tide me over until I find steady work? I will repay you for all you have done. I owe you. Please tell PapPap I love him. Tell him—read this letter to him if you have to. He'll understand.

Your sister,
Ruby

Nightmares invaded her sleep, hailstorms of babies in the arms of women with Malvina's and Ruby's faces. The chandelier above the bed cast sparkles of rainbow colors on the duvet when Nicole awakened, in sweat-soaked clothes, to midnight and the realization that gaps needed filling in. Where was she born? Why did her mother raise her sister's child?

"I wrote to Ruby." Gone were polite greetings and inquiries about Malvina's health.

"You wrote to her?" Malvina seemed confused.

"Did you think I'd run into her on the street?"

"I love you. You're my blood, Nicki."

"And if I never discovered Dad's picture?"

"Then time would have taken care of it."

"Meaning death?"

"Meaning whatever happens when a thing is over—life or a secret, no difference. Time meaning the healing of old wounds. Truth is, your father never wanted you to know. He said he didn't want to complicate our lives or yours, and I went along."

"So I'm stuck fixing your mistakes."

"Everyday I hurt, watching your father come apart. Making sure he knows where he is, who he is. Waiting for the day he'll confuse her name with mine. I protected my family, and I've never regretted that."

In the background, Squire shouted at the television, "Take the deal, take the deal."

Malvina raised her voice, "I considered including Ruby in your childhood." From time to time she had written letters, included a lock of hair, a clipped fingernail, a lost tooth—they never made it to the mailbox. They were hidden, destroyed after Nicole got into the cedar chest.

"No telling about that woman. Your father was my age, my classmate. I brought him home. And when he came back with his tail between his legs, it was me he turned to. I didn't care. My sister made her choice. And so did I."

"So, I know it's hard for you, Mother, but what's the point of dragging it out? Tell me the whole truth; then I can choose, if I have to."

Choice. Nicole hated that notion. That, and sacrifice. Her father spoke of sacrifice as often as he quoted Langston. Malvina, Nicole realized, singled out choices at every opportunity. The day Nicole finally accepted her marriage was over, she headed for her parents' house. Without a reference to the suitcase in her hand, Malvina had opened a bottle of her emergency bourbon and poured a shot for Nicole. After she gulped that one down and then another, Malvina declared that most men, and even women, two-timed their spouses with either heart or head. If the difference made sense to her, then Nicole had a choice to make.

She chose herself, but forgot when Clint came back. If Ruby was number one with her dad, and that position had been her habit, her choice, Nicole wanted to inherit that trait from her newly discovered mother.

"Don't put it off, Nicki. Find her. For me. I've got to know if she's dead or alive. I'd do it if I could."

28

Paris, February 1952

"Mistake mistake." Squire spoke at a pitch above a whisper so as not to offend, but with enough force to emphasize his dilemma. "Non, non. Rue de Vintimille in the ninth. *Neuf.* Don't stop here!"

"Ça va, Monsieur. Merci." Ruby dropped coins into the cabbie's outstretched hand. "I told him to bring us here."

They rode the elevator to Squire's room on the second floor, Ruby directly before him, her back to his front, her hair not even grazing his chin but close enough for Squire to take in her lavender scent. To say he stood woozy with the scent of her, was not all of the truth. It was Ruby herself, the nearness of her, the possibilities of a future, that made him giddy. They stepped into the corridor, triangles of light spilled from beneath doors cut high at the threshold, the lingering smell of bread and pungent cheese. At the door to his room, Squire paused and grinned.

"What's so funny, Bud? Cat got your tongue?"

"I'm not quite sure. I'm not, I don't know how I left my room. Mind if I go before you?"

"Squire Handy, you stepped straight into our little place this afternoon without a nod to me or its condition. Fair is fair." Ruby snatched the key from Squire's hand and unlocked the door. "Ain't a damn thing wrong with this room. You're the neatest person I ever met."

Back in Sheridan Squire hadn't shown much interest in his father's mill growing up; the dust, the bits and pieces of stray wood and splinters—they went against his nature. Never had one person from school or church or the center of town seen him with saw dust and mill dirt on his pants or shoes. Ruby never had, even when he had tried to court her. Now, he straightened his neck, seeming to adjust a crick. Inside his room, a narrow bed was pushed between the wall and a sink. A writing desk, catty-corner to the bed, held books stacked high, and pencils, tablets, and note-books to the right and left. Ruby plopped onto the wooden chair by the desk. "I could use a drink."

"I've been trying French wine." He hung his hat and jacket on the hook screwed to the back of the door. "Make yourself comfort-able." Ruby shook her head, kept shaking it back and forth. Squire handed over his handkerchief and reached below the basin for a bottle of red wine.

"Drink scotch or bourbon. French wine isn't good unless you pay a lot of money for it. At least that's what I hear." Ruby and Arnett had celebrated their one-year anniversary in Paris in a bis-tro with a two-franc bottle of red wine that cost the same as their two plates of food. She believed better-tasting wine was in her future.

"Well, then this is bound to taste real bad. Can't stand scotch. Or bourbon. Guess I'm-I'm not a drinker. Freddie Jones is a drinker." Squire removed the two glasses inside the cabinet, rinsed them in the shallow basin, then filled them with wine. He passed a glass to Ruby and sat on the floor. "I was afraid I was going to have to carry him out of the restaurant for all that man drank."

"Freddie's a good man. If it wasn't for them after Arnett..."

"Stay with me. I can sleep on the floor." Squire rushed to the tall bureau drawers filled with his belongings: handkerchiefs and knitted ties from Malvina, the last of a jar of chow-chow Martha had included in Malvina's last care package, a straight razor. Reaching into the bottom drawer, he withdrew a pair of striped pajamas, handed them to Ruby, and excused himself to the *salle de bain* outside and to the right of his room.

When Ruby opened the door for him five minutes later, posing the same as she had when he came to the rue de Vintimille, she wore the top of his pajamas. The seams that normally fit him square on the shoulders hung near to her elbows, the long hem close to her knees. He was provoked again by the urge to kiss her, this time on the crack behind her knees that separated thigh and calf.

Ruby climbed into the bed, leaving Squire to turn blankets, towels, and his winter overcoat into a makeshift bed. He collected her clothes from the chair and his bed and hung them in his closet alongside his two pairs of pants and five white shirts. He kept studying her, afraid she might disappear; afraid he might wake up from the best dream in all of his thirty years. He squatted and set her shoes at the bottom of the closet so that the heels of his two pairs were in perfect alignment with hers, but inches shorter in height, then he turned off the lights and crawled to the pad on the floor.

"What're you going to do, Ruby?"

"I'm going to sleep, that's what."

"I mean what're you going to do now that you're alone."

"I'm not alone, Bud. I have friends. You saw for yourself."

"I love you, Ruby."

"I know that, Squire."

"Then why, why didn't you call?"

"I told you before, I just don't know. What difference does it make now anyway?"

Squire sat in the middle of his improvised mattress and allowed his nose to adjust to the traces of lavender and oncoming spring and red wine. In the faint light from the streetlamps below his window, he scrutinized Ruby, her creamy profile, the curly hair, her face cradled in the arc of her arms stretched behind her head. He reached toward the bed and stroked the inside of her arm.

"Do you ever think about dying, Bud? Or how it feels? Dead. Done. Gone."

"No. I'm interested in the future. I think about how things are going to turn out, sort of a mystery. I try to figure out what it will be when it's solved."

"The dark makes me think of death. Arnett must have been feeling he was in the dark when he sat in that window. You think that's true?"

"I think I was worried about him having you; not getting to know him. He was different from me. But I can tell you, from what I saw, he loved you."

"I miss him."

"I know that."

"I'm tired, Squire." Ruby looked from the window to the single chair. "I know what I want. I just have to figure out the best way to get it."

"Let me take care of you, Ruby. That's what you should want."

Squire climbed onto the bed and scooted close to Ruby, the smell of her under his nose, addling his mind. She laid her head against him. He held his Ruby in his arms, her body, but not her mind.

"Arnett?" Ruby cried out startled hours later by the voices below the window. Squire grazed her cheek with his lips. She tugged at the lobe of his ear, ran her fingernails up and down his spine, touches that had pleased Arnett. In the dim light, she took Squire's rough hair for Arnett's curls, Squire's face, nubby at the line between cheek and jowl where he shaved, for Arnett's when he didn't. Then she drew him close and, for the first time in all the years of their acquaintance, Ruby kissed Squire with tongue and breath and body.

The bed squeaked when Squire climbed on top of her. She

opened her arms and her body, receiving him without regret, only the memory of a night in a car in a Mississippi woods filled with the notes of a saxophone and crickets and a hooting owl. If he never guessed, she would never let on. They were awkward in the newness of this connection. Squire let his manhood show him how to please her. When she moaned, he pumped slower, wanting to hear her moan again. Squire pushed, him calling her name in the dark, her silence rising to meet his body until they were wet together and calm. One falling into the past, the other into the future.

29

In both English and French, the imperative verb form commands an action. In French, if "let" is translated in the imperative it means requesting or giving permission.

prenez la lettre! (pren nay lah let truh)	take the letter!
apprendre (ah prahn druh)	to learn
écoutez! (aay coo tay)	listen!
vouloir (voul wahr)	to want

Monsieur Daudon switched his cigarette to his left hand, then shook Nicole's. "I was thinking, Madame, you left Paris without an *au revoir.* Not good, eh?"

"Monsieur Daudon, je vous présente Monsieur Bésson." Nicole introduced Laurent, leaving the decision of formality to the two men to decide. Inside, the store was empty save for the scudding footsteps of a very pregnant woman who approached Monsieur Daudon for the price of a spinning porcelain ballerina in the midst of a *tour jeté*. The electricity of Nicole's last visit was gone, replaced with the quiet of a middle-of-the-week, laid-back energy. Nicole motioned to Laurent, who maneuvered her boxes to the center of an aisle with the agile footwork of a soccer player.

One by one, he examined the album covers and records. Laurent muttered artist names and album titles with the reverence of a litany at high holy mass. Without stopping his exploration, he yanked reading glasses from his jacket and pushed them onto his face. The thick black frames worked against his face, not aging him, but giving him an off-kilter, scholarly demeanor. He scanned the liner notes and separated the albums into piles.

"Should I buy them?" Nicole whispered.

"If you don't, I will. You decide, after all, you found them."

Nicole started to let Laurent choose before her. She'd learned from her mother to give the best to others. No matter the meal or the occasion, Malvina gave Squire the filet on the T-bone steak, the chicken drumstick, or the last piece of coconut cream pie. Men, anybody but her, got the best and she accepted what was left. Nicole was prepared to make a random selection. Lyrics, not musicians, from long-ago Friday night parties jogged memories: "*Annie had a baby, she can't work no more.*" "*Caldonia! What makes your big head so hard?*" She poked at Laurent's arm. "Let me see."

When the lot was divvied up, Laurent waved to Monsieur Daudon and placed his credit card on the marble-topped counter, and Nicole did the same.

"These records are a fantastic find. Let's check the boxes before we completely forget why we're here. If your father's picture was in this one..." Laurent squatted to read the sides. A partial address was written on the second one—rue de Vint, smudged, but unmistakable. "We have to assume, because you found it with the books and records, that they're connected to your letters." Laurent consulted his *Paris par Arrondissement*, dragging his finger from where rue des Martyrs bisected Boulevard de Clichy and down to the street listed on the return address of Ruby's letters. "See? We're in the ninth, not far from rue de Vintimille."

Monsieur Daudon addressed Nicole, oblivious of the mystery her find had presented. "Ah, Monsieur, it can be of no use to you, or Madame. The boxes, I get from the home of one who is dead."

After Nicole described how Loot had waited for her, Laurent explained that his original meeting with Loot was part of his research for a piece on GIs in Paris. "I'm not surprised. It isn't that Loot doesn't like me. At least I hope he does," Laurent said. He and Nicole moved past congested intersections and a window packed with masks resembling leftovers from a New Orleans Mardi Gras.

"Does he have any reason to doubt your intentions?" Nicole grazed Laurent's bicep with her index finger, punctuating their conversation with touch.

"No. I'm a reporter—it's my job—and he simply prefers I don't ask so many questions." Laurent's hand brushed her shoulder. "Which always makes me ask more questions."

Eventually, the rue des Martyrs turned residential. Fewer boutiques and a greater number of stores filled with the necessities for everyday living: pharmacies, tailors, shoe repair. Laurent stopped, gazed to his left and right, and led Nicole to a restaurant a few doors down the rue Clauzel. A log-cabin façade and lace-covered windows plastered with newspaper clippings from U.S. papers and photos of Leroy Haynes stirring huge pots of collard greens.

"Chez Haynes. Not the original restaurant. It isn't the haven for black Americans that it was in the late forties and early fifties." He went on, with another history lesson. "Montmartre was the center of the Paris jazz scene between the two wars and filled with black soldiers, singers, musicians, and a few black expats." Now modernized wine shops and brasseries filled the famous clubs within walking distance: Le Duc where Langston bussed dishes; Bricktop's where the redheaded black woman taught the wealthy and royal to Charleston; the mysterious location of Josephine Baker's club; flappers, limos, socialites, and celebrities, music and dancing.

They continued to the corner of rue de Vintimille and a street that appeared to be unmarked. Ruby's stomping ground. Nicole stretched her arms into the doorway, now a hotel, wanting to believe that a hint of that woman remained in the wood, the plaster, the cement. Number thirty-two. She was tourist and Peeping Tom all in one. This whitewashed edifice was no different from others alongside it with weatherworn shutters and foot-wide wrought iron balconies. Endless patches of red and pink geraniums. This was a neighborhood where children played and families went about their daily lives. A place where Ruby might have lived.

In the lobby, Laurent approached the clerk. Her hair bounced when she shook her head no until he passed her his press card. Handwritten numbers and names filled the guest register and seemed, to Nicole, a leftover from a time before computers. The clerk ran her finger up and down wide columns in search of Ruby's and Arnett's names. "*Non.*" Her tone and reply needed no translation.

"Does anyone here remember them?" Nicole urged, broken French ready on her lips. "Y-a-t'il vieillards?" Laurent translated her question into correct French.

"A woman, she lives on the fifth floor," the clerk admitted. "Madame has lived in this hotel since after the war. Back then this place, it was different."

"Is she home now?" Nicole asked.

"I have not seen her, Madame, but how she comes and goes is private."

Nicole touched her right cheek. "Does she have a mole, right here?"

30

Paris, March 1952

Squire rarely wore his reading glasses around Ruby. He raised his book from his lap and leveled it with his face. He had no problem deciphering the words if he held the book half his arm's length away. The two sat upright, dressed in their day clothes, on the long side of his narrow bed. Ruby waited for Squire to finish a poem from the very book he'd carried through the war.

He took the pencil from his pocket and wrote on a dog-eared page while Ruby looked on: *RubyMae, this poem expresses much better than I could why I worry about you.* He cleared his throat, "'Passing Love,' by Langston Hughes," and dropped the book into his lap.

Ruby jumped up from the bed and faced Squire. "'Passing Love' by Langston Hughes." She mimicked his serious tone and erect posture. "Squire Handy, I do not need to hear that poem again. You know it by heart, and I've heard it so many times, that I now know it by heart. I get it."

"RubyMae, I want you to know how I feel."

"I already know. And it's Ruby, just Ruby. Can you get that through your head?" Ruby marched to the window. "Enough."

In their month and a half together, Squire and Ruby had fallen into a routine. Him doing homework at night, reading Langston and bungled French poetry out loud. Her listening, trying not to compare the poetry to the music Arnett played. In Mississippi, a younger Squire was a friend to talk to, to tease; a platonic love had filled her then. Arnett and the thrill of the forbidden had opened her to the world in the way she wanted to hold on to forever.

"Squire Handy, if I spend one more minute cooped up in this room while spring is trying to find its way to Paris, I'm gonna scream." She put on her coat, grabbed her purse, his hat, and opened the door.

Up until now Squire hadn't concerned himself with facts and details. He rarely left the Latin Quarter, and when he ventured from that *arrondissement*, he focused on his map. Not one foot had he set in the Métro, nor, except for the night he and Ruby returned to his room, had he ridden in a cab. He visited the Eiffel Tower, walked the Boulevard St.-Michel to the Seine and Notre Dame, then strolled back up St.-Michel to the Sorbonne. Anyone seeing him would have suggested he wipe the scowl from his face and enjoy, but remnants of it lived on his brow. A hint of his frustration crept into his letters to Malvina and filled the pages when he had no one else to talk to. The considerable structures of Paris made even Squire, a tall man by anybody's measurement, appear insignificant; the language, the gloomy winter, the sad faces sent him back to his room. The ongoing construction to resurrect Paris's glory. The rich Americans who pointed and asked what part of Africa he was from. The crusted bread. His mispronunciations, R's scratching the back of his throat. He hadn't captured his feelings in poetry. They lived in his head. Until now.

"I hate Paris."

"You're probably the only person who thinks that way." Given his agreement to wander again to another landmark, Ruby jumped at his declaration as they turned on rue Soufflot. Her early days in Paris, she diminished her curiosity by acquainting herself with the stone buildings so different from any in the States, certainly not in Mississippi: the Opéra, the Pont Neuf, Les Invalides, the Louvre. In all of their combined lives, neither Squire, Ruby, nor Arnett had been exposed to buildings so grand and dirtied with history. Arnett came close, taking into account the Empire State in New York and Chicago's Board of Trade with the statue perched at the top, the tallest buildings he'd claimed to have seen.

Ruby yanked at Squire's hand. "I've waited all my life to be here, and just think—for years, I didn't know it existed."

Two weeks wandering the city. Two weeks roaming through Paris. They had meandered the length of the Île de la Cité, marveling at the tiny island in the middle of the Seine, and wandered back to gaze at the curves and arches of Notre Dame and the gargoyles perched on its roof. They rested against cement balustrades edging the Seine and compared it to the Mississippi; and now they walked before the Panthéon, the church and burial place of the famous whose names and history neither of them had ever heard of. Squire appreciated books, not the columns and dome of this monument. He didn't marvel at the tribute printed in gold, *Aux Grands Hommes La Patrie Reconnaissante*, to the men buried inside. He ignored the dedication and scrutinized Ruby's face.

"It's circles of gold and light inside." Ruby tugged at his sleeve. "Do you want to see?"

"Nope." Squire shrugged. "You're what I love about Paris." They strolled the perimeter of the church, Squire observed Ruby and not the splendid architecture before him. He touched Ruby's arm. Accidentally or on purpose, his hands were on or never far from Ruby: her shoulder, her elbow, her cheek, her hair. When they reached the steps again, he hugged her.

Ruby squirmed out of his embrace and set her hands on her hips. "Squire Handy, there is more to Paris than me. You're missing everything." Ruby squinted and motioned to Squire to do the same. "And reach out your hand. See? Stretch and it seems you can touch the Eiffel Tower right from here. How can you not love Paris?"

"I love *you*."

"And I love Paris."

"You only came here because he dragged you. This isn't a place for Negroes. This isn't the place for us."

"You're wrong Squire. Mississippi isn't the place for us, if that's what you're thinking. Ain't nothing that place has to offer me but country roads and dust. Shameless gossiping. The same folk sitting next to you in church on Sunday, smiling and shaking hands. Everybody so pious and pure. Nothing going on. Nobody going nowhere. People hating you because of the color of your skin."

"That isn't the whole USA, and you know it." He moved to take her in his arms, but she pushed at him. "They say California's nice."

"I want to stay in Paris. I have friends."

"Friends? Those men? They're the friends you're talking about?"

"Yvette is my friend."

"She's French and all caught up in that fat trumpet player. You can't survive on singing." Squire choked, on the verge of tears. He swiped his palm over his face before lowering himself onto one knee. "Marry me, Ruby. Marry me and come home. I'll take care of you. I promise."

"Stay in Paris. Give me time to think. To let go of Arnett. It's only been a month."

Squire hung his head. These unbroken weeks together, loving her, her loving, was his Paris. He slipped up. He meant and hadn't meant to propose. Not now. Not this way. But the prospect of spring, the blue sky and cotton clouds, tricked him into thinking this was the place. This was where she was going to say yes. "Isn't what we do important to you? Aren't I important to you?"

"There are things I want." A plan came to her when Squire knocked on her door, her lucky number 21. The picture in her mind was clear: a black limousine waiting for her outside the Casino de Paris, men and women applauding and toasting her with champagne. She saw all types of men lavishing her with furs and diamonds, escorting her to fancy clubs and dancing until dawn.

"I want to sing. To be on the stage, the crowd swooning for me, not Josephine and Ella. My name in lights, posters all over the city."

"You're pretty enough to turn heads, Ruby. But you can't sing. Malvina can sing."

"Shut up about Malvina!" Ruby reached out her hand as if to slap Squire. Instead, she waved a finger in his face. "Don't tell me about can and can't. You think I got this far on can't?"

"No. But he didn't marry you," Squire whispered. "That's a can't right there. What kind of man is that to love?"

"You don't know a thing about Arnett Dupree. So just keep quiet, Squire Handy. Anyway, I'm not talking love. I'm talking dreams. Me and Arnett had dreams. I have dreams." Ruby marched from the Panthéon, Squire in her wake. They hastened past a woman with a rambunctious dog that nipped at Squire's leg, and a pharmacy, its windows filled with green bottles.

"You can have others. I can give them to you, Ruby. Different, yes, but ones that can come true."

"If he hadn't been so foolish, if he hadn't fallen from that ledge."

"Arnett didn't fall, Ruby, he did what he did on purpose. He jumped sure as if he was headed somewhere."

"We were on our way. It was just a matter of time."

"I don't have time, Ruby. I'm failing my classes. Paris isn't for me."

Ruby plugged her ears against the pining in Squire's voice. For the past month, he'd watched over her. Gone with her to the rue de Vintimille to tap on the *propriétaire*'s painted door and stand with his hat in his hand while Ruby spoke to the woman in broken French and told her she was a lost soul. When the *propriétaire* wanted to know about this new man standing so tall beside her and surely able to pay, Ruby whispered, in French, that he was her friend who preferred men to women and was unable to help with the rent. Squire, understanding none of the conversation, tipped his hat to the woman. "S'il vous plaît. Une semaine plus." Another week, he pleaded, and the *propriétaire* beamed at him and at Ruby as if to say, what a shame, so striking. But without new renters to take over Ruby's room, and all of her belongings that could be sold if the beautiful woman never returned, giving an extra week was practical.

"You think I was a fool to come here, don't you? You think Arnett messed up my life?"

"I think now we can be together."

31

The subjunctive verb tense is used to convey wish, doubt, denial, worry, emotion, and command. Beginners can practice the verbs "wish" and "doubt" to master this part of speech.

souhaiter (soo eh tay)	to wish
il est douteux que (eel ay doo tuh kuh)	it's doubtful that
il faut que (eel foh kuh)	one must, have to
craindre (kran druh)	to fear

From behind the painted wood door, a woman's brusque voice demanded that Laurent restate his name and purpose. The rasp of metal scraping against wood grew louder until, at last, the door opened. Nicole ducked behind Laurent, letting his shoulders block her view. "Bonjour, Madame." Laurent's tone was questioning. In rapid French, he repeated his name, apologized for the intrusion, and introduced Nicole as the daughter of Ruby Garrett.

Without shifting the door beyond the twelve inches she'd allowed it to open, Madame Simon guarded the entry to her apartment and glared at them over bright blue reading glasses.

Nicole stepped beside Laurent. The woman was taller than Nicole, despite her dependence on a walker, with a face filled with lines as complicated as a Métro map. No mole. Nicole wiped her hands on her shirt, not knowing what her reaction might have been if the woman had been Ruby. This woman's voice quivered. She didn't speak English. Laurent's intonations implied questions, her lengthy comebacks, answers. "Madame doubts she will be able to help. She wants you to step close."

Madame Simon motioned to Nicole. She spoke, Laurent translated. "She was the landlord when Ruby and Yvette lived here. You're the brown baby—and I'm translating here—that she took care of when your mother was working. She says, even after all these years, she sees you have her eyes."

"Well, I've never heard that before." Friends mentioned she favored Malvina, but never such a direct comparison, no shared features. Watching the woman watch her, Nicole shivered from the same cold chill, the same confusion she felt when she found out Ruby was her mother.

"I was born here? Where's Ruby, Laurent? Where's Ruby?"

Madame Simon shook her head and spoke without pausing for translation.

"She's saying when Ruby moved out, you weren't with her. She never saw either of you again. But Yvette lived here." The elderly woman's voice turned stern. She grumbled at their questions and invasion of her privacy. It was not respectful to share such private information with strangers, even with one with the eyes of a woman she'd known. Madame reached for the door handle, simultaneously pushed herself backward, and closed the door.

"And the records and books? Livres?" Nicole searched for the right vocabulary. "Does she know anything?"

Laurent received a curt answer before the door slammed. "She says many American musicians lived here over the years. No one else is left."

Nicole guessed from Laurent's face that he was thinking of the music that once drifted in these halls. She was thinking of Ruby—come out, come out, wherever you are. "Damn! Damn damn damn."

"It doesn't click. She was curious, otherwise she wouldn't have met with us."

"You call that a meeting? I say it's a wild-goose chase." Nicole jiggled the elevator call button.

"Give me a little credit, please." This time Laurent punched the call button for the sluggish elevator. "I do this for a living."

Without warning Madame's door creaked open, the space between the jamb and the edge narrow and unwelcoming. Without speaking, Madame glared at Nicole and tossed a matchbook at her before retreating behind her door.

Laurent retrieved the red matchbook from the floor. He curled his lips in his history professor smirk. "This is from the Casino de Paris."

"A casino? She wants me to go gambling?"

32

Paris, March 1952

Three days Ruby held the plan in her head. All those women she'd heard tell of—Josephine, Bricktop, Inez, even artists like Lois Mailou years before—they came to Paris and made it, even if it was just for a while. If they could do it so could she. On this fourth day, when the frustrations between her and Squire were unresolved, she began a new routine, a secret routine: out of bed and out the door as soon as Squire left. She headed for St.-Germain. In every café she passed, she searched for musicians. She paced the rue de Seine waiting for one to exit the Hôtel La Louisiane, the smell of fried chicken so strong her mouth watered. At Club Tabou, the janitor pushed his mop across the dirty floor, cleaning after the regulars and the tourists had danced late into the night. "Revenez ce soir, Madame," he ordered. Ruby didn't have to think twice: no coming back later that evening if Squire had his way. Club St.-Germain-des-Prés, Le Chat Qui Pêche—she went to these and others, with addresses and no names, in search of auditions. Finding singing gigs was a nighttime job, and Squire was not a nighttime man.

At the Café Tournon she dropped into a chair, lit a cigarette, and opened the little bar of chocolate she'd saved. Ruby ordered, splurging on coffee and a croissant instead of the dinner she was supposed to be shopping for. How long she sat, she did not know or care. She lingered over her coffee, grateful for the free refills the waiter poured in return for practicing his English.

She saw the piano player, his cheeks jiggling with every step, before he reached the café. Poppa. Ruby inched her dress up and over her knees and turned so that her profile was exposed to the street. A half grin crossed his wide face. Poppa, whose name Arnett spoke before he fell. Poppa, who'd told her man to go back home, to give up his woman. Poppa, whose gigs were one hundred percent steady.

He tipped his hat and sat opposite her without her invitation. "Sorry, I couldn't make the funeral. Haven't been to one since my brother got killed—Arnett reminded me a bit of him. He was a good man having a bad time." He spoke as if Arnett's funeral had been yesterday instead of over a month ago. "How ya doin', baby?"

"Ain't nothing I can't handle." She spat her answer.

"Hold on now, baby, you've got no call to be mean to ole Poppa."

"I'd say I do. Poppa." Ruby tilted her head, knowing sugar caught more flies than salt. "I'd say you owe me, don'tcha, Poppa?"

Poppa chuckled; his cheeks shook and his belly jiggled along. "What's that, baby?"

"I believe it's on account of you I'm in a predicament." She pouted. "You know what happened before Arnett jumped from that window? *You* told him he couldn't play, said he needed to get out of town. I'd say you owe me for that, Poppa, seeing as how it's your fault I'm on my own now."

"Now, wait a minute, baby, you can't blame Poppa for that. Everybody saw he was feeling low." A thin film of sweat popped onto his nose. He squirmed and kneaded the brim of his hat between trembling thumbs. In broken French, he ordered a double scotch on the rocks with milk on the side and another coffee for Ruby. "I can't help the way it turned out. You need money, food?" Poppa withdrew a wad of dollars from his pocket.

Ignoring the money, Ruby lifted the cigarette from Poppa's hand. He watched the cigarette move from her hand to her red lips. She inhaled a long drag, letting smoke curl in her open mouth. Arnett would want her to do it, for revenge. He would want her to make it in Paris, to do whatever it took. No going back—not for Arnett's woman. Living in some small, country town, forgetting she'd ever been in Paris, reducing her stay to a postcard locked in a dresser drawer. A husband and a passel of babies—was that what she came thousands of miles for?

"I was thinking you know a manager who'd give me a chance. Singing—not the star. But soon." She blew smoke into his face and waited for him to pour milk from a tiny pitcher into his scotch. He gulped down the entire drink. What he was thinking, Ruby didn't care. "You know, Poppa, a girl has to take care of herself. And you owe me."

"Ain't a whole lot of colored women making a living off of music in Paris. And you can't count Josephine, because she go way back with the French. Music is tough." He sniffed and wiped his nose with the back of his hand. "You oughta think about heading back home."

"But, I am home." Ruby lowered her head long enough for her lashes to flutter once, then twice. When she lifted her head, Poppa's bloodshot eyes were looking straight at her and she suspected this was not his first drink today. Every musician, colored and French, had heard he drank nonstop, but when he played his piano, no one, drunk or sober, could keep up with him. The faster they went, the faster he went, inverting chords and basing his improvisations on modes instead of keys, putting notes where no one else placed them. Riffs and improvisations that strung a song out for an hour. The night after he tried to play along, Arnett had cried at Poppa's comment: "Boy, when I come at you, you got to throw it all out on the floor."

"Now, you're not trying to tell me about my singing, are you, Poppa?"

"No, baby. I'm saying getting work is tough enough for a colored man. Can't imagine how it'd be for a colored woman on her own in this town."

"I know I can make it, Poppa. I just need a sponsor. Someone to give me a break."

Squire returned in the afternoon to find not his beloved Ruby waiting for him, but the echo of empty and the scent of silence. He sobbed loud enough for his neighbor to bang on their common wall and picked over what she had left behind on the bed: a blue, pocket-size French dictionary, a postcard, and a key.

On the face of the postcard, the camera captured a couple in the throes of a frantic dance. The woman's skirt blurred high in waves at her waist. The man's hands trapped in an eternal finger-pop. The saxophonist, the drummer, and the bass man caught in a single flashy note.

Ruby's scrawl spread over the back of the postcard. What wasn't written hurt most and made him feel foolish.

Squire,

The joint is jumping and so am I.

Ruby

33

Reflexive verbs are used in several ways. In general, these verbs denote action that refers back to the speaker.

se rendre compte (suh rahn druh compt)	to realize
déménager (day meh nah zhay)	to move
se douter de (suh doo tay duh)	to suspect
se blâmer (suh blah may)	to blame oneself

Oh, it's a music hall!"

"And a place where black dancers were welcomed during the fifties."

Lights and a grand marquee edging the Casino's façade announced concerts and upcoming shows. Beside it, the late afternoon sun reflected off a steel- and glass-fronted establishment Laurent described as having replaced one of trumpeter Sidney Bechet's nightclubs. An African security guard watched over the side door. He accepted the money Laurent slipped into his hand and touched a finger to his lips before allowing them to enter.

Nearly every inch of the lobby was red: quilted leather doors, floors, velvet walls, arched ceiling. Up a short flight of stairs and past the bar, two costumed dancers lounged on leather stools. Multicolored light, red, blue, and yellow the strongest, radiated from the stained glass window of nymphs playing musical instruments.

They retraced their steps back to the narrow staircase, the stairwell familiar and new to Nicole at the same time. She imagined leggy, bejeweled dancers dashing up the stairs and beyond to the door with a circle of glass near its top, a porthole to backstage. The skin on Nicole's arms rippled with goose bumps. She stumbled and fell against the wall, guarding her head with her hands. The swish of beaded gowns and the rustle of feather headdresses were the last noises she heard before she lost consciousness.

Nicole awoke to find herself seated in a chair. Laurent kneeling at her side. He rubbed the chill bumps on her arms until they disappeared.

"I'm taking you home with me."

"No. I'm hungry and cranky. It's a reaction to stress. I feel like sleeping for twenty-four hours. I'm sick of this freak search. I won't be good company."

"I'm not looking for company. You need to rest. In case you faint again. You don't need to be alone."

"If I stay, I have to say that with the mood I'm in"—Nicole grinned—"'staying' will be the extent of my visit."

Laurent shrugged. "When you stay with me, and I'm hoping that sooner or later you will, I want you to be one hundred percent present—not distracted by letters, Ruby, or fainting spells."

Two days later, Nicole relaxed on the living room couch. Tamara's suggestion to stay in an apartment, instead of a hotel, gave her the freedom to come and go whenever she wanted, to eat and lounge without interruption from maid service or hotel clerks, to feel at home, and to think. She figured, after her visit to the Casino, that Madame Simon had given them a partial truth. Returning, alone, to rue de Vintimille was an option to consider. To watch, a snoopy detective, the comings and goings of guests in that hotel. To scrutinize women's faces. Other than the mole, how was she supposed to distinguish Ruby from any older woman strolling with purpose? Nicole didn't know French law or how to translate stalking, but hanging out in the lobby or loitering on the corner weren't good alternatives. It came back to the letters, a cycle with no beginning or end; she'd search between the lines for other clues and hope for a place to cling to.

September 1952

Ruby,

I looked for you everywhere before I left. I was so worried after the June riots. They came close to the Monaco where Negro students often gather. Hundreds of North Africans arrested. I know no Negroes were hurt. You hid from me, not answering my letters then and not now. How could you be so mean? Even Yvette refused to tell me where you were when I returned to rue de Vintimille. So, I'm sending this letter to her, in hopes that she'll pass it on. Are you all right? I'm assuming you are. We were meant for each other, Ruby, and you let a cock-eyed dream ruin it. But I have moved on.

I wanted you to hear it from me. Malvina and I are getting married. She is a gentle and wise woman. She has stayed by my side while I've made a last ditch effort to get back my father's property. She's been a comfort to me. Ours will be a good match. A steady and caring marriage without the passion, I expect, or the fire you and I had. (I no longer wish for that kind of love.) But the love between Malvina and I will carry us through the years because we are solidly based in friendship, we understand one another.

Don't hold this against your sister. But then why should you, after all it was you that left me. I hope you will be happy. I won't bother you again. I'd leave you with Langston's words. But then, I don't have to write them out, do I? You took my book. Page 47. Read it and think of me. I am passing on your love, Ruby.

Not one day will pass that I will not think of you, not one minute that I will not love you. I hope that idea provokes you, and I hope, from time to time, you'll think of me, too.

Squire

The knock was polite and unobtrusive. When Nicole opened the door, Monsieur Large bowed deeply then thrust an envelope at her. "Une femme est passé, Madame. Elle a laissé cette lettre pour vous." Monsieur had a sense of the dramatic; he bowed again and headed for the elevator before Nicole learned about the woman who gave him this letter.

Ma chérie, Nicole.

That's part of the name my friend gave you. I'm glad to see that Malvina and Squire didn't change it. I waited at your door this morning, thinking I'd catch you on your way in or out. I wanted to surprise you, but I changed my mind. I want to see you. Can you meet me tomorrow? 1:00 for lunch at the café on rue de Buci opposite where the flower market is during the week. It's not far from you and returning to this part of Paris brings back so many memories. Please come.

Ruby

34

Paris, April 1952

A week after she left Squire, Ruby was living higher on the hog than she ever had. Poppa put her up in a real hotel to avoid the woman he lived with—a fine French woman who'd grown wide according to Poppa, and lost her sexual nature. His generosity came without effort. They rode in cabs, dined at Haynes's, ate steaks at a restaurant not quite as expensive or fancy as the famous Maxim's but close enough, and ordered champagne at a jazz club on the Champs-Élysées.

It was Monday when she allowed his slobbering lips to kiss her mouth, him a middle-aged man eager for a young woman. Ruby was careful not to let his lips stray far from her neck and square shoulders. Tuesday, he paid her week's rent and promised to pay when it came due again. Thursday night Ruby allowed his callused fingers to rub against her, like the middle C key on his piano, until her nipples stiffened through her dress from chill, not desire. He promised to buy her a new outfit. Saturday she sported a satin dress with sparkles at her neck and shoes with straps crisscrossing her high arches. Sunday evening, she let her robe slip from her shoulders as if she didn't know he was watching. Ruby closed the thin robe, her breasts clearly outlined under the fabric. Poppa's hands trembled and he sang a made-up song in his raspy voice. "I'm in love with a sugar woman, who don't give a damn if my love comes down."

That night Ruby sang four songs with the band. After she saw Poppa at the café and through the following Tuesday, she prodded at his manhood and poked at his guilt until she rid him of any notion of her giving herself to him. Without further displays or lovemaking from Ruby, Poppa went back to his afternoon double shots of scotch and his good-cooking woman, and forgot every promise he had made.

Without Poppa, no club owner took Ruby seriously. It was the gaunt photographer in the soldier's uniform, Loot, who saved her not with money but information: the American Negro woman who owned Chez Inez on the rue Champollion not far from the Sorbonne was hiring singers. Loot went with Ruby to the club, her watching for Squire. She surprised herself, half wanting him and half afraid to see the hurt that surely lined his face. If he loved her why had he given up? How could a man so scared of buildings and language, streets and foods with names he could not pronounce know where to start? How could a man who declared his love so fiercely, who hated Paris, not try? Ruby allowed herself to think these questions once, and then turned her attention to Chez Inez's.

The famous Inez was not at the club. Ruby waited until the manager toted a bottle of cognac and one glass to the table beside the platform that passed for a stage. Loot introduced Ruby and left. The manager, Delia, wore men's pants and a thick wool sweater, and smoked cigarettes in a succession suggesting agitation. When Ruby told her she had come to audition, the woman patted the empty chair alongside hers.

"You know singing, it is funny. You have it or you don't—I have never heard in between." Her accent bespoke her French citizenship, but her attitude was one hundred percent American. Delia filled a glass, downed that shot, and poured another without offering Ruby a drink.

"I've been practicing. A friend's been helping me."

"Ruby, you are the most beautiful woman I know, but, chérie, your voice, it is nice but not nice enough for my customers to pay to hear." Her voice was rasping and scratchy when she spoke again. "To tell you the truth, I don't think you can sing, but the men, they pay attention because you are pretty and sexy. But pretty does not fill a club and sexy does not buy drinks. Because of Arnett, I will give you the chance. If it does not work tonight, it will not work at all, anywhere. You dig?"

When Ruby could not move the zipper of her fancy dress past her waist, Yvette fashioned a deep V in the back and wove ribbons from side to side so that the dress stayed put. "You know I am not the expert, ma chère, but my mother she have four children after me, and the swelling I am seeing tells me a little one is growing inside you."

What Ruby contemplated, staring at her bulging midsection, was what her mother would say knowing her daughter had slept with two men within the course of a short month, married to neither, loving both. She didn't want Yvette to call her the name Martha had spoken as she laid her whipping stick on Ruby. *I can forgive a lie. I cannot a whore.*

Yvette hugged her friend. "This is okay, Ruby, this love, l'amour, it takes us women in many directions."

The deep cellar was crowded for a Thursday. Ruby sat at the bar and sipped a bourbon and water. The club was filled with regulars—Yvette, Loot, a bass player and trumpeter from the Club St.-Germain-des-Prés—and a few newcomers. She prayed that no one noticed her belly, forgetting that in clubs, in this world of throbbing beats, snapping fingers, smoke and booze, no one paid attention to anything except the music.

At the break, Ronald, the lefty drummer, came over to the bar. He pecked her cheeks in the way Paris Negroes accepted as their own. "You ready?" He blew smoke past her right ear.

"I'm ready." She hid her shaking hands in the gathers of her crinoline skirt. She had prepared for this night. Listening to Yvette's records, rememorizing Sarah Vaughan, Edith Piaf, and Juliette Greco songs, and writing their lyrics phonetically; repeating them until she was certain the song was her own. Days beforehand, Ruby had practiced, stopping and repeating according to what she recalled from Arnett's coaching. Seeing his face, that teasing twinkle when she got a song just right.

"So how we gonna do this set?"

"I've got two songs," Ruby said. Arnett had teased, and she believed he was happy, that she was wearing down the grooves on Sarah's "I've Got a Crush on You." She remembered saying he was doing the same with all the Charlie Parker he listened to. The easy songs were her favorites—no blues sad as Billie's, but songs that lingered on their way out her throat, songs no longer on the charts in the states but new in Paris, a tad slow, a mix of Sarah and Ella with her own spin.

"Come with me." Ronald motioned to the stairs.

No two *caves* were the same in Paris. Some were undersized, and men, women, musicians, and their instruments stuffed themselves inside. Some had harbored members of the Resistance during the war and were big enough for tables and chairs. Most all had stairways that led up and to the outside. Inez's place was roomy enough, but in every *cave* the staircases were the same. Ruby adjusted, her shoes longer than the steps she carefully climbed, resting her head against the craggy stone to let a touch of nausea pass.

Outside the club, Ronald reached into his pocket and brought out matches and half of a smashed joint. He sniffed, then lit the skinny stick and sucked. After his second hit, he waved the joint and exhaled in Ruby's face. "It's a good crowd. You can handle them, but this'll calm your nerves."

Arnett had smoked reefer to loosen up and make his licks come easy, teasing Ruby when she complained. "No mo Joe Below, baby, I'ma get paid." She inhaled, the drummer ogling her every move. The dope went straight to her head, leaving her giggling within seconds.

Inside, the stage resembled two sides of a fruit crate bound together. Along with Ronald's drums and cymbals squeezed close together, a trumpet man and a bass man, wide as the instrument he strummed, fought for space. Ruby ambled to the stage. Hot light beat the top of her head. Missing Arnett, particularly now, she imagined him sitting at the center table suggesting she begin. Unable to remember the touch of his fingers or call to mind his smell, she mixed that sadness into her song, "Since I Fell for You," a solemn one, calling for emotion.

Ruby mumbled through until she became accustomed to the smoke. She wanted a cigarette. She wanted another hit of the weed. The band led her into the second song before she caught her breath. The next show she would come down on her phrasing, "I've got a crush on you, sweetie pie," and stop to let the audience appreciate it, find a lone man in the crowd and sing to him.

At the end of the set, half the audience applauded—the other half had never abandoned their huddled conversations and liquor. The waiter inched between tables, trading overflowing glasses for empty ones. From the corner, a man shouted, "Hey, we're over here," to a thin man across the room, and everyone watched as a famous writer and his friends moved from the stairs to the bar. Ruby started her encore, snapping her fingers and waiting for the band to come in on the right note. The crowd's ruckus swelled over her faint beginning, letting her know they didn't want one. At least not from her.

35

The verb tense *passé composé* describes actions that took place and ended in the past or have been recently completed.

pas du tout (pah dew too)	not at all
pas mal (pah mahl)	not bad
n'est-ce pas? (ness pah)	isn't this?
n'importe quoi (nam port qwah)	anything

The afternoon sunlight bounced off the cut-glass brooch on Nicole's dress. Lipstick, a mist of perfume on her neck and arms—she was ready, but early. Squire considered promptness a sure sign of respect. Work or play, his habit was to show up early, and he expected everyone he knew to do the same. Unlike most of the others drilled into her head, Nicole followed her father's rule to this day. She surveyed the diners to see before being seen, to check out her birth mother before she raised her guard. The restaurant was packed, except for a couple of tables spilling onto the sidewalk. Men scanned newspapers, couples held hands, a smattering of young women sat alone.

Laurent had provided the stationery, addressed the envelopes to get swift and proper notice at the post office, and suggested what to write. He hadn't suggested questions. No prepping for the spasm in her chest or the challenge her knees presented as she tried to stand firm in her hiding space. What should she do? Crumple at the sight of a mother long lost and never known?

At ten minutes after the hour, a well-dressed woman situated herself at a table near the curb and scanned the menu. Low-heeled pumps, loose-fitting navy jacket offset by a bright orange scarf whose edge she fingered absentmindedly. She carried neither newspaper nor book and did not check her watch or glance up in expectation. She held a cigarette between her index and forefinger, a parody of a forties advertisement, her right hand poised close to her mouth. Instead of exhaling, she allowed the smoke to float from her mouth. This woman was petite and fragile, not how Nicole imagined the proportions of the woman in the photo. Her attitude, the effect she had had on Squire, and Malvina too, conveyed stature.

It wasn't that she reminded Nicole of Malvina Handy. It wasn't that Nicole saw herself in that face. After years of scrutinizing the photo, she simply knew. The mole, faded but prominent; painted or natural brows perfectly arched. The hint of brown in her creamy skin. Remnants of a scar on her chin. Nicole might not have distinguished her in a crowd. Without distractions, she was obvious. She spoke when Nicole approached her table.

"Roxane?" Ruby's voice was a lyric to a song; jazz and Mississippi tinged with France.

No remnants of Nicole's baby face. Her body had grown far beyond the chubby toddler in the family album. No longer were her cheeks round, her hair lustrous. She was startled by the sharpness of Ruby's recall and puzzled by what feature in her face made her recognizable from so long ago. Then, observing the Parisians walking the street in front of them, she became aware that Ruby knew her not from a feature she remembered, but elimination—she was the brownest of any passerby. For one minute, Nicole wished that the skin she loved were lighter, forcing Ruby to remember the face of her child. Ruby's heritage wasn't as identifiable. Hers was the color that, at home, might have caused a black person to glance twice or focus on her mouth, her nose, or the roots of her hair in search of a clue to her ethnicity.

"You *are* Roxane." Ruby removed a second cigarette from her pack and lit it with a metal lighter decorated with swirls of faded gold on both its sides. The lighter looked like an antique, but when she flicked the thumbwheel, it struck the flint and blue flame lit the wick nub. She offered the cigarette to Nicole and lit another. Nicole took a deep drag of the strong tobacco. An idiosyncrasy, or nerves, this mother and daughter had in common.

"Nicole-Marie. Nicole. Roxane is my middle name." Nicole exhaled.

"Sit, Roxane. You look like you've seen a ghost. You're not prone to fainting spells, are you?"

"Given my reason for coming, would you be surprised? And it's Nicole. Mother calls me Nicki."

The resemblances existed, not mirror images, but genes that made themselves evident. She wasn't seeing herself, although Ruby's eyes were hers. The similarity was in their voices, as if Nicole had dialed home and listened to herself on the answering machine.

"And look what you're wearing!" Ruby fingered the brooch on Nicole's dress then spread her fingers in a wide arc, suddenly animated. "That's my brooch. I never thought I'd see it again. Malvina bought it from one of her classmates at college and gave it to me for my sixteenth birthday. It was our secret."

Nicole scowled; the brooch was simply another one of the secrets and coincidences at the core of what she used to call truth. Ruby had been near, in the photo and the brooch. She fingered the surface of the costume jewelry; it alternated between rough and even. The blue glass formed blossoming petals, distinctive as the pot of impatiens sitting on their table. "Mother gave it to me when I turned sixteen."

"I stole the money she was saving when I left home. I didn't think it was stealing at the time, but it was." Ruby tossed her head distractedly, showing Nicole how men must have found her alluring. "I left the brooch hoping she'd know I was trying to repay her."

"What do you want me to say?"

"Malvina loved me back then. I thought you'd want to know." Ruby laid her hand on Nicole's; two friends reunited on a leisurely Sunday afternoon. Nicole jerked away and scanned the street for Loot or Laurent. She wanted their help. Loot as distraction; Laurent as journalist, savvy at interrogating.

"I want to know more than the story of a piece of costume jewelry."

"I thought someone was playing a trick on me and your letter was from Malvina, the handwriting was so neat. Did you know she won a prize for penmanship in high school? My sister."

Nicole equated their exchange to a game. She wasn't interested in chess, didn't understand it; even after she'd read that a man who taught chess to urban kids claimed the game encouraged strategic thinking. Nicole was tempted to ask if Ruby played chess: aversion was her strategy. Was that what the queen did, avoid capture by moving sideways instead of plowing forward?

"I'd like to hear stories, if you and I weren't birth mother and daughter meeting for the first time. As it is, I have tons of questions. If I were younger this conversation might be about being loved." Rejection, Nicole reasoned, hurt at any age.

"I'm sure Malvina and Squire loved you. I never doubted that."

"I'm merely doing what Mother wants."

"Are you?"

"You don't remind me of my mother at all." Nicole searched for a trace of Malvina in Ruby's face, and Ruby didn't shy from the scrutiny. Malvina's face had aged after her stroke, after becoming Squire's caretaker. Age lined Ruby's differently—worldliness, she speculated, not responsibility. From what Nicole observed, the sisters were not the same, not in spirit or physical features.

"Malvina and I have different fathers. Hers died in a farming accident, that's why we don't have the same last name. Our mother's genes weren't strong enough to make our relationship obvious."

A sole portrait in the family album comprised all Nicole's knowledge of her grandfather. When she questioned how a brown daughter came from a light-skinned father, Malvina's answer was that skin color played tricks on blacks. She didn't have the terms for genes or DNA back then, but Malvina made it clear that the tricks went back to the days when slaves and masters mixed. Blue eyes and brown skin. Freckles. Red hair, good hair. Light skin and nappy hair. With her partial revelation, Malvina's hesitancy was clear—she hadn't wanted to explain the truth that led to Ruby.

Ruby unfolded a handkerchief and dabbed at Nicole's cheeks where tears had started to streak her makeup. Nicole yanked the dainty cloth from Ruby's hand.

"Only my mother can do that."

"I *am* your mother."

"We could sit here forever and argue the meaning of motherhood. I don't even know what to call you." Sitting beside Ruby, Nicole wished for Malvina. For her sense of honor and unselfishness. Even in her moralizing moments, Malvina's actions came from love.

"Call me Ruby, if that makes you comfortable."

Ruby watched her daughter, and Nicole watched Ruby, amazed that an eighty-year-old woman was still so provocative. A server stopped at their table. Ruby ordered in fluid, effortless French; no hesitation, no trace of Mississippi. Within moments, the server delivered two *cafés crèmes* to the table. Ruby lifted her cup to pursed lips. She worked her mouth as if any minute important information would break through her lips.

"Which of my letters reached you . . . Ruby?"

"That's not a question to worry yourself with." Cigarette in one hand, coffee in the other, Ruby seemed a parody of how

Americans expected French women to behave. "What do you know about me?"

"That my father had it bad for you. That my mother wants nothing to do with you." Nicole pounded her cigarette into a flimsy tin ashtray. "They never told me who you were. Mother never mentioned a sister."

"You don't have a southern accent."

"I'm from California."

"So that's where they hid you." Stubbing the short butt in the ashtray, Ruby shook another cigarette from her pack and rolled it between her fingers.

"Did you ever try to contact me?"

"That's a better question for Malvina."

"Why didn't you keep me in Paris with you?" Nicole spoke quickly to hold back the emotion battling behind her eyelids. "Didn't you want me?"

"I never doubted you'd be in good hands. How is my sister?" Smoke swirled through Ruby's lips before it dissolved into the air. She reached to pat Nicole's hand again, and Nicole let it rest, momentarily, on top of hers. "She was so eager to have Squire. Has she been a good mother?"

"Ask her yourself." Nicole grabbed her cell phone and punched in her parents' number. When Malvina answered, Nicole hit the speaker button and set the phone on the table. "Say hello to Ruby, Mother."

"You see? A sister knows." Malvina's speech was heavy with the grogginess of sleep and surprise.

"Bonjour, chérie." Ruby pushed her hair back despite the length, too short to bother her face. She didn't fidget, didn't flip the sleeves of her cashmere jacket to check her watch. It was the corners of her mouth that suddenly wrinkled; Ruby was nervous, too.

"What does she—"

Ruby tipped the phone in her direction and jabbed the red button, disconnecting Malvina and the rest of her question.

"What are you doing?" Nicole called into the dead silence for Malvina. When there was no answer she shook the phone at Ruby. "My mother is the reason I'm sitting here right now, and you hung up on her?"

"You can't expect to fill in the gaps and tidy them up in a telephone call. I used to miss her, my sister. The tables got turned, didn't they?"

Anyone seeing Ruby and Nicole wouldn't have suspected that the older woman, not the younger one, was a risk taker. Nicole envied what had moved Ruby away from ordinary. That was the inheritance she wanted. Ruby tried to press her hands to Nicole's face. Nicole moved away. Over half a century to reveal the truth and, for all Nicole wished she'd known long ago, listening to Ruby now, she was unable to change these new truths.

"We're not long-lost friends catching up on good times." Nicole snatched her purse and tossed money on the table.

"Please, Nicole. Wait. Long ago, I had a speech ready, but it's long gone. And I came for you, not my sister."

36

Paris, Spring 1952

The gig at Club Inez ended the night it began.

After the last set, Ruby and Ronald, the left-handed drummer, ambled along a noiseless street far from the Seine and the crowds lingering at the river. "Your voice is okay, baby." Ronald's breath combined the worst of scotch and weed. "But you look better." He tilted his head, trying to kiss her lips; missing them, he continued to her ear and mouthed an invitation. "I can help."

Ruby backed away from the man, letting him know she was offended, but not enough to make him think his chance was gone. This drummer was no Arnett, or Squire. Shirt in sore need of a good pressing, hair cropped close to his scalp, tie dotted with food stains—he was a man who didn't bother with his body or clothes. Except for his hands: blunt fingernails, buffed from manicures.

"I can do it, you know." Ronald stepped to Ruby and stuck his tongue into her ear. "Take you from good to great."

Arms straight at her sides, fists balled into knots, Ruby let him mistake whimper for passion. He paid no attention to her face, and thus didn't spot disgust behind the feigned pleasure. She had slept with Arnett for love, with Squire for comfort. The drummer's sour smell, the queasiness that refused to settle. Wasn't this enough sex? Her simple, implied promise of it to Poppa got the rent paid, brought her new clothes, and helped to find a gig. Now her hopes roiled inside her stomach. The drummer's fingers slithered down the ribbons on her back. His eyes were shut, hers wide open, so that neither the rat scurrying between piles of garbage nor the outline of the man in the window above escaped her attention. Enough touching to feel the drummer's pounding heart, but not enough to open her mouth when his hands commanded her downward.

"Go on then," he shouted when she wrenched free. "Take your ass on home." He slammed his hat back onto his head and slapped it down. The drummer staggered down the narrow street. Not five steps later, he turned and fumbled through his pockets. When he found matches and cigarettes, he lit one, then puffed smoke rings into the scanty light. "You remember Verna Plessy? She was a beautiful woman, too. Music burnt her out. Now she's turning tricks to make it." Hand in his pocket again, he tossed money on the street. "You ought to think about that before you end up the same way."

Ruby came home to find Yvette reading the *propriétaire*'s demand for rent. Without speaking, Ruby unlocked her door. Yvette dragged Ruby's two striped suitcases and a trunk from the closet and tossed every piece of clothing, underwear, comb, paper, soap, Arnett's saxophone, his beloved records and the player, pots, and tea towels into it. When the suitcases were filled, Yvette wrapped the rest of Ruby's belongings in a blanket. Together they checked corners and drawers and under the bed, making sure nothing of Ruby or Arnett remained in the room. Yvette lugged Ruby's suitcases up two flights of stairs to the room she'd shared with Freddie Jones until he decided to go back to the States, and shut the door behind them.

The pile of bills from Arnett's pocket, Poppa's dollars, and even the drummer's crumpled francs lessened with every meal and the rent.

In the weeks after the Chez Inez flop, Yvette took in sewing and alterations, they scrubbed shirts and petticoats in the *blanchisserie*. Ruby searched for gigs. In Montmartre and the Place Pigalle, on the heels of men who stumbled in and out of clubs, manager after manager turned her down. They complimented her loveliness, yet their rejection was absolute, until one night a balding man puffed cigar smoke in her face and let her know that neither Parisians nor tourists needed another mediocre singer to bore them. Not when Sarah and Ella and so many other singers, black and white, were coming to the great city. Not when Josephine Baker, their national hero, was able to sing. Not when they had Piaf and Greco.

This day, Ruby sang along with the records, imitating Arnett's dedication, and considered how it must feel to have such talent. Or to waste it like Malvina, writing of her eagerness to have Squire, wanted to do.

She unlatched Arnett's saxophone case. The instrument was beyond use now, the crack in its bell aimed downward to the bow curve where Arnett had guided her fingers. The thumb rest was bent, most of the keys flattened. Her Arnett, cold in the earth, so downhearted that he threw himself to his death. He wished for the gift. He hadn't said it, but the desire had covered his face, disguised by weariness, and she had failed to notice. The road was too long, the reward dangling within her reach—if she played her cards right. She had not come this far to give up. How many can'ts must she hear? Her mother, her sister, colored folks, white folks, Jim Crow. She had scolded Squire. *You think I got this far on can't?* So what, she asked herself, if her talent was far from Sarah's reach, Ella's scatting, Billie's phrasing and ease. If all she had was a pretty face, and that was her gift, she was sure enough going to put it to good use.

Ruby rubbed her gloved hands together. Underneath her hands were red, her fingernails cracked from hot water and scrubbing stains from soiled clothes. Together outside the Casino de Paris

Yvette and Ruby stared at the posters of the dancers and upcoming events displayed on the walls.

"Let us peek inside of this beautiful place." Yvette led Ruby through the doors as if they had tickets to a performance.

The red lobby was carpeted from floor to tin cut ceiling. Sunlight from two large windows poured over the balcony, hitting crystal chandeliers whose prisms glistened with rainbows. A man in a pinstriped suit stepped up to them and directed them to the auditions being held on the stage. He was trim and elegant and, despite his skin color, he resembled Arnett. Ruby turned from the sight of the man. Yvette, leaving her request open to interpretation, asked for the stage. The man directed them to the stairs that led backstage and the dancers, before heading in the direction of the bar.

"We're not dancers," Ruby whispered, wanting instead to inspect that man's face again and hold on to his likeness to Arnett.

"But he does not know that, chérie. I dance a bit—that is how I met my Freddie. Let us see what we can do, Ruby. Do you think a rich man will want a girl with a washwoman's hands?"

The back of the stage was busy with women dressed in leotards, tights, and skirts of thin fabric tied at their waists, all stretched and pliéd in preparation for the audition. A few wore ballet slippers, one or two toe shoes. Yvette handed her coat to Ruby. She tugged at her waistline, rolled her dress up and over her knees, and kicked off her shoes. She stretched and mimicked the dancers. "Allons, Ruby. Il faut préparer."

The waiting dancers shuffled and stretched against the ballet barre. They pranced two steps up, back, two to the side, and back again. Ruby scratched her feet in a tight square, approximating not one correct step. Over four months with child, she was awkward and unprepared to present herself.

A short man rapped a long stick against the stage floor, then stepped forward. "Je m'appelle Monsieur Fortescue!" He counted ten women randomly, including Yvette, and herded them center stage. Monsieur choreographed steps for the dancers to follow. Barefoot, Yvette stumbled through the kicks. The tap steps she'd explained to Ruby she learned as a girl were useless in this line of skilled women. Her feet went left, the other dancers right, keeping her two steps behind all the while she was onstage. The music stopped. Monsieur Fortescue wound between the dancers tapping his decision on their shoulders. "Oui! Oui!" He tapped Yvette's shoulder twice. "Non! Non!"

Yvette limped from the stage to the curtains where Ruby waited, her head angled up and toward at the rafters. Ropes and pulleys hung from the ceiling. Beyond the stage, spotlights, covered with colored paper, beamed red and blue onto the backdrop. Monsieur Fortescue threaded himself through the dancers' lines and tapped Ruby's shoulder.

Breathing roughly, Yvette touched her toes. "It was good to have tried." She rubbed Ruby's belly. "And I suggest you do not try at all."

In all of his eagerness to move on to the next set of auditions, Monsieur Fortescue herded the women to the dressing room. Ruby and Yvette found themselves swept along with those Monsieur had selected with his shouts of "Oui, oui." They stood side by side in line, along with fifteen other women, facing mirrored walls, racks of costumes, and dressing tables crammed along the sides of the room.

"Us?" Ruby pointed to her stomach. "I know Monsieur didn't mean for me to be here."

"Shh. They think we are dancers, then we will act *comme les danseuses*. Oui?" Yvette rubbed her lower back and stretched. "We will have a little fun. We need a little fun, Ruby."

They followed the dancers to inspect the beaded costumes and feathered headdresses looped around hangers and wooden racks. A matronly woman with a paisley shawl hugging her shoulders demanded that the new dancers pay attention. She motioned for Ruby and Yvette to step into line, not recognizing them for the curious intruders they were, and insisted they all find costumes for the seamstresses to make whatever alterations were needed.

Yvette nudged Ruby with her elbow and nodded to a woman in the corner, separated from the others. "That is Madame LeDoux!" Bright lightbulbs encircled the mirror on the woman's dressing table. "She is on *l'affiche*, the poster outside." A seamstress, straight pins pinched between her lips, cowered beside the dancer. Madame LeDoux screamed at the top of her lungs, "Vous me torturez avec ces épingles! Vous détruisez ma belle robe! Faites venir une autre couturière!"

Yvette raced to the woman's side. She reached into the open sewing basket and grabbed needle and thread. "Il n'y a pas de problème, Madame. Je vous aiderai." Yvette turned to the pouting seamstress, who relinquished her work with a relieved sigh after demonstrating what needed to be done. Yvette pinned, tucked, and stitched until Madame LeDoux's gown was mended and perfect again.

"Parfait," Madame said without focusing on Yvette. She picked up her dress and examined the stitches. "Je ne vous ai pas encore vue. Vous êtes la nouvelle couturière?"

Yvette let the furious woman know that the reason their presence had gone unnoticed by Madame before was because they had come to the Casino to audition. She and her friend would happily work as seamstresses, if Madame encouraged management to hire them.

"Oui, oui!" she said and flicked her hand in the direction of the woman with the paisley shawl.

37

Paris, Fall 1952

During her entire pregnancy, Ruby worried over the wormy stretch marks that frolicked back and forth over her stomach and thighs; the swelling and spreading of her face, the extension of cheek into neck.

"A bit of butter, ma petite," Yvette recommended at Ruby's ongoing complaints. "You must rub your belly with butter to keep it without the lines."

These changes from the weight of her thickened body became as important as the baby inside her. She counted after the baby came in October instead of November. Counted to the day before Arnett's suicide when they had spent a rainy morning, afternoon, and night in the narrow bed, and Arnett was brooding and unstoppable; he needed her loving, needed her, needed to show her, to show somebody that he was a man. Counted the days afterward she spent with Squire.

No shouts or uncultured screams accompanied the child's delivery. Not that Ruby bore the pain of her twelve-hour labor in silence; she tolerated it, bit down on the cloth Yvette held to her mouth. Where some women called God or the name of their husband in either curse or praise, Ruby did not. Both men who could have fathered her child were long gone. She bit down on that cloth, squeezed Yvette's hand, and let the same woman who had helped prepare Arnett's body for burial tell her to push in preparation for the birth. When it was done, the pushing and pushing, and the infant's head crowned between her legs, and the baby slipped into the woman's hands, Yvette hugged Ruby at the sight of the crying newborn. The blood, so unexpected was the blood that covered the infant that Ruby did not want to be close to the girl. She waited, fretting that the pain would not leave soon, and waited until Yvette cautiously wiped every bit of the birth canal from the baby's skin.

When Yvette put the baby into her arms, Ruby complained. "I don't know what to do with this squiggling child."

"She wants the milk, Ruby. Put our little Roxane to your breast—in this way you will feed and come to love her, as I already do." Roxane Nicole-Marie. Yvette gave the child her name. Every evening the pregnancy had kept Ruby confined to their room, Yvette had read *Cyrano de Bergerac* to her for the story and the French. Ruby favored Roxane after the woman who inspired a shy long-nosed man to love.

When the baby girl lay sleeping and quiet beside her, Ruby stared at her face. Not as new mothers do—lips to nose, forehead, and ears, counting fingers and toes, pondering the blessing of life—but with an appraisal both vain and curious. She watched for reflections of her own face in the baby's as if the tiny child were a mirror. She searched for the hint of the baby's father: Squire's narrow forehead, Arnett's big ears.

"What does it matter, Ruby? When, this baby, she can have two mothers." Yvette cooed at the baby Roxane. "You will let me be her mother, too, Ruby?"

38

Faux amis, false friends, are words or phrases that appear to be easily translatable because of their resemblance to English, but have completely different definitions. The spelling resemblance is coincidental.

crier (cree ay)	to shout
assister à (ah sis tay ah)	attend a meeting or conference
un truc (trook)	a trick, a thing
la déception (lah day sep see ohn)	disappointment

Thunder came before the rain, a frantic summer squall. Mother Nature's sentimental metaphor for Nicole's threatening sadness. Christmas mornings in the Handy household, no presents were opened until both her parents awakened. Thirteen and tired of waiting, Nicole skulked into the living room and stripped shiny paper from a loosely wrapped box—a blue sweater and matching pleated skirt. Exactly what she wanted. Hours later, she faked excitement for the lovely set that was supposed to make her a real teenager. The thrill was gone.

That was how she felt: trapped between loyalty and curiosity.

Ruby had ruined her day, deflated her spirit. Ruby had eliminated surprise. When Nicole wrote the letters, she had visualized *her* calling Ruby, her setting the when and where. Time to cry, to get angry, to sort it all out.

What gave Ruby the right?

She needed to talk. A part of Nicole wanted to call her parents and feel secure in the safe space she returned to whenever the world treated her badly. Now they were the problem. Her fingers twitched; only a few digits to Clint's husky voice on the line, thinking he'd won. She punched the keypad.

"I found her. My mother."

"Ahhh, the thrill of investigative journalism." Laurent's sentence doubled through the echoing connection.

"Actually, she found me. I tried to get her to speak to my mother. She hung up on her. I hate Ruby and I love her. Does that make sense?" Cigarettes and coffee coated her tongue. Nicole spit into the handkerchief Ruby gave her—the only thing she'd ever received from this mother. She described how, with cigarette after cigarette, Ruby substituted smoke rings for real information. "I gave her my number. What do you think?" It registered that Ruby hadn't shared her information.

"In my experience, when you've got a source, you get all the info you can while they're hot. It's not often you get a second chance."

"I stared at her picture. I pretended to be her. I wanted to be her. This afternoon she was real and right in front of me. What do I do now?"

"You're upset. I'm sorry about Ruby, sorry your mother sprung her on you."

"Are you saying she won't call?"

"Who knows what she's thinking or what could keep her from seeing you again."

"She's interested," Nicole decided, trusting because she could trust Malvina—if she promised to call she'd call. "Wishful thinking."

"You want company?"

Nicole marked time with the expectations of others. Punch the clock at work. Document deadlines driven by court actions. "Come home, Nicki," Malvina demanded. Clint proclaimed, "I'm yours, you're mine." They all dictated when and what she should or should not do.

"Tempting, but I need to call my mother and make sure she's okay. I need to do this on my own time."

"Think of it as an adventure."

If getting here was the adventure, the adventure had changed: rummaging through Monsieur Daudon's store, meeting Ousmane and Laurent, a jazz club, a visit to another continent on the edge of Paris, a mother not her mother but her aunt. No bang. No pow. Just hot damn.

"Adventure? More like a roller-coaster ride."

"Well, roller coasters can be fun, too."

"Nope, they make me want to throw up." A perfect description, she thought, suppressing a gag at the back of her throat, of exactly how she felt.

"Whatever you decide, the trick is to know what you want from the next meeting—if there is one."

Waving to the concierge, Nicole asked him not to let anyone upstairs, especially if it was a woman. He agreed easily—casting doubt that he knew what she meant—and watched her skip the elevator and take the stairs. The notion stopped her halfway up that cold flight of marble. Without Ruby's answers, the story behind the story, all that was left was to fill in the pieces with the remaining letters—and whatever else Malvina chose to tell. All that was left was better preparation.

39

Paris, 1953

Dancers filed into the dressing room, their skin iridescent with sweat, their breathing hurried. The women wiggled out of their costumes, casting them on the floor, while Ruby and Yvette scrambled to pick up each fragile piece. They had work to do: sequins, fake pearls, and colored rhinestones to stitch back on, seams to repair, adjustments in the hips or stomach for weight loss or gain. Some evenings, the work was easy: mounting the skimpy costumes on hangers, then on racks to air-dry from the sweat that often soaked through the fabric.

For six months, Ruby observed the dancers pretending to work, memorizing the details of their style. She watched this evening: the powder swiped off their faces, the eyeliner reapplied, the hair brushed into chic chignons or puffy bouffant bobs. A few, naked, strutted the length of the dressing room, perfecting the balance of weighty headdresses. Ruby watched, committing their bearing to heart. It was important to Ruby that she, and Yvette too, blended in. Yvette, the better dancer; Ruby, the better body. Their legs as contoured, their bust lines as plump, their prance as tempting as any woman's in the chorus.

When the dancers were gone and the dressing room was quiet,

Ruby and Yvette stayed behind, as they did many evenings, holding the fancy costumes to their bodies, spinning this way and that. On nights such as this, Ruby imagined how it must feel to be onstage, not in the chorus, but the star—the reason the public paid good money to sit for two hours in the plush red chairs.

"I'm changing my name, Yvette."

"Non, Ruby, you have a lovely name, a jewel, eh?"

"RubyMae Garrett, she's a colored girl from Mississippi. Josette will be my new name." Ruby twirled the length of the room, until she came to the floor-to-ceiling mirror. "And Garrett is too boring for a woman named Josette." She would take Arnett's name. Dupree. Not spoken like back home stretching the E, but a French pronunciation, with an accent mark making it rhyme with stay.

Josette Duprée posed in the mirror now. Josette Duprée danced at the Casino, drank champagne, and spent her evenings in the clubs on the Champs-Élysées with her wealthy gentlemen callers. She wore furs and designer gowns. Rich men wanted her all to themselves. This woman had no experience with living in one-room apartments with narrow beds, toilets steps down the hall, bathhouses, or radiators that refused to work. Josette Duprée had not the slightest interest in baby bottles, burping, changing diapers; counting *sous* and *francs*, stretching scrawny chickens to last two weeks, or wooing drunken musicians for money to pay the rent. She never pushed a stroller beside the Seine to watch the river rush past, wishing she were off to somewhere.

"Josette Duprée." Ruby tested it on her tongue. "To you, I'll be Ruby, but to the rest of the world I will be Josette."

"You can be both," Yvette teased. "And our little Roxane will think that this Josette Duprée is her mother also, and she will be delighted that she has three, not two mothers."

At the beginning, she could not tell which man was the father; the baby resembled her mother in that innocent and pure face, in the creamy folds of skin, the loose curl of hair beneath her cap, the Indian lines of her nose, the heart-shaped lips. For all that should have spurred her love of the child, not the least of which was the maternal instinct, Ruby found obligation the strongest link to the fussy baby who demanded attention day and night, and turned browner with each passing day. Most often she handed the child over to Yvette, who cooed and rocked the baby to peaceful rest.

A baby. RubyMae Garrett had a baby and the baby put her hopes on hold. It was her decision to keep the child. Nature had lied to her with blood that spotted her panties through her third month, tricked her. Ruby loved the little brown Roxane. Perhaps that was what happened. Roxane could be the singer, the dancer. Perhaps mothers transferred their dreams to their daughters and reveled in their success. *Oh*, she pondered, now twirling in the mirror with this new name, *have I failed my own mother?* She deliberated on this and released it, telling herself, forever. But what of Josette Duprée?

"Josette Duprée is a woman who lives without regrets."

Yvette handed Ruby the coat they had haggled over with a feisty *marché* vendor, arguing that such beautiful women could honor his departed wife by wearing her fine coat. Reflected in the long gilt-edged mirror, Ruby to the left, Yvette to the right, they were sisters in style.

"You see how pretty you are, Ruby? No need to change your name."

"Then you can be Ruby, Yvette. You take her misery and her memories and be a colored girl. I am Josette."

"We will have fun, this Josette and I." Yvette followed her friend through the backstage door. Gone were the zealous suitors who regularly waited outside the stage door—fans with bouquets thrust at the dancers along with promises of champagne and caviar. Near the end of the short alley that wound to the front of the Casino a man, a latecomer, approached them.

"Pardon, Mesdemoiselles. J'ai beaucoup apprécié votre spectacle. Puis-je vous inviter à diner?" His greeting was in the unhurried pace of the south of France. He squinted into their faces, dividing his attention between Ruby and Yvette. He settled on Ruby, and she didn't dissuade him from the notion that, indeed, she danced at the Casino de Paris. He mumbled, bent in a deep bow, and pushed the blooming flowers into Ruby's hands. "Monsieur Prideaux. À votre service."

Ruby winked and extended the back of her hand for the nice monsieur to kiss. She considered this plain man. That saying the elders at home repeated when change was in the wind came to her mind. Opportunity was indeed knocking in the form of this Frenchman who would no more have spoken to her if she walked down the street with her baby, her brown baby, than he would have thought to speak to a simple seamstress exiting the hall. That this man, this Monsieur Prideaux, knew not one true fact about her—not that she was a mother, not that she had loved two men at the same time, not that she'd scoured the streets for months in search of a chance to sing, not that she was a colored woman on her own in Paris—set up possibilities.

"Je m'appelle Mademoiselle Josette Duprée. Je suis enchantée de faire votre connaissance." Ruby shot a warning glance at Yvette, who held her hand to her mouth stifling her giggles. Ruby's French was good, her vocabulary large, but such formality intimated that she was not a native speaker.

"Vous n'êtes pas française, Mademoiselle?" Louis's face was pleasant.

"Créole. Je viens de Nouvelle-Orléans." Ruby-Josette regarded Monsieur Louis Prideaux. Was he familiar with New Orleans, did he understand or prefer to speak English to her Creole French? "But in my hometown we barely speak to one another in this lovely language."

"I am français, and my English is not good. S'il vous plaît, Mesdemoiselles, permit me... We go to le café to know one another. Alors... allons-y."

Monsieur angled his arms, forming hooks at either side of his torso, open invitations to the two women. The three strolled to the Café Bijoux where, Ruby calculated, they avoided the Casino dancers and their suitors. Monsieur Prideaux ordered champagne served in a silver ice bucket. He was a talker, a man of distinct biases. He had no patience for Algerians or Africans. Or anyone who came into his country to take jobs from Frenchmen. He tolerated Americans, but not the rude ones who did not try to speak French. He did not approve of the jazz, or the invasion of *les noirs* in his country to play the confusing Negro music and try to win over French women. "I prefer Madame Piaf et Monsieur Aznavour." He talked nonstop, his English not as bad as he claimed. "And the music from before the war." He enjoyed an occasional night on the town, but he loved the southern France of his birth—the song of the *cigales* on a summer evening, a good cigar, a true burgundy, and a woman with good legs.

Monsieur did not ignore Yvette, he merely directed his questions to Ruby-Josette, less interested in her answers than her tempting rejoinders. "Your Nouvelle-Orléans, it is *comme* Paris?"

"New Orleans is pretty, *mais* Paris is beautiful," Ruby-Josette began. "New Orleans men are striking. French men are handsome." She parlayed the details she remembered from her visit with Arnett into her own truth. Jackson Square. The St. Charles streetcars. The misty bayous edging the city, the lima beans with rice and ham hocks big as fists. Arnett's words. Arnett's story. Ruby-Josette no longer remembered Arnett's voice, the scratch of his beard before he shaved, or the feel of his body against hers. Ruby-Josette forgot Squire's poetry and the tears he shed when he made love to her.

Ruby-Josette adjusted herself so that Monsieur Prideaux was able to see for himself the promise she held for him. She looked at his eyes, gray and dull, and believed they held a guarantee that Josette Duprée trusted was well worth pursuing.

After not quite two and a half months of her pestering, Monsieur Fortescue permitted Yvette to replace a sickly chorus line dancer whose role was to prance from stage right to stage left.

"Chérie, Monsieur will see if I will become a regular dancer." Yvette rushed into the dressing room. "But I will have to work very hard." For the months they worked at the Casino, Ruby-Josette worked to captivate Louis Prideaux; Yvette worked on Monsieur Fortescue.

"I am to attend *les répétitions*, the rehearsals, starting tomorrow. We must celebrate, non?"

"Yes! We'll tell Louis." Ruby-Josette kicked a chair. "But I promised Madame I'd be early tonight." The baby, the baby, always the baby to feed, to watch, to pick up, to keep her from going out, from getting back on her feet, from taking singing lessons. From being a star.

"Roxane will sleep. Madame, she will not mind," Yvette promised.

Louis and Josette had slipped into a routine. Him pacing at the end of the alley waiting for her long after the other dancers left with their admirers. Her watching for the dancers, having concocted a story: "So the other girls won't be jealous and tell Monsieur Fortescue to dismiss me! Then what would happen to your poor Josette?"

Louis stepped to the two women, grimacing at their noise as they approached. He complained again that Josette did not throw kisses to him in the midst of her routines onstage, and he was not able to pick his beloved out of all the dancers. He never confessed his need for glasses—blaming dim lights for his inability to read a menu or a program—or his inexpensive seat at the very top of the last balcony row, both of which kept him from recognizing any of the women onstage.

"Non, non! Monsieur, I can't do that." She batted her lashes, distracting him again from the truth. "Louis, tonight we must celebrate. Yvette has been accepted for a better position among the dancers." Josette nudged Yvette's arm.

"But I have the reservations." He raised two fingers and shifted the sparse bouquet of winter roses in his arms to Josette's. "And the special flowers." Since their fourth meeting, single flowers, and often none at all, had replaced the first bouquets Louis brought to woo Josette.

Yvette, gawking at the expensive bouquet, interrupted. "Tonight, I am so happy I will celebrate very much—I can wait, Monsieur. And I must attend to Roxane. Madame will be waiting."

With her tsk-tsks and not overly critical reports, Ruby-Josette changed Roxane into poor Yvette's child by an American colored man Yvette pined for, killed on the eve of their shotgun wedding. Josette hugged Yvette, thankful her friend loved tiny Roxane and was not attracted to Louis. Thankful her secrets were safe until Louis became enamored with Ruby-Josette's voice, her poor grammar, her left leg nudged against his right, her hand on his back, the cigarette held to her lips impatient for another drag. To give him the chance to fall in love with her. And for her to become accustomed to his formality, his preference for evening strolls and dining in small neighborhood brasseries. She could learn to ignore the impediment that made the end of his sentences seem as if he kept chewing gum in his mouth, the hairs that peeked from his nose, how he shoveled his food into his mouth and discouraged her from drinking spirits.

On many nights before this one, Ruby-Josette name-dropped the places the dancers mentioned—the Hotel Ritz, Tour d'Argent, Larue—but Louis remained frugal. La Grenouille was the nicest of the few restaurants they had frequented before this one. The restaurant named after a frog was not filled to its limited capacity, but not empty enough for Josette to feel lonely.

Louis motioned to the server, who waited for Louis to scan the menu and settle on braised chicken and roasted potatoes for two, including one glass each of champagne, which turned out to be drier than Josette favored. Josette drank half of her champagne in one sip, and when the waiter offered to refill her glass, Louis set his hand on top of it.

"I have thirty-eight years. I am not forever living in Paris. I come with *mes parents* from a *petit* village in the south near Arles because I am the single child." Louis used his English this evening to please Josette. "Before the war, my parents come to Paris. They want a shop for my father's leather goods. They are *morts*—my father from his poor digestion, my mother from missing him. I am never married."

Louis filled the minutes between ordering and eating with talk of living in the large home his family kept in southern France. He reminded her of his patience when escorting her home, the money for coffees and baguettes and slices of chocolate cake for Yvette's *petit bébé* to nibble with warm milk. The very dress Ruby-Josette wore, he had purchased for her.

He never challenged what Ruby-Josette said. In return she handed Louis a packet of lies neatly wrapped, the promise of her caresses and exaggerations of her stay in New Orleans. Tonight, she kept her lies to herself, preferring the champagne bubbles tickling the roundness of her chin.

Louis talked on after the waiter set their hot plates on the table, working through his chicken. He did not care about her age; her body, her wide hips proved she was perfect to birth the children he wanted.

As if he had practiced, he finished his speech and his meal, and scanned the restaurant. Seeing it nearly empty, he dropped to one knee, removed a pouch from his pocket, and opened it. A thin gold band rested on a velvet cone. Its diamond reminded Josette of the rhinestones tinier than her baby's fingernail she sewed to the dancers' costumes, the sparkling chips so minute that her vision had become strained from stitching them.

"Ma chère, I am full with the love for you."

She lowered her head, the coy woman she needed to believe she now was, the woman she wanted Louis to believe she was. "Why Louis, we've only known each other for a few weeks."

"Time does not make the love I have for you, Josette."

Quick was how love came to Ruby. Arnett fell for her in one

night—and she for him. Squire had cared for her since childhood, but he made love to her shortly after Arnett's death. Louis had loved her for a matter of mere weeks. Right now with him on one knee—surely on his way to bald—Ruby accepted that neither she nor Josette loved this man; nor was she sure if she liked him, so rigid was he in his thinking and faith. She could not have changed Arnett's death or Squire's disdain for Paris. Louis, so in love, on the verge of crying, she could change.

"Will you be my wife, Josette?" Louis's voice quivered.

She felt married to Arnett. They had been destined for a life together and marriage, when the fame they wanted was real. She had done all that a married woman could do for her man. Ruby had rejected Squire with the unwelcoming frostiness of cold bedsheets on an icy night. He'd mistaken his chance; no romance in his proposal except the Paris skyline and the dome of the Panthéon encased in mist. Yes, he'd bent on one knee. Yes, he'd spoken of a good marriage, love, and children. But his had been the promise of a sedentary life. Living out her days in a Mississippi town where the arrival and departure schedule of the Illinois Central train was the most interesting happening repulsed her. No returning to the States. Never.

She put a finger to her chin. "And my dancing, Louis? And I want to be a great singer."

"You will have what you want, Josette. I promise." Louis touched his lips to her hand. Wobbly and impatient, he pleaded, "You will honor me, Josette?"

"Oui." Ruby didn't care, but to Josette Louis's business, his devoted look, and the ring that could be traded for a larger one on an important future anniversary were her keys to a good life.

Louis slid the ring onto her finger. "May I kiss you, Josette?"

She nodded, amused that rationing her kisses had secured what she wanted. Now she would live in Paris forever. No worries about the rent, about working. About the baby. The baby. Whatever would she do about the baby?

40

In conjugating the three basic verb tenses, past, present, and future, note that past, present, and future can be spoken separately or combined in a sentence or paragraph.

la vérité (lah vehr ree tay)	truth
décrocher (day crow shay)	to pick up (the phone)
la poésie (poe aay see)	poetry
à demain (ah duh maa)	until tomorrow

November 1953

Dear Squire,

I'm hoping you don't crush this letter between your fists and curse me. And Malvina, if you read this before your husband don't you crush it either. and if neither of you crushes it, I hope you read on with a touch of affection for me. Just in case you DO decide not to read on, let me get my purpose out of the way quickly. I've had a child, Squire. A little girl just turned a year old. The little baby, she's a pretty child. She's got my eyes and a bush of my hair. Her skin is brown as the walnut shells Malvina and me used to gather in our backyard.

I deserve a chance, Squire. After all that's happened to me, I desire MY chance. So, with every bone in my body I'm begging you and Malvina to take this child. Give her what I can't. Give us both a chance.

I call myself Josette Duprée now. A new name for a new life. You know I've hated all tht race business at home. All the scraping and shining. In Paris no one cares or notices that I'm Negro. It just happened and kept happening. It was meant to be. And I'm not sorry.

I know you must believe I'm the devil for asking. I hope you understand and will agree to raise this child. Please find the kindness to help me.

RubyMae (who I will always be to you)

Without fail Ruby wanted—money, information, a favor—and Nicole promised herself to remember that greed, if they met again.

January 1954

You've got your nerve, RubyMae Garrett. Josette Duprée my black ass. Who do you think you're tricking with news of a baby? You have been prone to lies from the time you learned to talk to the day you ran off with that saxophone player to this probability of mistruth. My husband let me know before we married that he'd been with you. We left the past where it was. Why should I believe you?

I'm a God-loving woman. I know you're taking advantage of that, so don't think you're pulling the wool over my eyes, little sister. God knows I have to consider that this is the truth. He works His ways in His own precious time. I've lost two babies. After the last one, the doctor found growths as big as melons in my womb. He wanted to take away my womanhood, but I said no. That's when he told me that I could never, never have children. You can't imagine how that feels. But even if that were not so. Even if I had babies in my arms and hanging from my hem, I'd take this child. I see your baby, this opportunity, as a glass half full. So, we agree to accept this blessing, and raise your child as our own. I'll love her, as you do not. She'll never learn the truth from me.

But I'll be damned if you think you can change your mind. DON'T THINK I BELIEVE THIS IS THE END OF THE STORY. Don't think you've fooled me. You're selfish and I don't believe Paris or a baby have changed that. I'm taking that child on the outside chance she's Squire's and on the inside chance that if she stays with you, you'll ruin her life or worse.

SWEAR you'll never bother us. She'll be my child, our child. No changing your mind because a Frenchman has had enough of you—for whatever reason. No letters asking how the child is, no little Paris trinkets on Christmas or birthdays, no showing up on my doorstep one afternoon with your arms outstretched ready to take her back. If you have them, you will return to me all the letters that Squire ever wrote you. As a matter of fact, send back the one or two that I sent. You don't deserve to keep them. If you can give up his child, you can give up her daddy.

After that, I don't want to hear from you again. We'll work out the details of how to get the baby. Don't think you can trick Squire into coming. I won't let him. So you think about this now—long and hard, because I'm serious.

Malvina

Nicole dropped the two letters. The lesson of years of procrastinating finally unmistakable. Reading the entire collection before writing to Ruby, before meeting Ruby—their rendezvous would never have happened. Malvina had set boundaries she never had with Squire. She'd fought for Nicole, and at this moment, Nicole loved this mother more than ever.

"I tried calling you back. Is she pretty?" Malvina was not interested in the reason for the abrupt disconnect, and Nicole was glad she didn't have to interpret Ruby's feelings. "She probably made herself up for you."

"She was put together."

The woman who faced Nicole earlier was beautiful in a way Malvina was not. Neither woman was matronly or frumpy. They both had a natural energy, taut skin, and a tinge of color to their cheeks, but Ruby embraced her looks, Malvina didn't. Ruby acted pretty—even if the years had altered that. Her movements and primping confirmed that vanity didn't diminish with age. Nicole remembered—when she watched Malvina perform her morning routine—her mother lingering to wash her face, brush her teeth, and apply lipstick; a bit of rouge and face powder if she was going to a party. No more than that. Malvina's hair was hot-combed straight and flat against her head long before chemical relaxers came along. She described herself as smart. Never pretty or attractive.

"I thought about it, and her. What it must have meant to lose a child—different from the ones I lost before they were born—one that she'd held in her arms and cuddled and watched grow into a real person. I was afraid she'd change her mind. I didn't trust her then. I don't now. She probably told you a lot of lies."

"Can you forgive her?"

"I don't have anything to forgive. It's Ruby who needs to apologize." Malvina's temper never revealed itself in loud talk. Her mother was a nag, not a firebrand. "You can't understand."

"I think it's pretty clear, Mother. Your sister took your man, he came back to you, and then she sent you their child."

"Have I ever loved you like any child but my own?"

"You were, you are, a good mother." The Ruby Nicole met showed no expression that hinted a change of mind. "She didn't say anything important." With her cigarettes, the worn lighter, Ruby showed smoking was a habit. Her clothes and hair showed, true or not, that she pampered herself where Malvina didn't. "She smokes a lot. She seemed nervous. I was."

"What did you think of her?"

"I don't know."

In the near quiet between them now, Malvina made a mushy noise and Nicole realized she was sucking on cheek fat. Malvina's habit had worsened after Squire became ill. She'd shown Nicole the thick callus toughened by years of fretting after Nicole found her icing her cheek on the day she told them about her trip. "Are you planning on seeing her again?"

"So, how did I get from here to home? What about my birth certificate—how did you get listed as my birth mother?" All too elaborate a scheme, Nicole considered, for two uncomplicated individuals.

Silence again. It dawned on Nicole that it was four in the morning in California and Malvina hadn't complained.

"Ruby was beautiful. Starting with PapPap, every man was strung around her little finger." Malvina talked through hiccups. "We made a plan, Squire and I."

Her phrasing was matter-of-fact. Minutes after mailing her last letter to Ruby, Malvina and Squire checked their bankbook, hidden under the very mattress they slept on each night, and totaled that sum along with the money Malvina kept in an empty cold cream jar in the medicine cabinet. It was their house money; dollars, quarters, nickels, and dimes saved from their wages. They sacrificed; getting a ten-cent cone after a fifty-cent movie was a splurge. They lived with her parents and, despite the rent they paid to Martha, they put money aside every week.

All together it was enough. Enough for one, not both of them.

"Your father wanted to go, but I was afraid that if he did, if he saw RubyMae beautiful, holding his child, he'd never come back to me...I brought you home. I went to Paris."

"Here? Paris? And you never...oh, what's the use?" Swallowing quickly, Nicole wished she had hers, Ruby's, or anyone else's cigarettes right now.

"Nicki, let me finish while I can."

They drove to Jackson where two anonymous Negroes could make travel arrangements without worrying about it getting back to family or friends. They figured out the details on the ride up, playing with ideas to make everyone believe the baby was theirs. In Jackson, they went to a white travel agency, thinking that was safest. The agent made them wait for an hour. She helped white customers who came in after Malvina and Squire, fussed with her papers, went off to talk to another agent, then buffed her nails. When they sat, finally, a proper distance from her desk, and explained that they wanted a ticket to Paris, she made them show their money, their cash, before she considered booking an airplane ticket for two coloreds—no, one, they insisted—for so short a trip. And the questions: How did they get all that money? What did they do for a living? Why hadn't they found a colored travel agent in Sheridan to help them make their arrangements?

"Your father was calm. He showed me a side I didn't know he had—he lied without blinking. He made it clear to that stupid woman, I'll never forget, that I had a sister in Paris who was dying and I had to see her before she passed. He said he didn't want his in-laws to know about their youngest daughter, so he sold his truck and a little piece of land his daddy left him and then borrowed the rest so I could go to Paris."

Didn't she want to see all the sites, the travel agent inquired, didn't Malvina want to eat French food, stand on the Champs-Élysées, and get dizzy at the top of the Eiffel Tower—if they let coloreds do that sort of looking in Paris.

"'We'll take a ticket to Paris, from New York and back,' your father told that woman. 'Then my wife will take a train from New York to California. Oakland, California, and meet me because I have a job at the Army base.' Your father looked that white woman in the eye, the way he'd felt comfortable doing in Paris, and held her gaze until she started making the arrangements."

Squire did the calculating and the planning and wrote Ruby a letter with Malvina watching over his shoulder, giving dates and the name of Malvina's hotel. They gave Ruby a month or so to make her plan for handing the baby over. Without stopping for food or taking care of personal business, they returned to Sheridan and Martha and PapPap and repeated the story they'd settled into before they got home. In Jackson, they'd say, they found a doctor who'd help Malvina. And when the time was right, they'd let on that Malvina was already pregnant, and keep folks from visiting until the numbers worked out to fit the child's age. Telling Martha and PapPap was enough to spread the news—they were moving to California for a better job, good money. "It's wonderful!" Malvina declared. "My buddy has a job for me at the Army base," Squire announced. "And we're driving," Malvina blurted out. "In a month or so," Squire added. "Both my girls gone," Martha whispered.

"And what about my birth certificate?"

"We paid for that, too. Don't recall if babies needed passports. They probably did, but I was so nervous. I don't know how he did any of it. And one day your father gave me a birth certificate with our names on it and I believed him when he said it was filed in city hall." Malvina let go a moan, muffled, Nicole supposed, to keep Squire from hearing. She imagined the extension cord stretched into her old bedroom, Malvina rocking to ward off bad news. "Come home, Nicki. You're *my* daughter. I love you. I was wrong to keep the truth from you, I know that now. RubyMae is not what she seems to be. Don't let her take you away from me. Come home."

"I think I *am* home."

June 1954

RubyMae,

What I want to put down is best left to my thoughts and not this letter, or the poetry I rarely write these days. The baby is beautiful. She has your smile and your eyes. We call her Nicole—well, I call her Nicole, Malvina and everyone else calls her Nicki—it's American. Malvina isn't taken with the name Roxane, but she's agreed to keep it for a middle name. Of course, her last name will be mine—Nicole-Marie Roxane Handy. I hope that the bad blood between you and Malvina will soon heal. She is my wife. I respect her wishes, but if you're ever in need, write to us care of your mother. She has promised to forward the letters if you address them to Malvina. May God bless you for this.

Forever yours,
Squire

A letter near the bottom of the pile had a length of pink satin ribbon tucked inside. Nicole rubbed the empty space, the flat surface and lack of residue where a stamp and its adhesive belonged.

March 1954

Squire and Malvina

I'm as cruel as you think I am. I need this chance to see what I can be. I believe I've found the answers here. I know this is best for Roxane.

Ruby

What Nicole should've said to Ruby came to her. Ruby should know her: her right hand different from the left. The left hand fine-boned; the fingers slender and fragile, meant for wearing delicate jewels and sipping mint tea. Her right hand was her thinking hand, her doing hand. The fingers not thick or masculine, but sturdy and reliable. Nicole scraped Scotch tape from packages and goo from the floor with the thumb of that hand. Her right hand was for throwing punches, though she never had. She'd scratched Clint once with that hand. Ruby should know her; this afternoon she'd had her chance.

Each letter seemed filled with an electrical charge that jerked her in three directions—someone else's directions—secrets better spoken. Letters not meant for a child, adult or otherwise. Letters meant for lovers and sisters unable to get their lives right. The promises of this information were bombs blowing up Nicole's normal, ordinary expectations: a loving mother callous and hateful, a father strung out over a pretty face, a birth mother willing to let her child go. Was that the purpose of two mothers? One for the taxing work—Malvina; one for the delicate—Ruby.

Nicole collected the letters and envelopes, surprised at their number when their impact was so great, and headed for the kitchen. Gadgets of all lengths and shapes filled the drawers; skillets, pots, and pans in the cabinets beneath the counters. She settled on a wok, tongs, and a large skillet. Without paying attention to dates, old stamps, signatures, or envelopes, she scattered the letters in the wok and on the skillet's cast iron surface. She searched the cabinets, finding what she needed, and sprinkled olive oil over the letters. Nicole struck matches, tossing them one by one into the wok and the skillet until the letters smoked, then flamed. Standing over the burning paper, she flipped and stirred, a gourmet chef sautéing the meal of a lifetime. Monitoring the flames, lips taut, brows arched not from the smoke but from the combination of resignation and relief.

When the room turned smoky and threatened to trigger the

alarm, Nicole clicked the switch on the overhead vent and opened all the living room windows, letting smoke climb up and away into the Paris sky where it seemed this whole mess had begun. Let Paris have the ashes, the memories. She no longer wanted them. The letters burned to a crisp black, a mixture of ash and bits of paper dotted with sentence fragments: *Forever yours, Squire.*

41

In order to master the elements of grammar, the beginner must be able to conjugate verbs for current, completed, or ongoing action.

je suis, il est (zhuh swee, eel aay)	I am, he is
j'étais, elle était (zheht tay, ehl eh tay)	I was, she was
je serai, elle sera (zhuh seh ray, ehl seh rah)	I will be, she will be

---

Nicole resumed her vacation, determined to cram sightseeing and eating into her final week in Paris, unsure why she'd let the questions lurking in the back of her mind go unanswered or if she would ever hear from Ruby again.

Now Nicole and Laurent roamed the Musée Rodin garden, a museum not on her list, but filled with the master sculptor's most famous creations. When they reached *The Thinker*, Laurent stopped.

"You need the standard photos. Step in over there and strike the same pose."

"Do I have to?" Nicole followed another of Laurent's instructions and stood in front of the statue's three-foot stone base. "You know what I'd think, sitting in this lovely garden?"

"Raise your head a little. Now turn in the opposite direction."

"I'm thinking, if I had one question for Ruby, what would it be?" It was the "and then what?" that nagged at Nicole, the mystery of the woman herself and what of her had been quashed by Malvina's strict code.

"I have a present for you." Laurent joined Nicole at the base of the statue, stretched out his arm, then pressed the camera's shutter button. He handed Nicole a CD. *Madama Butterfly.*

"I love it. Strange, I know, but the opera reminds me of Ruby and my mother." Malvina had accepted another woman's child as willingly as the officer's wife. Was honor, similar to Cio-Cio San's desire to save face, Ruby's character, her reason for giving up her baby? Possibilities were tokens in a game that Nicole could maneuver in her head for hours, for years, without answers. "I can't help connecting the two."

"And now you won't forget you saw it in Paris—see, the liner notes are in French; that should take you a while to translate." Laurent dodged Nicole's quick punch to his shoulder. "If we hadn't met again at the opera, I wouldn't have been inspired with another great idea."

Nicole's cell phone rang, interrupting Laurent. With all that had been revealed over the last weeks, and a heart weakened by her stroke, Malvina's calls took priority.

"Allô, bonjour? Puis-je parler avec Nicole Handy?"

Expatriates, she'd heard, living long enough in France, never lost the accent of their native language. In the voice on the other end of the line, the southern drawl was apparent.

"Chérie, this is Josette. Ruby." She offered no reason for taking so long to get back to Nicole. "We should meet again."

"I'll come to you. What's your address?" A casual question in Nicole's mind.

Laurent wrote on the back of the museum brochure, *Want me to go with you?* Nicole shook her head. The two-beat hesitation before Ruby answered was more than Nicole needed to understand she had to see Ruby on her own.

"After I married, Yvette and I met at the Cimetière de Montmartre every week. Most folks visit Père-Lachaise where so many celebrities are buried. I go to Montmartre to think. I visit less now, once or twice a month. It's not crowded. Can you meet me there?"

Meeting newly found mother surrounded by the dead, in a place few visited. Nicole agreed without argument, knowing that everyone had their reasons for keeping outsiders from their door.

A bridge had been constructed over an entrance to the cemetery. From Nicole's vantage point metal strips, hammered with equally spaced iron studs, framed Ruby sitting on a cement bench. Nicole watched her, scrutinized her, erect and expectant, and tried to find hints of herself in Ruby. Outside of a version of her eyes, hair, and good posture, whatever else she'd inherited was difficult to see, from that distance. Taking her camera from her bag, Nicole zoomed the lens and snapped four times, uncertain if the memento was for her, her mother, or her father.

Ruby sat next to a six-foot-high sign anchored by cement posts, comfortable with the death about her. A man with a cane paused between the bench and the sign. For a brief moment, Nicole wished he were the one who'd put the gold band on Ruby's finger; that Ruby wanted to introduce him, an opening into her secrets. The man glanced from Ruby to the sign; his hand moved up and down its height. Ruby referred to her watch and spoke. The man tipped his hat and moved on. Nicole continued from the bridge and down the steps to the entrance under the busy overpass. No other noise except the whoosh of passing cars, the drone of tires on the bridge's rough grate, and the occasional mewl of a stray cat.

"Ah, Roxane. Nicole. You're brave, that's good. My sister wasn't. Malvina believed in ghosts." This was news to Nicole, but how often had she talked to Malvina about death? A conversation touched on when her parents signed their wills and Malvina mentioned her preference for cremation rather than burial.

"I see you wore my brooch again." Surrounded by this solemnity, Ruby seemed in charge. "I search for tombstones. This sign has the names of all the famous people buried here. Let's try Dumas, the son." She directed Nicole to a path on the left and Nicole followed in search of #34, *Alexandre Dumas, fils*. Ruby's step was sprightly, with remnants of what Ousmane called sway. "Does it bother you, dear? Death?"

"I'm more afraid of being dead than I am of dying."

"There are worse things. Being dead while you're alive. I hope you never know how that feels." She turned onto a sunlight-dappled path without giving Nicole a chance to pursue her cryptic comment.

For all its somberness, Nicole found the graveyard beautiful. No white rectangular tombstones or military sites, or simple arches, angels, and scrolls. Sepulcher was a scriptural word from Catholic school. From Jesus rising from the dead. Here lesson met reality—arches, stained glass windows, miniature mansions—sepulchers, varying in height, marble and granite tributes to the dead beneath them. One monument, the size of Nicole and Ruby head to head, displayed portraits in the granite and told the story of relatives, a family of Jews, not buried but killed in a concentration camp and memorialized on this site, their sacrifice never to be forgotten. A few of the living had reserved their spaces: Gaston Collet, 1939–. Agathe Collet, 1935–.

They stopped before a twelve-by-twelve-foot plaque squeezed in the ground between several two-foot-high headstones. Louis Prideaux, July 31, 1915–. Under Louis's a second name, Josette Duprée Prideaux, September 19, 1928–. Not far from this grave was another engraved headstone: *Yvette Marie Arcenaux chère amie August 31, 1922–February 8, 2009.* Ruby stooped, agile and quick, and whisked fallen leaves from the stone.

"Yvette loved it here, too. I bought this plot beside us, so she would never be alone. At the time, Yvette and I believed Monsieur Prideaux was a wealthy man. My husband doesn't even know she's buried here. She was the best friend I ever had." Ruby made the sign of the cross. "She was my sister, more than my sister."

Ruby recounted the story she'd fabricated for her then gentleman caller, that Nicole was Yvette's love child, as if she'd never told anyone the truth. "Yvette was your mother, too. She cared for you and loved you. When I started seeing Monsieur Prideaux, Yvette covered for me. He didn't want me around Yvette. He had such high morals. So Catholic. But when he proposed marriage, I panicked. I didn't know what to do. Did you talk to Malvina?"

Nicole nodded and clutched Ruby's outstretched hand to help her stand. "She wasn't as surprised as I expected. She wanted to know if you were still beautiful."

"Women who aren't ask that question." Ruby laughed, finally connecting herself to Malvina. They both cackled; unexpected behavior from such genteel women. "She always worried about such silly things."

"Mother taught me that any woman can be pretty, given the right clothes and makeup. She wanted me to be smart."

"And are you smart?" Ruby paused. She scrutinized Nicole's face, her dress, and the sweater draping her shoulders. "You're different from me. And her. Pretty enough, with those ears and all."

"Are you typically this blunt?"

"I've never found the need to beat around the bush." She delivered this line lightly as if brushing bothersome lint from her shoulder and went on as if Nicole hadn't spoken. "Are you musical?"

"I wanted to play the piano. Mother said we couldn't afford lessons. Musical, smart or pretty, none of them is worth a damn if you don't do anything with it."

"And what did you want to do?"

"I wanted to be a lawyer. I wanted men to fall all over me. I wanted to balance the world on my fingertips." She wanted to be the woman in the picture.

“And what have you ended up with?” Ruby’s gaze was intense, her voice tender.

She had done it again, and Nicole didn’t know how, but it was a trick she was eager to learn. Maybe Ruby sensed that Nicole welcomed her questions so that her birth mother would know her. Nicole felt drawn in to the mystery of Ruby, the breezy air about her, her ability to get what she wanted.

“Ordinary, I got ordinary. A few lovers, a marriage that lasted a year, working with lawyers that I’m as smart as, and hiding that fact from them for the sake of a paycheck. A mother who isn’t my mother. An aunt who’s my aunt and my mother.”

“Ordinary isn’t so bad. We all have to live with our choices.” Ruby’s face let on that her declaration was for the both of them.

“Mother didn’t find yours acceptable.”

“Except for taking you, I could say the same about hers.” Ruby double-checked her worn cemetery map. Leaves, furled and browned, lay between the headstones and the path, crunching under their soles.

“I’m ready to leave. I don’t care if we find Dumas’s grave,” Nicole said. “Stepping on these graves is creepy.”

“The dead are dead. Six feet of dirt and who knows what else between us and them. They don’t feel. They don’t care.”

“But I do.”

“You’re sensitive. Squire too. Does he still write poetry?”

“I used to hide under their bed. That’s where I found his poetry journal, between the mattress straps. Dad’s not well.” Nicole summarized the effects of Squire’s disease, his measured slip into a living grave. His body was turning into a sepulcher—worn and brimming with inaccessible memories.

“Squire was a good man.” Ruby shook her head, reminding her of Malvina’s reaction whenever she heard sad news about old friends.

“Did you love him?”

“He was a man to love. A good friend.” They reached the place where their exploration started. Ruby dug into her purse and dropped money into the slot of a green four-foot-high square column with an acorn carved on its top. The coins clanked inside the hollowed-out pedestal, alms for the poor of Paris.

"Did you love him?"

Ruby rested against a polished granite crypt, ignoring the fleur-de-lys ironwork protruding from its side. "It doesn't matter anymore, and I'm not sure it's any of your business. Anyway, not one thing we do or say can change the past. And dwelling on it is a waste of time."

42

In general the final consonant in most French words is silent. The letters c, f, l, and r are frequent exceptions.

un mot (ahn mow)	word
avec (ah veck)	with
pas (pah)	not
dans (dawhn)	in, inside of

Ruby sneered at a young boy jumping on the bench beside the sign of celebrity plots and his excitement over a famous man who carried the same name as his own. She waited for a pickup truck rumbling down the graveled path to pass, its flatbed filled with bags of dead leaves and multihued workers. Then she beckoned to Nicole to accompany her beyond the guard station where a man waved from behind a glass wall.

"I suppose Malvina hates me. I didn't talk to her when she came for you. I was afraid she'd try to make me go back with her, or not take you."

The letter from Squire had come, addressed in Malvina's flourishing hand, a month before she was scheduled to arrive. Ruby was shocked her jumpy big sister was brave enough to take an airplane. When she received the letter, she wished that Squire had decided to come. She might have changed her mind; taken Squire for her own again and never let him go back to Mississippi, or Malvina. Strange, she told Nicole, her feelings for Squire and Arnett. She loved them both. She didn't love the man she married, but when he wooed her, she regarded him as a means to all she desired. "Surely, you've learned about survival by now. As women, we do what we must."

The younger sister had turned up her nose at the inexpensive hotel that Squire, not knowing any better, chose in the neighborhood where he had lived. When Malvina arrived the hotel clerk handed her a note describing when to meet Ruby at the popular Les Deux Magots. Ruby wanted Malvina to know how worldly her baby sister had become and be impressed by the famous men and women who frequented that place, if Malvina had even heard of Wright, Sartre, and de Beauvoir. Ruby planned to bring Yvette along because she calmed the fussy toddler who fidgeted, so eager and independent.

On the morning they were to meet, Ruby packed a suitcase with the baby's papers, clothes, bottles, blankets, toys, and Yvette's worn copy of *Cyrano de Bergerac*. She dressed her baby, Roxane, so that she was beautiful; a baby to be proud of, even though the child's skin was brown and her ears poked out of her yellow bonnet. When the day and hour came to meet, Ruby waited beside the Chapel of St.-Germain and watched her sister arrive at the restaurant and seat herself in the front row of caned chairs. Ruby had chosen an early hour, before the arrival of tourists, the beats, and existentialists—what that meant was beyond her interest, she'd learned it from Louis and his annoyance with the young men and women dressed defiantly in black.

The woman who ordered a coffee from the waiter with the confidence of an experienced traveler was not the sister Ruby remembered. Her sister's appearance, her almost beauty, shocked Ruby and froze her to the spot by the old church. Malvina wore a suit with a dragon sprouting colored threads of flames along its bodice. Her hair was swept up in a mass of pin curls on top of her head. In her lap, she held a yellow blanket and a diaper bag.

"Malvina looked so in charge, I was afraid she was going to fuss at me for taking Squire from her, for living in Paris. It's a power older sisters have over younger ones. When we were little, she made me do her chores or hide Momma's whipping stick when we acted out."

Yvette begged to keep the baby. The baby's color made no difference to her. She loved Roxane. Again and with certainty, Ruby denied her friend. Yvette carried Roxane in her arms on the last trip from rue de Vintimille to the Boulevard St.-Germain. She rubbed the toddler's head, adjusted the bow tied under her chin, and tickled her tummy and made Roxane giggle. Then she held her to Ruby, who kissed the baby's forehead and sent them off.

Malvina rose from her chair when she saw Yvette, the only woman on the busy street with a child, a brown child. Ruby watched from her hiding place. The two women shook hands. Yvette sat holding Roxane, a mother in spirit unwilling to let go of her child. The two women chatted—about what, Ruby never asked—Malvina tickling the baby and finding ways to make her laugh. By the by, Malvina stretched out her hands and Yvette handed Roxane to her. Malvina fussed with the child and sang to her with that voice Ruby wished was her own.

"She took your shoes off and counted your fingers and toes. She kept kissing your face and little belly and talking and singing. She cried and you cried, too. But you liked her. You were finicky, but new faces never troubled you. Yvette and Malvina got along like best friends. I don't know how long they sat. I don't know how long I watched. I remember that when they parted they hugged and Yvette kissed Malvina's cheeks and then Malvina copied Yvette and kissed her cheeks. I could hear them laughing."

"It's a miracle we don't all hate you."

"The past is dust, Nicole. Just like the people in this cemetery. Gone. We can't fret over it." She moved in the direction of the courtyard and stopped at a flower vendor's bouquets of irises and bright yellow dahlias. "It's a lesson you better learn. That's why I come here. To remind myself that I can never go back."

"Didn't you ever want to know about me?" If Ruby had married her father, Nicole guessed that her years before leaving home might have been dreadful. A child raised by an unhappy woman would never be appreciated.

"I had to take my chance." Ruby fumbled for cigarettes in her bag. Nicole watched her rub her thumb against the same brass lighter. Nicole observed details unnoticed at the restaurant on rue de Buci—heavy powder creased in the shadows beneath Ruby's eyes, frayed jacket cuffs, roots a sooty gray not the dark brown of its ends, fingertips tinged a smoker's dark yellow.

"Ordinary touches us all, Nicole. What I've done, who I've been is unimportant. We've got to decide, you see, what we mean to each other now. If we are important to each other. I'm old." Ruby held up the backs of her hands; brown freckles dotted each one. "My husband is old and difficult. A prince who turned out to be a pauper. He lied to me as I did to him. He doesn't know I have a child. He doesn't know I'm a Negro."

"And so you gave me away." Nicole set her brown hand beside Ruby's pale one. Malvina, Nicole remembered, said on many occasions that it was easy for one black to see black in another, even when a person tried to hide it. "Shame, shame on you, Ruby Garrett. And did passing make you any better than you would've been in the States, with a Negro child?"

"Don't you understand?" Ruby snapped. "It was my chance and Louis was not a man to tolerate differences. He was so nosy, wanting to know why he wasn't able to court me at my home, why I depended on Yvette. I couldn't put him off any longer, he was going to change his mind—we married right after I gave you to Malvina."

Ruby stopped. Hers was the face of a woman on her way to the confessional. "I packed up all my belongings, everything that identified me as Negro." She had already sold Arnett's fractured saxophone to keep all three of them eating. She combined his records with Yvette's. The photograph Nicole found, hair creams, dark stockings—all of these belongings she left with Yvette to keep her secret. She avoided the sixth, and if she had to go back, she avoided the jazz clubs and cafés. Any song she sang, if she sang at all, was American—Doris Day, Rosemary Clooney, Patti Page. "Louis believed I lost my belongings in a fire."

"Do I have brothers and sisters?"

It was easy to see Ruby toy with her answer. Her hands trembled as she watched the florist, and a group of mourners waiting on the sidewalk. Nicole supposed Ruby feared being overheard.

"I was pregnant, once, but Yvette helped me. And after that, I was careful with Louis—checking my cycle; we hardly had sex. For sure, that's one reason he soured on me. And now we're both too old to care." Even as a girl in Mississippi she'd heard talk of folks passing—women killed by their white husbands when the babies came out black. "What if a woman whose white husband believed she was white had a brown child?"

"What if a light-skinned black woman has a brown child and wants to be white?"

No need for an answer. Ruby waited for Nicole to come to her own conclusions. It struck Nicole then, another variance between Malvina and her mother/aunt. Malvina showed compassion missing from the woman beside her. If the tables were turned, and Malvina were revealing this truth, she would've consoled Nicole; she'd done it after their squabbles. Ruby's passing, and the guts to have made and stuck to such a weighty commitment, was spellbinding. She had not one bit of solace for her abandoned child.

"That's why you didn't invite me to your home? You're afraid he'd figure out you're black?"

"There's no reason for you to meet Louis. I'm not so stupid to think he'd find a resemblance between us. To him, you're Yvette's child." Ruby fingered Nicole's brooch again, seeing, it seemed, the past rising from the dust she'd declared it was. "We'll meet again, before you leave. Day after tomorrow. There's a restaurant on rue Lepic in Montmartre—the one with a checkered floor. You'll come?"

Nicole unfastened the brooch and pinned it to Ruby's jacket. Then Ruby did it again—took Nicole's face in her hands—and, this time, Nicole let them stay.

43

No language can be learned all at once. The beginner should seek a comfort level with conversation by speaking in simple phrases and sentences before moving to an advanced level.

la chance (lah chahnce)	luck
le parapluie (luh perrah plooey)	umbrella
la nuit (lah newee)	night
ailleurs (eye yur)	elsewhere

Neither Malvina nor Squire—in his right state of mind—were the sort to deny his or her own flesh and blood. Squire's brother, temporarily down on his luck, had lived with them when he came to California. Her parents made it clear to Nicole that helping him was their duty. They tithed, refused to defraud their taxes, fed stray dogs, and watered vacationing neighbors' lawns. Nicole considered them down-to-earth with a strong belief in family, home, and God. They practiced fundamental decency and raised Nicole to do the same, and she figured she should follow their lessons.

Ruby and Nicole parted at the bottom of the cemetery steps with kisses to both cheeks. Ruby mounted the stairs slowly. Neither her carriage nor her steps were fragile; she was strong in her movements. At the top, she glanced from right to left at the oncoming traffic, then the blue of the brooch on her shoulder flashed as she turned and faced Nicole. She stared at Nicole from the top of the steps, lips expanded in the broadest smile, and waved. Nicole saw in her a flash of that young, willful woman who dared to change her destiny. Reality hadn't met Ruby's expectations; she took what she could and stayed with it.

Not that Ruby had taught her about being on the other side of a three-way relationship, but Malvina's sadness, her fifty-odd years of worry, was the reality this discovery had revealed to Nicole. If it were appropriate, and she were braver, she'd write a letter of apology to Clint's wife. But this afternoon offered Nicole better lessons. To never be with another woman's man again—the consequences, like dirt swept under the rug, left a lot of work to be done. And the best one: let go of Clint and every man before him.

Following Ruby's example, Nicole decided to be a woman who put herself first, without regrets. That, too, was her unspoken message. And this was Paris. Montmartre back to the sixth, Nicole made the trek, veering left and right at whim. She wanted to see Paris the way she wanted Ruby to see her. Paris. What had she learned from this lover? That simple beauty was a must: a pot of flowers posed on a chair, a sprig of heather in the window of a *tabac*. Attention to detail forged in wrought iron, handwritten bistro menus, women who cared for themselves—a scarf, well-maintained shoes, a spritz of perfume. Reverence for history: stories, people, structures. Paris demanded moments to muse and reflect, a lesson she needed to take home.

It was a night to celebrate. That was her reasoning when Laurent phoned, and she was happy that he pursued. This was what he promised when he came to her door. He kissed her, a lengthy, auspicious kiss, as if this were how they greeted each other. She kissed him back because it was how she wanted to be greeted.

Laurent bowed and presented Nicole with a wine bottle streaked with dusty remnants of a hasty swipe. She had dressed for him this night in the one close-fitting, low-neckline dress she'd brought. A bit on the front and a lot of kickback on the *derrière* put French clothes out of her reach. Not one mannequin in all of Paris represented her body type. Shoes, however, were another story, and tonight, in bright red ones, she flaunted a pair of designer offerings.

"I met Ruby at the Montmartre cemetery this afternoon."

In the kitchen, Laurent worked a wine opener into the aged cork while Nicole described how they'd meandered the graveyard's crunchy gravel paths.

"She's passing and has no intention of telling her French husband that I'm her long-lost black child. She goes by the name Josette Prideaux."

"That's why we couldn't find her." Laurent passed the purplish, stained cork underneath her nose close enough for Nicole to smell blackberries and smoke.

Bottle and wineglasses in hand, they moved to the living room and the spread of food arranged on the coffee table. Nicole considered returning to Chez Papa, because she loved its cozy chic. Background music, low lights; clichés for the romance she wanted—in Paris, the city of love. Instead, she'd bought cheese, bread, chicken rubbed with tarragon, and crispy roasted potatoes from a vendor on rue de Buci. She didn't care that the food was so basic, so American. She cared that she spoke French when she ordered and the man at the deli complimented her simple sentences. Straightforward entertaining seemed appropriate.

"So how are you feeling? It happened pretty quickly."

"Dull. So she's black. Her baby was black. Hello. It's the twenty-first century. Can you say President Obama? I think I'm mad, and a bit sad for her and Mother." She sipped the wine, the taste rich and fruity on her tongue. Laurent went through a complicated description of the wine's characteristics and its change from the tip of her tongue to the back of her throat. Nicole didn't care. "Bottom line, I'm numb and a bit in awe of someone who carried off a serious lie for such a long time. I feel detached and completely intrigued."

They settled on the couch and listened to a CD compilation of French singers from the fifties. "We agreed to meet again at a restaurant on rue Lepic. I'm curious to know how her mind works. But for now, I don't want to talk about RubyMae-Ruby-Josette Garrett-Prideaux, whoever. That's how I really feel."

"Keep 'feeling' until you don't want to." Laurent kissed her. Different from the doorway. With hands, with body, with passion.

He rose and headed for the wall lined with built-in shelves. He selected a CD and inserted it into the player. The pianist started off slow. A contemporary musician Nicole didn't know. She didn't care. Jazz for lovers. The piano was like the saxophone. Sexy. Nasty. It reached deep down and under her blue dress. She wanted to dance, to feel how Laurent moved. She stepped into his open arms, familiar and new. Energy vibrated in his body. They two-stepped in a contained circle, ignoring the wider floor. A saxophone joined the piano and pulsed, burning through Nicole's body. The song ended; they stopped dancing, clinging to one another, wanting but not wanting to separate.

Laurent led Nicole back to the couch, his hand hot on the small of her back. She appreciated a man who took his time. They nibbled at the food and finished the wine—which was better by the end. Her red shoes fell to the floor. His suede loafers dropped beside hers. All on their own, her fingers tugged at his hair, got lost in his chaos. His hands found her zipper, slid it down past the curve of her back. And when his hands slipped inside her dress, Nicole sighed at his warm touch.

"Take me to my bed." Clichéd, unoriginal, or downright trite, that was what she wanted. That was what Paris commanded.

For a man of words, he was a silent lover. Without a huff or a moan he lifted Nicole in his arms and headed for the bedroom, her recently made bed, her freshly laundered sheets and uncluttered room.

Lips to lips. His nose brushed against her neck, the pulsing veins, then downward. They were cautious explorers. Her tongue running down his body, skipping a patch of fuzz, catching on the outline of his ribs. Both of them stroking now, releasing mind and body, unafraid to explore. Over the highs and lows of each other with fingers and tongues, pinpointing pleasure. A shiver, a moan. Making music, skin against skin. Pushing, rolling, sinking into one another; this was what Nicole needed. Laurent was in charge, and that was what she wanted. His body on hers, hers to his side, above him, under him again. Friction. Sweat. Chaos. Like wine, they were better by the end.

44

For the better part of the following days Nicole and Laurent retraced Paris's jazz footprints, sat in the Tuileries Garden, explored the Marais and the Picasso Museum. Now Laurent and Nicole held hands, content as a couple on a postcard, and watched one of the bridges on the Canal St.-Martin gradually rise and make room for a tugboat. The canals of Paris were no secret to Nicole. She was positive she'd seen an article stuffed in her file folder—the folder she planned to toss when she returned home. Holding on to the adventures of others was not how she wanted to live.

"I've got good news. I planned to tell you the day you met Ruby. I've been offered another assignment." Laurent put his arm around Nicole. She accepted his affection, and her comfort in it.

"So, the editor was pleased with your opera story?"

"She was indeed. But this is a freelance assignment. On jazz, and I owe it to you. Going to the sixth and talking jazz, its influence on the French music scene, and the black musicians who came here, I pitched a piece." They walked over the bridge when the two heavy sections clanked shut, waving to the man inspecting the bridge's connection.

"I have to decide on an angle, a person. People think the history of jazz is simple and clear-cut. Not true. It's complicated, but I'll start in the States, probably New York, New Orleans, Kansas City. You ever been there?"

"I heard three different places. There where?"

"I know that, Madame. If I went, would you meet me there where?"

Nicole frowned, considering what to share and how sorely her inner being needed repair. Can one, should she, fall in love with a man she just met?

"Don't be so serious. It's an invitation, not a marriage proposal. Paris is about love. You found love here, you know that, don't you? Ruby's love—to what extent, you have to find out—but it's love. I'm not making a declaration or making an appeal for one. But it's an option worth exploring."

This was the conversation she should've had with Clint the night he offered marriage. A discussion that spoke to an emotional connection. An exchange that should've preceded his proposal. She was well aware love was an odd emotion. Necessary, but not absolute in shape or size, or kisses and outrageous declarations. Every so often it was stern—that was Malvina's love—or gushing or distant and contrived. Or irresponsible or infringing.

"My mother wants me to take care of her and Dad. Not an unusual request. But now I think she had a feeling. Maybe that, with all of Ruby's charm, she'd lose me to her sister. Even though she had my father, she lost a part of him to Ruby. Her request was really a plea. Who knows who or what I might have been if they hadn't accepted me. I love them. And they love me."

"I bet they have a record player—a hi-fi. I'd like to hear the records you're taking home."

"My mother is a saver—if you couldn't tell from the letters. Their record player is dusty, but I'm sure it works. And I'm sure she'd love to hear what you have to say about the records, Professor Bésson."

Of all the Métro stations Nicole wandered in and out of over the course of her stay in Paris, Abbesses was the most intriguing. Tiled surfaces and dark, squared letters marked the station name on the wall and she assumed the station was close to street level. Nicole ignored the elevator, stumped by its necessity, until she started up the stairs. They went on and on, so many flights that when she reached the top she held on to a poll supporting the glass-topped entry. Waiting for her breath to regain its even tempo, she poked through her purse until she found her cigarettes, then tossed the pack into the trash.

The sidewalks rose at a steady incline. The second meeting Ruby had lured her to in Montmartre. This one was, as it should've been, planned and agreed to. Winding through the streets now, Nicole imagined again that her steps intersected Ruby's, not Josette's, Ruby's. For a woman who traversed an ocean on the blind promise of change, Ruby seemed no different from Malvina, who'd ventured from Mississippi to California. But then Malvina had crossed an ocean, too. She'd come for a baby she was ready to love. The connection to husband by lies, not love, confirmed for Nicole that RubyMae Garrett had ended up where she didn't want to be. Maybe adventure had burned her out, burned itself out. She'd stepped on those she loved, even Yvette and possibly her saxophone-playing boyfriend, to get what she wanted. But she chose to move on. That was the choice Nicole was determined to acquire.

Ruby had hidden from Malvina when she came for Nicole. Now Nicole waited in hiding for the aged Ruby. From a *pâtisserie* on the opposite side of the street, Nicole's view included both the tiny, crowded terrace and the restaurant inside. A sign above the door marked the year a crew filmed a movie onsite.

Baked goods perfumed the air. Observing the scene before her, Nicole guessed that to a few jaded Parisians, Paris might be considered ordinary. In the restaurant, diners sipped wine and coffee, and lunched on salads and sandwiches dripping with gooey cheese. A mother sipped a beer with one hand and, with the other, rocked her child cradled in a car seat atop the bar. The bartender tickled the baby's cheeks.

Ruby was nowhere to be seen. Somehow, Nicole imagined, if Yvette were alive, hers would be the face she anticipated. Long ago, Ruby feared Malvina. Nicole was convinced that was Ruby's story—she was afraid to be seen with a black woman, thinking she'd be pegged black by association. Ruby was intriguing; her story was intriguing. Nicole didn't love her—not as Ruby had preened in the café and not as they sat in the cemetery and spoke of the past—but she respected her guts.

What struck Nicole was that Ruby hadn't cried when she met the daughter she gave away. Nor had she apologized. Challenging Ruby, breaking her down until they both cried—that, Nicole realized, was what she should've done. Ruby's actions were unalterable, and Malvina, out of the three of them, bore the most. Every kiss, every hug, every part of Nicole must have reminded her of Ruby. That she even existed meant Squire had loved Ruby, had kissed that mole, been inside Ruby and pined for her. In giving Nicole to her parents, Ruby blessed her child with a life of unconditional love. And ordinary.

Nicole left the *pâtisserie* and headed in the opposite direction, toward the edge of the Place Pigalle. Conceivably, Ruby, too, was hidden, waiting. In the end, Nicole no longer cared, nor did she care to continue with comparisons.

Her flight home was scheduled for late afternoon. Nicole's adventure was at an end. The couch, the antique coffee table, the rugs, the hum of Paris outside her window made for the perfect spot to reflect. She'd made it to Paris, on her own. An unexpected bombshell, Ruby, had set Nicole on an adventure. Laurent could be that man to snuggle with her in front of her fireplace. The cliché worked: she'd never forget Paris. She left the apartment, letting her tears fall as she strolled to the fountain of the conquering angel, ending where her trip had begun. The fountain was filled now with a prankster's sudsing bubbles. She disregarded the tourists, the fashionable women, the students, and others trying to take pictures.

Nicole elbowed her way to the fountain's edge. She pulled a handful of coins from her pocket and tossed half of them into the water. If her parents had been in better health, she considered, they might have made good travel companions. There were sacrifices, she was sure, they'd made for her. "I wish peace for Mother and Dad."

She jiggled the remaining coins in her hand and blew on them, like a gambler hoping for good luck before rolling a pair of dice, then threw them into the water. "Let me come back to Paris soon."

Oh yes, she'd return, not for Ruby, but for the sight of the Eiffel Tower at night, for the taste of Berthillon ice cream, nougat candy from the shop on the Île St.-Louis, the Sunday crowds in the Marais, and the efficiency of the Métro. And even Laurent.

Nicole headed back toward the Quai des Grands-Augustins for the last time—this time around. Paris was not a city to release all of her secrets. No, a skilled poker player, the city held her winning hand close and dared her visitors to ante up.

"Loot!" Nicole shouted at the slight figure of a man inching through the crowd. She realized her mistake. She wanted to see him. His quirky hobble, his dated uniform. His grin. She wanted to tell him she had found Ruby, and he could, too, if he scoured faces for a woman not all she seemed to be. Nicole went back to the café on the corner, checking side streets for Loot. The barista who'd served her and Loot greeted her when she arrived.

"Bonjour. Vous avez vu Monsieur Loot?"

"No, Madame." The barista passed her a coffee. She drank slowly, half expecting Loot to dance through the door at any minute. In return, she pushed an envelope to the barista. "For Monsieur Loot. Three coffees. Hot."

Her final goal was to find Monsieur Large, give him an envelope with a few euros inside to acknowledge his graciousness. When she pushed open the outer door, the concierge rushed up to her, a package in hand. "Bon voyage, Madame." He thrust the parcel into her hand and bowed.

"Merci, Monsieur." She handed him the envelope, gratitude for his vigilance.

"Il n'y a pas de quoi, Madame." He kissed her hand and scuttled to his door. His quiet protection was important to Nicole. The French were, Nicole decided, dear to her. From the concierge to Monsieur Daudon and the strangers in between who had helped her find her way, read a menu, buy a newspaper, speak their beautiful language.

No return address on the rigid, thin package; familiar handwriting. Two layers of brown paper covered the book inside. It was well worn, its pages yellowed and dog-eared: *The Dream Keeper*, by Langston Hughes. Pencil lines underscored stanzas on every page. A book loved and enjoyed. A cream-colored envelope peeked from the top. Two old pictures with pinked edges fit inside a folded letter. Both as preserved as Squire's in the Army and Ruby in her glory.

The first was of a man and woman standing in front of the Club Tabou—a place Laurent and Loot had described. The woman carried a clutch bag and wore wrist-length gloves and a cocktail dress with a flouncy skirt. Her scarf was knotted under her chin and the ends tied at the back of her neck, as if she were ready to step into an off-camera convertible. The mole on her face was prominent, and she posed to show off it and her clothes. The man held a saxophone in his big hands; oversized ears peeked from beneath his tilted hat. They smiled at the camera, warm and open and bursting with promise.

The second black-and-white image was dull now: two smiling women seated side by side. The women were both beautiful. One blonde and statuesque. One petite, with curly hair—Ruby for sure, the dark mole distinguishing her and no one else. Yvette must have been the second woman, for their body language, their intimacy, spoke of friendship and affection. Ruby held a child in her arms, a lovely brown baby with big ears peeking through her thick, curly hair.

Dear Nicole Roxane,

I am a coward. You see I've been here so long, I no longer remember the young girl who set her feet in Paris close to sixty years ago. A lot of Negroes cried when they got here, not me. I kissed the ground. I was never going back to the US. Or Mississippi. I could never be a colored girl again scorned or worse, hankered for like an animal in heat. It took me a while to understand what that meant, and if my Arnett had been stronger our lives would have been different.

Thank you for my brooch—you see I believe it is mine after all these years. I'm glad Malvina gave it to you, it ties the three of us together, don't you think. Anyway, it will remind me of you and the better times between me and my sister. Tell Malvina not to be mad. I loved Squire, but he wanted to put me in a poem and that was not where I wanted to be. I hid this book and pictures from Louis all these years. You found the picture Squire gave to me. He was so proud. It must have been among Yvette's belongings. When my poor friend passed she only had her music and her memories.

This was Squire's book. He read his poems every day. He nearly drove me crazy, but after a while the poems became him and I loved them too.

When you reach a certain age, Nicole, you'll look back on what's happened in your life more than you look forward to the future. You'll find you cannot waste the precious little time you have left fretting over mistakes and half truths. That is what I want you to learn from me. Whatever the future has in store for you, if adventure is what you want, I hope you find it. But I will tell you this—adventure is only a word. Don't be so fixed on finding, live and in that the adventure will come.

Ruby

P.S. See page 47. "Passing Love" was Squire's favorite poem. He was a romantic and so worried that I would leave him. But I would have hurt him if I'd stayed. The poem seems right for this moment as it did back then. Please read it to him and give him my love. Maybe poetry will jog his memory and he'll find a kind word for his RubyMae.

Nicole shook her head, not quite understanding what Ruby was trying to tell her besides goodbye; she'd left much unsaid. But then, she realized, that was Ruby, not a straight shooter. Wasn't she supposed to have remembered that?

The moldy smell of aged paper left Nicole with no option but to inhale it when she opened the book. The poems were annotated with Squire's handwriting: *read this one to Ruby*, or *this one is for the troops*, and a note meant for Ruby. At an already dog-eared page 47, Nicole read to herself.

Because you are to me a song
I must not sing you over-long.

Because you are to me a prayer
I cannot say you everywhere.

Because you are to me a rose—
You will not stay when summer goes.

Fragments of her father's neat cursive, his notes and memories of him standing by the fireplace, pipe in hand. The pride on her mother's face for both husband and daughter. Nicole reread the poem, speaking the title and author out loud as Squire would if he could. "'Passing Love,' a poem by Langston Hughes."

Acknowledgments

Once again, I'm amazed by the power of intentions, the potential of possibilities, and the importance of dreams.

Thank you, women of the Finish Party—Alyss, Deborah, Farai, Lalita, Nichelle, Renee, ZZ—for friendship, great ideas, wise counsel, and support. You've proved, yet again, how blessed I am to have such wonderful mentors, teachers, and friends in my life. May we never finish!

As always, I'm grateful for my Number One Fan, my mother, for her positivity and love; and for my sister's thoughtfulness and ongoing encouragement.

There were so many details to get right and such great people to help me: Sarah Raphael, for helping with my French, Dick Mathias for the saxophone jargon and music discussion, Julia Brown and Ealy Mays (Walking the Spirit Tours) for my insider's look at Paris.

Many thanks to my publicist, Linda Duggins, and editors, old and new, Karen Thomas and Helen Atsma, for their diligence and attention.

Onward!

Reading Group Guide

A Conversation with the Author

Nicole wondered how Jacqueline knew so much about Paris, today and in the fifties. Grand Central Publishing offered her this opportunity to interview the author. (Ruby declined to participate.)

Nicole-Marie Roxane Handy (NH): The last half of *Searching for Tina Turner* took place in southern France and Paris. All of *Passing Love* takes place in Paris. What is it about Paris that makes you keep writing about it?

Jacqueline E. Luckett (JEL): Obviously, I'm in love with Paris. The fascination started with my father and my uncle, both of whom spent time in France during World War II. Then there's my name, Jacqueline, spelled the French way, and my sister's name is French as well. I visited Paris for the first time in around '86. Somehow I was able to recall my high school and college French, though I understood more than I spoke. Except for the one time I might have ordered horsemeat, thinking it was beef, I was able to make my way around without any problems. I feel comfortable there. The language is lovely, and I continue to study it. My fascination comes from the language and Paris is... Paris.

NH: You have lots of details about Paris in the past and the present. What kind of research did you do?

JEL: I knew from the beginning that *Passing Love* would take place in Paris. Although I'd been there twice, it was important to go back to capture the essence of the story. I took pictures of the oddest things: cobblestones, garbage, signs, fences, tables, feet, and more. Then I put together an album that I referred to when details skipped my mind.

There is so much black history in Paris. I took a couple of tours from people who specialize in Black Paris. Ricki Stevenson, Black Paris Tours (http://blackparistour.com/default.aspx), has a wealth of information and knows lots of people. Because I really wanted to know about jazz and black expats, I made arrangements for a private tour with Walking the Spirit Tours (http://walkingthespirit.com). Julia Browne and one of her guides, Ealy Mays (http://www.spiritofblackparis.blogspot.com/), know the city inside and out. Discover Paris! (http://www.discoverparis.net/) conducts tours of Paris and has great information in their newsletter about restaurants and out-of-the-way places. They recently added a tour of Black Paris. I took my own walking tour using Discover Paris! owner Monique Wells's book (cowritten with Christiann Anderson) *Paris Reflections: Walks Through African-American Paris*. Though it's hard to find, Michel Fabre's *A Street Guide to African Americans in Paris* was another good resource to discover Paris and create your own walking tour.

NH: I wanted to see more of Paris. Did you make up a lot of the places that you describe in the novel?

JEL: Your story, and Ruby's, was more important than all the descriptions of Paris. You can go back, you know, and I hope you do. Some clubs' names are made up, but based on real venues. A few were actual hot spots popular during the forties and fifties—Club Tabou, Haynes Restaurant, Chez Inez, Café Tournon. The tourist sites and buildings are all real.

NH: Where did you find all of this information? And how did you decide to write about Paris in the fifties?

JEL: Paris was popular with black soldiers, musicians, and expats between the end of the First and beginning of the Second World War. The city was a hot spot and refuge for African Americans starting with Jimmy Europe's band performances on the streets of Montmartre. African Americans experienced a freedom and acceptance that most never had in the States. Ask Ruby—what she experienced is based on fact. The more I read, the more I liked the period after World War II because it was part of the evolution of jazz.

There's a wealth of information on the Internet, in books, and magazines about Paris during this time. I focused on blacks in Paris. I found articles from *Life* magazine, photographs of Paris with blacks in every place in the city imaginable. Here are a few of the books I used for my research. The list is much longer, and I've included it on my website.

Black American Writers in France, 1840–1980, Michel Fabre

Harlem in Montmartre: A Paris Jazz Story Between the Great Wars, William A. Shack

Into a Paris Quarter, Diane Johnson

Manual of Saint-Germain-des-Prés, Boris Vian

Notes of a Native Son and ***More Notes of a Native Son***, James Baldwin

Paris in Mind, edited by Jennifer Lee

Paris Jazz, Luke Miner

Paris Noir: African Americans in the City of Light, Tyler Stovall

And if you can find the video or CD of the movie ***Paris Blues*** (Sidney Poitier, Diahann Carroll, Paul Newman, and Joann Woodward), watch it. The story takes place in the sixties but it's not much different in attitudes than what Ruby experienced.

Discussion Questions

1. Ruby is as anxious as Arnett to leave the South. Was Paris her dream or Arnett's? Would she have been happy if they had stayed in New York or New Orleans?
2. Nicole rejects Clint's proposal. Did she reject it for the right reasons? When do her reasons become clearer to herself and not just a clichéd response?
3. The term "postracial" is used often since Barack Obama was elected president of the United States. When Laurent and Nicole discuss the differences in Parisian and U.S. attitudes toward race, how does postracial apply to their view and the U.S.? Can that term be applied to France, or any other country in the world?
4. Ruby mentions that if Squire had come back to Paris to get baby Nicole, she might have considered being with him. How do you think Squire (married to Malvina by then) would have reacted if he had seen Ruby with the baby and she had asked him to stay?
5. Ruby and Nicole go to Paris thinking that their lives will change. Did the city succeed in meeting their dreams? Did

Paris fail to be all they thought it would—or was the failure Nicole's and Ruby's?

6. Is there any U.S. or international city that makes you feel the way Nicole does about Paris? What triggered that passion? What did Nicole learn from stretching past her fears?
7. Ruby's and Nicole's stories are told in alternating chapters. Malvina's character develops through her letters. How would chapters telling Malvina's story have affected the novel?
8. Squire loves Ruby, yet continues to accept Malvina's care packages and love. Can he be considered a cad for his behavior? If he were able, what would he say about his relationship with Malvina?
9. Nicole understands she's destroying her history when she burns her parents' letters. Was there a way for her to keep the letters? Why would she have wanted to?
10. When Nicole meets Laurent at the opera, she describes Paris as the City of Coincidence. Have you experienced coincidences that have shifted or changed your life?
11. Nicole touches on the issue of race, yet the reader knows she is comfortable in her own skin. Ruby toys with passing even in her hometown. Imagine a conversation between Nicole and Ruby on race. Do you think Ruby would regret her decision? Would she have taken the same path if she had stayed in the U.S.?
12. What is it about the tone of the two stories that reveals Nicole's and Ruby's characters?
13. Nicole is a procrastinator. She put off a trip to her beloved Paris, and she put off ending her relationship with Clint. What could she have done differently early on in her life to change? What lessons would she have learned if she'd stayed at home?

© Ashley Summer

Jacqueline E. Luckett is the author of *Searching for Tina Turner.* A San Francisco Bay Area native, she lives in Oakland, California. For more information, and to read her blog, you can visit www .JacquelineLuckett.com.